# BROWN EYES

**Also by Mary-Jo Holmes:**

Gianna … a love story

# BROWN EYES

A Romance

Mary-Jo Holmes

Award-winning author of *Gianna*

iUniverse, Inc.
New York Lincoln Shanghai

# BROWN EYES

iUniverse books may be ordered through booksellers or by contacting:

iUniverse
2021 Pine Lake Road, Suite 100
Lincoln, NE 68512
www.iuniverse.com
1-800-Authors (1-800-288-4677)

Because of the dynamic nature of the Internet, any Web addresses or links contained in this book may have changed since publication and may no longer be valid.

This is a work of fiction. All of the characters, names, incidents, organizations, and dialogue in this novel are either the products of the author's imagination or are used fictitiously.

ISBN: 978-0-595-47700-5 (pbk)
ISBN: 978-0-595-91963-5 (ebk)

Printed in the United States of America

For all those who have the heart to go the distance for love.

# *ACKNOWLEDGMENTS*

Thanks to all my family and friends for their love and support during the creative process, especially:

Sierra—for inspiring the title and cover art.

Capri—for her enthusiasm and sense of humor.

Matthew—for his patience and male perspective.

Sharon—for her wit and wisdom and tireless friendship.

Vicky—for indulging my romanticism over her better judgment.

Melissa—for her relationship philosophy, advice, and laughter.

Andrew & Lillian—for always believing in my happy ending.

*I saw the angel in the marble and carved until I set him free.*

... Michelangelo

# PROLOGUE

"Oh, God."

Hesitant, St. Peter approached, reluctant to disturb Him on such a busy night in which everyone worked in diligent quiet except for a choir of angels whose reverence resounded throughout the halls in glorious harmony.

"Yes?"

"I'm sorry, Father, to bother You this eve during the preparations for Your son's birthday celebration tomorrow, but I thought You needed to see this." St. Peter handed Him the parchment paper containing the man's prayer.

"It's his first," God commented as He sat down on His throne. "Accurately transcribed?"

"Of course. Triple checked by three angels."

"There aren't many of *his* kind here."

"Did you hear the one about the priest, the rabbi, and the—"

God silenced St. Peter with a wave of His hand.

"Give Me a moment," He said, beginning to read a portion of the man's prayer aloud. "'Now, God, I'll be the first one to admit that there are a lot of things I don't understand—may never understand, and I don't want to be pointing fingers or playing the prosecutor, but this world You made has a lot of flaws in it. So, I'd contend that You've made Your share of mistakes, too, so that's why I feel I can ask for a favor. And it's not for me; it's for Callie....'"

From inside the luminous room, St. Peter caught sight of an angel with blazing red hair who motioned him to the alabaster door. Leaving God's side to meet the winged woman, St. Peter whispered, "How may I help you?"

"I wanted to play my flute for Him so that I may be selected for the birthday orchestra."

St. Peter shook his head.

"Now is not the proper time. He cannot be disturbed. Let's go from here to the choir room where you can practice with the others."

"All right. I'm sorry if I acted improperly." She fluttered her wings in nervous anticipation, the slight breeze stirring the folds of her gown. "I've just arrived—it's taken me several months to get here—and this process is quite new to me. Everyone is so joyous in anticipation of the celebration, and I want to be part of it. I never imagined that heaven would be so much fun."

"Yes," St. Peter said with a solemn smile. "We do have fun but there is much work and responsibility that comes with this eternity."

Confused, she looked at him with surprise.

"Does this *fun* you speak about come only once a year?"

"We do have our daily smiles," St. Peter mused, taking her hand to lead her to the choir chamber. "Did you hear the one about the priest, the rabbi, and the—"

God interrupted, "Angel, you have a question for Me?"

"Oh, Father," she bowed her head to avoid meeting his eyes and stepped backward into the hall out of view before St. Peter prodded her forward into the throne room. "I-I-I intended to ask a question of You, but now I—I'm afraid."

"Angel, you cannot know courage without fear. Please ask your question."

"I wanted to play my flute for You. I thought, perhaps, that I may play *O Holy Night* for the celebration tomorrow."

"Tomorrow, the senior angels will play." He tri-folded the parchment paper that St. Peter had given Him and placed it in His pocket. "However, I want you to learn Pachelbel's *Canon in D* for you to play six months from this very day—a very special celebration—and the world will hear your music."

She bravely looked up into God's face, a radiant glow accompanied by a reassuring smile offered to dispel any embarrassment or fear a naïve angel could feel.

"Father, can they hear our music on earth?"

"When I want them to."

The angel looked down again and stared at her silver instrument.

"Angel, I see sadness in your heart."

"I'm sorry, Father, but I did want to play my music tomorrow."

"Angel, you cannot know true joy without sadness."

# CHAPTER 1

"No, Mom, I don't think you need to call an ambulance for Dad. Just put some ice on his knee, and I'll be by in a little while to look at it."

Less concerned about her father's bruise in the wake of her mother's perpetual over-reaction to things like this, Callie found herself more annoyed that her 60 year-old father had been outside shoveling snow when she had arranged for the neighborhood boys to do this heavy work. Nevertheless, Callie prepared to close up shop an hour early, but a prospective customer at the front window delayed that action.

"Mom, I gotta go. There's a customer. See ya soon. Love you." Callie snapped her cell phone shut and shoved it into her jeans pocket. Slugging down a gulp of caffeine, she stepped back into her high heels, sure to keep one eye on the window-shopper. A quick tug on her green turtleneck sweater and a fluff of her long brown hair put her into sales mode.

The fellow steamed the glass with his warm breath as he looked at the display of diamond rings set in a festive exhibit in the front window. Ever since the coffee shop opened next door, her uncle's jewelry store seemed to draw more attention, even on blustery December days such as this. The tall guy at the window continued to study the shiny stones while maintaining his position as the full force of the wind shook his stance. He swayed for a moment, then regained his balance and pulled up the collar of his black wool coat for extra protection as his dark hair danced in the winter's wind, his cheeks red from the brutal cold.

*Come in already,* Callie said to herself, the caffeine kicking in to add to her antsy-ness to be on her way to see her dad. *Come in or go away.*

In the warmth of the store, Callie watched him for nearly five minutes as he stared at the engagement and wedding rings. Seemingly about her age—early thirties, he had kind but penetrating eyes and a prominent nose, an almost royal face, with a kingly stance. As impatient as she was to get going, Callie admired his tenacity, braving the bitter cold while scoping the different stones and settings—all for the precious lady in his life.

The shop had been busy earlier in the day with Christmas shoppers, mostly men buying jewelry for their girlfriends or mothers. Now, near closing time, the store was empty, and Callie had nothing to do except wait and hope the browser might come inside and purchase a ring—maybe an expensive ring. She knew her uncle needed the money to offset the medical bills from her aunt's sudden heart surgery. Every-one in the family had offered financial assistance, and Callie had even given her time, choosing to work in the store on her days off from the art gallery so that her uncle could spend more time at the hospital.

The young man at the window glanced up and caught Callie staring. He smiled, and she reached for a pen and paper to pretend to look busy. There was nothing worse than appearing desperate for business. She sketched for a moment, using her favorite ring in the store as a model for her drawing. It wasn't the typical engagement ring so her uncle hadn't included it in the window display, but it had a small heart-shaped diamond set in the middle of two ribbons of tiny diamonds so that it resembled a sparkling bow. Sentimentality connected Callie to the ring despite the broken relationship with a boyfriend that would have placed that ring on her finger permanently.

Strange how she never thought about *him* except when the ring stirred up memories that now seemed best forgotten. It was another time and a series of circumstances that she refused to regret despite her want to be married. Living with regret equated to swimming with rocks in her pockets … the weight would eventually drown her, and she had entirely too much to live for.

The jingle of the bell on the front door jarred her attention, and Callie looked up to see the window browser entering inside.

"Good evening." Her welcoming tone carried the subliminal sales pitch of *buy something!*

"You're still open?" the man asked as he closed the door behind him.

"Yes, till seven. We have extended hours during the holiday season." She eased herself off the stool and watched him fold down the collar of his coat and unbutton it. "A bit chilly today, huh?"

"It's brutal, but I love New England." His smile stretched across his face—a dazzling smile that seemed to rival the shimmering stones in the cases. "Couldn't imagine living anywhere else."

"Me neither."

Callie returned his smile, now noticing the finer details of his appearance as he turned completely toward her. With a handsome face that squared slightly at his chin, the well-dressed man possessed soft lips and brown eyes, a paler shade of his sable-colored hair which was cut short and parted to the side. As he finger-combed his bangs off his forehead, he casually glanced around the showroom.

"Is there something I can help you with? Something particular you're looking for?"

"I'll know when I see it."

Politeness forced another smile before he strolled to the center island case and peered through the glass at the jewelry.

"I noticed you looking at the engagement and wedding rings in the window. Would you like to see some of them?"

"Sure."

Callie unlocked the window and reached into the exhibit, removing several of the velvet-covered displays. She set them upon the center island and waited for him to select a ring. He stood still in silence, apprehensive or perhaps waiting for her permission, so she took the initiative and picked up one of the finer engagement rings.

"This is a two-carat marquise diamond in a platinum setting." She tilted the ring slightly to catch the light. "Notice the clarity."

"Hmm, yes."

Sensing his indifference, Callie selected another ring.

"This one is pear shaped. It's one and a half carats, and it's tipped by tiny diamonds. This is white gold."

"I see." He eyed it then asked casually, "What's the difference between platinum and white gold, besides the price? They look the same."

"Platinum is more durable than white gold, and because of its more pure form, it's preferred by people who are allergic to other metals."

"Oh, I didn't know that."

And by his flat tone, Callie surmised it was a fact he didn't care to know. She looked around for the nearest wall to smack her head on. He turned away from her and glanced at his watch. Not wanting to lose the sale, she quickly chose another ring with a smaller stone and cheaper price tag.

"This one is yellow gold. The diamond is one carat, round. It's flawless."

"Ah."

His eyes were unfocused as if his thoughts were elsewhere, looking at her yet through her … the worst kind of customer.

"How about I teach you a little bit about diamonds?" Callie attempted to inject some energy into the sale and put the ring in his hand. "The value lies in the colorlessness and the clarity of the stone. This diamond is an F, which means it's virtually colorless.

"Oh, I thought F meant flawless."

Callie smiled, pleased with his growing interest.

"Flawless means no visible imperfections at 10% magnification. What do you think of this ring? Do you like it?"

"It's nice." He handed it back to her.

"I'm sensing you're not loving any of these rings," she declared as his eyes took on that far-off look again. "Do you have any idea what you're looking for?"

"Not exactly, but I'll know it when I see it."

He smiled and shoved his hands into his pockets like a little boy, bored.

"Maybe we should start with price. Are you working within a budget?"

"No." He pursed his lips. "Price doesn't matter."

"Okay. What about the stone? What size diamond? Half a carat? One carat? Two carats?"

"That doesn't matter. *Size* doesn't matter, does it?"

The seductive question coupled with the heat of his princely eyes momentarily rendered Callie speechless before she pulled herself together.

"Well, actually," she replied, her voice soft with disquiet, "size doesn't matter unless we're talking about boats or flat-screen TVs or paychecks." Callie laughed when he laughed, relieved that her quirky sense of humor didn't blow the sale but rather brought them to common ground. "In all seriousness, when it comes to diamonds, *size* does matter to most women. They seem to equate the size of their diamond engagement ring to how much they're loved."

"No," he said with mock incredulity, raising one eyebrow suspiciously as he slipped off his coat and laid it on the counter. "You're telling me that the bigger the diamond I purchase, the more I love my girlfriend?"

"Well, I can't speak for *you* or your girlfriend, but most women think that way."

"What about you?"

"Me? Well, I'm not *most women*. I believe in the thought, the gesture. Love comes from the heart, not from the diamond."

He gave her another charming smile then a wink as if to say he had just been teasing her. Leaving Callie's side, he walked over to the glass cases where she had been sketching and bent at the waist to survey the encased jewelry.

"Anything catch your eye?" she questioned, still wanting to make a sale yet doubting this man was sincerely interested in purchasing a ring. She labeled him dubious and suspected he merely wanted to warm himself inside the store before battling the winter night once more. "Most of those rings in that case have colored stones—rubies, sapphires, emeralds—not the traditional engagement ring."

"What do you suggest?" He moved slightly to the next glass casing.

"I wouldn't. That's a very personal decision."

"Perhaps."

*Perhaps? It's your engagement!*

Callie peered over his shoulder at the clock on the wall, tired of his indecision and subtle sarcasm. She needed to be on her way to check on her father. The customer pulled himself upright and turned around to face Callie, leaning against the showcase.

"Well, if you were getting engaged," he paused and looked at her—directly and unabashedly, seemingly baring her naked, "what kind of ring would you chose?"

One time, she had chosen, and it jinxed the whole relationship. Callie glanced over at the heart-shaped diamond in the case ... and remembered *him.* Her quiet caused the customer to repose the question.

"What kind of ring would you chose?"

"I—uh—do you want to see these rings anymore or shall I put them away?"

"You didn't answer the question."

"Neither did you," she said, gathering up the velvet boards on the center island.

"Leave the rings there," he replied. "Now, your turn."

"What was the question again?"

He playfully rolled his eyes then refocused on her.

"If you were getting engaged, what ring would you chose?"

Callie eased out a sigh along with a half-truth.

"I wouldn't. *He* would chose. Isn't that the whole idea of the proposal?"

"I suppose that's a little old school." The fellow turned his back to her before she could debate the issue. "Hmmm. This one is nice. Let me see this one."

Callie moved to his side.

"Which one?"

He tapped the drawing on her sketchpad.

"Where is this ring?"

"There."

She pointed to the ring—*her ring*—below in the glass case.

"Let me see that one."

She unlocked the case and removed the ring, placing it in his open palm.

"It's really beautiful, but the stone is only a half carat."

"Could you try it on for me? I'd like to see how it looks on the hand."

"Sure."

Callie reached for the ring, but at the same time he took her left hand and gently slid the sparkling diamond on her ring finger. For one magical moment, she dreamed of *him,* being in love and engaged, snuggled up in front of a fire, lost in romantic conversation. A hazy image of her former lover floated before her, a love lost to her career. Callie's stomach curdled. The moment had come, the ring was on her finger … and as she stared at it, she had an epiphany of sorts as she thought about her life at this very moment. She had nothing to be sad about, and suddenly her anguish turned to elation. She was finally over *him.*

"It fits you perfectly," the customer observed. "It's almost as beautiful as your brown eyes."

"Thank you." Callie slipped the ring off her finger. "I must confess it's my favorite ring in the whole store."

"Then why don't you buy it?"

"Diamonds possess a mythical magic, a power of virtue and wealth and strength, which disappears if not given as a gift. I suppose that was the gods' way of cursing egotism and Cupid's way of blessing the proposal."

Silent, uncommenting, eyes glazed in a fixed stare at the ring, he seemed surprised by her little story or maybe he was just consumed with his own thoughts. Callie resumed her saleswoman mode.

"So, are you interested in this ring? Notice how it catches the light." She rotated the ring under the florescent fixtures. "The diamond is only a half a carat but it's absolutely flawless. Timeless, I would say."

"Yes." His rich voice took on a quiet tone of contemplation. "Your fingers are so delicate. Her fingers are a little fatter. Not that she's fat or anything." He shook his head. "She's pretty. And nice."

"This ring is a size 6."

"Oh." The corners of his mouth dropped. "I suppose I would need a size 7."

"We can resize it for you. The owner will be in on Monday."

"I wanted it before Saturday." His voiced turned glum. "Plus, the diamond is rather small. I wouldn't want her to think I didn't love her."

Callie smiled at his presumed humor, then watched him return to the center island display of engagement rings for another inspection.

"Do you have any size 7 rings here?"

"Yes, but not there; in the window." Callie locked the case, and he followed her to the window display where she removed a velvet board of diamond rings. "These are all size 7."

As he reached for the board, he knocked it loose from her hands and it fell to the ground, sending the rings scattering about the carpeted floor.

"Oh no! I'm so sorry," he apologized. "Here, let me help you."

They both dropped to their knees in search of the diamonds. Callie felt ridiculous crawling around the casings, scavenging for the rings like a jellybean hunt. When the rings had been gathered, the fellow apologized again and helped Callie to her feet.

"These things happen," she said, gently blowing the lint off the settings as she rearranged them on the velvet pad. "What about these rings? Anything catch your eye?"

The fellow picked up a tear-shaped two-carat diamond surrounded by smaller baguettes. "This one is nice. It'll do."

Callie creased her brow.

"Nice? It'll do? That's not what you should be saying." She waited for him to respond, but he just looked at her with a puzzled expression on his pleasant face. "You have to be absolutely sure. You have to *love* it, adore it. 'Nice' isn't good enough. You're going to be seeing it every day for the rest of your life. Even if you're not wearing it, it's a statement of who you are, who she is."

He continued to stare at her with that mystified expression. She thought an art analogy would better prove her point since that was her expertise after all.

"It's like buying art," Callie explained. "The painting must capture the essence of your soul, who you are, what you believe in. Whether it's hanging in your home or in your office, there must be something within that artwork that is inherent within you."

"Oh." The man smiled at her, his brown eyes gleaming with some indescribable emotion, obviously overwhelmed by her passionate discourse. "You can wrap this one up. Do you take American Express?"

"No."

"But your sign in the window says you accept American Express."

"No, not that. We accept credit cards. I'm talking about the ring. I don't want to sell it to you."

"Why not? What's wrong with it?"

"Nothing. There's nothing wrong with the ring. It's you—your attitude. I don't think it's the right ring." She shook her head, agitated. "Nice just won't do. It's not the word you use to describe anything when you're in love. Nice is ordinary, plain, blah."

He laughed at her, a great big hearty laugh.

"May I help you down off your soap box, Miss English Teacher?"

"No, it's just that this is an engagement ring, and I think you're making a rash decision and not making a good investment."

"Talk about no sales pressure. Do you turn all your customers away?"

"I'm not turning you away. I'm just suggesting that—"

"Thank you. You're sweet. But I want to buy this ring." He reached for his wallet and handed her his credit card.

"It's non-refundable."

"I'm okay with that."

Callie reluctantly accepted his credit card and glanced at the name.

"I'll ring this up, Mr. McGregor."

"Call me Aidan."

As she processed the paperwork, Callie admonished herself for getting so involved with the customer that she nearly lost the sale. This wasn't her art gallery; this was her uncle's jewelry store, and he needed the money.

"Well, here you go." Callie handed the gold bag and the credit card to Aidan. "All the paperwork is inside, including the appraisal certificate." She smiled. "Good luck."

"Thank you."

"If you don't mind me asking, how do you plan on popping the question?"

Aidan's face glazed over with that former look of uncertainty. He shrugged.

"I'm not sure yet."

"Well," Callie said, "whatever you wind up doing, I'm certain it will be *nice.*"

♥              ♥              ♥

Aidan sat on a cracked-leather stool at the Towne Tavern, an out-of-the-way pub known for its historic value and greasy burgers. The beamed ceilings and log structure transported him back to his childhood days when he spent Christmas in Maine at his grandmother's cabin. He always enjoyed his stays there, and distinctly remembered thawing out in front of his grandma's stone fireplace after a long afternoon of skiing. Those once-a-year visits influenced his decision to attend college in New England, and after graduating with a degree in journalism—a major that would allow him to work in any part of the world—Aidan decided to make his home in Massachusetts. The only thing he left behind in sunny California was his sister, and no amount of persuading could uproot her to the East Coast.

Journalism proved to be too competitive and not as lucrative as his lifestyle demanded. Consequently, Aidan attended law school and joined a private practice. He maintained his publishing contacts, and that was how he came to meet his girlfriend Grace. A chance meeting in a corporate cafeteria led to a two-year relationship and the purchase of the diamond ring.

Aidan glanced over the paper menu, abandoned his usual entree of grilled chicken and baked potato for the sinful cheeseburger and deep-fried onion rings, and drank a beer, waiting for his friend Tony to arrive. A private practice attorney dealing mostly in family law, Tony had an aptitude for diving through the muck and getting to the heart of a problem. He dished out advice like a man twice his age with twice his experience. Honest, Tony always told it like it was, harsh sometimes to the point of brutal. Tonight, Aidan needed a heaping of frank talk.

Tony and his fiancé Eve were the common thread linking Aidan to Grace. Over his philosophic brew, Aidan contemplated fate and how life had brought him to this moment.

*Was it all meant to be or did I have a hand in my own destiny?*

Aidan loved Grace; he knew that. But over the past few months, something changed. Something was different yet nothing he could put his finger on. They didn't fight; never argued. They talked but never about deeper, intimate issues. Sexually, she still aroused him; although, their work schedules didn't leave that much time for passion.

*Passion. Just how important is that in a relationship, in a marriage? And does it come naturally or does it require effort? Love ... is it science or is it poetry?*

Tony entered and brought with him the winter chill as a swift breeze blew through the bar. He parted the crowd like Moses and the Red Sea, bee-lining for the barstool next to Aidan as he slipped off his leather jacket. He wore jeans and a gray-speckled pullover sweater—attire quite different from his usual legalese three-piece suits that Aidan was more accustomed to seeing him in during the workweek.

"Aidan, good to see you, man." He patted him on the back. "Manny, I'll have my usual," Tony told the bartender, then turned his attention back to Aidan. "So, you got the ring."

"Yeah, I got one."

"Let me see it."

Aidan pulled the velvet box from his coat pocket and placed it on the bar. What he really wanted to do was toss it into Boston Harbor or, better yet, return it to the jewelry store and see that girl again.

"Wow," Tony commented as he opened the box. "Nice rock."

"Yeah, *nice*." He could hear the girl's voice lecturing him again about *nice*.

"How much did it set you back?"

"Enough." Aidan took a long swallow of his beer as Manny set his cheeseburger and Tony's drink on the counter. Tony snapped the black box closed.

"Well, she's worth it."

"Is she?"

Aidan knew the question would spark a flame in Tony.

"What's this all about?"

"I met a girl tonight."

"Yeah, that much you said on the phone. So what about it? You meet a girl and suddenly you don't love Grace anymore?"

"How can I even think about proposing marriage when I have feelings for someone else?"

"Feelings? You just met this girl. The only feelings you could possibly have are between your legs."

Aidan laughed, not sure if Tony was joking.

"Seriously, how can I think about spending the rest of my life with Grace when I can't get this other girl out of my head?"

"It's just the jitters. The same thing happened to me before I proposed to Eve. Every girl I met seemed a better prospect. I doubted myself, doubted Eve, doubted my entire life."

"Yeah, but it's not every girl. It's just this one girl—this amazing, beautiful brown-eyed girl."

"I hear a Van Morrison song," Tony mumbled through a swallow of his drink. He set his glass down and looked Aidan squarely in the eyes. "Grace is beautiful, and she's got that curly blonde hair and baby-blue eyes. A brain to boot coupled with street sense. On top of all that, she's a sweetheart, at least when she's not kicking ass in the office, as Eve tells it.

Bottom line, my friend, is that your girlfriend, future fiancé, wife-to-be, is really a nice person."

"Yeah, *nice*." Aidan punctuated it with a sigh.

"What's wrong with nice? Do you wanna marry a bitch?"

"No, no. It's just that maybe I'm settling. Ya know what we did last night?"

"What?"

"Nothing. And the night before? Nothing. And last weekend, nothing. She works on her laptop, and I click through the channels."

"Yeah, but she's up for a promotion. And how many nights during the year do you bring work home, writing briefs, preparing for depos or trial?"

"Point taken, but—"

"No buts. How could you even think about dumping Grace? You've got a good thing. You've been together for two years. You don't even know this other girl. With all the crackpots, whackos, and diseases out there, why would you ever—" Tony swallowed his frustration along with a large swig of his rum and coke. "Where did you meet her?"

"At the jewelry store."

Aidan smiled, half owing the feeling to her beautiful face that had just re-entered his mind, half knowing what Tony was going to say.

"She sold you your frickin' engagement ring? That takes the cake!" Tony drank down the rest of his drink. "You can't compare her to Grace. Grace is successful, a soon-to-be vice president of a publishing company, and the other girl is a sales clerk in a jewelry store. Is that really the type of woman you want to spend the rest of your life with?"

"It's just a job. The fact is she's stunning and smart, incredible brown eyes."

"I wouldn't know about the stunning; haven't met her. And as for smart, I presume all you talked about was rings. That's her job. She's gotta know her product."

"No, she said a few other things." Aidan fell quiet remembering her little snippet of mythology. "I just know I couldn't take my eyes off her."

"Let me set this up," Tony began, using his hands to figuratively draw a storyboard. "You're shopping for an engagement ring for the love of your life, and while you're looking at all these gorgeous diamonds, Miss Brown Eyes—?"

"Yeah, sexy brown eyes and long brown hair."

"So while you're looking at all these gorgeous diamonds, Miss Brown Eyes behind the counter is the one that catches your eye."

"Exactly."

# CHAPTER 2

Callie's art gallery, Appassionata, bustled with a steady stream of workers from the catering company. The holiday season, disappointingly, offered little income in way of art sales. Most people purchased more practical gifts that fit under the Christmas tree. However, Callie rented out Appassionata for holiday parties, and the gallery proved to be the perfect atmosphere for celebration. Between the expanse of spectacular artwork gracing the walls and the enormous floor space ideal for dancing, the gallery appealed to the more sophisticated corporate or private gathering. Furthermore, by opening her doors in this way, Callie could secure the attention of innocent attendees—or prospective buyers as she liked to call them—who could not resist the incredible paintings and sculptures offered for sale. Most would return at a later date to purchase a piece that had caught their interest or tugged on their heartstrings.

That seemed to be Callie's most proud accomplishment: selling artwork to people who had absolutely fallen in love with it. *I have to have it! It's beyond breathtaking! It speaks to me, drawing me into its canvass.* How she loved to hear these statements—such adoration bubbling forth as her patrons sometimes paid thousands of dollars for one fantastic painting, by Callie or some other hopeful yet undiscovered artist, that meant the world to them. And so, whether creating her own majestic masterpieces or selling another artist's splendid work, Callie exuded the passion that had inspired her to name the gallery Appassionata.

"Excuse me. Are you the owner?"

Callie turned around to greet the husky voice. He wore a heavy, navy blue jacket with the words "Sycamore Florist" embroidered in thick, white stitching.

"Yes, I'm Callista Emerson. How can I help you?"

"I'm delivering the flowers for tonight's party. Where do you want them?"

"I want the white poinsettia pots on each step along the railing all the way up to the loft, then the red poinsettias should semi-circle the dance floor. The mini Christmas trees should be set on opposite sides of the front door, and the floral vases need to be on the guest tables as center-pieces."

"Okay." He glanced around the gallery and repeated her instructions. "White up the stairs, red on the dance floor, vases on the tables, and the Christmas trees by the front door?"

"Yes. Thank you."

Callie turned her attention to a pile of tiny white lights on the floor—myriad strands needing untangling before hanging. She took a seat on the carpet and began the tedious task of unraveling the twisted wires. She pulled at knot after knot, trying to protect the bulbs as she unweaved the wires. As soon as one strand was successfully unsnarled, another presented itself in a hellish twining. Callie reached in her pocket for an aspirin and popped it in her mouth, washing it down with nothing but the spit of irritation. Somewhere along the 20th strand as her bed beckoned, she felt a tap on her shoulder.

"Hello, Callie. Nice to see you again."

She recognized the man's voice and reluctantly turned her head to acknowledge her former boyfriend's presence. *Him.* It was a Casablanca moment where she wondered, *Of all the galleries in all the towns in all the world, he walks into mine!* She reached in her pocket again but could only find a breath mint, not exactly the prescription for seeing him standing next to his pregnant wife.

"Hi, Joe," she replied, rising to her feet while maintaining hugging distance. Callie smiled at his wife who strolled over to a wall of art and rested her arms on her belly as she viewed the paintings. "Congratulations. When's the baby due?"

"Next month. It's a boy." His eyes resonated with pride.

"That's wonderful." Callie cleared her throat and forced a tone of sincerity. "I'm very happy for you."

She wished she meant it, knowing that were it not for a twist of fate, she would be married to him. She remembered the night. How could she ever forget? It was December 1st, their two-year anniversary of dating. Joe had reserved them a suite at the Copley Plaza in Boston, and made reservations for 7:00 p.m. in the Oak Room for a celebratory dinner. With every intention of heading straight to Boston, Callie left her apartment at five but decided to make a quick stop in Sycamore at her parents' house to check on her father who had recently been discharged from the hospital after a bout of pneumonia.

When she arrived at her childhood home, Callie found the neighbor, Mr. Bennedetto from down the street, over for a visit, saying his goodbyes before he packed up and left for Florida for the winter. During the midst of his grumbling about the upkeep of his property while away, Callie offered to buy it. She loved the farm across the street, especially the big old barn that she dreamed of converting into an art gallery. The old man laughed at first, thinking she was joking, but when Callie insisted that the offer to buy was genuine, he began to seriously contemplate the sale and put a price tag on the property.

With a dollar amount giving shape to a real transaction, Callie's father tried to dissuade her from making such a serious purchase, so she found herself having to convince both men of her intent and plan for success. After an hour's discussion, Mr. Bennedetto agreed to sell his farm, and they called Callie's cousin, Peter, an attorney, to come over with a contract to finalize the terms before Mr. Bennedetto left for Florida in the morning. She wouldn't take ownership for several weeks, but at least she'd have a signed contract in her possession.

When Callie realized the time, how late she'd be for dinner, she called Joe to apologize and share the good news. He didn't answer his phone, so she left him a brief message explaining what had happened, then headed for Boston in a desperate hurry. It was well after eight when she entered the hotel's restaurant. With no sign of Joe, she asked the front desk clerk for a key to the suite, eager to tell Joe about her purchase. Callie had been waiting for the right place, the perfect location to situate her gallery, and the barn on the farm was ideal.

Inside the suite, the lights were on and the bed turned down, but Joe wasn't there and none of his things were inside. He was always one to unpack and set his toiletries on the bathroom vanity. The sink's counter sparkled in its emptiness. Callie pulled open the drapes and peered out onto Copley Square, thinking of a way to apologize to Joe, but no *I'm sorry* could rectify this wrong. Too many times she had put her work, her art, ahead of their relationship. That was three years ago.

"I was going to propose to you that night," he said as if reading her silence, her eyes.

"I suppose it just wasn't meant to be." She mustered another mouthful of sincerity as well as a smile. "You're happy now."

"Yes. And you?"

"Yes, the gallery is doing quite well."

"I didn't ask about your work, Callie."

"My work is a large part of my happiness, Joe." From the corner of her eye, Callie caught sight of his wife heading in their direction. "So what brings you to my gallery? Looking to buy some art?"

"Yes." Joe reached for his wife's hand. "My parents visited Italy this summer and loved it. We thought we'd buy them a painting for Christmas, and some friends of ours recommended we come here."

"I do have some beautiful paintings of Italy in the next room." She led them across the foyer.

Joe pointed at one of the paintings.

"That's the one. It looks just like the café in Sienna they were photographed in front of."

"I suppose," his wife agreed, her voice quiet, almost timid. Not the mate Callie would have expected Joe to choose.

"Who's the artist? Anyone famous?" he inquired, still focused on the details of the painting. "It's amazing how he's captured every minute detail, and the color is so real."

"The artist would be me. I painted this two years ago after a trip to southern Italy. This particular café was so picturesque, almost Parisian, with its canvas awning and ivy crawling along the windows. They would serve these delicious loaves of Italian bread." Callie pointed to one of the terrace tables in the picture where a couple sat eating. "I only wish I could have captured the scent as well. It was the best bread I've ever tasted."

"Well, the painting is beautiful. So realistic, so much detail. It's like we're standing right in front of it. Mom and Dad are going to love it. It comes in this gold frame?"

"Yes, as is. I could change the frame if you want."

"No, it's perfect. We'll take it."

Callie smiled, pleased to have sold her painting, yet pained by the fact that it had taken all these years for Joe to really appreciate her work.

"I'll pay for it today," he said, "but is it okay if I don't pick it up till a day or two before Christmas?"

"Certainly. We're closed Christmas Eve, but why don't you come by on the 23rd. I'll have it wrapped with a bow for you."

"That's very nice of you, Callie."

"No trouble at all." She proceeded to the front desk and wrote up a transaction receipt while Joe and his wife meandered about the gallery, trying their best to stay out of the caterer's way.

Before leaving, Joe stopped at the desk to retrieve his credit card and receipt. He smiled, paused—hesitated—cleared his throat as if he had something important to say. Callie looked up, wondering, waiting. It seemed an eternity. But he said nothing—just merely nodded then walked away. Maybe some things were better left unsaid. She wasn't one for apologies.

♥          ♥          ♥

"Hurry up, Aidan," Grace called out to him from the bedroom. "I don't want to be late."

Aidan opened the bathroom door, his face full of shaving cream. "I can't opt out on this one? It's *your* company's Christmas party, not mine."

Grace sat on the bed and pulled on her stockings. Spirals of blonde curls fell across her shoulders.

"No, you can't not go." She looked up at him, and her blue eyes nearly turned red. "You're not shaved yet! Come on, Aidan. I can't be late. I'm chairing this party. I'm supposed to be there early."

She stepped into her gold shoes and stood up. At the closet, she slipped her gold and black gown from the hangar, and Aidan watched her slither into it. Grace had a full body, round ass, and each one of her curves teased him through her dress. She turned around and caught him staring at her.

"Don't just stand there staring at me. Get shaving!"

"As soon as I find my razor."

"It's in your hand." She rolled her eyes. "You're going to be the death of me with all your procrastination. Please put punctuality on your list of New Year's resolutions. I hate being late."

"Then you go ahead, and I'll meet you there."

She wasted no time considering his offer.

"All right. You know where it is?"

"No. Leave me the address by my keys on the dresser." From the mirror, Aidan watched Grace spritz on some perfume then slip a business card under his keys.

"Love you, honey. See you later." Her voice trailed off as she exited the room.

"Bye."

Aidan wondered why he was having such a hard time saying *I love you* lately. Ever since the purchase of the engagement ring a few days ago, it seemed the words choked in his throat. Tony had convinced him at the bar that he just had a case of cold feet. Simple nervousness, nothing else. Just nerves trying to sabotage a great relationship.

*After you're engaged,* he told Aidan, *it'll all go away.*

Aidan believed him, but now sitting on the edge of the tub, he contemplated what "it" meant.

*It'll all go away. Did Tony mean nervousness? Confusion? Doubt? But what if all the love went away?* Aidan scolded himself. *Fine time to think about all this—the night you plan to propose to Grace!*

Aidan remained seated on the cold porcelain for a long while thinking about his life. He wanted to get married. He wanted to start a family. At 36, with a secure job and beautiful house, the timing couldn't be better to settle down.

*Then why all this indecision?*

After he dressed in a black suit, Aidan retrieved the diamond ring from the back of his sock drawer. Although Grace hadn't officially moved in, she spent enough time at his house that Aidan felt a need to keep the box hidden from her innocently finding it. Picking up his keys, Aidan glanced at the business card. *Appassionata Art Gallery.* He thought it was an odd place for a Christmas party, but maybe the perfect place to propose marriage … that is if he could shake the doubts about Grace from his mind.

*When she says yes, everything will be fine.*

Through the woodsy town of Sycamore with towering pines and rustic farmhouses, Aidan drove in search of Appassionata. He needed to stop for directions and consequently followed a winding road that led to the art gallery. It was a sight right off a Christmas card. Tiny white lights framed the huge building, which seemed to have been converted from a barn. More lights trimmed the four large, arc-shaped windows fronting the gallery through which Aidan glimpsed partygoers on the first floor and dozens of paintings on the second floor. On the expansive lawn sat a fleet of straw deer, lit with hundreds of white lights, their heads and bodies in different positions for a true-to-life look. All the tall pine trees on the premises, too, had been decorated with lights, each tip topped with a sparkling star.

Aidan parked his car, and walked up the shoveled path lined with glittering angels stationed to welcome visitors with their piped-in music of Christmas carols. If anyone needed a dose of holiday cheer, this seemed to be the place to get it. Inside, the decorations and lights rivaled outside, and the party blared in full force.

Met at the door by a white-shirted man with a red bow tie, Aidan handed off his coat to him, then took a minute to look around for Grace. He spotted Tony at the same time Tony saw him, and the two men met at the bar.

"Seen Grace?" Aidan asked, scanning the room for her.

"She and Eve and some of the other wives are upstairs in the loft looking at the paintings."

"This place is incredible."

"Yeah, the owner Callie outdoes herself at Christmas. Eve and I stumbled upon this place last year when we were looking for some paintings for the new house."

"It's sure out of the way. I got lost three times before I had to ask for directions."

"Well, now you know where to go for art. Callie's very talented, very creative. Everything in this gallery was either done by her or by local artists."

"She only paints? I see a lot of sculptures, too."

"Most of those are Polinsky. He's a local known for his couples—bound together in some erotic embrace. I got Eve one for her birthday this year."

Aidan nodded, remembering.

"That's the piece in your dining room."

"Yeah. For Christmas, I bought Eve one of Callie's angels. I'm no art connoisseur, but these angels are really beautiful. She uses some ancient Japanese process where she actually sets them on fire. It's incredible."

Aidan spied Grace descending the stairs, talking to one of her coworkers. She held up the hem of her gown so as not to trip on it.

"Is Grace mad that I'm late?"

"Oh, she'll get over it when you propose later. You remember the ring?"

"Yeah." Aidan patted his pocket before asking the bartender for a beer. "I still have my doubts, though."

"What's it now? Not that silly girl from the jewelry store?"

"No, I haven't thought about her since that night, thanks to you."

"You're welcome. Then what? What's your problem?"

"I don't know, but something's not right."

"Yeah, you. You're not in your right mind."

"Probably." Aidan downed a mouthful of beer and then waved Grace over.

"Hi, Honey. Glad to see you finally made it," Grace said, hooking her arm through Aidan's. "Isn't this place fabulous?"

"Yeah, it's great." He moved to kiss her, but she turned her cheek to him. He whispered in her ear. "You look gorgeous. Do you want to dance?"

She wrinkled her nose.

"Not now. I have a lot of mingling to do. Come on. There's some people I want you to meet." Grace turned to Tony. "Would you go retrieve your wife from upstairs? Tell Eve that Mr. Minoshowa should be here soon, and I need her to find me when he arrives."

"Is he the computer guy?" Tony asked.

"He owns a technology company, and he spent $2.8 million in advertising in our four magazines this year. Nobody calls him the *computer guy*, especially my assistant's boyfriend. That's absolutely offensive."

Aidan tried to diffuse her irritation.

"Lighten up, Grace. He only meant—"

"I know what he meant," she said quietly, taking her anger down ten notches, "but a comment like that could destroy my chances for the promotion. You know—you *both* know how important that is to me, how hard I worked for that."

Tony walked away.

"Grace, you can't treat our friends that way. It doesn't matter that Eve works for you. They're our friends first, and nothing—no job, no promotion—should ever supersede that."

Grace looked at him with quizzical eyes as if searching her mind for a reply, but a young, red-haired woman tapped her on the shoulder and stole her attention.

"Ms. Sullivan, you remember my husband, Jonas." The woman smiled brightly as she introduced her spouse, a tall, bearded fellow with square-rimmed glasses.

As Grace turned to shake hands, Aidan heard the band in the bordering room announce a short break. Through the throng of people that began to disperse, he noticed an angel ice sculpture standing tall above a fountain of red punch. And then he noticed *her*. Just a quick glimpse before the crowd eclipsed his view, but he recognized her face, her smile, her lovely long hair, and her enchanting brown eyes. It was the girl from the jewelry store.

*But, no, it can't be.*

Aidan doubted that angelic vision of her in a white dress, and tried to peer over and around the people to see if his eyes were playing tricks on him. With no sight of the woman anywhere in the room, Aidan applied reason, and thought that his doubts about Grace had seeped into his head and caused a subconscious hallucination.

"Come, Aidan." Grace's voice broke through his delirium. "I see my boss at the buffet table."

"Who was that girl you were talking to?"

"That was Sara. She writes copy in the Marketing Department."

"Isn't that the girl that was married in September?"

"Yeah, that's her. And that's all she talked about for the longest time. Now it's Eve getting ready for her wedding in June. Wedding this, wedding that. You'd think it was the most important day of her life."

Grace said it with such seriousness that Aidan couldn't tell if she was being sarcastic since he had only the back of her head to look at as she led him through the room. They never really talked about it—marriage or even their getting married, except one time in Las Vegas—but for

Aidan the thoughts had always been present, somewhere in the corner of his mind, from the first day he met Grace. He had asked himself then, *Could I spend the rest of my life with this woman?* And though he couldn't answer it at that time, he repeatedly asked himself the question over the course of their relationship and yet again on the wing of his proposal … *Could I?*

Their walking came to a halt.

"So nice to see you, Mr. Bronson. You remember my boyfriend, Aidan McGregor."

Aidan extended his hand as Mr. Bronson looked up from his plate of sliced roast beef. The man balanced the dish with his left arm in order to shake Aidan's hand, nodding cordially before a basket of rolls courted his attention. Grace insisted on conversation.

"You met Aidan at Sara's wedding in September."

"Yes, yes. How's the law business?"

"Good."

Grace piped in, "Aidan's the trial attorney for the Morrison wrongful death case. It's all over the newspapers these days."

"I read a bit about it. Medical malpractice," the man remarked. "Expecting a verdict anytime soon?"

"The defense has few more days of testimony, then it's in the jury's hands."

"Well, good luck." Mr. Bronson looked down at his plate indicating his desire to eat.

"Wonderful buffet," Grace commented, obviously wanting to extend the conversation to keep in her boss's good graces.

"Yes, Grace, you did a superb job, but then I expected no less." His smile equated approval. "Now, if you'll excuse me, I'd like to join my wife."

Grace stepped aside, her eyes gleaming with happiness. She waited till her boss was out of ear range then squeezed Aidan's hand.

"Did you hear what he said? He has complete confidence in my abilities. That promotion is nearly mine!"

"Congratulations."

"Well, it's not mine yet," she said as Aidan watched her glance around the room for someone else to schmooze.

"I'm starved. Let's eat, Grace."

"I've no time for eating. I have to mingle. Plus, Mr. Minoshowa is due any minute." She kissed Aidan on the cheek then wiped at the lipstick mark it left. "You'll be all right without me, won't you, honey?"

"Of course, but I don't know why you drag me to these things if you're going to abandon me for the night." He marked his sarcasm with a serious frown. Touching the ring box in his pocket, Aidan again doubted his decision to propose.

"Oh, I do no such thing. It's just a little mingling. I'll be back before you even miss me." Grace kissed the air next to his cheek, then sauntered off to a small circle of people gathered by the stairs.

Nearly two hours had passed before Aidan could capture her attention again. Dessert was being served, and many guests were saying their goodbyes for the night. He saw Grace standing by a huge, arch-shaped window, the moonlight and the room lights bronzing her blonde hair as she chatted with a group of people. She looked like a goddess with her curly hair draping her shoulders. If the proposal was ever going to happen, now seemed the time.

"Come with me." Aidan took her hand.

"I don't have time for this," Grace protested.

Ignoring the pleas, he led her upstairs to the loft—a spacious area partitioned by giant canvases from which hung large and small portrait paintings. Aidan perused the loft for guests. Seeing no one, he took Grace into his arms and kissed her. She responded with a soft purring that pushed every doubt out of his mind.

"I love you, Grace."

"I love you, too."

"We've been together for so long—three years now, and I can't imagine my life without you. We've had our ups and downs, and we've been able to work through them. I don't think there's anything we can't overcome together."

"I know. I feel the same way."

"And there is no one else I want to be with. Only you. And that's why I think it's time we make this permanent." Aidan dropped to one knee and took her left hand to his lips, kissing her fingers. "Grace, will you marry me?"

# CHAPTER 3

Callie brushed off the top step of the stairs leading to the loft and sat down, hoping not to dirty her white dress. Although noisy down in the main area with the party and band at full volume, she could clearly hear the voices in the loft. Someone had just proposed marriage. Callie didn't want to intrude on such an intimate moment, so she perched herself on the step, eavesdropping, waiting for the woman's emphatic and ecstatic *Yes*! There was a long silence where Callie assumed the couple was kissing in celebration of their most romantic moment.

"I love you, honey," the woman began. "Our time together is wonderful, and there isn't anyone else I want to be with either, but I can't marry you—not now."

Callie stifled a gasp. It had been such a passionate, endearing proposal. "No" just didn't make sense. Callie listened as the woman continued her explanation.

"There is so much going on with my life right now."

"At work you mean?" he asked.

"Exactly."

"The promotion?"

"Yes, the promotion," she answered. "You know how important that is to me."

"So we'll have a long engagement. No one's saying that we have to get married tomorrow. We'll wait a bit."

"No, that won't work. I can't be engaged. That ring symbolizes you and family and a dozen other distractions that will eliminate me as a candidate for the vice-presidency of my department. I know it, and I'm not going to risk blowing the opportunity of a lifetime. I've worked too hard for it."

There was a long silence, and this time Callie knew it had nothing to do with kissing. The fellow was obviously hurt and at a loss for words.

"And what if you do get the promotion in February?" he asked, his voice tainted with turmoil. "What's going to change then, Grace? I can only imagine that your workload will be even greater. Where does marriage and family fit in?"

"It doesn't—not now. Let's talk about this in six months."

"No, we have to talk about it now. I'm not going to put *my* life on hold till you figure out what you want in *your* life. It doesn't work that way. Either we both want the same things or we go our separate ways."

"You're breaking up with me?" Insult coated her voice.

"I see no other option. We clearly want different things. I'm ready to be married. I want to start a family. I'm 36; you're 35. I don't want to start having kids when we're in our 40's."

"But—"

"I won't—"

"—it's almost Christmas."

"I can't just be your companion, someone to fill your free time. I need to be a priority." His voice became a bit louder and more frustrated. "Damn it, Grace, I deserve that."

"But I love you."

"At a point, those become just words."

Callie couldn't listen anymore. Feeling his pain, she descended the stairs and waited near the front door for the couple to return to the party. She was only half-surprised when the woman—who Callie recognized as Grace Sullivan, the person from the publishing company in charge of the details for tonight's party—had come down from the loft alone. Callie thought about approaching her, but Grace looked relatively calm and collected with no tear-stained cheeks as she rejoined the party.

Callie continued to wait for the man to exit the loft, but he never came down. After a few minutes, Callie went up to make sure he was okay.

As she turned the corner around the first partitioned area, Callie saw the guy and recognized him as the man from the jewelry store.

"Hello," she said.

Aidan, leaning against the wall, looked up, surprise replacing his sad face.

"Hello. You're the brown eyes—uh—girl from the jewelry store. You work for Graymoore Publishing, too?"

"No." Callie shook her head. "This is my art gallery. I'm Callista—Callie Emerson."

"Nice to meet you again." Aidan shook her hand. "And you also own the jewelry store?"

"Oh, no. That's my uncle's store. I only help out there sometimes." A silence fell between them as she hesitated asking about his popping the question. "So, can I show you some art?"

"If it's gonna be anything like you showed me rings, I'll pass. I'm not up for a lecture."

Callie chuckled.

"Come on. I'll show you some art."

He shrugged his shoulders.

"I wouldn't know good from bad, not a creative bone in my body."

"There is no bad art—at least not in my gallery."

"I didn't mean—sorry." He stammered over his words. "Sure, show me something, but nothing abstract. I like to know what I'm looking at."

"All right. Step around to the other side," Callie instructed.

Aidan scanned the wall of various sized, black-and-white pictures framed dramatically in onyx or chrome casings.

"These are photos, not paintings."

"That's right. They were taken by Deardra Manning. She's a freelance photographer. She's got a slew of credits to her name, including having worked for *The American*."

"Really. That's impressive."

"People, faces are her specialty." Callie watched Aidan look from one photo to the next.

"This one." He pointed to the black-and-white photo depicting a ballet dancer, puddled on the stage, clutching her ankle.

"That's *Death of a Dancer.*"

"There's so much pain and sadness in her face," he commented.

"And fear, too. That ballerina is Jill Urakowa. She danced for the New York Ballet. She was fabulous, so graceful. This particular night, during the performance, her ankle snapped. And what Deardra caught is Jill's mixture of emotions at age 30 knowing that her career had come to an end."

Aidan stared at the picture, his face taking on some of the same sentiment as he obviously thought about his relationship with Grace coming to its own end.

"How did the proposal go?"

He shot her a guarded look.

"You know?"

"I overheard some of it." Callie winced seeing the pained expression return to his face. "I'm sorry."

"I feel like a total idiot. I should have seen it coming." He gestured to the many portraits surrounding them. "I feel like all these faces are staring at me, mocking me. It's as if I've died and gone to hell."

"Come with me." Callie reached for and grasped his hand. "I'll show you my little bit of heaven."

They walked to the back of the loft, behind another immense canvas supported by chains hanging from the beamed ceiling. The space, painted a very pale blue, was draped with white lace and tiny white lights. Six long tables covered with a similar lacey fabric formed a semi-circular shape, and on these tables sat over fifty glorious angels of different heights, all with golden brown hair and blue eyes.

A subtle palette defined the ceramic angels with their hands steepled in prayer or clasping candles or holding hymnals. Their wings, some of them spread for flight, as well as their dresses glistened with iridescent lusters of green-blues, golds, and copper. Each one so beautiful and so special to Callie's heart. The angels were her most prized creations, her most cherished pieces of art. And here in this space, the farthest corner of the loft, it actually felt like being in the clouds, beyond her universe known as Massachusetts.

"So, what do you think?" she asked, bubbling with pride.

Aidan haphazardly glanced around the room.

"I can't believe I got shot down. I just wasted the last two years of my life." He paced along the arched tables. "Spent so much time looking for the right ring, and I didn't even have the right woman. Damn it. I feel like a complete idiot."

"Don't. You fell in love, and that's never a bad thing. It takes two to make a relationship work. Maybe she'll change her mind."

"Grace? Yeah, right," he said sarcastically. "You don't know her. Grace strategizes everything, and right now her plan of action is her career. Me, marriage, and children don't fit into that plan."

"Well, at least you found out before you married her. Divorce is hell. My sister, Maisy, had—"

"I wish I found out two years ago. What a waste of time. Now I'll have to start all over again, and let me tell you—several of my friends are single out in the dating scene, and they tell me it's slim pickings. Try and find beauty and brains and sexy in one woman. It's nearly impossible."

"It'll happen, I'm sure. When you're least looking for it, she'll be right in front of your face."

Callie watched Aidan look distractedly from the table and up at her.

"Would you like to go out sometime?"

"Me?" She widened her eyes. "I don't think so."

"I'll buy you a drink, a martini maybe."

"I don't drink vodka."

"Dinner then?"

"I don't think so."

"You sure?"

"Yes, I'm sure. You're on the rebound, and I'm not interested in being anyone's transitional girlfriend."

"Oh, I didn't mean—not that way." He shook his head and fumbled for words. "A date? He laughed. "God no. It's just that you're easy to talk to, and I thought that—well, never mind." He pulled his business card from his pocket and gave it to her. "If I can ever repay the favor, Brown Eyes, call. I'm going to be on my way now."

Callie followed Aidan down the stairs. He went out the door, and she headed for the bar.

"I'll have vodka and cranberry juice; hold the cranberry juice."

♥                    ♥                    ♥

The next morning, Callie woke to a solid rapping at her front door. She glanced at the clock, then jumped from the bed seeing that it was 10:00 a.m. She grabbed her robe and darted down the stairs. A quick peak out the window confirmed it was Nick, and she opened the solid, red door of her farmhouse to her dear friend.

"Nick, I'm so sorry. I overslept." She stepped aside as a blustery wind escorted his six-foot frame inside. Pulling his knit cap from his blonde hair, he shook his head and brushed the static from his short locks.

"It seems someone had a party that I wasn't invited to." Nick scratched at his morning stubble as his green eyes perused the adjoining living room for some sign of a previous night's celebration.

"*I* wasn't even on the guest list. A publishing company rented out the gallery for their Christmas party last night." She closed the door and stepped into a puddle of wet snow that had dripped from Nick's boots. "Darn it." She pulled the soggy sock from her foot. "Make yourself comfortable. I'm going to put on some dry socks."

"I'll be in the kitchen."

Nick slipped off his jacket and hung it on the coat rack in the hall. He wore a thick navy ski sweater with two tan stripes woven around the collar and cuffs. Callie watched him wipe the slush from his boots onto the braided matt. Casually, he inspected their dryness, and seeing that they were too wet to traipse through the house on the wooden plank floors, Nick unlaced his boots, pulled them off and set them near the radiator.

A shudder ran through him as he stepped on the cold floors with his socks.

"Mind if I start a fire?" he asked.

"No, please do." She stopped mid-stride on the stairs and leaned over the handrail. "I brought some extra wood in last night. It's still in the mud room by the back door." Continuing up the stairs, she halted her ascent, and back-stepped down the stairs. "I'll help you."

"Go!" He shooed her up the stairs. "I'll take care of it. Go now. And comb your hair while you're up there, and put on something a little less frumpy. If I wanted to see frumpy, I'd spend Sunday mornings with my mother." He pointed to her red terry cloth robe. "Good Lord, Callie, I hope you don't wear that thing around your boyfriend."

"I don't have a boyfriend, remember?"

"Yes, yes, no wonder, wearing bed clothes like those." He snapped his fingers at her. "Give me that horrific robe. I'll use it for fire kindling."

Callie smiled. She absolutely loved Nick and his sense of humor. He had been in her life for a year now, and she couldn't imagine herself without him. They had met when Nick came to Appassionata to purchase art for his new restaurant in Boston. On a tight budget, he had traveled outside of the city to Callie's gallery to find affordable but classic art. He had chosen eight of Callie's paintings—all landscapes but eclectic as to location—from the sunny beaches of southern California and the ridged mountains of Sierra, Nevada, to the snow-kissed hills of Austria and the magical Blue Grotto of Capri.

Through the hours Callie spent with him choosing the artwork, a natural rapport developed. Consequently, she reduced Nick's original purchase price by 50 percent. He was grateful; she was enamored. Nick possessed all the qualities she sought in a man—kind, considerate, outgoing, humorous, sexy—but Callie soon learned she was not his type. His type was male.

"Mimosa or latte?" Nick asked upon Callie's entrance into the kitchen ten minutes later. As gallant as a knight, he smiled and pulled the chair out for her, then resumed his cooking at the stove, wielding his spatula and wooden spoon with the medieval deftness of a Viking and his jewel-encrusted sword.

"Caffeine, please. I'm still not awake yet."

"So tell me about this party last night," he said, glancing over his shoulder before reaching for the coffee pot. "Who catered it?"

"A restaurant outside of Boston." Callie paused as Nick handed her a cup of coffee to which she added sugar and milk. "I don't remember its name, though."

"Details, Callie, details. These are the details that I crave: name of restaurant, dishes on the menu." He turned back to the stove where he took a half-dozen eggs and cracked them into a bowl. "Tell me about the food. How was the food? Not as good as mine, I'm sure."

"No, of course, not. If I'd had my way, Nick, I would've hired you."

"So, tell me," he persisted with a fleeting look in her direction, "what was served?"

"The usual hot trays, ziti, chicken marsala, sausage and peppers."

Nick let out a gasp of disapproval.

"Ziti. So blasé. Anything out of the ordinary? Salmon crepes wrapped in prosciutto?

"No."

She looked up from her coffee to see Nick smiling, obviously taking great pleasure in the fact that he cooked dishes of exceptional taste, unique with his own brand of ingredients, seasonings, and garnishings.

"What about the desserts?" he asked. "Anything delectable?"

"Nick, you're making it sound like the food was awful. It wasn't; it was good, just not anything near as good as what you cook."

"Thank you. I appreciate the compliment. And had you showered this morning, I'd could toss one back to you."

"Humph," Callie moaned as she grabbed a scrunchie from the counter and pulled her hair into a ponytail, completely self-conscious in her flowered nightshirt and thick grey wool socks. "Just for that, let me tell you how much everyone raved over the cheesecake last night."

"Really? Did *you* rave?"

"I did better than rave. I brought a piece home."

"Let me taste it."

"You're joking, right? We're about to eat breakfast."

"I don't joke about food." Nick turned off the gas and moved the pan from the burner to a butcher-block board, insistent on sampling the cheesecake. "Let me taste it.

As hungry as she was for breakfast, Callie trudged to the refrigerator, removed the plastic-covered plate, and set it before Nick on the table. Like a doctor examining a patient, Nick removed the plastic wrap and inspected the cake. He sniffed at it, held it up and studied it from all angles.

"Fork, please," Nick said.

Feeling like his nurse, she handed him a fork from the table and watched him taste the cheesecake. First, he nibbled then he took a larger bite, savoring the piece in his mouth for nearly a minute before swallowing. Finally, he slammed the fork on the table.

"I know why it tastes so good," he said in an omniscient voice riddled with disgust.

"Why?"

"It's mine."

"Yours?"

"Yes, mine."

"You baked this?" she asked, giving into her rumbling stomach and dipping one finger into the side of the cheesecake and licking it.

"No."

"They bought it from you?"

"No."

"I don't understand, Nick." She attempted another finger-swipe at the cheesecake, but he stopped her hand mid-flight.

"They stole the recipe from me."

"You're joking."

"Callie, I told you I don't joke about food. It's my livelihood."

"It's cheesecake, Nick. There are a million recipes for cheesecake. How do you know it's yours?"

"I know. Believe me, I know. There're two ingredients in this cake that no one's ever put in cheesecake but it gives it a rather distinct taste. Plus the way it's decorated. My recipe is very specific about the nut mixture of the crust being one-third up the side, full circumference. Even the chocolate is drizzled in my same pattern." He handed the plate back to her as if sending a spoiled meal back to the chef in the kitchen. "Get this away from me."

"Nick, don't you think it's just some weird coincidence?"

"No, I don't, considering this is the second such incident I've witnessed. I'm sure I have a spy in my restaurant."

"What do you mean 'second such incident'? You never said anything to me before."

"Well, before, I thought it was just some *weird coincidence* with my veal saltimbocca recipe, but now I have no doubt. Someone is stealing my recipes."

"Who?"

"I don't know but I'm going to find out."

"What was the name of the restaurant that catered the affair last night."

"I can't remember. I'll have to check the gallery. I'm sure there's a business card somewhere."

"Thank you."

"Well," Callie said, puttering to the stove and relighting the burner. "Let's discuss suspects over the omelet."

"No, let's talk about something else," he muttered still distracted with thoughts of the thief. Nick sipped at his coffee then seemed to realize that Callie was cooking at the stove. "Here, let me do that. Go sit your pretty self down."

"*Pretty self.* I guess we're back to compliments."

"Callie, you know I think you're gorgeous, especially when you're all dolled up as I suppose you were last night, turning a hundred heads. Any handsome men at this party?"

"None you'd be interested in."

"And what's that supposed to mean?"

"You know, Nick, it's like I always say: The good ones are either too young or married or gay."

Nick laughed.

"Well, number three poses *no* problem for me, but I wasn't asking for myself. Remember that chef I told you about?"

"Michael?"

"Well, we've gone out a few times."

"And?"

"And we get along, so I'm not looking for anyone else right now. I was asking for *you*. We got to get you on the market again, Callie."

"Don't do me any favors. It's not so pleasant out there. And even if you meet the right person, it just may not be the right person."

"Okay, now I'm dizzy." Nick spun his eyes. "Could you not talk in circles?"

"One of the guests at the party proposed to his girlfriend who actually said no." Callie hitched herself up on the counter stool and told Nick about Aidan's rejection.

"Could the whole Aidan/Grace thing be bothering you because it hits a little too close to home? Sounds a lot like you and Joe."

"Oh my God. I didn't even tell you who stopped in the gallery yesterday!"

"I'm thinking it might be Joe."

"Yes! Along with his pregnant wife." Callie used her hands to show how big the woman's stomach was. "She looked ready to burst. And he—well, Joe looked great, but it was really uncomfortable seeing him with her."

"Jealous? If not for a twist in fate, it could've been you pregnant with his child."

Sighing, Callie tried to push those thoughts from her head.

"I can't change the past."

"No, but you can learn from it." Nick sprinkled some cheese into the omelet. "Did he buy anything?"

"Matter of fact, he did. He bought a painting for his parents—one of *my* paintings."

"Congratulations. Which one?"

"Café Capri."

"In the piazza in Italy? I loved that one." Turning his attention back to the stove, Nick lowered the gas on the burner. "So did you two talk? Did he have anything to say about—"

"About us? Nothing. What could he say? It wasn't his fault; it was my fault we broke up."

"What about the gallery? Did he say anything about your art?"

"He bought my art. That says a lot. It's weird that it took him this long to appreciate my work."

Nick cocked his head to one side, a sure-tell sign that he was going to say something profound.

"What's weird about it? It took you this long to appreciate *him*."

♥              ♥              ♥

On Sunday afternoon in the midst of re-organizing the gallery after Saturday night's party, Callie received a phone call from her uncle.

"Callie, my pooch," he said in the fondest way. He had nicknamed Callie "pooch" when she was a little girl because she had a hard time pronouncing her name, always referring to herself as "Collie." Since then her uncle affectionately called her "pooch."

"Hi, Uncle Don. How's Aunt Agnes feeling?"

"Better everyday. She'll be able to have family visitors this week. You must go and see her."

"I will."

"Now, pooch, I've been going over the receipts since Thursday tonight, and I don't see anything for the 2 carat platinum diamond that was in the window. Allan worked Friday and Saturday, and he said he didn't sell it or see it. He thought you sold it Thursday."

"I did sell a diamond on Thursday. The receipt and credit card transaction should be there."

"Yes, I do see one for the 2 carat tear-shaped diamond set in white gold, but not for the other ring."

Callie thought for a moment. She couldn't have lost the ring. She remembered locking the cases after Aidan left the store. But then she recalled how the rings had tumbled to the ground, and he had helped her pick them up. Had he pocketed one of the rings? Callie remembered how he quickly chose a ring after that, probably because he wanted to distract her with a purchase, then leave the store before she noticed the ring missing. Aidan had obviously stolen the ring.

*Oh, Lord, I can't let Uncle Don know how irresponsible I've been.*

"Hello, pooch? You still there?"

"Yes, I'm still here. I'm sorry about the mix-up. I did sell another ring on Thursday. I forgot all about it. The customer paid cash, and I didn't want to leave all that money in the store's safe, so I brought it home with me. I have it in an envelope at the house. I'll bring it by in the morning."

"Oh, that's a relief. I would have hated to see that ring go missing or, worse yet, stolen. It's got a $7,000 price tag."

Callie had money set aside for the bathroom being installed in the studio to accommodate the school children from the field trips she hosted. Callie would have to withdraw those funds to give to her uncle until she could get the ring back from Aidan. Just how she was going to do that, Callie didn't yet know.

Four days had passed, and still Callie wasn't any closer to devising a plan to meet Aidan and convince him to return the ring to her. She had his business card, but she couldn't just pick up the phone and say *Aidan, it's me Callie, the woman from the gallery. Remember, we met in the jewelry store when you were STEALING one of my uncle's rings. NOW GIVE IT BACK!*

No, that wouldn't work. She needed a plan, a subtle approach … so smooth that it would be like stealing the ring back from him.

"Aidan McGregor, please." Callie waited a patient second while the receptionist put her on hold.

"Good afternoon, Mr. McGregor's office," a sprite young voice said.

"Hi, Aidan McGregor, please."

"And who may I say is calling?"

"Callie Emerson."

"One moment." The classical music on the hold button calmed her jitters. Although she was the honest one here, Callie couldn't help feeling like she was doing something deceptive.

"Callie? Brown Eyes from the gallery, right?"

"Yes, that's me."

"Nice to hear from you. What can I do for you?"

"Well—" She heard the quiver in her voice and paused for composure. "I was wondering if you'd like to have dinner tomorrow. Thought you might like to talk some more."

"You have perfect timing. I—actually my firm won a big case today, and we're having a celebration of sorts tomorrow. How about you drive over to my office at three?"

"Well, that's a bit early but I suppose—"

"Great. I'll see you at three."

"Okay. See you then."

"Oh, Brown Eyes, one more thing."

"What's that?"

"Pack a bag."

"Pack a what?" she asked, doubting she had heard him correctly.

"Pack a bag. You know, just a few things to get you by till Sunday."

"Sunday! Where are we going?"

"Las Vegas."

"I couldn't possibly—"

"Sure you can. It'll be fun."

"Aidan, I don't think—"

"Don't think. Just say yes. Where's your spontaneity? Be a little adventurous."

Traveling with a stranger wasn't spontaneous or adventurous. It was downright dangerous. She wanted to trust Aidan; he seemed nice enough, but then again he was a jewel thief.

*Damn!*

Callie forgot for a moment the whole purpose of her seeing Aidan. The ring. She had to get the ring back.

"All right," she conceded, realizing she hadn't only lost a diamond ring.

*I've lost my common sense, too!*

# CHAPTER 4

Twenty thousand feet in the air kept Callie from walking out on her jet mates: three young, pompous attorneys and their even-younger blonde girlfriends who sat like trophies, adorned in gold necklaces and bracelets and rings, while their boyfriends paradoxically celebrated a $3 million jury verdict resulting from the tragic death of a promising young actress. Not a single mention of sadness over the girl's death, just repeated pats on the proverbial back for their exemplary legal strategy and questioning of the negligent doctor.

"Do you need some aspirin?" Aidan asked her. "You keep rubbing your forehead."

"I already took two when you dozed off. I'll be fine." She looked out the first-class window through the feathery clouds to the hard ground and wanted nothing more than to push out the cabin door and plunge to her death.

"Aidan," one of the partners called from across the aisle, holding up a glass of some clear alcoholic beverage. "Here's to you and your silver tongue or should I say *gold* for your exquisite cross-examination of Dr. Pizat." He took a sip of the liquid and then cleared his throat to imitate Aidan's voice. "'Let's recall for a moment, Dr. Pizat, your journal article, already marked as Exhibit 64, published exactly four months prior to Miss Dublon's surgery, surgery which you testified in detail about how you performed. Is it true that you acted outside your *published* method of procedure and that deviation from your own recommended standard of medical procedure resulted in a hemorrhage....'"

Callie looked again out the window. Using her mental canvas for escape, Callie painted a picture, but she could find no color, only stroke after stroke of black—an ugly picture that captured her mood. Aidan patted her hand and smiled, oblivious to her upset. Although he didn't contribute to his partners' egoist conversation and their spin on justice nor gloat about the verdict, his silence annoyed her just as much.

Callie tried valiantly to think of Aidan in a positive light. She looked at him wearing a diamond design shirt of fall colors; at least he had style. Maybe he was different. Maybe he was one of the *good* lawyers like her cousin Peter—one who put people ahead of profit, one who had honest pursuit for truth and justice, one who advocated for the weak and elderly, one who made Lady Justice proud. However, Aidan sat silent next to her. Not a single word to define his character as anything but a self-serving attorney ... and jewel thief.

*The sooner I find that ring, the sooner I can get away from this man.*

Las Vegas sparkled with color. Red, blue, yellow, silver and gold glittered among the massive buildings with neon letters taller than small New England trees. The avenue beckoned tourists with an assortment of restaurants from six-dollar buffets to bohemian cuisine, replica monuments like the Eiffel Tower and Statue of Liberty, and headlining entertainment. From every corner people bustled with dogged determination to get from one place to another.

Though Christmas season, shopping and gifts didn't seem the intended destination for when Callie stepped into the hotel's casino, there she saw the lure of Las Vegas: gambling. One-armed bandits shook hands with hopeful slot-players as short-skirted waitresses catered to their beverage needs. In other areas, black jack, roulette, and craps invited bets from smartly dressed men in cordoned off areas with potential payoffs seemingly worth the gamble.

As Callie walked through the casino with Aidan to the front desk to check in, she could hear the machines' bells and the rustle of chips coupled with the moans and praise attributed to luck. *Luck's against me today! Luck's doubled our money!* Callie didn't believe in luck, chance, or the proverbial throw of the dice. She felt that each person was responsible for his or her own life—by means of solid or reckless choices—not left to the mercy or ill humor of luck.

Standing in line waiting to register, Aidan whispered to Callie, "I'm sure they reserved us one room. If you're uncomfortable with that, I'll get you your own room."

Callie thought for a moment, realizing she had to throw fate a bone. If Aidan had brought the ring to Vegas, as she suspected in order to pawn it out of state in a place where the exchange of valuables for cash was an everyday occurrence—no questions asked—the only way to recover the ring was to have access to Aidan's luggage, and that would be nearly impossible if they had separate rooms.

"No, Aidan, one room's okay. I'm sure you'll be a perfect gentleman."

The room turned out to be a very expensive luxury suite with a vast view of the city's landscape once the thick blue drapes had been pulled open. Intricate moldings detailed the perimeter of the room, and a dazzling gold chandelier hung from a fresco ceiling. A gleaming black marble bathroom with a spa tub and glass shower courted Callie's attention away from the bed.

*One bed.*

The suite had one king-size bed.

*Where am I gonna sleep? Where's Aidan gonna sleep? Oh, God!*

A pain shot over her shoulders and down her back.

*Lord, must I carry this cross alone?*

"Let's go," Aidan urged, taking her hand, leading her out to the hall and the elevators.

"Shouldn't we unpack first?"

"Later. Let's explore." His voice held excitement like a child's. "There's so much to see. I don't want to waste a minute. We only have the weekend."

They wandered through the hotel and the gaming rooms, past some expensive shops with designer clothes and stylish handbags. Callie felt a bit underdressed in a pair of jeans and white silk top, but her red lace-up ankle boots drew sufficient attention from Aidan and a few passerbys to uplift her spirit.

"Hungry?" he asked, heading outside towards the strip. "I'm starved." He held her hand and strode with a purposeful gait as if he had a plotted course. "I know a great restaurant, but it's a bit of a walk to the other casino. Can you make it in those sexy shoes or should I hail a taxi?"

"I'm fine walking. So, you've been here before?"

"Yeah, last year."

"Another verdict celebration?"

"So to speak."

They paused to cross the street.

"I don't understand how you can celebrate these verdicts," Callie griped at the risk of offending him. "Your clients are people who've died or are maimed. It just doesn't seem right."

"You're not looking at it the right way. I fight for their causes, their payment for wrongful death or pain and suffering." He spoke with reverence. "Yes, I get a percentage when we win the case, but the fact is I—my partners and I work really hard to get those verdicts. There's usually years of paperwork preceding the trial."

Aidan's humble explanation in contrast with his partners' bragging kept Callie from harping on the subject.

"How long have you been an attorney?"

"About eight years. We got our first big verdict about four years ago, and it got a lot of press, and after that, the practice just grew with good cases."

"Good cases," she repeated.

"I feel a legal brief coming on. What do I have to say to convince you I'm one of the good guys?"

"You make money at the expense of others."

"No, Brown Eyes, I make money *helping* others. Our legal system is twisted and complicated, and without lawyers like me, these people would have no recourse to get the compensation they deserve." Aidan let go of her hand and met her stare with raw spirit. "I won't let you put down my profession. We can debate this all night; I'm gonna win."

"Okay, okay. I'm sorry. I never really looked at it that way."

"All right." He took her hand again. "No more legal talk, okay?"

"Okay."

They continued up the avenue, and a young couple, wearing the smiles of *Just Married*, emerged from a taxi at the entrance to a hotel. The woman wore a white gabardine wide-legged pantsuit and a veil and held a bouquet of red roses trimmed by a white lace ribbon.

"I was hoping Grace and I could elope last year when we were here, but she hated the idea."

"So you proposed to her last year, too?"

"Not really. It was just one of those things, you know, walking past a chapel, getting swept up in the moment and saying, 'Let's get married.' She stomped on the idea immediately. I didn't take it personally, though. I just thought that she wanted a formal proposal and a big church wedding. Looking back now after what happened with—" Aidan shrugged. "I should've realized then that Grace just didn't want to get married period."

"Everything happens for a reason. You gotta look at the big picture."

"Yeah, I hope it involves some winning bets later tonight," Aidan joked but his eyes still looked sad.

"You're a good gambler?"

"Good? Hmm, I'd say *somewhat skilled*."

"You really mean *lucky*, don't you? Isn't it all about luck on your part, the gambler? It's the casinos that are skilled. These buildings weren't built on luck, ya know. The owners know how to win, they've calculated the odds, and they know you're gonna lose more often than not."

"Gee, another sparring match?" he quipped. "What's got you in a snit? Your shoes tied too tight?"

"Sorry. I just believe that people have to own up to their choices. Luck doesn't shape our lives. We make our lives."

"We're talking about gambling, Brown Eyes, black jack, craps. Don't be so serious. This is Vegas." He tugged her hand. "Sometimes you just gotta let life happen. Put $500 on red."

"Five hundred dollars is a lot of money to a lot of people. I couldn't make a bet like that without a lot of thought first."

"Yes," Aidan concurred, "I suppose so, you being a starving artist and all that."

He said it with such seriousness that Callie couldn't tell if he was teasing her. She pulled her hand out of his grasp and gestured grandly.

"I consider myself a very successful artist. My gallery does quite well."

"Oh, I didn't mean—I was just kidding around, Brown Eyes. Your gallery's great." He reached for her hand again and squeezed it in a patronizing sort of way. "I'm not much of an art aficionado, but I'm sure you could teach me. You gave me quite a lesson on diamonds last week."

*Yes,* Callie thought to herself, *so good a lesson that you stole the most expensive diamond in the store!*

Callie just wanted to go home. All she could hope for was that she'd find the ring among Aidan's personal belongings. Either that or maybe she'd give luck a try with a dollar in the slot machine to solve her $7,000 problem.

Later after dinner, Callie and Aidan met up with his partners at the black jack table. Their girlfriends were noticeably absent, so while Aidan deliberated the value of his first hand, Callie slipped away from his side and returned to the suite. She quickly unpacked her bag then tried to settle her stomach as she opened Aidan's small suitcase.

Feeling like a criminal herself, Callie perspired with panic at every noise seeping in from the hallway. Sure she would be caught, she rehearsed an excuse while lifting out his clothes and placing them on the floor. She searched the side pockets and unzippered pouches for the ring. Nothing. She opened the black satchel containing his toiletries and rummaged through bottles of shaving cream, cologne, deodorant, toothpaste, toothbrush, velvet box, razor, nail trimmer, dental floss—VELVET BOX! Callie grabbed the box and flipped it open to find gold cufflinks.

*Damn.*

Disappointed, Callie figured Aidan must have kept the ring on his person, probably in his pocket. Maybe that was the reason for the exploratory walk: to scope out a pawnshop. Callie didn't remember seeing such a place, but then again, the city in all its glitz had clearly distracted her.

After Callie repacked Aidan's suitcase, she set it by the bed, then turned on the gas fireplace, curling up on the sofa in front of it. She wished she were home in front of her own fireplace under one of the blankets her mom had crocheted. It seemed odd to be somewhere rather warm without snow one week before Christmas. Callie missed home, missed Massachusetts.

A click of the door signaled Aidan's return two hours later.

"Brown Eyes, you asleep?" He used quiet words and gently closed the door behind him.

"Hi, Aidan," Callie mumbled, not fully awake. Still in her street clothes, curled on the couch by the fire, she had drifted in and out of sleep over the past hour. "Sorry about ditching you, but I'm still on East Coast time. How did you do downstairs?"

"Won $3,000."

His smile gleamed through the shadows of the dimly lit room. He emptied his pockets onto the desk near the sofa, and Callie quickly focused on the pile for the ring. Nothing but cash and coins.

"That's great. You're good at black jack."

"Nah, just *lucky*." The emphasis on *lucky* referred back to their afternoon conversation. "Not a bit of skill except that you gotta be able to add to 21."

"Yeah, I would think that's a prerequisite."

Aidan picked up his suitcase and set it on the bed. He stood there for a long moment, not opening the suitcase but just staring at the bed as if it were the first time seeing it. Callie imagined the thoughts going through his head.

"I guess I should've asked for a room with *two* beds," he finally said rather apologetically. "You can have the bed. I'll sleep on the couch."

"Actually, Aidan, I'd rather sleep by the fire, even if it's a gas flame. It reminds me of home. I have this drafty old farmhouse, and some nights when it's really cold, I'll grab a quilt and sleep in the living room in front of the fire."

"Are you sure?"

"Yes, just toss me a pillow and blanket, and I'll be fine."

In the bathroom, Callie washed up and changed into a pink nightshirt. When she emerged, she saw that Aidan had fixed her a comfy bed on the sofa.

"Thank you," she said, neither of them making direct eye contact, though she glimpsed him in a white t-shirt and black boxers. "The bathroom's all yours."

Callie fought sleep till Aidan came out of the bathroom, said goodnight, and turned off the lights. Somewhere in the middle of a crazy dream where she was speeding along an icy road, Callie woke up to the sound of the toilet flushing and Aidan nudging her.

"Brown Eyes."

"Hmm? What's wrong?"

"I've got a ripping headache. Do you have any aspirin?"

"Yeah," she replied, sitting up to reach for her purse on the end table. "Here." She handed him a travel package of pain relief.

"Thanks."

Aidan popped two pills in his mouth, then returned to the bathroom to wash them down with water. He studied himself in the bathroom mirror. He looked old; he felt old. His bloodshot eyes stared back at him with no sympathy. At times he could be his own worst enemy. He blamed it on Grace. He missed her. God, how he wanted to deny that, forget her, be done with every memory of her. Yet even the Capitol of Vices couldn't distract him long enough to keep Grace from seeping into his mind. Why was he having such a hard time letting go—letting go of somebody who had already let go of him? Aidan turned off the bathroom light.

"Sorry I woke you," he mumbled on his way back to bed.

"Come here." Callie propped the pillow on her lap. "Lay down. I'll rub your head."

"You don't have to do that."

"I know." She patted the pillow. "Come on."

Aidan laid his head on the pillow, and Callie began stroking his scalp. She combed his hair with her fingers and massaged his forehead and temples. Her angel hands smoothed the pain from his head and hurt from his heart.

"That feels so good, Brown Eyes," he managed to say as his eyelids grew heavy.

"Why did you become a lawyer?"

It was a thought-evoking question that he didn't have the energy to answer.

"A lot of reasons. Why?"

"Just wondering." Her fingers continued their stroking. "Why did you tell the waiter in the restaurant tonight that you're an accountant?"

"Oh, I do that because it's easier that way. When I tell people I'm an attorney, I either get a dozen legal questions seeking my expertise or I get the cliché lawyer jokes."

"Did you hear the one about the honest lawyer?" Callie asked.

"No."

She laughed before dishing the punchline.

"That's because there are *no* honest lawyers."

"Yeah, funny. See what I mean."

"Sorry."

There was a long stretch of quiet, and Aidan closed his eyes as Callie's gentle touch soothed the ache in his head. His mind cleared of all thoughts as if she had poured whiteout fluid in his ear to erase all stressful memories. Nothing to think about, Aidan felt himself giving in to sleep.

"Aidan," Callie said softly through his layers of slumber, "did you ever think about opening your own practice?"

He just wanted to sleep, but he asked anyway, "Why?"

"I think God has a special plan for you."

"I don't believe in God."

"Really? You don't believe there's a higher power watching over us, helping us?" She paused for his answer, but Aidan didn't have the energy to debate the point. Callie continued, "I believe in God, not for what He does for me or what He can do for me but for what I can do for Him, the life I can live and the people I can help to better this world." She yawned. "And you have the power to do so much, Aidan, to help so many. I think you're smarter than your partners."

"This headache is my fault," he mumbled.

"I don't know about that." A long quiet bridged her next sentence. "I just think the gambling, the partying, the drinking—it's all out of character for you." Callie stopped rubbing his head, and Aidan felt her disappointment rip through him.

"My partners are good guys. They like to have fun. They're young, enjoying life, and this is Vegas." He sighed, wishing again for the silence to fall asleep. "I drank too much downstairs. That's a given, but that's my fault, not theirs."

"You're not like them, Aidan. They thrive on the win, and you—"

"I want an easier life." He knew that sounded shallow, so he added an explanation. "When you have your own practice, you work hard to generate a profit over expenses. You have rent, insurance, staff. In a group practice—"

"You have the same expenses."

"Yeah, but the income is multiplied by four, six, eight, however many attorneys are employed. In my firm, there's four of us. I work less; reap more."

"What exactly is *more*, and when is *more* enough? When will *more* make you happy? When will *more* bring you love? It seems you're letting the things you own define you, compromise you."

"Sure, I've compromised some things but it's allowed me a better life. I have a beautiful house, cars—"

Another long quiet surrounded them as Callie resumed rubbing his head. The last thing Aidan heard her say before he fell asleep on her lap meshed in dreams for many nights to come.

"It's allowed you to buy some things, but there's other things, Aidan, once you pawn them, you can't ever get them back."

♥ ♥ ♥

"How was your weekend?" Deardra asked as Callie looked up from the computer in her office. Deardra, a forever friend, a former and famous photographer, now worked part-time at the gallery paying bills and commissions so Callie could spend more time in the studio.

"My trip was educational."

Callie pressed the enter button on the keyboard, then logged off the computer.

"Two days in Las Vegas. I don't think anyone has used that word to describe that city."

"I'm talking about Aidan. I learned a lot about him. We bonded. He's a really nice guy."

"Did you find the ring?"

"He didn't steal the ring. He couldn't have. It'd be completely out of character for him."

"It's called temptation," Deardra blurted, derailing Callie's defense. "An expensive diamond glittering in his palm. It's only the most honorable man that denies the most primeval urge."

"He's honorable. We shared a suite, and he was a perfect gentleman. Not one primeval urge the entire weekend."

"If he didn't take the ring, then where is it? Somebody took it."

"I don't know what happened to it. I just know Aidan didn't take it. I really believe that."

"Boy, I want you sitting on my jury one day." Deardra lowered her voice to a deep bass to mimic a prosecutor. "Miss Juror, here's the smoking gun, the fingerprints, the forensic evidence, the motive, and you still vote not guilty?"

"Aidan's a good guy, Deardra. He didn't do it."

"Sounds like you're falling for him."

"No, it's not like that at all. We're friends. That's it. He's still recovering from his breakup."

"He'll be over her someday."

"And when that someday comes, I'll paint that picture. Right now, the canvas is bare."

"What about the ring? What about the money you're out?"

"You can't put a price tag on friendship."

"Maybe so, but I can put a price tag on that bathroom in the studio. How are you going to pay for it?"

"Don't worry about it, Deardra. It's my cross. I have till the end of the week to figure it out. If I could just stall the contractor for a few weeks, January has always been a good month, and I already have a few sales pending."

"I'll say a prayer."

"No!"

"What?"

"Don't waste your prayer on something as silly as this. I sometimes think that we only get one prayer answered, and I would hate to think you wasted yours on me."

The jingle of the front door bells alerted them to a visitor, and the Patriots cap, green eyes, and wide smile declared the man to be Rich Mackenzie, the general contractor.

"Morning, Ladies," he said, taking off his hat in a polite gesture.

About forty years old, Rich had lived his entire life in Sycamore, about three streets away from Callie's home, so his was a face she had grown up with. Built like a football player with a strong neck and formidable stance, he exuded that manly-man charm that reckoned him a force that could conquer any problem and protect young damsels from all distress. A hard body with strong hands, a bright mind, and a soft heart. That made him very attractive, especially to the single women who needed a helpful hand around the house from a knowledgeable man with a contracting license.

Rich placed a white box on the front desk.

"Puccini's pastries. Thought you might like some with your morning coffee."

"That was so nice," Callie gushed, more excited over the fact that he hadn't come into the gallery to ask for more money to cover the studio expenses.

"Well, I was in town picking up the tile for the bathroom."

"Does that mean the studio's almost done?" Callie tried not to sound panicky.

"Almost. We're a few weeks ahead of schedule." He smiled but seemed to pick up on her less-than-enthusiastic attitude. "Is there a problem? I thought you'd be happy to get it done and get me and my crew out of your hair."

"No, no, I'm happy. It's just that—well—I won't have the final payment till January, and we agreed that I'd pay you the last installment when the work was done."

"Oh, Callie, don't be frettin' over something like money. I know it's the holidays and everyone's pockets are dry. You pay me when it's convenient."

"Thanks, Rich, but—"

"No, buts about it." He put his cap back on. "Now, I better be gettin' back to the studio."

"Here," Callie said as she reached into her jeans pocket for a five dollar bill. "Let me at least pay you for the pastries."

"Nonsense. It's my treat." He zipped up his winter jacket. "You know where to find me. Bye."

"He's so nice," Callie said to Deardra, who had opened the box and was nibbling on a cheese danish.

"And sexy," she managed to say with a full mouth.

"And *married*. Like I always say, the good ones are either married or gay." Callie took an apple turnover from the box and headed to the back office with Deardra following behind. Callie sat at the desk, wrote out a check, and handed it to Deardra. "Merry Christmas. It's your bonus."

"You can't afford this. It's too much."

"It's not enough. You're another friend I can't put a price tag on. You've been an unbelievable help to me."

"Well, maybe next year when Liam starts school, I can put in some more hours."

"Whatever you can manage. I have an intern starting at the end of January. He's an art major, really talented. I think he'll be a help to both of us—me in the studio and you here in the gallery with sales and marketing."

A jingle of the Christmas bells on the front door alerted the girls to another visitor.

"Maybe Rich forgot something."

"Callie, my dear pooch, are you here?"

"Yes, Uncle Don," she called from the office as she made her way into the front room to see her aging uncle in a dark green cable knit sweater with a zipper neck. Never one to wear a jacket, even in the brutal winter, the man rubbed his hands together in a warming fashion. "What a surprise!" Callie hugged him. "How's Aunt Agnes doing?"

"Fine. Better than we all expected. I just had coffee with your mother. She's going over to the house today for a visit."

"Oh, that'll be good for both of them. How about you? Do you need any help this week at the store?" She hoped he didn't say yes. She couldn't afford to lose another ring.

He smiled at her while pulling a small velvet box from his pocket. He held it in his hand and opened it so that its contents shined in her direction. It was the ring. *The missing ring.*

"Where did you find it?" Callie exclaimed.

"So you knew it was lost?" His disappointment was clear.

"Yes, I knew it was lost. I lost it. I'm sorry."

"Then why did you lie to me?" He pulled an envelope from his pocket. "And where did all this money come from?"

"I'm sorry, Uncle Don. I lost the ring, so I paid for it. Accidentally, a display of rings fell to the floor Thursday night. I thought I gathered them all up, but obviously I didn't. By the time you let me know the ring was missing, I figured the cleaning crew or another customer had found it and taken it. I didn't want to upset you with all that's going on with Aunt Agnes, so I just—"

"Paid for it yourself. You have a good heart, pooch," he said handing her the envelope.

"Can I ask where you found it?"

"It was wedged between two cases on the floor. If I hadn't dropped a ring myself, I never would have found it."

Callie giggled.

"So, I guess I inherited my butterfingers from you."

"Yes, your clumsiness from me, but your heart from God. Thank you, pooch, for trying to do the right thing. Here's your money back."

Callie glanced over at Deardra and, through her smile, mouthed the words: *I told you Aidan didn't take it.*

At the Towne Tavern, Aidan met Tony for drinks after work. Quick to slip off his jacket and unknot his tie, feeling strangled and browbeaten by a stressful day in court, Aidan ordered a beer and hoped to unwind with Tony.

"Cross-examination today?" Tony asked as he similarly hung his pin-striped suit jacket over the back of the chair. "You should give up criminal defense work."

"After the day I had today, I'm seriously thinking about it. It was the typical nightmare when your client fails to tell his attorney all the facts, and the prosecutor has a field day ripping him apart."

"Why did you even put him on the stand?" Tony tossed a $20 bill on the counter as the bartender served the drinks.

"Believe me, it wasn't my idea. He insisted on telling his story, which was just that—a story."

"Hey, it's happened to all of us."

"Yeah, but when Rottendam is prosecuting, it's even worse."

"She's tough, no denying that."

"Days like today make me want to quit the practice and start writing again."

"It's just a bad two weeks," Tony said as he reached for the menu. "After what happened with Grace, I think you're doing just fine."

Aidan was surprised Tony mentioned her. They had agreed Grace was a subject best not discussed.

"How is she?"

"About as good as you. Eve says it looks like someone else is in line for the promotion."

"Too bad," Aidan commented, feeling more numb than sad for her.

"Ya know, it's Christmas this week. You could pull this relationship back together if you wanted to."

"And why would I want to do that? Promotion or no promotion, her focus is far from marriage and family. Even if she shifted her focus back on us, I'm sure it wouldn't be long before some aspect of work took priority again." Aidan drank a long swallow of the brown ale and thought about Callie and some of the things she had said in Vegas. "The fact is I got to make some changes in my life, Tony, and the only thing my past has got to do with my future is to serve as a marker of big mistakes."

The next day at the courthouse, Aidan tossed his keys in the plastic bin, placed his briefcase on the conveyor belt, and stepped through the metal detector. The machine wailed, so Aidan stepped to the side and raised his arms for the security officer to wave another metal-detecting wand around the perimeter of his body. Used to the daily search, Aidan smiled at the guard as he got the green light to proceed. Aidan reached for his keys and briefcase, then hurried up the marble steps.

The architecture of the spacious lobby formed an acoustic echo as the din of voices and the beeping of the security machine below carried to the third floor where a sculpted eagle greeted Aidan on his way to Judge Clemson's chambers. Rapping twice, Aidan heard a *Come on in*, and entered the judge's office.

A small space darkened by thick green drapes and bordered by shelves of books, Judge Clemson's chambers seemed to suck the breath out of Aidan, the dingy office compacted by stacks of papers and bound folders piled on the floor near the window. The radiator hissed with forced hot water as it struggled to warm the cold concrete walls, and the floorboards creaked under Aidan's heavy step.

The judge glanced up from his phone call and waved Aidan over to one of two black leather chairs opposite the desk. The Honorable Robert Clemson, with white, cropped hair, a grandfatherly face and honest eyes, wound up his conversation and hung up the phone.

"Thanks for seeing me," Aidan said and stood up to shake the judge's hand.

"No problem. What can I do for you, Mr. McGregor?"

"Well," Aidan began, not sure how to broach the subject without eating a large piece of humble pie. "Sometime ago you asked me about doing some pro bono work and mentoring some of the interns."

"Yes, and you flatly stated that you had no desire to do any such thing."

"Yes, sir, but—" Aidan felt his stomach churn with remorseful indigestion.

"But what, Mr. McGregor? You're one of the highest profiled attorneys in Boston, with an eat-em-up, spit-em-out attitude that's made you quite successful." Judge Clemson frowned which soured what Aidan thought was a compliment. "Though your ethics can't be disputed, your motivation at this point in time leaves me quite dumbfounded." He clasped his hands almost reverently, and Aidan felt like he was in a priest's confessional rather than a judge's chambers.

"Judge, sir, I've had a change of heart or an epiphany, as one might say. Law has been good to me, afforded me a comfortable practice and a nice home. It's opened doors and provided opportunities through which I've met my best friends as well as role models, such as you. It's also challenged me to excel and prevail through some mighty stressful circumstances within the courtrooms of this building and others. For all that, I'm thankful. I've gained so much. Now, it's time to give back."

"Are you sure about this or is the holiday spirit just tugging on your heartstrings?"

"I feel like I took the gift given me and pawned it for a million dollar practice. Well, lo and behold, it's a few years later and I still have the gift, and now I want to share my experience with those who truly need it."

Judge Clemson leaned back in his chair and looked Aidan over with prosecutorial eyes. He wore the expression of uncertainty as he did in his courtroom where he donned his black robe and handed out justice like spoonfuls of castor oil to those disdainful of his medicine.

"So what exactly are you saying, Mr. McGregor? You're quitting your firm?"

"No, Judge, but I'm opening up some hours, and thought you could help me pencil in a few appointments."

Aidan paused and waited for the verdict and the accompanying lecture, but Judge Clemson had nothing but a smile.

# CHAPTER 5

"All right, Aidan. Have a wonderful Christmas with your sister in sunny California. See you when you get back."

Callie pushed out the jewelry store's door into the biting New England air. While she slipped her cell phone into her purse, she looked back over her shoulder to wave goodbye to her uncle. Suddenly, she felt someone plow into her and nearly knock her to the ground. If it weren't for her quick shuffle of the feet and the person's strong hands to hold her steady, Callie would have landed on her backside.

"Sorry," she apologized, knowing full well that it was her own fault for not paying attention to where she was going.

"Callie?"

Callie glanced up to his face. She didn't recognize him.

"It's me Nick—Nicholas Ashton."

She felt her smile stretch across her face. She couldn't believe it was him. Nicholas. He didn't look anything like he did in high school. His brown hair had been shaved to the scalp with just a layer of peach fuzz covering. Lines aged his face with maturity, and he had put on some weight. He was no longer the lanky teenager she remembered. And he had grown taller, too, for now he towered over her 5'5" petiteness. So much of his appearance had changed except for his brown eyes and bright smile. Those gleamed with all the intensity of his youth.

Callie remembered that graduation party as if it were yesterday. The senior class talked of little else that month of June during the last weeks of high school. Because the principal's own son was graduating, he had planned for a graduation gala in the gym. Food, a band, dancing—everything a senior could want after picking up his or her diploma. A fine way to say goodbye to high school.

"I'd prefer you didn't go," Callie's father had told her as he sat in his brown leather recliner, his shirt untucked and a can of soda in his hand.

He seemed a permanent fixture in that chair in the family room, positioned six feet from the television and ten feet from the fireplace. It was a beautiful room of a pale shade of green with plank floors, high ceiling, and paned glass windows providing a view into the expansive backyard whose tall oaks stretched beyond the edge of the property. Callie had liked to sit on the couch in that room when she was younger and take long afternoon naps after her eyes had grown heavy from gazing out the windows into the sky. It was a room with an aura of peacefulness, often marred by her father's presence, deep-rooted opinions, and erupting temper.

"No good is gonna come from a party like that,"

"Please, Daddy, don't say I can't go. It's my graduation party."

"Callie, you're leaving for art school on Monday," he grumbled, perturbed to turn his attention away from the television. "I've already gone against my better judgment to let you go there."

"But my art—"

"Yeah, I know all about your art. You don't make a living with art. Today you're an artist, and tomorrow you're unemployed and starving and living off your parents till you're 40."

"Jake, that's enough," her mother said softly, so frail looking in her blue cotton dress and apron. "We're talking about a graduation party."

"All I'm saying is that we've already extended ourselves far enough by letting her go to New York for six weeks."

"Daddy, I'm 18 years old. You've got to trust me. I'm a good girl. I've never done anything to disappoint you or Mama."

"There's always a first time. Remember what happened to Maisy?"

Her father's stare of intimidation brought drops of weakness to her eyes. Why did she have to be punished for her sister's mistakes?

"Please, Mama, talk to him."

"Joan, don't say a word," Callie's father barked, raising his hand to silence her. "And you stop your sniveling. I didn't raise you to be a crybaby. God, why couldn't I have sons?"

"Jake."

"I mean it. Boys don't cry; boys don't wanna be artists; boys don't get ra—"

"Jake, we're talking about a simple graduation party."

"This party has PROM written all over it."

"It's not a prom," Callie dared to speak under the glare of her father's eyes.

"There's no coupling up," her mother explained. "It's just the senior class getting together for a little social gathering. It's on school property, and it's chaperoned. She won't leave the gym."

"Please, Daddy. Can I go?"

The last thing Callie wanted was to be precluded from another high school event and have to sit home with her parents on Saturday night while they played bridge with the neighbors, and she stayed in her room watching television with only five working channels. Not while all her classmates celebrated their graduation.

A long silence accompanied her father's scowl. His forehead creased with worry lines as he announced his decision with a dramatic wave of his hand.

"All right, Callie, you can go, but you're home by ten."

Callie shot a pleading look at her mother who quickly said, "Eleven. We'll pick you up after our bridge game with the Williams."

"Eleven," her father restated as if he had made the decision. "What're you wearing?"

"I bought a dress," Callie admitted quietly.

"Out of your allowance?"

"No, out of the money from working at the deli on weekends."

"I thought you were going to buy new brushes for art school with that money."

"I did, but I had some money left over so—"

"So you bought a dress." He punctuated his disapproval with a slap of the armchair. "I guess it didn't occur to you that you would need spending money while at art school. Did you think your mother and I were going to flit the entire bill?"

"No, Daddy. I have extra money saved up from Christmas and my birthday."

Callie saw her father's face sour. He hated not getting his way or not being right.

"Very well then, Callie. You can go to this dance, but don't make me sorry for saying yes."

"Thank you."

"Now, Joan," her father said, still abrasive as he turned his attention to his wife, "what's this about bridge with the Williams? You know Harold cheats."

"Jake, he doesn't cheat. You just hate losing."

As Callie's parents began bickering over their bridge game, Callie ducked out of sight and ran off to her room. In the closet, she pulled off the plastic garment bag to expose the pale pink satin gown that she had bought in a consignment shop in Boston. Brand new in a boutique, the dress would have cost $300. However, Callie purchased it for $80 in the second-hand store. She especially loved the halter top and open back as it hung elegantly from the hanger. She pressed the dress up against her body and looked in the mirror. It was lovely, and Callie couldn't wait for Saturday night to wear it.

The gym had been transformed into a nightclub with dimmed lighting, a rotating disco ball suspended from the ceiling, a six-piece band playing on the stage, and table upon table of home-baked food from fried chicken and shrimp to brownies and chocolate mousse. Callie carried in her own foil-lined tray of baked ziti and placed it on the table, careful not to spill anything on her gown. She saw groups of the students clustered together in their cliques—the jocks, the brains, the dopeheads, the punkers, the cheerleaders, the nerds, the bullies, the drama queens—as they posed for pictures signifying the end of their circle of friends for the past four years.

"Hey, Callie!" someone shouted. "Come get in the picture!"

She saw Emma waving her hand, motioning Callie over to their group—the artsy girls. Emma, the flutist; Jill, the dancer; Brianna, the stylist; Deardra, the photographer; and Callie, the artist. Scooting in between Brianna and Jill with Emma and Deardra pushing in from the ends, Callie hugged her friends as the moment was captured on film. The teacher handed the camera back to Deardra.

"How's it feel to be on the other side of the lens?" Callie asked her golden-haired friend. Deardra was a kindred soul, passionate about photography the way Callie adored painting. With a camera hanging from her neck or tucked in her bookbag, Deardra's quirkiness annoyed most but inspired Callie to always be ready to capture the randomness of everyday moments. For that, Callie kept a sketchpad in her car motivated for that spontaneous sunset or storm or swooping hawk with outstretched wings.

"You know me. I like taking the pictures, but tonight I feel like a glamorous model."

"You are," Callie praised her friend. "You're absolutely stunning in that gown."

Deardra twirled full circle as the shimmering white gown swished with her pirouette. Subsequently, she fixed the spaghetti strap that had slipped down over her tanned shoulder.

"I wish you were coming to London with me, Callie."

"Me, too, but at least we have six weeks together in New York."

"Yeah, it's gonna be great. Are you packed yet?"

"I've been packed for a week," Callie confessed. "Not a thing to do tomorrow except count the hours."

Deardra turned her attention to her camera and rolled her thumb over the button to advance the film.

"Look at this camera my parents gave me for graduation."

"It looks expensive," Callie commented.

"It is. It's got auto and manual focusing plus changeable lenses for close-ups and distance. I absolutely love it. Here, let me take your picture."

"Sure."

"That pink dress looks great on you," Deardra said while focusing the shot.

"I love your dress, too," Emma complimented as the other girls chimed in with their own ooo's and ahh's as the camera's flash flickered.

Emma, considered the mother of the group because of her bossiness, wore a black lace dress and three-inch high heels that raised her to Callie's height. Emma's blonde hair had been expertly styled, pulled up and wisped across her head, secured with silver beads and pins.

"Thanks, Emma," Callie replied. "I really love your hair tonight."

"Thank you. Brianna did it."

Brianna grinned proudly. With model beauty, Brianna easily claimed the title as the prettiest girl in their artsy group. She had big blue eyes, which were highlighted by perfectly placed glimmering blue eye shadow and eyeliner. Knowing exactly what colors brought out her best features, Brianna usually wore blue or red to bring attention to her eyes and lips. Though a natural brunette, Brianna bleached her own hair blonde and weekly dyed the roots to hide any traces of her former color. She liked to crimp her hair, then pull it up off her forehead, letting two spiral curls frame her face.

"Callie, let me do your eyes," Brianna said, pulling a makeup case from her purse.

She carried a makeup case the way Deardra carried a camera and Callie carried a sketchbook. Brianna's post-high school pursuits involved hair styling and cosmetology. Ever since Callie could remember, Brianna had been making over her friends, fixing their hair, painting their faces, and accentuating their eyes with bold colors. Each of them had been a willing participant in her recreation because Brianna always seemed to color them beautiful. Then Deardra would snap a picture for their scrapbook of memories.

"They need a little brown or bronze," Emma suggested.

"Yeah," Jill quietly agreed.

Rather shy, Jill had sexy Asian eyes and long silky black hair, which she always pulled into a ponytail or bun that seemed to make her round face even more symmetrical. Self-conscious about her thin body and flat chest, Jill had asked Brianna to teach her to paint her eyes so that they would be her most predominant feature. However, Callie felt that no matter how attractive her eyes were, Jill's finest attribute was always going to be her legs—legs that seemed to extend to the sky. Long, lean, and muscular, she epitomized all dancers Callie had ever seen. Good enough to graduate from high school and go directly to a professional dance company, Jill opted instead to study at Julliard. Callie admired her discipline and commitment to ballet, but knew that Jill would have to overcome her performance anxiety if she were to become a truly successful dancer.

"There," Brianna said, brushing on some russet powder over Callie's eyes. "Gorgeous."

"Definitely gorgeous," the male voice behind Callie said. "Would you like to dance?"

Callie looked at Brianna who smiled at the fellow standing behind Callie. Keeping her back to the boy, Callie took a few steps away to give Brianna some privacy with the young man.

"She walks away. I'll take that as a *no*," the fellow said, too much smug in his voice to be hurt.

Realizing the question had been directed to her, Callie turned on her heels to see who had asked her to dance. There stood Nicholas Ashton—her secret crush since kindergarten—the boy who always said hi to her in the hall, at church, in the deli, but who never seemed to actually *see* her. Yet now he stood in front of her, gazing at her, admiring her—the center of his attention.

Nicholas raked his brown eyes over Callie as his smile widened. Surprised by his attention, she stepped backward onto the bottom of her gown, causing her center of gravity to shift backward, which only made her take another step in reverse, still treading on her gown as it began pulling her to the ground. If it weren't for Nicholas's quick action and strong hands to hold her steady, Callie would have landed on her backside. Through all that, he never lost his smile.

Callie couldn't believe that it was 15 years later and Nicholas was standing in front of her, holding her up again, that charming smile of his still plastered to his handsome face.

"My God, it's good to see you," he said. "You haven't changed a bit."

"Thanks—I think." A strong gust blew her hair across her face, some strands sticking to her lip gloss. She brushed them back behind her ears. "You sure have changed."

"You think so?"

"Definitely. Taller, broader." She returned his smile. "More handsome."

Another lash of wind whipped them, and Callie pulled her unbuttoned coat more fully around her for warmth. The cold stung her cheeks, and she turned slightly into Nicholas's body to shield herself from the winter thrashing.

"Do you want to go somewhere and have a cup of coffee?" he asked putting his arm around her to give her additional protection from the wind.

"Yes."

Without hesitation, she cuddled in under his arm and led him next door to the coffee shop. The bell on the door rattled as they entered. Callie nodded to Katie, the petite blonde clerk behind the counter whose youthful innocence showed with each gum bubble she blew. Oblivious to the coffee stains spotting her yellow striped apron and the impatient customers needing their midday caffeine, Katie moved with sloth speed as she grinded flavorful beans and frothed milk.

Callie walked to the back of the shop where the booths were situated. Nicholas helped her off with her coat, then she slid in one side as he sat on the other. He took off his gloves and shrugged out of his suede coat, letting it rest behind him. He wore a thick camel-colored sweater that matched the light brown tones in his eyes—eyes that continued to hold her in view, ignoring all the coffee cup decorations begging for attention on the walls. Nicholas drew his hand through the stubble on his head, and for a second he seemed almost embarrassed for not having that youthful head of hair.

"I like it," Callie complimented.

"Like what?"

"Your short cut hair."

"Oh that," he said. "I'm still getting used to it."

Callie smiled at him. He was easy to look at just as he was so many years ago. He had a very handsome face, clean-shaven, and athletic features with a strong neck, broad chest, and muscular arms that pulled the sweater taught at his biceps. As Callie rubbed her hands together, warming them, Nicholas reached across the table and took her cold hands into his.

"You're a radiator," she remarked.

"Warm blooded."

"Well, you know what they say about cold hands."

"What's that? Poor circulation?"

"No." Callie laughed. "Warm heart. Cold hands, warm heart."

"Oh, I already knew that about you."

Callie smiled and pulled her hands gently out of his but he retained a hold, keeping his fingertips upon hers. She pleasantly noticed that he didn't wear a wedding ring. She wondered if he had noticed that about her, too.

"Shall I go stand in line?" he asked.

"No, Katie will come over in a few minutes."

"So tell me about you, Callie. What have you been doing since high school?"

"Oh, you know, this and that, art stuff."

"I assumed as much. So tell me about it. How was art school?"

"Actually, art schools. They were great."

"And?"

He leaned in toward her as if she would disclose a huge secret. Callie looked at him perplexed. He couldn't really want to know about her art. Yet his eyes held wonder like a kindergartner on his first day of school.

"And I wound up getting a Bachelor of Fine Arts and a Masters in Visual Arts Education."

"Whoa. Let's go back a few years and take this from the beginning. After high school, you went to New York for art school, right?" He began to massage her one hand as she used the other to assist with her descriptions.

"Yeah, at Parsons. That was just a summer program, but it was a pivotal time in my life, being on my own, away from home. New York is such a fabulous city, so much culture 24-7. Museums, churches, restaurants. Everywhere you go, there's art ensconced in the buildings and architecture." She paused for a moment, distracted by the sensual stroking of her hand. Nicholas rubbed each finger, gingerly plying the skin with deft tenderness.

"New York, it's an amazing city," he said, leading her back into the conversation.

"And the people—a stew of every walk of life. I became very humanistic there as I began to ungroup people and perceive their individualism."

"I think that's called growing up."

"Probably, but it was more than that. You know how in high school everyone seems to be grouped, labeled in some clique?"

"Yes." Nicholas turned her hand over and softly traced the lines in her palm. His finger traveled in different directions following the creases that veered up and down and across her hand. Callie again lost herself in his rhythmic touching. Nicholas glanced up at her. "And you were saying?"

"Oh. And I think most people continue to do that their whole lives—grouping. It's an innate character flaw, I suppose, and I think it relates even to us as individuals. We lose or simply ignore those qualities that set us apart, and we suddenly become gray."

"And gray's a bad thing?" He nodded, expecting her answer.

"Blue and red and green can be bad things, too, if you segregate them and that's all you see. What you have to do is look deep within yourself and see that you're a little of each of those colors. We are amazing human beings, myriad colors, living in a richly landscaped world. When you're able to see your hues and shades and then recognize those distinguishable characteristics in other people, that's when the painting becomes exciting, real, profound."

"That's very philosophical but true."

"My art took on such depth as I got to know myself, discover the world beyond Sycamore."

"That was a little town."

"It wasn't so much the town. It was my parents—actually, my father, who sheltered me from the world." She used her free hand to gesture to Katie who had forgotten to take their order. "But once I got to New York, tasted freedom, met people, experienced life without rules and expectations, I could explore all that on canvas or in my sketchbook. It was probably the most important six weeks of my life."

Nicholas leaned in again, and Callie saw every hazel spec in his eyes. He had the kindest eyes, soft, inviting—almost provocative.

"So what happened after that?" he asked.

"I came back home a changed person. With so much knowledge and so many ideas on how to develop my talent, it was hard living in a house where I had to suppress my thoughts and opinions. I suppose my father thought that six weeks of art school was going to get it out of my system and that I'd drop my major and enroll in another college focused on another career, but I came back from New York determined to be an artist. I convinced my parents to let me live on campus, and I attended the Art Institute of Boston. That was another phenomenal experience where I became truly aware of art's impact on every facet of our lives. I developed a solid foundation in art history, all the while continuing to develop my personal style and creative direction."

"Which led you to what?"

"*Where* should be the question." Callie paused and pulled her hand from Nicholas's as Katie approached their table. "Katie, this is my friend, Nicholas."

"Hi," the waitress said, snapping her gum.

"Busy day?" Callie asked.

"Don't you know it." Katie glanced over her shoulder at the door as the bell signaled another customer coming in from the cold. "The colder, the busier. So, what can I get for you?"

"I'll have a latte," Callie replied.

Nicholas leaned back in his seat.

"I'll have a large coffee with milk and sugar."

"Coming right up."

The girl smiled and meandered back behind the counter.

"You can call me Nick, you know. My friends all do."

"I can't. I have another friend named Nick and, well, it'd be too confusing. Besides, you'll always be Nicholas to me."

He smiled again and reached once more for Callie's hands.

"So, getting back to what you were saying, tell me *where*? Where did your art take you?"

"Everywhere. Italy, Rome, Milan, London, Paris. I took workshops, worked for local artisans, painted on the banks of the Seine. I spent a lot of time abroad."

"And then? You're how old at this point?"

"Then—let's see, 26. I came back to Boston and got a job as an art teacher and worked part time on weekends as a tour guide in a museum. It was good—the teaching part, not the money part, but I had a goal, and I saved as much as I could. I loved working with the children, though. They're so creative at that young age. It's all about coloring outside the lines. No boundaries."

"So you're a teacher."

"Not anymore. I own my own gallery."

"Really? That's terrific!" he interjected, proud like a parent.

"I've always wanted my own gallery."

"I would think every artist wants a place to create and display his work."

"Exactly. And that's what Appassionata is all about, but not just my work. All the local artists have an opportunity to exhibit their works from watercolors to oils to sculptures to computer-generated designs. It's an incredible place. And having the gallery allowed me to be creative again. I kinda shelved my own ambitions when I was teaching because I was so focused on my students and developing their talents. But now I'm back to painting and sculpting."

"I'm impressed, Callie. You've done quite well for yourself."

"Thank you. I'm happy."

"So you don't teach anymore."

"No."

Katie approached the table carrying a tray with two piping hot cups of coffee. They let go of hands as the waitress set Callie's latte in front of her, then placed the other cup in front of Nicholas.

"Anything else?" Katie asked, tucking the tray under her arm.

"No, thank you," Callie answered and looked to Nicholas for his reply.

"This is fine. Thanks," he said.

"All right. Enjoy." Katie smiled and walked away.

Callie pulled the very large orange cup closer to her and blew on the steaming foam. She heard the tinkle of the spoon as Nicholas stirred his coffee. When she glanced up, he smiled at her.

"Where has the time gone, Callista Emerson? It is Emerson still? I didn't hear you mention any marriage or husband."

"No, no marriage or husband. I came close once, though, but my art got in the way."

"Your *heart* got in the way?"

"No, my *art* got in the way."

"Your art can't *get in the way*. It's who you are."

"I know." She shrugged. "He didn't see it that way." She tried taking a sip of the coffee, but it was still too hot. She blew on it again, then set the cup down. "I just saw him a few weeks ago. We've been broken up for three years, and out of the blue, he walks into my gallery. I don't think he knew it was my gallery."

"That has Bogart written all over it."

Callie laughed.

"Exactly."

"So, he was happy to see you again?" His tone held reluctance as if he didn't want to know the answer to his question.

"I don't know. He was with his wife—his very pregnant wife. And all I could think about was that it could've been me—maybe *should've* been me. I think about the last three years of my life, and outside of the gallery, there isn't much to brag about. I really want to be married and have children. I want a family."

Nicholas smiled.

"Sounds like a simple name for one of those *groups* you mentioned before."

"Family can be the worst group or it can be the healthiest. I think it has everything to do with your parents. Some are overbearing, intimidating, limiting. Those kinds of people keep their children from exploring their minds and the world around them. And other parents live or want to live their lives through their kids, pressuring them to do things like sports or be things like doctors because that's what the parents never achieved. I think it's so sad that the people who are supposed to love you the most, who gave you life, deny you your right to live that life." Having just described her own parents, Callie felt ashamed and looked away from Nicholas's stare.

"It's a sad fact. You and I grew up in those kinds of families." His voice was raspy, almost sad. He touched her cheek. "Despite all, we survived. Your parents still alive?"

"Yes. Yours?" she mumbled.

Nicholas started talking, but Callie couldn't hear a thing. His touch of her cheek had drawn her back to the graduation gala where he had caressed her cheek in the exact same way.

"You are so beautiful, Callie," Nicholas had said to her that night 15 years ago as they danced to some slow music in the gymnasium. She almost believed him by the gleam in his eye. No one had ever looked at her that way before. "By far the prettiest girl in this gym, this school, in Sycamore, in the whole darn state of Massachusetts."

She let his compliments paint a smile on her face.

"You're such a charmer."

"I mean it. I wouldn't lie to you."

Nicholas touched her cheek, and the warmth of his hand flowed through her. She felt her heart beating outside her chest, pumping furiously as if her gown's halter top would snap at any moment. Weak with this new emotion, she clung a little too tightly to him. He moved slowly, his weight barely shifting from one foot to the other, as his hands rested on her hips. Callie liked being in his arms. She could feel his breath on her ear, and occasionally he would whisper something sweet, a compliment about her eyes or her gown.

"I love the way you smell," he muttered. "I could breathe you forever. If I could bottle you, I'd be rich, but no—I'm already rich because this moment is golden, and it's going to stay with me the rest of my life."

"Callie."

Nicholas knocked on the coffee shop table, drawing her back to reality. She focused in on her latte, fingered the rim whimsically, then took a long gulp. She wondered if he remembered that night and the things he had said, if that moment had really stayed with him forever.

"Where were you?" he asked.

"With you."

Callie curled her lips into a smile. It was that comfortable feeling that he always gave her that made her want to be nowhere else but with him. Just sitting with him now, picking up conversation as if they had been out of touch for only a week instead of a half a lifetime, seemed perfectly natural. Maybe it was the familiarity of having grown up together that produced that comfort zone where she could be completely herself with no guarded attitudes. Callie loved the ease and effortlessness of being with Nicholas. Maybe after all these years, they could let fate take its course and have a relationship. Callie liked that possibility.

"You were saying something about your parents?" she asked.

"Yeah, my dad just had heart surgery—double bypass."

"I'm sorry to hear that. My aunt just went through the same thing. It's a long recovery. Is your dad still in the hospital?"

"No, he got out a few days ago. He's recuperating at my sister's house. My parents kinda moved in there till he's back on his feet."

"Your parents still live on the Cape?"

"Yes, but my sister lives in Connecticut, so I drove Mom and Dad down there, stayed for a few days. I was supposed to go home tomorrow, but it's chaos in that house between my sister's kids and my parents. I said my goodbyes this morning and headed out."

"So, you live around here?"

He jumped over her question and asked his own.

"So how is your sister doing?"

"Talk of Maisy is better done in a bar than a coffee shop," she said matter-of-factly as Nicholas looked at her peculiarly. "She drives me to drink."

"Oh," he laughed. "That bad?"

"My sister is a series of catastrophes. She dropped out of college, moved to Los Angeles to be an actress but couldn't support herself, kind of went missing for a year where no one really heard from her, then she turned up married in Chicago to some guy we never met. Anyway, she sang his praises, and my parents relaxed thinking she had finally settled down, but over the course of two years and several visits, we came to realize that her husband was beating her. Too many bruises to explain."

"God, that's awful."

Callie took a sip of the coffee, recalling the night her sister called from the emergency room with a broken nose.

"Maisy finally admitted to the abuse. Her self-esteem was at an all-time low, so it took a lot to convince her to leave him."

"I can only imagine."

"You know, Nicholas, my sister's never been known for her good judgment, but I think all of her problems in the past years have stemmed from the rape. My parents never put her in therapy, which was a huge mistake. They just kinda swept all her pain under the rug and never dealt with it directly. But Maisy has a distinct victim personality that attracts trouble. I've been encouraging her to go to therapy for years, and just last year she took my advice. She's doing much better now, though she still has a few vices like chain smoking. But she's got a new job as a secretary with a sports management firm, and she's moved out of my parents' house which may or may not be a good thing."

"What do you mean?"

"Well, it's great that Maisy's being independent and responsible living on her own, but when she was living with my parents, they kinda kept an eye on each other. She looked after them, helped around the house, and my parents made sure she stayed out of trouble. Now, it's fallen on my shoulders to keep an eye on everyone."

"And you have time to paint *when* exactly?"

Callie laughed.

"Whenever I can. I've got such a great working environment that it's hard not to be inspired 24-7. My gallery and studio and house are just down the street from where I grew up."

"Where?"

"The Bennedetto farm. I own it."

"You're kidding."

"No, it's mine, really. Remember that big old red barn?"

"Yeah."

"Well, that's the gallery. I renovated it and added a huge addition, then I converted another of the smaller barns into a studio."

"Amazing. So, where do you live?"

"There. Remember the farmhouse?"

"Barely."

"Well, it's cozy and drafty and everything I love. In fact, my favorite place to paint is in the conservatory." She noticed the surprise on his face. "It's not really a conservatory; I just call it that. It's actually a porch that I closed in with windows and sliders and skylights."

"Sounds great. I remember how pretty that area was, especially in the summertime," he said, gently squeezing her hand. "I can't believe you still live in Sycamore."

"Where do you live? Near here?"

He took a large drink and finished the entire contents of the mug. He leaned back in the booth as his eyes darkened to espresso.

"No, I live in South Carolina."

"South Carolina," she repeated, hearing the disappointment in her own voice.

Callie looked away for a moment, down at the table. She felt fate's cold hand slap her then cruelly poor black paint over the fantasy she had just painted. South Carolina. He could've said *Iceland*. It seemed as far away.

Tapping her hand to regain her attention, Nicholas inquired. "So, your parents still live in Sycamore?"

"Yeah." Callie looked up again, her head still spinning over his state of residence.

"They're retired?"

"Who?"

"Your parents."

"Yes." She tipped her head to the left. "They putter around the house, get on each other's nerves." She tipped her head to the right. "Play bridge every Saturday night and get on each other's nerves. It's a vicious cycle," she joked, "but they'd say they're happy. I'd debate it, but at least they're healthy. My father had a bout with pneumonia three years ago that hospitalized him for two weeks. He could barely breathe. I really thought he was going to die."

"God, that's awful." Nicholas empathized with a long sigh, having just gone through a similar situation with his own father. He tried not to think about it—death—and the mortality of his parents.

"Actually, it was a good thing, because it softened him up a bit, you know. A brush with death will do that, makes you mortal, makes you think about your life and what's important."

"Don't you think that it's sad that people can't realize how precious life is without death knocking on their door?"

Callie nodded as Nicholas continued with his philosophizing.

"Some people think they're going to live forever, that the sunsets will be there tomorrow or next year to look at or that the people they care about are always going to be there, but one day, it could all be gone in a second. Then you have nothing but regret, and that's a horrible thing to live with."

"Sounds like you have none of that."

"Regrets? A few." He leaned forward as he proffered the next question. "How about you, Callie? Any regrets?"

He waited anxiously for her answer, looking deep into her brown eyes for a fleck of sadness, guilt, remorse. She was quiet, contemplative.

"Not a single one," she replied too soon, too pleased with herself. Nicholas felt his smile fade. He sat back in the booth and casually withdrew his hand from hers. He couldn't believe she just said that. Surely, *he* had to be one of her regrets. Was she really that callous? Nicholas wasn't going to stick around to find out. Hiding his hurt and irritation, he pushed up the cuff of his sleeve and glanced at his watch.

"Gee, it's getting late." He slid out of the booth and put on his jacket. Reaching inside his front pants pocket, he pulled out a $10 dollar bill and laid it on the table. "It was nice seeing you again."

Callie wiggled herself out of the booth and stood to hug him.

"It was *great* seeing you, Nicholas, even though I hogged the conversation and didn't get to hear what you've been up to all these years."

"Not much, really."

"Well, I'd love to hear about it." She kissed his cheek and tugged playfully on his scarf. Her brown eyes twinkled, almost flirtatiously, as she gazed at him. "If you don't have any plans for dinner, I'd love—"

"Actually, I'm meeting up with some old friends."

He looked over her shoulder, around the room, at the money on the table—everywhere but in her eyes. He couldn't look in her eyes and lie.

"That'll be fun." She reached across the table for her purse. "Here's my business card. Give me a call the next time you're in town."

"Sure," he said, forcing a smile as he took a step backward. "See ya, Callie."

"Bye, Nicholas."

There was so much he wanted to say, yet he swallowed his hurt, his disappointment and walked away, adding yet another regret to his list.

# CHAPTER 6

❀

Outside the coffee shop, the cold air hit Nicholas with a mighty punch that knocked him back to the graduation gala. He found it so ironic that 15 years ago, it was Callie who dashed away as he begged for more time with her.

"I want to kiss you, Callie," Nicholas had said as they sat high up on the wooden bleachers in the dimmed gymnasium.

He didn't care if it was in the gym in front of his friends, her friends, or in front of their former teachers. He just wanted to kiss her. And she wanted to kiss him, too; that he could see in her eyes as she gazed at him through half-closed lids dusted with glittering powder.

For a few moments, he was oblivious to everyone and everything except Callie—the way she talked with inflective tones and dramatic gestures, how she smiled with dimpled cheeks, the provocative way she licked her lips so titillating, and the adorable way she crinkled her nose when she laughed. Most of all, he liked the way she held his hand, stroking it as if he wore mink gloves. Her touch, so innocent, was so sensual.

"I want to kiss you," Nicholas whispered again as some other kids sat down near them. "But not here. Come with me."

He took her by the hand and helped her down the bleachers. Holding up the bottom of her gown, Callie stepped carefully to the final row where Nicholas gallantly grabbed her at the waist, lifting her over the last bleacher rung.

"Where are we going?" she asked as he led her to the gym's exit.

"Outside. I want to be alone with you."

Callie stopped mid-stride.

"I can't."

"You can't what?"

"I can't go outside." She back-stepped towards the dance floor. "Let's dance again."

"We've been dancing all night. We've posed for pictures, talked with your friends and mine." He moved close to her, his voice barely a whisper. "Now I want to be alone with you, just the two of us. I want to kiss you, Callie, and I know you want to kiss me, too."

Callie momentarily closed her eyes, denying Nicholas access to her heart. But he didn't need to see her eyes to know what she was feeling. He was inside her soul—a place Callie could not refuse him admittance for somewhere in the past three hours, through their dancing, their talking, their joking, their laughing, Nicholas had stopped being a fellow student and earned her affection. They had shared private things, dreams and fears, hushed secrets not even revealed to their closest friends.

"Come on." He tugged at her hand.

"I can't, Nicholas."

"Why not?"

"I promised my father I wouldn't leave the gym."

"I'm not going to hurt you, Callie. You can trust me."

"That's the same thing the boy said to my sister before he raped her."

Callie's statement rocked Nicholas. He felt like he had been stabbed with a dozen knives. Suddenly, all that blood that had been rushing from his heart to his head ceased pumping and allowed his brain to start functioning again. Nicholas now saw the panic in her eyes.

"I'm sorry that guy did that to your sister, Callie, but I'm not that guy. I'd never hurt you."

She glanced at her watch.

"It's late. I've got to get going."

"I'll walk you to your car."

"No, my parents are picking me up. They're probably already parked in the front circle outside."

"Can I see you tomorrow? I want to see you before you leave."

"I've got a lot of packing to do." She looked at the floor, at the clock on the wall, at the band on the stage—everywhere but in his eyes. "Bye, Nicholas."

♥          ♥          ♥

Callie drank the rest of her latte and motioned to Katie to bring her another. She didn't want to go outside yet and brave the cold. She just wanted to bask herself in warm thoughts of Nicholas....

The day after the graduation gala, Callie had escaped her father's endless list of New York City do's and don'ts by taking an afternoon walk across the street, past the Benedetto's big red barn, and down the incline towards the waterfall. It certainly wasn't Niagara Falls by any means—just a constant trickling of water running off the mountain. In the wintertime, it would freeze and become one giant icicle.

Callie focused her sight on the gentle flow peacefully dripping down the mountain but her head still clamored with her father's instructions for art school.

*Don't talk to strangers.* But, Daddy, how do I make friends? *You don't need any new friends. Keep your door locked at all times. Don't look up at the buildings; you'll look like a tourist.* But, Daddy, I *am* a tourist. *No, you're a target; and if you're not careful, you'll be a statistic. Don't go to any parties. Get to sleep early. Make sure you and Deardra stay together. Don't forget to call home every night.*

"Callie!"

A male voice broke through her thoughts and startled her. She hadn't seen anyone on her trek to the falls and now nervously scanned the brush and boulders lining the stream for the person calling to her. Her father's warnings of the city had caused an unusual terror to rip through her.

"Callie! Over here."

She now recognized the voice as Nicholas's and turned her head to see him sitting on a tall rock waving at her, the sleeve of his red shirt snapping with each movement like a mast on a ship.

"Hi," she called, forced to walk in his direction.

She wished she were wearing her bib overalls instead of the more provocative cut-off shorts and white tank top. Her father's paranoia continued to peck at her brain.

*Don't be alone with any boys. You can't trust them. Don't put yourself in such a situation. You'll have only yourself to blame. Remember what happened to your sister.*

Callie's head spun with her parents' warnings and Maisy's tears.

"Hey, Callie, finish all your packing?"

"Yeah. Thought I'd take a little walk. This is one of my favorite spots."

"I know. You said so last night. I was hoping you'd come by today. I wanted to see you again before you left."

Seated high on the rock, Nicholas looked like a mythological god, smiling warmly upon her, with the sun's golden rays gleaming through the trees and the waterfall his backdrop. As Callie scaled the rock, he extended a strong arm to assist with her climb. When she sat next to him, Callie noticed she had scraped her knee on the way up. Using her finger, she dabbed at the blood.

"Oh, God," Nicholas said as he emptied his pockets in search of a tissue or scrap of cloth.

"Don't worry about it," Callie assured him. "It's just a scratch. I'll live." She glanced up and saw that his face had paled, almost a ghastly white. "What's wrong?"

"I—nothing."

"No, tell me."

"I can't stand the sight of blood." He bowed his head, seemingly embarrassed.

"The music must have been really loud last night 'cause I thought you told me you're going to study medicine at BU."

"Yeah," he replied quietly.

"Um, Nicholas, doctors usually come in contact with blood."

"I know."

"And you don't like blood."

"I know."

"Then I think you need to pick another major."

"I know." They both laughed at the same time. "What I don't know is how I'm going to tell my parents that."

"They want you to be a doctor?"

"More my father than my mother. My dad wanted to be a doctor—actually a surgeon, but the Vietnam War put a wrench in that. He came back with nerve damage in his right hand, probably from the high-powered guns he used. Who knows?"

"So he made his dream your dream?"

"It's not my dream."

"What is your dream?"

"You promise not to laugh?"

"Yes."

"Writing." His admission caused him to hang his head again.

"What's wrong with writing?"

"Nothing for girls, but tell any of my friends that I love to write, and they'd think I'm gay."

"And you're—"

"Not gay."

"I knew that."

"How'd ya know?"

"By the way you held me last night."

Nicholas took hold of her hand, and that feeling of excitement from the prior evening raced through her again.

"I like holding you," he confided softly.

Callie needed to keep the conversation going or become lost in the rising emotion.

"So tell me about your writing. What do you write or want to write? Books? Poems?"

"Everything. I've written a few short stories—mysteries and suspense. That's fun because before I even start writing, I know the ending so all through the story I drop clues here and there for the reader; and just when you seem to figure out who dunnit, I'll twist the story in a new direction."

"Wow. I admire you. It's not everyone who can use words in a creative way. I don't read much outside of assigned school reading, just some poetry like Emily Dickinson."

"Have you been to her house in Amherst?"

"Yeah. It's so sad, though, that her world was that house." Callie realized that, but for the grace of God, her own life could easily revolve around Sycamore.

*Lord, I can't wait to go to New York!*

Nicholas opened a white paper bag that had been hidden next to him.

"Here," he said, taking a cannoli and handing it to her.

"Oh, I couldn't." She gently pushed his hand away.

"But you said last night that they're your favorite dessert."

"They are. I love cannolis, but I haven't had dinner yet."

"And dessert before dinner would be a serious crime?" His sweet mockery caused Callie to smile.

"All right. Just one bite." She held out her hand, but Nicholas chose to feed her, like a bride. Callie bit into the delicious pastry and savored the sweet cream in her mouth before swallowing. "That's so good. It had to come from Puccini's Bakery."

"How did you know?"

"They make the best pastries. It just melts in your mouth. Take a bite; have some," she encouraged. He took a bite, then fed her the rest of the cannoli. "Thank you."

"My pleasure."

He was the nicest boy she had ever known.

"So what else have you written?"

"Not much else, not with my schedule this past year. Between schoolwork and sports, I had little free time."

"Which sports?"

"Soccer and baseball. And you play volleyball in the fall and run track in the spring."

"Yeah, how did you know that?"

"I've had my eye on you for a while."

"Really? Since when"

"Since kindergarten."

Callie looked at him skeptically.

"You can't be serious."

"I am."

"And you wait till graduation to let me know?" She leaned against him playfully. "Your timing stinks."

"Well, it's not entirely my fault. Word around school was that you weren't allowed to date."

"Oh." Callie felt her face redden with embarrassment.

"I hope that's true because otherwise I'd really hate myself for not asking you out."

It was probably the nicest thing he could say to ease her shame.

"Yeah, sort of. My parents—my father is overprotective. After Maisy was raped, life changed for me."

"I suppose it would."

"But it shouldn't have. I wasn't raped. I didn't do anything wrong. Not that Maisy did anything wrong except trust someone who shouldn't have been trusted. She used bad judgment going out with a boy like Finny in the first place, but that's not my fault. I knew better. I was 13; Maisy was 17, yet I knew the boy was a creep. I told her so. But I'm just a kid. No one listens to me. I'll be 30 years old one day, and they'll still not be hearing what I say."

"I know how you feel."

"They put me in a box here in Sycamore thinking they're protecting me, keeping me safe, but they're suffocating me. In their infinite wisdom, they forgot to poke air holes in that box. I can't breathe. That's why I'm so excited about going to New York."

"How did you manage that? I'm surprised they're letting you go."

"Believe me, it took a world of convincing. A 4.0 GPA, an awesome portfolio, and a recommendation from my guidance counselor, art teacher, and principal were just the beginning. I had to have my friend agree to come along and room with me."

"Which friend?"

"Deardra."

"The photographer. She takes some amazing pictures."

"You've seen her work?"

"Yeah, in the school newspaper. Actually, I wrote a few articles and a short story for the paper under the pseudonym, Ashly Kohl."

"Oh my God. I illustrated her story—your story. Was that really you?"

"Yeah. I loved your drawing."

"I loved your story. *Getting Out Alive*. About this guy who goes skiing and gets caught in an avalanche, but survives. It was great, very descriptive. I could picture myself there, buried in the snow, dying." She chuckled, more to herself. "It could've been Sycamore, you know, with leaves instead of snow. I could definitely relate."

"You're gonna go on to do great things, Callie Emerson. I believe that."

"My father thinks I'm silly, that there's no future for me as an artist."

"Don't listen to him, Callie. You gotta believe in yourself. Sometimes you gotta follow your heart when everyone and everything in your head says something contrary." He kissed her hand. "You're gonna paint great pictures."

"Maybe I'll illustrate great books." She leaned into him again playfully. "You'll write great books, and I'll draw the covers."

"I like that. We'd be a great team. Emerson and Ashton."

Callie smiled at his gallantry, positioning her name before his. Nicholas put his arm around her shoulder and nudged Callie closer. She sat under the warmth of his protective assuredness, quietly staring down at the rippling stream. The water created a hypnotic trance, crashing into rocks and spilling over twigs as it danced determined to forge ahead to the river. Nicholas touched her face, and she turned to look at him. He had the kindest eyes.

"You are so very beautiful, Callie," he complimented.

"You're sweet, but I'm very average. Wait till you get to college, then you'll see what beautiful really is."

"I know what beautiful is. It's an angelic heart, a bright mind, a vivid imagination." He touched her cheek and slid his finger to her lips. "It's luscious pink lips and gorgeous brown eyes."

Callie's heart doubled its beat as Nicholas tilted his head slightly to kiss her. His lips were soft and spongy, a warm and wet playground of intense emotion that Callie freely explored. Exhilarated, she responded with a sweet purring that elicited a deeper, more ardent kiss. She touched his cheek, felt it hot with passion, a fiery response to the growing excitement between them.

Nicholas's hands drifted through her hair, down her back, along her arm. His touch, though soft and gentle, seemed deliberate in its roaming as if she were composed of Braille and he didn't want to miss a word. His fingers continued their reading as Callie grew a bit uneasy over the powerful sensations he exponentially produced in her. Every minute in his arms seemed to mold her to him, shaping her heart into his, twisting their bodies into a lovers' knot. It was just a kiss but Callie knew it was so much more.

She pulled back from Nicholas and opened her yes. She saw his brown globes gleaming back at her—a parallel universe with deep oceans of emotion and vast continents of desire and longing. Minus from his speckled eyes of happiness were her islands of fear.

"I'm going to miss you," he said.

"What're you gonna to do this summer?"

"Miss you. Count the days till you're back."

Callie faked a laugh, though she knew he was serious.

"No, really, any plans?"

"We have a summer house on Cape Cod. I work at one of the restaurants there."

"How nice. It's beautiful there."

"Yeah, not as beautiful as you." He leaned forward and kissed her again. "You have such soft lips."

"Thanks," she mumbled, shyly. The faint din of clanging metal sounded. "I gotta go."

"You'll call me when you get back?"

"You'll be on the Cape."

"I'm not sure where I'll be. My folks are thinking about selling the house here and moving permanently to the Cape. My sister graduated college last month, and she got a job in Stamford, so she moved to Connecticut. There's only me left in the house, and I'll be living on campus at BU. My dad wants to sell, but my mom's hedging because of all the memories in the house. I don't know what they're gonna to do, but I doubt anything drastic is going to happen in six weeks. Just know that wherever I'll be, I'll be thinking of you."

Callie tried to be flippant as she slid down the rock.

"Oh, I'll be a distant memory by the time my feet hit the ground."

"I don't think so," Nicholas said, trailing behind her.

She reached the ground and turned to him as he leaped from the boulder to her side.

"Why's that?"

"Because you're special, Callie, and maybe I'm falling in love with you. Maybe I want you to be my girlfriend."

The sound of the bell grew louder, and Callie welcomed the urgency with which her mother pounded that God-awful cowbell to summon her to dinner.

"I gotta go," she said, ignoring his revelation. "The natives are getting restless."

Callie kissed Nicholas on the cheek then darted up the hill towards her house. She had a connection to Nicholas; there was no denying that. However, she didn't want to be anybody's anything.

*I just want to be me.*

But at 18 and having lived under the thumb of an oppressive father, Callie had no clue who she really was … just an artist waiting to paint herself.

# CHAPTER 7

Nicholas knocked on Drew's hospital door before entering. His best friend lay in a white-sheeted bed amidst an offensive odor—a stomach-churning mixture of medicine, meatloaf, and antibacterial spray. Drew's wife, Annie, with her southern belle blonde curls and smile, sat perched on the side of the bed rubbing her husband's hairless head as he slept, breathing through an oxygen mask.

The lunch tray revealed the remnants of a salad, pot roast, potatoes, applesauce, and jello—partially picked through like a fussy child not liking what was offered. Though usually a hearty eater, Drew now disliked his meals, contributing his lack of appetite to the cancer and its treatment. Despite Annie's efforts to keep the weight on her husband, Drew had deteriorated in six weeks from 200 pounds to 175. The once strapping man with a will of iron was beginning to look worn and beaten. Nicholas was concerned.

"Hey, Nick, you're back from Boston?" Annie said softly, trying not to wake Drew. "How's your father?"

"He's fine, you know, recuperating at my sister's. What's going on here? I stopped by your house, and your mom said Drew was admitted yesterday. He couldn't breathe?"

"Bronchopneumonia. We didn't realize that the chemo was killing off his white blood cells along with the cancer. His immunity is down. He caught a cold last week, and it just progressed down to his lungs."

"He's gonna be okay?"

"Yeah, Drew's a fighter."

"Well, he's got you and the boys. That's a lot to fight for."

Drew's eyelids fluttered open. He shifted himself to a more upright position and removed the mask from his mouth to speak.

"Hey, Nick, how you doing?"

"I'm fine. How are *you* feeling?"

"Like shit. I'm sick of being sick. I just want to get healthy again."

Annie leaned over and kissed Drew on the cheek. Her fragile eyes held hope.

"You will, honey. This is all gonna be behind us real soon, and you'll be out in the yard playing with the boys again."

"Yeah, I'm looking forward to that." Drew's voice became raspy forcing him into a coughing jag.

Annie rubbed at his back as he tried to get up the mucus. After spitting into a tissue, he put the mask back over his mouth and took a few deep breaths.

"This sucks," Drew mumbled.

"Hungry?" Nicholas asked, handing a white paper bag to Annie. "Picked up some lunch for you two. Thought the hospital food might not be so appetizing."

Annie peeked in the bag.

"Ah, heroes. What kind?"

"Sausage and peppers."

Drew took off the mask again.

"You're a good guy, Nick. How's your dad?"

"He's going to be okay. He's lucky they caught it in time. Two of his arteries were completely blocked. The doctors say that once he's recovered, he'll be able to do so much more."

"I bet it's like having a brand new heart," Annie commented as she took the foil-wrapped sandwiches from the bag. "How was the weather? Lots of snow?"

"Yeah, it's always cold there this time of year."

Nicholas remembered the bitter gusts that whipped him and Callie and the way her long brown hair danced across her face and over her shoulders. He could still see her brown eyes peering at him through her curtain of hair.

"Who is she?" Drew asked.

"Who's who?" Nicholas replied, blinking Callie's memory away.

"The girl you were just thinking about. I haven't seen you smile like that since—hell, I don't think I've ever seen you smile like that. It's gotta be a girl."

Nicholas shrugged off the remark with a laugh.

"It's no one."

"Are you seeing someone?" Annie asked. "If not, there's this new girl at my office, Zendra. I could fix you up with her."

"No, please don't."

"So you're seeing someone," Annie said, peeling the foil back on the sandwiches.

"No, I'm not seeing anyone."

"Then why were you thinking about her?" Drew asked, narrowing his eyes with suspicion.

"Look, you guys, I gotta go. Enjoy your lunch." Nicholas took two steps to the door.

"Wait a minute," Drew called. "You can't leave without telling me."

"There's nothing to tell."

"Nick, this could be my last day on earth." Drew faked a cough that turned into a real coughing fit which, after several minutes, produced another ball of mucus. "I don't want to die with this cloud of mystery hanging over my head."

Nicholas extended a sympathetic look.

"You're not going to die."

"I know. Me and Annie wouldn't miss your wedding for the world."

"I'm not getting married. Geez, she's just some girl from high school that I ran into up there."

Drew wrinkled his forehead in thought. Without that usual black head of hair, Drew's scalp visibly pulsated with his detective brain waves hard at work.

"She's not *the one*, is she?"

"The one?" Annie asked.

"There was this girl that Nick fell in love with at the end of high school," Drew began. "She went off to summer camp—"

"Art school," Nicholas corrected.

"—and was supposed to call him when she got back. She never did. Needless to say, rooming with Nick freshman year at BU was hell. He was so much in love with her and was having a hard time dealing with her just blowing him off like that." Drew looked from Annie to Nicholas. "What was her name again?"

"Callie."

"Is that all true?" Annie posed the question to Nicholas.

"Pretty much. Callie and I had this unbelievable connection. I felt it; she felt it."

"Passion?" Annie hinted.

"Innocent passion. I just kissed her once, but—" He thought for a moment how to put it into words, how to describe the magic without it sounding completely foolish. "I can't explain it."

"Pure teenage lust, I'd say," Drew added.

"No," Nicholas shook his head. "It wasn't just the kiss or how pretty I thought she was. It was the way we connected mentally. We could talk about anything and everything. We saw life the same way. She was smart and funny and everything I wanted in a girl." Embarrassed by his rambling, Nicholas bowed his head. "That was a long time ago."

"So she went off to art school and never called you again?" Annie seemed confused.

"Yes."

"Why didn't you call her then?" she asked.

"Exactly what I said all those years ago," Drew exclaimed and kissed his wife's hand. "That's why I love you, Annie. You think rational thoughts."

"Nick, why didn't you call her?" Annie repeated. "If you had such strong feelings for her, how could you let her walk out of your life?"

"She was supposed to call *me*." Nicholas tried to defend himself. "She obviously didn't feel the same way about me when she came back from

New York, otherwise she would have contacted me. I figured she met someone else. I just had to accept that."

"Yeah, but it took a while." Drew explained, "We college guys did our best to distract him, make him forget about her." Drew turned his attention from Annie who was using a knife from the lunch tray to cut the sandwiches into more manageable pieces. "Did you get to talk to her this time, Nick, or was it one of those sightings from afar?"

"No, I got to talk to her. We sat for a while and had a cup of coffee. She told me what she's been doing since high school. She owns an art gallery now."

"Still pretty?" Drew asked.

"Gorgeous."

"Married?" Annie inquired.

"No, not married."

"Boyfriend?" she persisted.

"I don't know."

"So how did you leave things?" Drew asked.

"It was like that summer all over again. We had that same powerful connection, attraction, easiness—whatever you want to call it. Somehow we started talking about regrets, and I asked her if she had any. I was sure she was going to say *us*, that she regretted not calling me, seeing me, something—anything about that summer, missing me, missing the chance to be with me, but she just smiled and said she had no regrets, *not a single regret*." Nicholas shook his head. "I'll never understand it." Goosebumps prickled his arms as he recalled Callie hugging him, pressing herself so close as she kissed his cheek as they said goodbye. "Who cares really?"

"I think you do," Drew said as he bit into the sandwich. "It's a few days later, and she's still on your mind. Why don't you call her? Did you get her number?"

"She gave me her business card; told me to call her the next time I'm in town."

"So call her."

"Why bother? It's an impossible relationship. We live in different states."

Drew shook his head.

"That's a non-issue. She's an artist. She can work anywhere."

"You could definitely have a relationship." Annie pulled a tissue from the box and wiped her mouth. "Think about it, Nick. Maybe it was meant to be, you know, meeting again after all these years and still having the same chemistry. It's romantic. It'd make a great novel, Mr. English Professor."

Nicholas chuckled.

"I'll think about it."

"Calling her?"

"Writing the book." Nicholas teased. "I think it'd be easier."

Drew inhaled a deep breath of oxygen then pushed the mask aside to speak.

"Call the lady. The best advice I'll ever give you."

"Yeah, the same advice I got 15 years ago."

"Maybe you'll actually take it."

Nicholas shook Drew's hand.

"Feel better, man. I'll call you tomorrow. Got an appointment with the barber now."

"Hey, it's growing in. Leave it alone. It looks good," Drew said.

"Nah, I'm getting it shaved again. I made a promise to you till yours grows in. Solidarity, my friend, solidarity."

Annie walked over to Nicholas and hugged him.

"You're a great friend, Nick. You're gonna make some lucky lady very happy one day."

Nicholas silently wished that lucky lady were Callie. He couldn't get her out of his head. Thoughts of her, the scent of her—everything about her made him want to call her and see her again. Nicholas vowed to contact her. He was tired of living with regret.

♥          ♥          ♥

Another Christmas Eve alone. Callie took her malaise to the window seat in her bedroom and stared out onto the darkened sky bordered by a million stars. She played dot-to-dot, forming her own constellations of sadness and melancholy, only to be interrupted by a late night phone call.

"Merry Christmas," she answered prematurely.

"Hello, Brown Eyes."

"Hi, Aidan, how are you?"

"Fine. Good to see my sister."

"How's the weather there in California?"

"Just fine, but not white. It's just not feeling like Christmas without the snow." He laughed off his sadness. "How's everything with you?"

"Great," she lied, not wanting to confess her loneliness. "I'll be spending Christmas tomorrow with my parents."

"Did you get the present I sent?"

"Oh, yes, yes. Thank you so much. I love that ring."

"It looked great on your hand that first day."

Aidan's voice trailed off. Callie knew he was thinking about Grace again.

"You didn't need to buy me a Christmas present, especially such an expensive one."

She couldn't tell him that she never wore the ring, would never wear the ring, that she couldn't even look at it because it reminded her of Joe and her mateless life.

"Think of it as a mythological thank you gift, bestowing upon you all its magical powers."

Callie cried to herself.

*Alone on Christmas Eve—obviously the myth is a lie.*

"Thank you, Aidan, but you shouldn't have spent so much money."

"For all your listening and counseling. Much cheaper than a psychiatrist. I don't know how I would've gotten through the past weeks without your friendship."

"Did you call her?"

"Grace?"

"Yes."

"No. Not that I didn't think about it, but it's better I don't. It's over, ya know. No sense banging my head on a closed door."

"You still love her."

"Yeah, but it never was about me and what I was feeling." Aidan sighed. "Anyway, thanks again for being such a good friend. I really appreciate it. I'll call you when I get back, okay?"

"Sure. Merry Christmas, Aidan."

Callie returned to the window seat and resumed her solitude. Not the usual one to indulge in self-pity, she permitted herself a few sad minutes to think about her life and why everyone she knew was coupled up except for her. She couldn't understand it. Then she looked outside of herself and thought of Aidan and his pain. Being alone was one thing … being alone when you can't be with the one you love is horrible.

Callie putted around her kitchen baking cookies she had no intention of eating. She hadn't much of an appetite yet she had an abundance of nervous energy that caused spring cleaning to arrive with the onset of the new year. Dusting this and scrubbing that, Callie had busied herself all day in the house, not even venturing across the lawn to the gallery. When she saw Deardra's red scarf blowing in the January wind, Callie hurried to the front door to let her in.

"Hi! Come in."

Deardra stamped the snow from her boots and entered the foyer.

"I can't wait till spring."

"Well, that's not coming any time soon."

Callie closed the door and followed Deardra into the kitchen. Her friend planted herself on the stool at the island and breathed in deeply.

"I smell something good, and surprisingly it's not paint for a change."

Callie laughed but secretly wanted to cry. She hadn't painted in a week and worried about her loss of creativity. Her mind could only think of Nicholas … wonderful, delicious, naughty fantasies of a man she craved to be with. No reprimanding her subconscious could quell these desires that ran rampant, pulling her from her artistry.

"I'm being domestic today. I'm baking cookies. You can take them home to Keith and little Liam."

"Want to see the latest picture of my men?" Deardra pulled a photographic masterpiece from her wallet—a snapshot of her husband and four-year-old son ice-skating.

"Gosh, Liam gets bigger every day. Was this taken over on Breemer's Pond?"

"Yeah. Remember how we used to skate there and sled down Riker's Ridge?"

"I never sledded down the ridge. My father strictly forbade it."

"Oh, your father was always a killjoy." Deardra took off her coat and laid it over the chair. She pushed up the sleeves of her sweater bearing a brilliant mix of colors. "God, it seems like ages ago. You know, I never feel old till I start reminiscing or see my son doing things I used to do as a kid."

"Don't be calling yourself old, 'cause then you're calling me old, and, well, I'm too young to be old."

Deardra shrugged her shoulders in defeat.

"Take the battery out of the clock if you want, but the fact remains we're not getting any younger. Got any coffee?"

"Just made some. Help yourself."

Callie pulled a cup from the cabinet and handed it to Deardra who poured herself a mugful of the brew. She laid a napkin on the countertop and placed two cookies on it.

"I can't remember the last time I baked. So what's up? Cookies and a sparkling kitchen, not quite the Callie I know."

"And you working on a Sunday afternoon. Not the Deardra I know."

"I wanted to close out the books for December. You really had a good month, Callie, the best December ever. Plus, the parties were an added bonus. Not counting the other artists, you yourself sold nine paintings and 32 angels. You could make a fine living all by yourself without com-

missioning out the other artisans, but since I'm one of those appreciative artisans who you so kindly let display and sell my photographs, I'll
not encourage you to close the doors to us."

"Never. The gallery would be absolutely boring with just my work."

"Oh, yes," Deardra said sarcastically. "A gallery full of Monet would
be simply boring."

Callie opened the oven door and removed another tray of chocolate
chip cookies and set it on the stove to cool.

"So, why the urge to bake? Has Nick finally gotten to you?"

"Nicholas? How did you know about him?"

Deardra skewed her mouth.

"Callie, Nick has been a friend of ours for a year now."

"Oh, Nick—that Nick. Yes, sorry, not him." She tripped over her own
words.

"Then who? Who is Nicholas?"

Callie sponged the granite top island in an effort to appear nonchalant.

"Oh, um, Nicholas from high school."

"High school?"

"Yeah, Nicholas Ashton, from high school. Remember him?"

"Yeah. Why are you thinking about him?" Deardra couldn't hide her
puzzlement.

"I ran into him last week—literally ran into him outside my uncle's
jewelry store. We had a cup of coffee, chatted for a little bit, and then he
left."

"And?"

"Nothing."

"You're baking. That's something. He's got you baking."

"It's nothing, really. We had a nice talk and—and—" Callie wanted to
come clean and confide in her friend. "Since then, I can't seem to shake
him from my mind. God, Deardra, he was so handsome, and the way he
held my hand—"

"He held your hand?"

"Just casually, you know, across the table. It didn't mean anything, yet it meant *everything*. It was like that day at the waterfall all over again—the connection, the anticipation, the kiss—"

"You kissed?"

"No, not this time, but it felt like he kissed me."

Deardra's face lit up. She sat for a moment speechless, just smiling, shaking her head at the mere coincidence of it all.

"Imagine that. After all these years, Nicholas Ashton is back in your life."

"No, not really. We just had coffee. Actually, he lives in South Carolina."

"So he was up here visiting his parents for the holidays?"

"Something like that. His dad had an operation."

"I told you that summer in New York to call him, but you never listened to me," Deardra chided and bit into one of the cookies.

"I couldn't. You read his poem in that book he sent me. He was falling in love with me, and me—well, I was falling in love with the world."

"I suppose you were too young. So, what's he do for a living now?"

"We didn't really talk about that." Callie remembered their conversation in the coffee shop and how she had drifted in and out of memories while he was talking. "I guess he's a doctor. That's what he went to college for."

"Did you exchange numbers, e-mail?"

"I gave him my business card and told him to call me the next time he's in town."

"Which could be never," she added, ever the realist.

"Gosh, I hope not. I'd really like to see him again." Callie rinsed the sponge and considered cleaning some other surface before abandoning the thought and tossing it in the sink. She stared out the window towards the woods, towards the waterfall, but before drowning herself in memories, she turned toward Deardra and sighed. "I'm never gonna see him again."

"Just call him," she insisted.

"I don't have his number."

"Well, if he's a doctor, he can't be hard to find. Do a search on the internet."

"I suppose I could." Callie scrunched her nose and feigned pain.

"What's wrong?"

"Inasmuch as I'd like to see him again, part of me says *What's the point?* There's no denying I'm attracted to him, and seeing him again will only add to that, but the fact is he lives in South Carolina."

"The real fact is he's a doctor and he can practice medicine *anywhere* he wants. If things progress and he wants to be with you, he'll figure out the geography and make it work."

After Deardra left, Callie used the computer to find Nicholas's contact information. She first performed a global search of doctors in South Carolina. Once she had that database, Callie entered "Ashton" as the keyword. The resulting information showed no data for a Nicholas Ashton. Staring at the screen, Callie realized she faced a dead-end in locating Nicholas. Their fate of ever meeting again now rested solely in his hands.

On her bedroom shelf, she found the poetry book Nicholas had sent her while she was at art school. She blew the dust off of it, and fanned through the verses to the last blank page where he had written in blue ink an ode to Callie:

> *At last I can breathe*
> *For she has awakened my senses*
> *With her sweet scent.*
> *I want to breathe her.*

> *At last I can feel*
> *For she has touched me with*
> *Innocent strokes of tender passion.*
> *I want to hold her.*

> *At last I can taste*
> *For she has pressed her lips to mine*
> *And filled me with delicious desire.*

*I want to kiss her ... again.*

*At last I am alive*
*For she has stirred my heart*
*With soft whispers and endless longing*
*I want to love her ... forever.*

♥               ♥               ♥

Three days later, Callie logged onto the computer at the gallery. Within her e-mails, she opened the one with the subject line: 15 years and counting ...

*Dear Callie:*

*It was wonderful seeing you again after all these years and catching up a bit at the coffee shop. My apologies for running out, but I'd like to make it up to you by taking you up on your offer to get together the next time I'm in town—which will be this weekend. Perhaps, we could have dinner Friday night and reminisce some more. After all, it's 15 years and counting.*

*Sincerely, Nicholas*

Callie smiled and pondered a reply.

*Hi Nicholas ... Yes, it was great seeing you, too. I'd love to get together Friday night for dinner. Let's meet in Boston at The Nick of Time. Attached find directions. If you're going to be staying on the Cape, and you'd like to meet somewhere else that is more convenient, let me know. Otherwise, I'll see you at the restaurant at 7:00 pm ... Artfully yours, Callie*

By three o'clock Friday afternoon, Callie had rummaged through the contents of her closet twice in search of an outfit for dinner with Nicholas. Turtle-neck sweaters, ski sweaters, button-down sweaters, low-cut sweaters, tight sweaters, cashmere sweaters, silk blouses, linen blouses, jeans, low-cut jeans, black jazzy pants, short skirt, leather skirt, corduroy skirt, long skirt, vintage skirt, frilly skirt, v-neck dress, spaghetti-strap dress, knit dress, knee-high stiletto heel boots, cowboy boots, granny boots, strappy sandals, pumps … not a thing to wear!

Callie lay on the bed in her black satin bra trimmed with tiny red silk roses and matching panties. Deciding on her underwear had been easy enough, but then again, nobody was going to see it. Certainly, not Nicholas … though Callie smiled at the thought of the possibility. Maybe it was the history between them that surfaced those kinds of thoughts … or maybe it was the passion.

When Callie arrived at the restaurant, she saw Nicholas seated at the bar, handsome in a black shirt and black pants. She glanced at her watch: 7:00 p.m.

*God, I'm so on time!*

She hoped she didn't appear too eager, yet he was already there with a half-empty glass sitting on a coaster in front of him. While Nicholas conversed with the bartender, Callie took a second to check her appearance in the mirror at the coat-check room. She had finally settled on a cream-colored corduroy skirt, black cashmere sweater, and black boots. Casual yet classic. Dressing required so much more insight than painting.

Nicholas saw Callie's reflection in the mirror over the bar as she came up behind him and placed a kiss to his cheek. She radiated beauty in the simplest way. Much the same since high school, Callie still had that wholesome, country-girl, dipped-in-milk look that set heads turning when she walked into a room.

"Hi, Nicholas. So good to see you again. I hope everything's okay with your dad for you to be back here so soon."

"He's fine, Callie. Thanks for asking."

*What would she think if I told her I made the trip just to see her?*

Callie boosted herself up onto the stool next to him, then crossed her legs, flexing her booted foot to rest upon the brass bar of his stool. It created a bridge between their bodies—one he wanted to walk with his fingers. God, she had gorgeous legs.

"What would you like to drink?" he asked.

"A Marguerita. I think I'm gonna have the fajitas tonight. They're delicious here."

"So, you eat here often?" Nicholas motioned for the bartender.

"Often enough. The owner is a friend of mine." She turned her attention to the bartender who flipped a napkin on the counter in front of her. "Nice to see you, Charlie. Busy night, huh?"

"Just the way I like it," he answered. "Even better when I get to serve pretty girls like yourself. What can I get you, Callie?"

"I'll have a frozen Marguerita, salted. By the way, this is my friend Nicholas Ashton."

Nicholas felt her warm hands on his back as she made the introduction.

"Yes, we met before. The English professor from South Carolina."

"English professor?" Callie's surprise arched her eyebrows. "Wow, you really did it. You really changed your major." She smiled, obviously pleased. "So you teach English?"

"Creative Writing at the university. Though, sometimes I think it would have been easier to be a doctor," he joked. "The body, the bones, muscles, tendons—they're all joined one way. Words can be joined a million different ways, and there's usually no definitive right or wrong."

"I suppose it's very much like art. There are no *bad* paintings."

Nicholas shook his head and raised a disbelieving eyebrow.

"You can honestly say there are no bad paintings?"

"Okay," she chuckled. "There *are* bad paintings. Not mine, of course."

"Of course. And there is bad writing, too. I have a few of those students. It's painful just reading their stories. They try—Lord, they try so hard to put their thoughts on paper and create a story, but it's so stifled and disjointed." He paused as Charlie placed Callie's drink in front of her. "Then I have other students—the English majors—who just flow with words. Everything works for them from plot to character development. I suppose the best part of my job is developing the mediocre writer into an exceptional talent. It's challenging, but the payoff is when someone gets published."

"Are you published? Have you written any books?"

Callie put her lips to the glass and suddenly Nicholas's mind emptied of all reasonable thought. She had such sexy lips, full and red with a shiny lipstick that left its mark on the rim of her glass.

"So, written any books?" she repeated.

"Um, yeah, I've dabbled in fiction with several short stories, a collection of essays, and a contemporary suspense. Two of my mysteries are still collecting dust on my publisher's desk, and I'm in the middle of another novel, as we speak."

"As we speak?"

"A good writer always absorbs his surroundings. It may or may not make it into the text, but the more you have to draw upon, the more people you meet and emotions you encounter, the greater likelihood of capturing the truth in everyday life. And I think that's what makes a compelling story—that sense of realism. That's what I try to impress upon my students, to delve to the core and tap the honesty."

"That's the essence of art, too. It's funny, don't you think, how parallel our lives are?" Her hand found his. "You with words, and me with pictures, both of us trying to touch the world in a profound way. I want to read your stories." She playfully tugged at his fingers in a pleading sort of way. "When can I read them?"

Before Nicholas could answer, he saw Callie's eyes brighten as she caught sight of someone approaching from the kitchen area behind him. He glanced over his shoulder to see a good-looking fellow slipping on the jacket of an expensive Italian suit. Appearing to be in his thirties, the man had a European face with chiseled cheekbones and a broad smile, which he directed to Callie.

"Callie, gorgeous, happy New Year. We all missed you at the party," the fellow said as she hopped off the barstool and into his arms for a hug.

"Sorry. I had an exciting night with my parents."

"They were asleep before midnight?"

"Exactly." She laughed and raked her fingers through her hair. "So, dish the gossip. Who was here?"

"Maisy."

"My sister? She's such a brat! *She's* the reason I canceled. She bailed out on my parents claiming a headache."

"Well, by the way she drank champagne, I'm sure she had one the next morning."

"Unbelievable."

"Good news is that I sold your painting of Bourbon Street."

"To who?" she asked.

"To whom," Nicholas quietly corrected, an involuntary reflex as an English teacher.

"Hmm?" Callie suddenly remembered Nicholas and realized her rudeness. "I'm so sorry Nicholas. Nick, this is a friend of mine from high school, Nicholas Aston. Nicholas, this is Nick Roccia. He owns this restaurant."

"Nice to meet you," Nicholas said, standing to shake hands. "Beautiful place."

"Thank you, but Callie deserves much of the credit. All of the art and murals, from the ceiling to the floor, were painted by this lovely lady. The food may be good, but it's the atmosphere that keeps them coming back."

Nicholas hadn't really taken notice of the art, but found interest in knowing that Callie had donned the brush. Glancing around the bar into the dining room, he glimpsed a partitioned area where tables were nestled near a full-wall mural of the beach and ocean and setting sun. Its perfect depth and coloring set a romantic scene of dinner on the beach at dusk. A fisherman's net draping each table and bucket candles added to the authenticity.

"Ready to eat?" Callie asked, rejoining Nicholas to the conversation.

"Sure."

Nicholas carried his drink and her Marguerita, and followed Nick upstairs to another dining room. More formal and elegant with white lace tablecloths and stem candles, this room held Callie's paintings in gold-leaf frames positioned asymmetrically on the walls. A pianist sat motionless behind a mini grand situated in one corner of the room while a harpist strummed softy but methodically in the other corner.

As Nick escorted them to an out-of-the-way table near the window, Callie touched Nicholas's arm.

"I thought we'd be eating downstairs," she whispered. "It's a bit more casual, a lot less romantic. I'm sorry."

"Don't be sorry," he responded, quite happy to be seated on the quieter, more intimate second level.

"Here you go," Nick said, laying two menus on the table. "I've some business to tend to in the kitchen, but I'll be back later on. Enjoy your dinner."

"Thanks, Nick," Callie replied. She sat quietly for a moment, watching her friend depart the room, then she looked at Nicholas and smiled. "I'm so glad we're doing this. I didn't realize how much I missed you."

"Over the past 15 years?"

"No, the past two weeks. I hoped we'd get together again."

He reached out and touched her hand, connected by skin yet the pulse of passion weaving a strange but familiar bond. There was something in Callie's brown eyes, something unspoken, something that needed to be said.

"You're adorable. Why is it no man has snatched you up yet?"

"Not all that many prospects."

"Is that so? Just tonight, the bartender and Nick both seem to adore you."

"Well, Charlie is married, and Nick sits on the other side of the fence."

"He lives out of state?"

"No," she laughed, then lowered her voice. "He's gay."

"Oh."

"It's as I say, the good ones are too young or married or gay." She flashed a mischievous smile. "Or they live in South Carolina."

Such quick wit caused Nicholas to smile. He pondered a moment the reference to his being an out-of-reach prospect.

"I have to ask, Callie, why you never called me all those years ago after art school."

She sighed then sipped her drink.

"I was young with a different set of priorities. You wanted a girl-friend, and all I wanted was to paint." Her voice matched the melan-choly in her eyes. "Should I apologize for that? Do I regret it?" Callie shook her head. "No. It's those experiences—all of them—that have made me the person I am today, and I really like who I am." A quick squeeze of his hand preceded Callie's picking up the menu. "Besides, I was so focused on me and my art that I wouldn't have been a very good girlfriend. You would've come to hate me, and 15 years later we wouldn't be sitting here now talking about what might have been." She peered up from the menu for one quick second, smiled, then turned her attention back to the list of entrees. "The shrimp scampi sounds deli-cious. Maybe I won't order the fajitas."

Nicholas sat there completely charmed by her personality, beauty, and answer to his question. It hadn't been another fellow after all that kept her from calling. It was art that had claimed her attention, her ado-ration, her love. Nicholas found no jealousy in that; he smiled.

"I suppose you're right. I wouldn't have Adam in my life," he added.

Callie dropped the menu to her lap.

"You're gay?" The sound of her voice indicated more disappointment than surprise. Mentally, Nicholas saw her reaffirm her statement: *The good ones are too young or married or gay.*

"No, I'm not gay," he chuckled. "I'm a father."

"You have a son?" Now, Nicholas heard surprise. "You're married?"

"No, not married, but I have a son. Adam is great. He's five now. In kindergarten, reading already."

"No doubt with you as his dad. Do you have any pictures?"

Callie waited as Nicholas pulled his wallet from his pocket and handed it to her.

"Nothing recent, though. My mom pilfered some pictures on my last visit."

Flipping through baby photos when the boy seemed no more than two, Callie smiled at the blondish-brown-haired little boy.

"He's adorable. Looks a lot like you."

"Yeah, that apple didn't fall far from the tree." Nicholas readied himself for the onslaught of questions about Adam, but Callie asked none.

Handing him back the wallet, she simply smiled and said, "You seem to have life sitting in your palm. Family, a great job, published books...."

As Callie continued talking, Nicholas tried to read her face for some sign that she wanted to be included in that life. Those eyes of hers—those doe eyes, wide with a mixture of emotion—were impossible to read.

*What does she want? Could this develop into something more?*

Callie touched his hand.

"I want to read your books, Nicholas. When can I read them?"

"I can send you a copy, I suppose, or you can find them in the bigger book stores or online."

"Their titles?"

"The collection of essays is called *Nowhere to Run,* and the novel is *Badges.*"

"Great titles. How do you come up with them?"

Nicholas didn't want to talk about this. He wanted to push past the trite conversation and get to something meaningful.

"Titles? I try to keep it to three words or less, something eye-catching that hints what the story is about."

Callie took on a pensive stare, detective-like.

"Badges. I guess it's about cops?"

"Yeah, a mystery, you know, good guys, bad guys, homicide." *Absolutely nothing I want to talk about right now with your sexy self sitting across from me.*

"It sounds spine-tingling. I can't wait to read it. What about the other ones you've written not yet published?"

He hesitated and looked around for the waiter or waitress to take their orders and interrupt this nowhere conversation.

"Those manuscripts are with my editor. I'm hoping I'll get the green light soon."

"Can I read them? I don't care if they're published or not. You wrote them. They *have* to be fabulous."

Nicholas gave her one of his self-deprecating shrugs.

"They're just entertaining stories. They're not going to change the world."

"If you can make a difference in one person's life, then you've changed the world." Callie picked up her glass in a toast, glancing off in thought as she moistened her lips with a flick of her tongue. When her eyes settled back on him, they held promise and certainty. "Here's to that one person whose life you're going to change." She clinked her glass to his.

# CHAPTER 8

❀

Driving through the old neighborhood the next afternoon, Nicholas turned left and right until he came upon Callie's street. This piece of small town America hadn't changed much over the past 15 years except that the pitted gravel road has been paved and there were about only half the working farms as he remembered. Callie's childhood house looked the same—still light yellow with dark green trim and shutters. The landscape, too, remained as he remembered except the Emerson's flowerbeds were covered in two feet of snow.

Nicholas continued slowly down the road. There on the opposite side, he came upon Callie's property—the old Benedetto farm. The big red barn stood bigger and redder, proud almost, with large arched windows careening to the sky. Over the door hung the sign *Appassionata*. Several cars were parked in the circular drive, and he could see people moving about inside the gallery.

Further down the road he drove, trying to peer over the four-foot high rock wall that surrounded Callie's property. Nicholas remembered the Benedetto farmhouse as shabby, but now it bore fresh white paint, brick red shutters and door as well as a new front porch. A slate path, shoveled free of snow, connected her home to the gallery. Once past the house, he could glimpse its rear, and there he saw a wall of glass—the sliders of Callie's conservatory, the once screened-in porch she had told him about.

The ground was thick with snow, and the barren trees offered a full view deep into the woods. Nicholas's mind clicked off memory after memory of cutting through the Benedetto property to hike into the woods to fish in the creek or pulling a sled to Riker's Ridge with his friends. Those were good times.

Nicholas turned the car around and drove back towards Appassionata. He parked in the half-circle in front of the building. It was hard to imagine it ever being a barn with hay and horses and cows. Inside, walls of paintings and drawings and tables of sculptures and pottery appeared at every corner. Nicholas followed the sound of Callie's voice, and found her with customers. She greeted him with a smile.

"Hi, Nicholas. I'm going to be a little bit longer."

"That's okay."

"Feel free to look around. Deardra's exhibit is upstairs."

Callie had told Nicholas over dinner the previous night how she and Deardra stayed friends over the years. Wandering through the gallery, he observed some of the finest art he had ever seen. Callie seemed to find the essence of life within each painting she created. Though most of her work revolved around scenery and landscapes, each picture touched on some human element—a couple holding hands, a mother rocking her baby, two girls swimming in the lake, skiers racing down the mountain, a pair of sandals left on the beach at sunset. Subtle yet defining.

Callie had an incredible eye for detail. Not that Nicholas considered himself any expert on art. Having visited the university gallery a few times, he had learned a little bit about the different artists, impressionism and Cubism. All that didn't matter except to add to his appreciation of the effort behind the art.

Upstairs, Nicholas found Deardra's photographs. She still had an innate flair for capturing the truth in life. Some of her pictures stemmed from her freelance magazine work. Others depicted everyday events and the humanity accompanying them. She, like Callie, portrayed honesty to the core. He continued through the loft until he came upon an altar of some sort. Awestruck, Nicholas peered around the space at all the ceramic angels. It was like he had stepped into heaven, and all the winged angels greeted him with glorious smiles.

"So, what do you think?" Callie asked as she stepped up behind him.

"I didn't know you were so religious."

"Not religious really. Rather, I'd say I'm more spiritual. That's why I love the angels so much. They're not saints. They're not martyrs. They're not perfect. I believe they were just ordinary people who lived regular lives—worn thin sometimes by everyday life." Callie picked up one of her angels and touched its face. "They had families and friends and jobs. They were mothers, fathers, daughters, and sons, policemen, paramedics, secretaries, waitresses, writers, attorneys, artists. They laughed and loved and lost their tempers at times. They were the imperfect in this imperfect world but who always tried to do the right thing." Setting the angel back down, Callie turned her smile to Nicholas. "In this day and age with all the pressures of family and work and economic stress, with the threat of crime around each corner, and with our own ingrained instincts to keep to ourselves, I don't think any of us could aspire to more. I believe there's an angel in all of us, just that with some, you have to chip longer at to unearth the goodness."

Nicholas picked up one of the angels and examined its delicate shape and color.

"This is so beautiful … the face, the wings. And I love the swirl of color. How do you paint that? They're all so different yet so alike."

"It's the fire that produces that luster."

"Fire? You mean the kiln." He set the angel down and picked up another.

"No, I mean fire. After the angel is glazed and set, she's put in a paper-lined metal can and set on fire. After I put the lid on and the fire goes out, the angel cools. When she's cleaned off, the color and pattern are miraculously formed."

"Amazing."

"Take one. Pick any one out as a gift from me to you."

Nicholas liked the one he was holding. It resembled Callie with delicate facial features—winter-kissed pink cheeks and soft smile. The only difference could be seen in the eyes. The angel's were blue.

"I'll take this one."

"Terrific. I'll wrap it up for you."

"Thanks." Nicholas felt overwhelmed with reverence in the small space. "You know, I haven't been to church since I graduated high school, and even when I did go, I never really prayed for anything."

"That's good, 'cause I believe we only get one prayer answered in our lifetime, and you should save it for something really meaningful. I used mine on my sister, but I'm still waiting for that one to be answered."

"Is hoping praying?"

"It's only praying when you invite God in on your conversation."

Callie led Nicholas back downstairs to the front desk. Pulling tissue paper from a drawer, she folded it around the angel and placed it in a bag.

"This gallery is incredible, Callie. I can't believe the way you transformed the place."

"Thanks. No one ever believes it was a barn until I show them old pictures."

"I'd love to see those."

"Oh, they're in the office. Right this way," Callie said.

Nicholas followed Callie into the small office. She pointed to the picture on the wall as Nicholas stepped behind her to observe it. She felt his breath on her cheek as he looked at the photo from over her shoulder. The room seemed to shrink by the second as Callie became more aware of the close proximity of Nicholas and the response her body produced. Her pulse quickened, and she felt the need to touch him. But he was off limits. Nicholas's disclosure of a son last evening, though she hadn't asked for details surrounding Adam's birth or his mother, clearly signified a life rooted in South Carolina.

Clasping her hands, Callie said, "So, it's after two. I can close early. What would you like to do?" She turned her head and saw in Nicholas's eyes a reciprocal affection.

"I want to be with you."

His reply rippled through her, washing up memories of the graduation gala and the afternoon at the waterfall, but this time she didn't want to run from him. Callie wanted to fall into his arms and kiss him, but despite their attraction, she knew he belonged to another place, another state, and maybe another woman. She had skated over all of that last night, not asking any questions, not wanting to know the facts that would keep their story fiction.

"Why don't we go for a drive?" she suggested. "I'll show you the old neighborhood."

"I've a better idea. Let's go sledding."

"Sledding? You're joking, right?"

"No, I'm serious. Do you have a sled?"

"Yeah, at my parents' house. They're old sleds, though, from when me and my sister were kids."

"Well, let's have a look. I bet a good scrubbing and a wax candle will get 'em going."

"I'm sure my parents are home," she said in tone meant to discourage.

"Should we invite them along?"

"No, of course not," she laughed. "I just don't know if—do you really want to subject yourself to my parents?"

"Callie, I'm a teacher. I meet parents all the time."

"Okay, but I warned you."

Callie's mother must have been watching from the window as they walked up the driveway, because as soon as they stepped onto the front porch, her mother opened the door.

"Hi, Mom." Callie stomped the snow from her boots, and Nicholas did the same.

"Callie, what a nice surprise."

Bearing no resemblance to her daughter, the slender, gray-haired woman in a brown sweatsuit and blue slippers stood at the big oak door. Fine lines creased her mouth and forehead as she smiled and arched her eyebrows in a welcoming expression. Her glasses hung from a chain around her neck, and she put them on to get a better look at her guest.

"Mom, this is a friend from high school, Nicholas Ashton."

"Hi, Mrs. Emerson." Nicholas offered his hand to her.

"Ashton, Ashton," the mom mumbled, tapping her forehead as she sidestepped to allow their entrance into the house. "Didn't your family own the house on Pinewood Road?

"That's right. They sold the place my first year in college. They live out on the Cape now."

"How nice," the mother replied.

"It's bitter cold there this time of year with the wind blowing in off the water," Callie's father added from earshot of the kitchen. He clicked open a can of soda, waved a polite hello, then shuffled back to his chair in the family room.

"Mom, we're gonna borrow the sleds in the basement."

Nicholas took off his cap.

"Oh, a marine," the mother said, looking at his haircut. "You're a marine."

"No, I'm not a marine." Nicholas smiled.

Callie's father leaned back in the chair and glanced into the living room.

"He's not a marine, Joan. That's an Air Force haircut. Wyckowski's son is in the Air Force. He's got a cut just like that."

Nicholas self-consciously rubbed at his head.

"No, I'm not in the Air Force either. A friend's got cancer—"

"You got the cancer?" Callie's mother exclaimed. "Oh, lordie, Jake, he's got the cancer."

"I—" Nicholas tried to interrupt.

"Well, it's not the end of the world, Joan. Buzz had it, and they chopped out his prostrate two years ago, and he's still walking around," Callie's father stated.

"I suppose it depends on what kind of cancer you have. Flora Kennedy—no relation to the famous Kennedy's, mind you—just had a mastectomy. Just awful, you know. You have to check for those lumps.

Callie, do you check for those lumps? You have to feel around in a circular motion and—"

"Mom, I know how to check myself."

"Well, good, 'cause you can't be too careful these days. It shows no prejudice that cancer, old and young." The mother looked at Nicholas. "What kind do *you* have?"

"I don't have cancer. My best friend has cancer, and when the treatments made his hair fall out, I shaved my head as a show of support," Nicholas explained to everyone's astonished looks. Callie's father turned his attention back to the TV.

"That's a wonderful thing," Callie said, petting Nicholas's arm.

"What can I get you two to eat?" her mother asked.

"Nothing, Mom. We just stopped by to borrow the sleds."

"Where you off to?" her father inquired from his chair.

"Riker's Ridge," Nicholas announced.

"No, that's too slick. It's way too dangerous," the man said flatly. "Go over to Carson's hill. They always got a nice packed hill."

Callie knew better than to reply or argue with her stubborn father, and silently led Nicholas to the basement where they spent a few minutes wiping down the sleds and waxing the steel rudders with a candle. After they said a quick goodbye to her parents, Callie and Nicholas set off down the street.

"Carson's hill is this way," Callie said, tugging Nicholas to the left.

"I know, but we're going to Riker's Ridge." He saw doubt then excitement cross her face … or maybe it was fear. She didn't say much else except comment about the weather during their half-mile trek to Riker's Ridge.

Big feathery flakes floated whimsically overhead like baby birds on their maiden voyage. Callie felt like a teenager again holding Nicholas's hand and trudging through virgin snow while the anticipation of soaring down a hill on steel rudders grew by the minute. When they finally reached the top of the slope and sat on the sleds, Callie resumed her age.

"I don't know if this is such a good idea, Nicholas. I never sledded down Riker's Ridge before. It looks a little dangerous."

"It's safe. Me and my friends did it a thousand times when we were kids."

"*Kids*. That's the operative word here. We're not kids anymore."

He came up behind her and knelt down in the snow. His breath steamed the air.

"I wouldn't let anything hurt you, Callie. Trust me." As he pushed the sled, launching her down the hill, Nicholas's words propelled Callie back to when she was a kid and her father warned her never to sled down that hill. *You'll get hurt, break something, and wind up in the hospital. Then who's going to help around the house?*

Callie's sled came to rest in a drift of packed snow just seconds before Nicholas's sled petered to a halt next to her.

"Safe and sound?" he asked, taking her gloved hand to help her up.

"Yes, that was so much fun. Let's do it again!" Callie charged back up the hill, again feeling like a kid, slipping and laughing as Nicholas plodded behind her pulling their sleds. This was one of the last of her father's *don'ts* that she had adhered to. It was a *do* world ... and Callie wanted to do everything, be a little reckless, eat new-fallen snow and feel it melt in her mouth, drink milk on the expiration date, and flirt with a man impossible to fall in love with.

♥              ♥              ♥

After sledding, Callie cooked dinner while Nicholas shoveled the driveway and pathway to the gallery. He must have drove into town because, upon returning inside, he brought with him a bottle of Chardonnay and the familiar white bag from Puccini's Bakery containing cannolis.

"You remembered."

"What's dinner without dessert?"

"How are the roads?"

"A bit slick. I was detoured past Breemer's pond because some crazy teenager took the hairpin curve on Maple Street too fast and crashed into a tree. Crazy kids, always in a rush. I tell my students that speeding only gets them there five minutes faster, and what's five minutes weighed against a lifetime?"

"You're right." She opened the utensil drawer and retrieved a cork-screw. "Would you do the honors? Dinner's ready."

While Nicholas poured the wine, Callie turned on the radio to the classical station, which provided perfect background music to their continued reminiscing about grammar school, high school, former neighbors and childhood friends. When dinner was finished, dishes remained on the table in lieu of washing as Callie and Nicholas moved to the living room and the warmth of the fire.

"Did you have fun today?" Nicholas asked.

"The best time. I can't believe I missed out on Riker's Ridge all these years. Overprotective parents."

"How long have they been married," he asked, pushing up the sleeves of his blue knit sweater. He rested his back against the couch as he sat on the floor bordering the hearth.

"Forty years this September 27th."

"Planning anything?"

"Maisy and I talked about it. I want to throw them a party, and she wants to give them a trip. I don't know what we'll agree on. My parents rarely travel, and when they do, it's by car. I think a party with the family and their friends would be more appropriate." She skewed her mouth in indecision. "What I do know is that they deserve to be congratulated for staying together all these years, despite their dysfunction. Again, let me apologize for this afternoon."

"Don't be silly. They're not a whole lot different than my parents."

"Well, I'm sure your father would have gotten up out of his chair for a proper introduction. These days my dad's a permanent fixture in that chair in front of the TV."

"My dad likes his chair, too. He hails the remote as the best invention ever."

Callie laughed.

"My dad always had a remote even before there were those hand-held devices. He had me. Callie, go change the channel. Callie, turn up the volume."

Nicholas chuckled.

"And my mother" she continued. "I still can't believe her little demonstration on the fine art of breast exams!"

"I can help you with those, you know. Breasts are my specialty."

"I'll keep that in mind." She sipped at her wine. "Is your friend with the cancer doing any better?"

"Drew is amazing. He was my roommate in college. He's a detective on the police force in Greenville. He's gonna beat the cancer; I just know it. He's such a fighter, but then again he has so much to live for. His wife Annie is a sweetheart, and they have two boys, ages 2 and 5, who he adores. They got a great life, married ten years. This cancer thing is just proof how strong their relationship is."

"Why is it that some couples can last 10 years or 40 years like my parents, and others have a meltdown in two?"

"There's a lot of variables in relationships, Callie," he replied all too quickly as if he had been asked this question before. "Sometimes what brings people together doesn't keep them together. There has to be sacrifice and compromise."

"True. And support of the differences that make you individuals. I believe in the best of relationships you can be who you are and not lose your identity yet—"

"Love as one."

"Such a paradox, don't you think? We being such experts on relationships and neither of us married." They sat facing each other on the floor in front of the fire, roaring with bright orange flames from the last log Nicholas had tossed into it. "What about the relationships in your life, Nicholas? Short term, long term? Any proposals?"

Callie wasn't sure she wanted to know but she had to ask. That was the strangest thing about getting to know someone—wanting to know everything yet not wanting to know anything that might hurt.

"My freshman year in college is a blur. I don't remember a whole lot except thinking about you, about us, waiting for a call or letter, wondering what went wrong."

"Nothing went wrong—"

"Well, now I know that, but then I had so many questions." He cleared his throat. "Anyway, when I got my first D ever, in English no less, it shook me back into reality. My friends fixed me up with some nice girls, but they all reminded me of you—molasses nice, blah. Then I dated a few wild types, but that wasn't any better. I was drinking too much, drowning myself in liquid pity."

He ran his hand over his head and forehead as if he had a headache, silent for many minutes as Callie presumed he was censoring some of his memories from those days. At last he inhaled deeply.

"After graduation, I started teaching outside of DC, got my Master's down there. I was out one night with some friends at a bar," Nicholas confessed, "and the lead singer of this punk band bought me a drink. We went out a few times and wound up sleeping together, and she got pregnant."

Callie saw the regret in his eyes as Nicholas continued with the sordid details.

"It was stupid. *I was* stupid. I knew better. Anyway, she was young, 22, and I offered to marry her, but she didn't love me and I didn't love her. She moved back home to South Carolina to be with her family, and when a teaching position at the university down there came up, I applied. Adam had already been born, and the baby was just too much for Pru to handle. We agreed that I'd have full custody, and she'd have extended weekends when she wanted them. I hired a nanny."

"So, it's all working out. Adam gets to see his mom?"

"Yeah, Pru joined another band after he was born, but they just played locally. About a year a go, she got a steady job at a radio station, so now she just plays piano at a lounge on the weekends. She's settled down a bit. Her hair's not pink anymore. She's a better mother now. I think it's partly because Adam is older, and she can relate to him as a person. He spends at least one weekend a month with her." He took another deep breath then exhaled. "So that's my sad story."

Callie sipped her wine.

"It's not so sad. You look happy now."

"I am. I have a great job at the university, and I'm assistant coach of the soccer team."

"You played in high school, didn't you?"

"That I did. In college, too. I like coaching, though. It's different from the sidelines."

"How do you mean?"

"Well, when you're on the field, it's all about the goal, the win. But from the sidelines, it's more about the technique. My perspective is different. And that's what I try to ingrain into my athletes. It's definitely how you play the game. And that directly relates to life. It doesn't matter what you accomplish if you've had to compromise yourself along the way. It won't mean a thing."

Callie nodded her agreement as she stepped down off the pedestal that Nicholas had put her on this weekend. Her life seemed a series of compromises. She changed the subject.

"Any special lady in your life now?"

"No," he answered abruptly. "How about you? Are you in love?"

"No." She sipped again at her wine. "But the potential is there."

"With me?"

Callie laughed.

"I was speaking of the man I've been seeing."

"Oh, and you're falling in love with him?" His question carried reluctance, as did his eyes.

"Oh, no, I'm no where near feeling that yet. We're still friends at the *news, sports, work, and weather* stage."

"Huh?"

"Our conversations tend to revolve around those topics: news, sports—"

"Oh, then what do you mean by *potential?*"

Callie wondered for a moment about a relationship with Aidan. He certainly wasn't over Grace yet, but in due time their friendship could blossom into something more.

"Well, he's a great guy," she finally answered.

"Like me?"

"Yes, like you."

Nicholas shifted closer, and Callie was all too aware that their knees and thighs now touched.

"Tell me about him."

"No." She couldn't help shooting him a peculiar look over his odd request.

"No? Why not? I wanna hear about this guy who's making his way into your heart. I wanna know what's he like, if he's good enough for you."

"Oh, watching my back, are you?" Callie chuckled. "Well, let's see. He's thoughtful and kind, and he makes me laugh. We have fun together."

"I see. Like me."

"Yes, like you."

"Then why not me?" He paused a moment, looking into her eyes, waiting for an answer. "Am I thoughtful?"

"Yes, you brought me cannolis and this bottle of wine."

"Maybe I was trying to seduce you."

She smiled at his playful teasing.

"You're thoughtful, Nicholas."

"Am I kind?"

"So kind. You helped shovel the sidewalk and built this fire while I cooked dinner."

Callie let the flames warm her face as she gazed at it, lost in a snow-globe of memories from their afternoon together.

"Do I make you laugh?"

Nicholas took her hand and kissed the inside of her wrist, and suddenly Callie was back in the moment.

"Yes, I love your stories and reminiscing about growing up in this old town."

"Am I fun?"

"Absolutely. Not many men would find their inner child and go sledding."

Nicholas nudged even closer, and Callie breathed in the sweet smell of wine floating between their lips.

"Then why not me?"

Callie chose not to answer.

Nicholas whispered, "Does he share your love of art?"

"I suppose he respects my art."

"I *love* your art, your paintings, with each stroke defining the essence of who you are, what you think, and every angel so masterfully sculpted and created that they almost breathe." He paused. "Can he relate to growing up in a small town in a strict home?"

"I don't know. We haven't talked about that."

"Does he know about Maisy and what happened to her?"

Callie looked off into the fire again, admitting softly, "Some things are too personal."

He kissed her wrist again and let his tongue linger on her skin for a moment before asking another question. His lips, soft and seductive, were an invitation she couldn't accept.

"Did you tell him your dreams and aspirations?"

"Outside of art?"

Nicholas touched her cheek and redirected her gaze towards him.

"About love and marriage and children and family?"

"No," she sighed. "I only told you."

"Have you been in his heart since kindergarten class 28 years ago?"

Callie smiled and shook her head.

"When he looks at you, does his eyes hold you with desire?" Nicholas gazed deep into her whiskey eyes—pure intoxication. "When he kisses you—" He leaned forward and put his lips to hers. Ever so gently, their tongues touched. He withdrew slightly from the kiss, and she looked into his eyes so drunk with desire. "Do you feel his kiss deep in your soul?"

"No," she confided.

"Then why not me?"

Nicholas cupped her face and let their attraction draw them into a soul-drenching kiss, very much the same as their first 15 years ago. His lips were soft as she remembered, and his hands began a familiar exploring as his fingers moved from her face to her hair and down her back. The magic of yesteryear on the rock at the waterfall surrounded them in a surreal, passionate moment. She wanted it to last forever, never leave his arms.

"Why not me?" he repeated.

"Don't," Callie said lightly, leaning back, away from the temptation of his lips.

"Don't what? Don't fall in love with you? I'm serious, Callie. Why not me? Give me one good reason."

Callie took a long, dramatic sip of wine and used the impending seconds to quell her pounding heart and think a rational thought.

"I'll give you a thousand. You live in South Carolina, and I live in Massachusetts. That's a thousand miles."

"Besides the geography."

"Oh." Swirling the wine in her goblet, Callie thought for a moment, but she was having a hard time concentrating on anything since his kiss. She felt Nicholas touch her chin and turn her face slightly towards his as he pressed his chest to hers for another kiss. Again, a fire burned through her, igniting all the parts of her that had been dormant for so long. Her body responded to him, and she found herself pulling him closer for a deeper, more intense kiss.

"You're incredible." His voice was raspy, appealing in a masculine way that cultivated her desire. "So sweet and sexy. I could kiss you forever."

"Mmmm," she purred. "You have great lips." She moved her finger gently over his soft lips till his tongue drew it into his mouth where he sucked on it. So erotic it sent chills up her spine. Callie smiled. "*You* are very sexy."

"And you're a dream come true. I've waited a lifetime for this moment."

They sat there for a long time just gazing into each other's eyes. His fingers caressed her hands, warmly stroking her palms and inner wrists.

"Who are we fooling?" she asked, daring to break that electric connection between them. "You know this is impossible."

"Nothing is impossible."

"We have lives—very full lives with family and friends and work—in different states, far away states, a thousand miles apart. Our being together is next to impossible."

Nicholas kissed her again.

"Nothing is so settled that there couldn't be a move. Stop thinking; stop worrying; stop plotting against us. Just lay back and let me kiss you."

Callie smiled, pleased that Nicholas was willing to move to be near her, to be with her. He had dipped her world in sugar ... how sweet it tasted!

# CHAPTER 9

Nicholas woke to the smell of coffee brewing in the kitchen. For a moment his surroundings confused him, then he realized he was in Callie's living room, obviously having slept the night on her couch. Early morning light filtered in through the curtains, and he went to the window to see how much snow had fallen during the night—at least 12 inches. Surely not enough to cancel his flight later in the day. In South Carolina, a 12-inch snowfall would shut down the whole state, but in Massachusetts, hardly anyone would blink an eye at that accumulation. Needless to say, hoping for a delay at the airport was out of the question, so that gave him the remainder of the morning to spend with Callie before leaving for the airport. God, how he wanted to take her home with him. He found it uplifting just knowing Callie would move to be with him.

"Good morning, Sweetheart," he said, entering the kitchen where she busied herself at the stove with a half-dozen pancakes in a green nightshirt that fell to her thighs, just barely covering her ass. "Smells delicious."

"Thank you. How did you sleep?"

"Fine."

"It's a comfy sofa, but you could have slept in one of the bedrooms upstairs."

"With you just one room away? I don't think so. The temptation, the attraction was so great last night that I needed at least a floor between us."

Callie laughed at his sarcasm, but seeing her in that nightshirt, smelling the sweetness of her perfume in her hair as he kissed her neck made him want to make love to her. And there was no good reason why they shouldn't be intimate except that he was a gentleman.

"I'm just a woman, you know."

"Oh, no, my dear. Great novels have been written about temptresses such as yourself."

"Really? You think I'm a temptress?" She turned off the burner and transferred the pancakes to a serving dish, then used a spatula to flip the bacon still cooking in a separate pan.

Nicholas brushed another kiss to her neck then found her lips in tender moment.

"I think that every moment alone with you entices me to—"

The phone rang.

"Hold that thought," Callie said, stepping back towards the phone then quickly returning to the stove as the bacon crackled. "Could you answer that for me?"

"Sure, Love." Nicholas picked up the receiver. "Hello?"

"Hello," a very angry female voice barked. "Who's this?"

"Who are you?"

"Who the hell are you? Where's my sister? Put my sister on the phone!"

Nicholas stretched the cord to Callie.

"It's your sister. She sounds *mildly* upset."

Callie rolled her eyes. She didn't want to deal with Maisy on a perfect Sunday morning. She handed the spatula to Nicholas, then took the phone.

"Hey, Maisy. What's up?"

From the pained expression on Callie's face, whatever Maisy was telling her was not good news. Nicholas lowered the gas and flipped the bacon one more time as he listened to Callie explain that she had company.

"Maisy, can't this wait or, better yet, isn't there someone else you can call?" Callie asked. There was a brief silence. "No, don't call Mom and Dad. Someone *besides* them."

Again, another expression of pure stress on Callie's face as Maisy's screechings echoed from the phone. Nicholas dished out the bacon, and set the plates on the table. Pouring two cups of coffee, he sat down at the table while Callie finished the conversation with her sister.

"All right, all right. Calm down for Pete's sake. It's just a car. I'll be there as soon as I can."

Callie's slam of the phone surprised Nicholas, jarring his full attention. She stood at the counter for a moment, seemingly composing herself.

"Sorry," she apologized. "Your temptress has an occasional temper."

"Whew," he laughed, wiping fake sweat from his brow. "I was beginning to think you were perfect."

Callie's smile returned.

"Maisy's a four-aspirin headache that just won't go away."

"What's the problem today?"

She sat down at the table and rubbed the stress from her forehead, groaning in aggravation.

"It seems my ever-so-smart sister neglected to park in her assigned parking space at her apartment complex last night, opting instead to park on the street, in a no parking zone, mind you. Anyway, lo and behold, she wakes up to find they towed her car during the night."

"Too bad."

"Yeah, and top that off with a $250 towing bill."

"Wow, that seems a little high."

"Something to do with weekend rates. I don't know." Callie buried her face in her hands and moaned. "I could barely understand her with all her yelling and cursing."

"Is she always like that?"

She looked up and shook her head.

"No, she's prime rage today. She quit smoking three days ago. Need I say more? Anyway, the tow company is open from nine to twelve today. I'll go later after breakfast." She spooned sugar into her coffee cup, then served Nicholas and herself several steaming pancakes heaped with butter and syrup.

"I'll go with you."

"You will?" She bit into a large forkful of the flaky, syrup-dripped pancakes. "What time's your flight?"

"Not till four."

"You don't have to come along. I won't be long."

"That's okay. I want to meet my future sister-in-law."

Surprise turned to laughter as a red-faced Callie choked on his words. Spitting tiny bits of food onto her plate, she reached for a napkin and covered her mouth.

"Sorry." Her cheeks reddened with genuine embarrassment.

"A temptress, a temper, and a spitter," Nicholas laughed and reached for her hand to kiss it. "I think I hit the jackpot."

Standing at Maisy's door, Nicholas took off his glove and knocked while Callie apologized for bringing him along.

"I'm so sorry for dragging you along."

"You didn't drag; I offered." He touched her gloved hand. "I only wish I could always be here for you." She leaned in closer to him. "God, it's cold today."

"Yes, it's—"

The door flew open, and Maisy appeared in torn jeans and an oversized navy blue sweatshirt. Her hair, an almost orange-red, appeared uncombed as it skewered in different directions. A gray cat scampered up to the door, and Maisy used her foot to block its exit.

"Finally," Maisy huffed. "I've been waiting *all* f-ing morning."

"You've been waiting an hour," Callie replied. "You could've used that time to shower, maybe dress up a bit."

"Had I known you were bringing company—"

Nicholas interrupted Maisy's sharp reply. "I'm not company. I'm Nicholas. Are you ready to go?"

"Just a minute." The cat purred, and Maisy shooed it away from the door. "Damn cat." She pushed a smile to her face. "Callie, could you look at my computer real quick and see what's wrong. It died three days ago, and I can't get it working."

As Callie walked inside, Nicholas followed. The interior of the apartment was as unkempt as Maisy. Unmatched furniture from different time periods was arranged haphazardly throughout the living room. A red country sofa, a green plaid Queen Anne chair, a gold-fringed contemporary ottoman nestled together for unpleasant conversation. Cluttered stacks of magazines and newspapers cloaked the tables in the living room and what Nicholas could see in the kitchen. Empty containers of take-out food brimmed the garbage can near the computer. The curtains were still drawn, and the room had a tainted odor of cat urine.

"Maisy, you've got to change the litter box," Callie said, putting her hand to her nose to breathe in the fresh scent of soap.

She sat down at the computer and tried typing on the keyboard. Nicholas stood beside Callie, looking around the room, not wanting to sit down on anything.

"I know, I know," Maisy whined, pulling open a dusty curtain. "I just haven't had a free f-ing minute."

Callie slammed her hand on the desk.

"Enough of the cursing already."

"Sorry, but it's all *your* fault making me quit smoking. It's driving me shit-crazy."

Callie glared at Maisy. Nicholas again intervened between their sparring.

"I think the computer would work better if it was plugged in." He pointed behind the desk.

"What?" Maisy exclaimed. "Damn cat! Always knocking things over and causing trouble. Where are you, you little hairball? You better hide!"

"Can we go now, Maisy?" Callie got up, brushed cat hair from her jeans, and walked to the front door.

"Yeah, but do you have any money?" Maisy reached for her Prada pocketbook and emptied its contents on the sofa. Lipstick, coins, tampon, keys—all spilled out, some slipping into the cracks between the cushions. "I was out last night and—"

"No, I didn't bring my purse," Callie snapped. "Nicholas drove."

Maisy stepped into her boots and peered up at him.

"How about you, Lover Boy? Got any money?"

"Stop it, Maisy. We'll take you to the ATM. Now, let's go!" By Callie's tone and her dogged stride, her patience neared the end. "Please, God, answer my prayer."

As Callie headed out the door, Maisy tapped Nicholas on the shoulder.

"Got a cigarette I could bum off you? My quittin' days are over."

"Get the *patch*," he said.

Maisy pulled up her sleeve and revealed two patches taped to her arm. She dramatically ripped each one from her arm, taking with it a layer of dry winter skin, then crumbled them into one sticky ball.

"They don't work," she replied crassly.

Nicholas's patience, too, had reached its limit, and he morphed into an angry professor scolding a lazy, immature student.

"Just remember, Maisy, you're the *older* sister."

"What's that supposed to mean?" She recoiled, backstepping like a frightened child, her red hair running down her face like clown tears.

"Think about it."

A day had passed since Nicholas's visit. Callie missed him, so the trill of the phone sent her running to answer it.

"Hello?"

"Brown Eyes, do you want to go for a swim?"

Callie enjoyed Aidan's spontaneity; however, today she was hoping for someone more predictable.

"Aidan, it's January, this is New England. You're not in California anymore."

"Very funny. I was inviting you to my health club. Thought we'd burn a few calories then put them back on with a dinner somewhere. What do you say?"

Callie continued to hedge.

"I don't know, Aidan. My bathing suit's packed away for the winter."

"I'll buy you one at the club. There, that's settled."

"Gosh, there's no arguing with you. You'd make a great lawyer."

He laughed.

"Love the sarcasm. Now go check your e-mail, Brown Eyes. I'm sending you directions. See you later."

"Bye."

In one of Boston's poshest health clubs, Callie sat on the edge of the pool drying off under the warmth of a large yellow cotton towel. She watched Aidan continue to swim laps back and forth across the long pool. His strong arms pulled the water in heaving strokes as he glided like a fish from end to end. A person walked by and stirred up a breeze that caused a chill to run down Callie's spine. She pulled her knees to her chin and tucked her toes underneath the towel. Thinking warm thoughts, she remembered her weekend with Nicholas and felt his kiss burn through her.

"Hey, Brown Eyes, you ready to get some dinner?"

Aidan splashed up next to her as he hoisted himself out of the pool. Beads of water trickled from his bangs and down his face. He looked rather sexy all wet and somewhat naked.

"Sure, anytime you are." She handed him a towel. "You're really in great shape."

"Thanks. I haven't been here in a while. Grace's idea of exercise was shopping. She was supreme at finding the best deals at the most out-of-the-way places. Probably how she found your art gallery."

"Probably." Callie didn't care to talk about Grace, but she was Aidan's favorite topic, as every conversation seemed to segue into stories about Grace or them as a couple in happier times. Six weeks had passed since the breakup, yet Aidan's continued rehashing annoyed her. He couldn't seem to let go, and Callie hated that about him, simply hated that. Turning those emotions inward, Callie had tried to help him cope with a sympathetic ear, but today she had no interest in soothing his ailing heart, so she redirected the conversation away from Grace.

"What else do you do for exercise?"

"Eh, mostly tennis and golf. The country club Grace and I belonged to—"

Callie interrupted in an enthusiastic voice, "I like to ride my neighbor's horse."

"That seems like more exercise for the horse than for you," he laughed.

"Well, I bike in the warmer months. Most of my free time is spent painting or sculpting or working around my property, especially in the springtime. I love gardening and planting flowers."

"Don't know anything about that. My landscaper handles the property." Aidan toweled off his hair and pointed towards the ladies' locker room. "Go shower and change, and I'll meet you back here in 20 minutes."

Callie stared at him in disbelief.

"Twenty minutes? It takes me about that long to dry my hair."

"Brown Eyes, do your best. It's not the ball with Prince Charming, just dinner with me."

Callie smiled. Aidan had a self-deprecating way of using humor to put her at ease, and she adored that about him … simply adored that.

"Thanks for coming with me today," Drew said, reaching for a magazine he had no intention of reading. Nicholas knew his friend had too much on his mind to concentrate on any articles in the magazines in the doctor's office.

"Don't mention it."

"How was your trip north? Things go well with Callie?"

"Yeah, it was great. We spent a lot of time together." Nicholas's thoughts veered off for a minute as he remembered their weekend. "Callie's an amazing woman."

"She's still *the one*?"

Nicholas confided, "If I had to pick a soulmate, Callie'd be it."

Drew thumbed through the pages, stopping a moment to feign interest in an article before tossing the magazine on the side table.

"Soulmate, huh? So what drives the attraction?"

"I guess the way how she balances life so well. Her commitment to her family, her friends, her work—they each pull her in a different direction, yet she's centered, grounded, with traditions and values. It's probably what I love most about her." Nicholas spoke quietly as he assumed other patients in the waiting room were listening to his conversation with Drew. "Besides that, she's incredibly sexy. I miss her already."

"So what's the plan?"

"Status quo for now."

Missing Callie was easy. Nicholas's heart involuntarily pumped those sad sensations to his head every day. Wondering about their future was hard—much harder. Smart enough to know he couldn't judge a lifetime by their few days together, Nicholas wanted a chance to explore a real relationship with Callie, and that meant her moving in with him. Though she had agreed that a move was possible, he didn't want to press her too soon. He knew that there would be much involved in leaving Sycamore, and he could only hope that in the next few months Callie could arrange for a smooth transition.

"I suppose you've discussed her moving here." Drew fidgeted in his chair as the nurse entered and crossed off a name from the sign-in sheet. The woman peered into the waiting room and motioned to an older man sitting with his wife. "When does Callie plan on making the move?"

"We spoke briefly about a move, but that's gonna take some time, ya know."

"It's funny, Nick," Drew began, leaning closer and speaking in a conspiratorial tone. "I always thought time was on my side, that I would have years and years to do all the things I wanted to do, and now—"

"And now you're gonna go into that doctor's office, and he's gonna give you a clear bill of health."

"He's gonna chew me out for not wanting anymore chemo."

"It's four months since the surgery. You had a lot of treatments; you played by their rules, and it was wearing you down."

"I just want to be normal again. I just want to make love to Annie again." Drew rubbed at his bald head. "That's the worst part, not having any drive, ya know, to do what—" He sighed. "The chemo may have killed the cancer, but it also killed my libido. I hate what I've become."

"You've become healthy again. That's the way you gotta look at it. Now, you gotta do what's right for you, Drew."

"I know." He buried his face in his hands and held that position for several minutes. He groaned, but no one in the waiting room seemed to notice. Leaning back in the chair, he whispered, "It's just that I'm so tired of battling death. I just want to start living life, being a full man again, and I can't do that hooked to an IV or with my head in a toilet."

"I hear you."

The nurse re-entered the room, scratched another name off the sheet, and called for Drew. Nicholas watched him walk down the hall with a bowed head, dipped shoulders, and sagging jeans. Although his bulky shirt attempted to camouflage his leanness, nothing could hide Drew's feelings of despair. As Nicholas thought a minute about Drew, he remembered what Callie had said in the angel loft.

*Maybe we do get only one wish, one prayer during our lifetime.*

Nicholas thought this was a good time to use his.

# CHAPTER 10

Callie and Nicholas began a tender exchange of long-distance, late-night phone calls that usually began with nostalgic reminiscing but always ended with passionate sighs of *I miss you* and *wish you were here*. E-mails from Nicholas delighted Callie just as much as hearing his voice for he could make love to her with words, caressing her with provocative prose as well as impressing upon her the enchantment of kismet. Suddenly, the nights weren't so cold.

*Darling Callie,*

*Kiss me. Close your eyes and feel my hands on your shoulders, gently caressing your warm skin, my fingers massaging you, relaxing any worldly stress that dares to distract you from us. Pull me into the circle of your arms, close, so close that I can feel the rise and fall of your chest, the delicate, rhythmic pounding of your heart, and you can hear my heart and feel each hard muscle of my body responding to you and your sensuous touch. Breathe deeply and smell our scents mingling and enveloping us in an erotic moment of anticipation as my mouth nears yours. Taste my lips as they meet yours. Linger in deliberate playfulness, torturing me with want as the need of passion burns deep to my soul. Open your mouth to mine and let our tongues dance together, mating in the wetness and tenderness of a feverish kiss that grows hungrier with each second. Kiss me deeply, passionately, softly, tenderly ... kiss me like only you can ... then open your eyes and look deep into mine and see the essence of my soul, that I am someone whose lips want only yours ... kiss me again.*

*Nicholas*

*Sweetheart Callie,*

*I find myself missing you at the most inopportune moments such as in the middle of class, in staff meetings, while out to dinner with friends. My mind begins drifting away with delicious thoughts of your eyes, your sexy smile, those luscious lips, then my fantasies become vivid daydreams of us in many states of undress. I'm quite embarrassed that I've been caught by my students and colleagues and friends with a silly grin on my face. They all want to know "who she is" and I desperately want to unveil you to the world as not only the girl from my childhood but also the woman of my dreams. I love you.*

*Missing you … Nicholas*

The first time Nicholas declared his love was in that e-mail. Callie reread it over and over again. *I love you.* Was it a misprint? Did he really mean it? Callie's second encounter with those words came at the end of a phone call, followed by a short pause as he waited for her reciprocal response. Callie couldn't say it. *I love you* was a commitment, and with a thousand miles still between them, she just couldn't make that commitment … not yet. The awkward silence hung between them till Callie changed the subject. That scene happened often, always leaving her feeling guilty, almost ashamed.

Work proved to be a welcome diversion. It consumed Callie's attention with boring and tedious business details. Bills and commissions needed to be paid, and new contracts needed to be reviewed and signed. Though Callie preferred the creative side to art, she couldn't neglect the responsibility of managing her growing gallery.

Callie had just locked the front door to Appassionata when the phone rang. Though February was traditionally a slow month for art sales, she found this first Saturday of February to be unusually busy. Appassionata had reached the point of independent success. Callie no longer needed to spend large sums on advertisement. The gallery had rooted itself in Sycamore, blossomed into something rare and beautiful that attracted attention like botanists to hybrid roses.

"Hello," Callie answered. "Appassionata Art Gallery. How may I help you?"

"Brown Eyes, how about dinner and a movie?"

Not one to beat around the bush, Aidan skipped the introductory chitchat that always drilled through Callie like a streetworker with a jackhammer.

"I'm fine, Aidan. Nice of you to ask. And how are you?" She accentuated each word, purposefully underscoring her want for the niceties of a greeting.

"Sorry, Brown Eyes. How are you on this brisk February afternoon?"

"Wonderful. I was just locking up."

"Good day?"

"Exceptional day. Sold five commissioned pieces and two of my angels. You remember my angels?"

"Oh, yes," he said in a contemplative voice as if remembering the night of the proposal. "So, what do you say, Brown Eyes. Up for dinner and a movie?"

"Hmm?" Callie thought for a moment, but there wasn't much to think about. With no plans for Saturday night, she'd happily accept Aidan's offer. "What movie?"

"Any movie. Your choice."

"Gosh, that's a loaded gun. I could drag you to a chick flick, one of those sappy *he loves me, he loves me not* movies."

He laughed at her spunk.

"I guess I'm taking my chances then."

"Pretty desperate for a date, aren't you?"

"I'm just not up to poker and cigars with the boys. Thought you could intrigue me in some way."

A flirtatious tone hung in the air.

"Did you? Well, if it's mystery you want, let's go see that new thriller, *In the Shadows!* It's getting great reviews."

"All right. Sounds good to me. Shall I pick you up at the scene of the crime?" His reference to the gallery and the rejected proposal was none-too-subtle.

"No, that's okay. I'll head into the city. Let's meet at Nick of Time at six."

"Great. See you then."

Callie loved a long drive. It obviously had something to do with her childhood and her parents' not wanting to take any other form of transportation when traveling. In the car the family would go, sometimes traveling two days by car rather than two hours by plane. Maisy always got car sick, but Callie enjoyed the long routes, gazing out the windows, sketching and sometimes dreaming about the destinations long before they even arrived.

Now, driving was a little less fun. Not having the luxury to lose oneself in the landscape as a passenger, Callie used the 40-minute treks into the city for clearing her mind. Driving let her think all those thoughts she was too busy to do during the day. And on this particular trip, she thought about Nicholas and how wonderful it would be when he moved and they could finally be together on a daily basis.

Nick of Time streamed with customers, but Callie easily spotted Aidan at the bar. With a black sweater and gray pants, he sat supremely center of the bar conversing with Nick. He had a dogged attorney look on his face as if making a particular point as Nick nodded in agreement, too polite to disagree with a customer. Callie walked over to rescue Nick.

"Hi, Callie," Nick greeted, leaning across the bar to kiss her cheek and change the topic of conversation. "What can I get the prettiest woman in this bar to drink?"

"I'm driving tonight, so how about cranberry and orange juice?" She put her arm on Aidan's shoulder. "Nick, this is my friend Aidan. He's a—" Callie halted her introduction as she remembered Aidan's dislike of people knowing he was a lawyer. "He's an astrophysicist."

Nearly falling off his stool, startled by her statement, Aidan flashed Callie a wide-eyed expression of confusion.

"Really," Nick said, extending his arm for a handshake. "What exactly does an astrophysicist do?" His tone resonated with genuine interest.

"I don't quite know. You're going to have to ask Callie," Aidan responded with a hearty laugh. "She's trying to cover for me. I don't usually tell people I'm a lawyer."

"Oh," Nick smiled and nodded, then pulled a glass from the rack overhead.

"I usually say I'm an accountant." Aidan turned to Callie. His eyes still held that boyish surprise. "Why'd you say *astrophysicist?*"

"Accountants are so ordinary, you know, numbers and decimals. I thought I'd give you an exciting career."

"Brown Eyes, that's the whole point. Ordinary doesn't invite attention. What's to ask an accountant; unless, of course, its tax season."

"Oh." Callie bowed her head meekly, her cheeks warming with embarrassment. She slid herself onto the adjacent stool and watched Nick busy himself behind the bar.

"And if I do get a question, at least I can fake my way through it. Astrophysicist!" Aidan laughed again. "That's right up there with epidemiologist and nuclear physicist. Next time stay away from any job ending with 'ologist or physicist."

Callie's cell phone rang, and she happily welcomed the diversion from Aidan's innocent mockery. She pulled the phone from her purse and glanced at the number.

"Ugh. It's my sister," she told Aidan then looked at Nick. "Maybe you should put a shot of something in my drink. I got a feeling I'm gonna need it." Callie answered the phone. "Hey, Maisy. What's up?" She fell silent for a minute. "Can you speak up? I can hardly hear you." Plugging one ear with her finger, Callie smiled at Aidan before walking out of the noisy bar and into the much quieter lobby.

"Ever meet her sister," Nick asked.

Aidan shook his head. "No. What's she like?"

"Ever see a load of strawberries fall off a truck?"

"No, can't say that I have, but I can only imagine that it's a mess."

"That's Maisy exactly. A mess. And Callie—the doll that she is—continually cleans up after her." Nick set Callie's drink on a napkin. "I would've washed my hands of her a long time ago."

"Who? Callie?"

"No, Maisy. Callie's a keeper. She's one of those succulent peaches—pretty and tempting on the outside and dripping with sweetness on the inside. If I were a different kind of man, you wouldn't be dating her now."

"Oh, we're not dating," Aidan quickly replied.

"Could've fooled me. I see the way you look at her and the way she is with you. You're quite the couple."

"You know I've thought about us that way, taking our friendship to the next level, but I get the feeling there's someone else in her life."

"Callie can be a bit tight lipped when it comes to her personal life. However, she's—Aidan, I'm not telling you what to do, by no means, but the fact is—" Nick paused to wipe the bar counter with a white terry cloth towel. He swirled the rag in deft circular motions as if cleaning away a thousand years' dust to reveal ancient hieroglyphics. "It's Saturday night, and she's out with you. That, to me and you, should say everything."

Aidan smiled.

Callie returned to Aidan's side and resumed her seat on the stool. Brushing a fuzz from her sweater, she apologized for the interruption.

"Everything okay with your sister?" Nick asked.

"Yeah." Callie rolled her eyes. "She was frantic because she couldn't find her cell phone and she needed to go out. So, what does she do? She calls me as if I'll know where to look for it. I told her to hang up with me and call her phone number then follow the ring."

"And?" Aidan asked.

"She must've found it 'cause she didn't call me back."

Nick laughed and shrugged his shoulders.

"Typical Maisy."

"Enough about her," Callie said, picking up her glass that Nick had rimmed in orange sugar. She took a long lick of the sweet rim then paused before taking a sip of the juice. "What are we toasting tonight?"

Aidan felt the warmth of her erotic licking streak through him like a bolt of lightning. He stopped staring at her lips long enough to answer Callie's question.

"Peaches." Aidan lifted his glass and touched it first to Nick's then to Callie's.

"Peaches?" She grinned that adorable wide-lipped grin and raised one eyebrow quizzically.

"Yes," Nick said. "My favorite."

Callie added, "They're out of season this time of year. A good peach is hard to find."

"Yes," Aidan agreed as he peripherally caught Nick winking his approval. "A good peach is hard to find."

Later, after the movie, Callie and Aidan walked a block to a coffee shop for a bite to eat and discuss the movie, which had one of those endings that prompted after-thought and deep conversation. The line in the café curled around the tables with moviegoers and—comers, preferring to pay an extra dollar or two for a richer cup of coffee than that offered in the theater. This particular shop offered a delicious variety of pastries and slices of decadent cakes. Callie stood with Aidan and mentally debated ordering the strawberry cheesecake or the chocolate mousse cake.

"Still thinking about that ending?" Aidan asked.

"Hmm? The movie? Oh, yeah," she lied not wanting to appear so shallow, completely absorbed in a thicket of thought over dessert and a cup of coffee that would rid her of the February chill.

"What I can't understand is if the twins switched identities, how come nobody checked the dental records when one was found dead. Surely, the attorney for the other brother would have wanted some positive identification that his client was really his client and not the twin brother. Any good lawyer would've done that. I know if that was my client—"

"Excuse me." The woman behind them tapped Aidan on the shoulder. She smiled under a wool hat and thick black scarf, her eyes shifting from Aidan to the floor in shyness. "I couldn't help but overhear. Are you a lawyer?"

"No," Callie interjected. "He's a dairy farmer. You know, cows, milking, pasteurizing."

Callie smiled at Aidan who laughed under his breath.

"Oh," the woman replied meekly as her eyes lost their inquisitiveness. "I just thought—never mind. Sorry I bothered you."

Aidan put a strong arm around Callie and pulled her into whispering range.

"Dairy farmer," he chuckled. "Brown Eyes, you—I love you."

Callie heard the air of lightness in the remark, but it immediately made her think of Nicholas and his very serious declarations of love. She missed him; she missed doing things like this with him—standing in line, seeing movies, making jokes—all the little things that ultimately grow into one big and wonderful relationship. Moments like these made the truth of the situation so much harsher ... one thousand miles was just too damn far.

♥         ♥         ♥

As she walked between the tables in the studio, Callie felt a small hand tug on her shirt. She looked down to see five red and blue fingerprints embedded on her smock.

"Miss Callie, can you help me make my flower smile?" the second grader asked, peering up at her with pleading eyes.

"Smile? What do you mean?"

"Well," the little girl explained, "your flower on the wall seems so happy, and mine—well, it looks like it wants to cry."

Callie knelt down next to the sandy-haired girl and inspected her picture.

"Well, I think your flower is beautiful just the way she is."

"But I didn't say anything about it being pretty. I said it looked sad, and I want it to be happy."

Callie realized the child had a point.

"Okay. What do you do when you're happy?"

"I sing or dance or play with my friends."

"Then let's give your flower some friends."

Using her fingers like the school children, Callie dipped them in the paints and swirled the colors into four spring flowers, two on each side of the girl's original flower. The leaves from each of the stems reached out to touch the others as if the flowers were all holding hands. The child's face brightened.

"She's happy now." The girl clapped her hands in joy. "She has friends. Thank you, Miss Callie."

Long after her students had left on the bus back to their school, Callie remained in the studio painting. Being around the children inspired her to sit on the floor and see things through their eyes. Callie immersed herself in painting the loveliness of the woods as seen from the window in the studio at a child's height. What she got was an amazing picture of the tips of trees, prickly against a cold blue sky, with a lone bird dipping down towards a branch.

Callie's cell phone rang. It still puzzled her why she could get service in the studio, but a hundred yards away in the house, she couldn't make or receive cell phone calls. Flipping open the high-tech gadget, she heard Aidan's voice on the other end talking to his secretary.

"Mark that bill 'No Charge.' That client's part of my pro bono work."

"Aidan?" Callie cradled the phone between her ear and shoulder and continued to paint.

"Hey, Brown Eyes, how are you?"

"I'm fine. You?"

"All things considered, just great. I'm calling to see if you have any plans for tomorrow."

"No, no plans." She desperately wished she had plans with Nicholas. That February day was earmarked for being with him. She missed him so much. Dabbing the brush against the canvas, Callie added more brown to the bird's wings.

"Want to have dinner tomorrow night."

Callie hesitated with her reply while her stomach knotted.

"You know what tomorrow is?"

"Yes, and I thought we could keep each other company while everyone else is paired up doing the romantic thing for Valentine's Day."

"I don't know, Aidan."

She planned on renting a sappy movie, soaking in a hot tub, then feeling sorry for herself because the guy she liked couldn't be with her on the most amorous day of the year.

"Oh, come on, Brown Eyes. I know this great restaurant in Boston, low key, good food, quiet music."

"Sounds romantic," she balked and used a smaller brush to tip several of the trees with snow.

"No, absolutely not. They don't even have tablecloths."

"Oh, then it sounds absolutely dreadful," she teased. "Why bother?"

"Don't make me beg." He sounded rather sad. "I'd rather not be alone."

"Why don't you call Grace?"

Callie winced when she said her name. Aidan hadn't mentioned her in two weeks, and here was Callie resurrecting someone he had put in the past.

"No." He said it with a sigh, and Callie heard his staggered, distressed breathing. She prepared herself for some long-winded story of one of Grace and Aidan's Valentines together. "What do you say? Dinner?"

"I don't know."

"Okay, now I'm begging."

"All right," she begrudgingly agreed, feeling it a betrayal of some sort to Nicholas.

"Great. Can you drive into Boston and meet me at 7:30?"

Callie paused to consider the next day's schedule while mentally trying to talk herself out of going.

"You there?" he asked.

"Yes, I'm here. E-mail me the details—address, time, so forth—and I'll meet you tomorrow in the city."

"Terrific. Bye."

Callie dropped the phone to her lap as she carefully inspected the canvas. She tinted the sky with several shades of blue then set the canvas against the wall and observed it from a distance. It was perceptually per-fect, but something about the painting bothered her. Callie dipped her brush in brown then returned to the canvas to paint in another bird.

♥          ♥          ♥

When Callie entered the restaurant, she found Aidan waiting in the foyer for her. Black suit, red tie, disarming smile, impeccably handsome as always.

"Punctuality is not your best quality, Brown Eyes," he said, helping her off with her coat. "Though red dresses are. Man, you are quite a stunner tonight."

"Thanks. Sorry about being late. I was over at Nick's, and he was try-ing to persuade me to stay."

"If you'd rather—"

"Oh, no, this is fine."

Callie peered around the lobby and into the dimly lit bar where patrons sipped cocktails in patient wait for a table. View of the dining room revealed an upscale but casual environment with porthole win-dows, mustard-colored walls accented by plank flooring and dark-stained wainscoting that extended around the perimeter of the room. The tables bore red napkins in celebration of Valentine's Day, and observing the women in the room, Callie noticed that they, too, donned some article of pink or red.

"They've been holding our table, Brown Eyes, so we'll have to bypass the bar."

Single-file, they followed the hostess to the table situated in the cor-ner. A tea candle lamp, topped with a beaded shade, stood center of the table, providing just enough light to read the menu.

"The specials tonight are our rack of lamb for two and our seafood platter which includes lobster tails, coconut shrimp, and scal-lops—enough for two." The hostess smiled graciously. "Your waitress is Tara, and she'll be right over to take your drink order. Enjoy your din-ner."

"The seafood platter sounds good," Aidan commented, not bothering to pick up the menu. "Are you hungry or did Nick feed you?"

"Actually, he tempted me with a half-portion of crème brule."

"Dessert before dinner?" He raised an eyebrow with purposeful sarcasm. "Did your parents teach you nothing?"

Callie laughed at his prosecutorial questioning.

"Oh, rules are made to be broken."

"Rules are what keeps this society together."

She put down the menu and eyed him directly.

"I feel a legal brief about to begin."

"Sorry." Aidan smiled and held up his hands defensively. "We did agree in Vegas not to have such talk."

"It's just that we have different ideas about the legal defense system."

"It's called due process, innocent till proven guilty."

"It's not those vague cases I'm talking about. It's the ones like the Smythe case where he's caught with both hands in the proverbial cookie jar or should I say cocaine jar, and you defend him."

"Due process," Aidan responded matter-of-factly.

"Just wait till you have kids of your own, and these guys are on the street trying to sell them drugs. Then you'll think twice about letting them back on the streets."

"Touché. Point made and taken."

"Your moral compass is leading you directly to hell," she commented.

"I don't believe in God, remember?"

"Yeah, you said that in Vegas. What's up with that? Were you raised that way?"

"No, I was raised Catholic, but all the rules handed down from the pulpit restricting the way you can think and live. I just don't respect a god who intended a life like that for us."

"So you do *believe* in God, you just don't respect Him for all these rules He's imposed on us." Callie smiled. "And what's that you were saying before about rules being what holds this society together?"

Aidan expression of indifference turned to surprise. The corners of his mouth turned upward as he nodded in reluctant agreement.

"Touché. Again, point made and taken. You're a lawyer in the making with that golden tongue of yours." He lifted his glass to toast her but stopped short when seeing she didn't have one. "You need a drink. Where's our waitress?"

"I have to use the ladies' room. Order me a club soda with lemon."

"No, no, not tonight, Brown Eyes. How about I order us a bottle of wine?"

"No, really, Aidan, I'm driving tonight."

"If you get pulled over and arrested, I know a good lawyer."

The waitress appeared at the table.

"Are you a lawyer?" the girl asked. "My father's a lawyer, well, a corporate lawyer, and I'm pre-law at BC. I'm thinking about interning for the public defender's office." She seemed anxious to discuss her future career. "I'm so nervous about the LSAT's."

Callie dared to interrupt. "No, sorry, he's not a lawyer; he's a mortician."

"Oh," the waitress managed to say as her face lost its color. "W-w-what can I get you to drink."

"We'll have a bottle of chardonnay," Aidan said, avoiding the stark expression on the waitress's face.

"Dear, is that blood on your shirt or is that my lipstick?" Callie winked at him.

"Ap-petizer?"

"No," Aidan responded. "Just the house salad, and we're going to share the seafood platter special."

"Yes, I-I'll get this order in, and I'll be b-back with your bread."

Aidan and Callie held their laughter till the waitress left the room.

"Brown Eyes, I do believe you're getting quite good at that. Straight face and all." He laughed again and glanced over his shoulder to make sure the girl was out of earshot. "Mortician. That certainly silenced her questions."

"Yes, I know, but I'm beginning to feel awfully bad about that. Here she is working nights trying to put herself through law school, and all she wanted was a little advice. I'm sure you could have put her on the right path."

"I can't save the world," Aidan said with a half-smile seeming more like a half-frown.

"Tough day at the office?"

"Tough day period."

Considering the day, Callie assumed it had more to do with his love life than his law practice. She didn't take the bait; she didn't want to resurrect Grace. In a minute of awkward silence, they sat looking at each other. Callie noticed the candlelight settling in on the tiny creases at the corner of Aidan's eyes. He had movie-star good looks, and Callie oddly pondered if that had persuasive powers over the juries. During the course of dinner, her thoughts drifted in and out with other curious wonderings, such as if he had strong hands to give good neck massages and what it would be like to kiss him. Embarrassed by her own musings, Callie found herself drinking a second glass of wine to wash away her peculiar feelings of attraction.

"Let's dance." Aidan reached across the table for her hand.

"Dance?" Callie looked towards the small parquet floor and the three couples swaying to the soft music and instantly thought of Nicholas. "I don't think so, Aidan."

"Why not?"

"Because we don't dance."

"Sure we do. *I* am a fabulous dancer." He held onto her hand and leaned closer for a more private conversation. "It all began when I was five and my Uncle Julia—it used to be Julio but an accident with a fan on a hot day—" Aidan winced. "Need I say more?"

Callie laughed. "You're joking."

"*Of course.* It wasn't a hot day at all. It was 15 degrees in the middle of winter, but who would believe Uncle Julia liked a brisk breeze on his—"

"Aidan, stop," Callie pleaded, moved by his charming sense of humor. He had the innate ability to make her laugh with something completely ridiculous.

"Do you want to dance or should I continue the rest of Uncle Julia's story?"

"Dance," she conceded against her better judgment, but dancing with Aidan, being held in a man's arms for just a short while, proved to be medicine for her aching heart. They danced several more times that night, and Callie felt almost whole and happy.

After dessert and espressos, Aidan paid the check and walked with Callie outside the restaurant and down the block towards the parking garage. The tall buildings provided little shelter from the brutal night's wind. Callie pulled on her gloves and dug her hands deep into her pockets. Reaching the end of the sidewalk, Aidan held her arm as she stepped into the street over a mound of snow. They continued silently till they reached the neon lights of the parking garage.

"You'll be okay driving home?" Aidan asked. "I'll call my car service for you."

"Thanks for the offer, but I'll be fine. I'll be home in an hour."

"You could follow me home and stay at my place." His eyes seemed to twinkle or maybe it was just the reflection of the florescent lights overhead.

"Thanks, really, but I don't mind the drive."

Aidan stepped closer and pulled up the collar of her coat, letting his hands rest on her shoulders.

"I'm not being entirely altruistic. I'd rather this night not end." He touched her face, softly, tenderly, and tipped up her chin. "I want to kiss you."

Before Callie could speak or react or even entirely comprehend his words, Aidan kissed her. At first, his lips barely touched hers, just a warm breath like the summer sun rising in the morning. Callie craved the warmth, and the kiss turned deeper, more intense. A gust of wind pushed her fully into Aidan's arms; her knees shook. Though the kiss lasted only a minute—or so she thought—what Aidan said next stayed with Callie the long ride home.

"I *really* like you, Callie." His voice, his expression, his stare—all penetrated her with seriousness. "You're somebody I want to fall in love with."

# CHAPTER 11

The 60-minute drive home didn't help much to put Aidan's kiss and statement in perspective. *It is Valentine's Day*, Callie rationalized. He was lonely; she was lonely and, admittedly, a bit flirtatious. They ate; they drank; they danced. *We shouldn't have danced.* Her lonely body didn't need another lonely body to brush against. But it felt so good to be held … just for a while.

And the kiss—*it meant nothing, didn't it? Who am I kidding? Of course, it meant something.*

Clearly, Aidan desired to take their relationship to the next level, and that in itself would pose a sleepless night over whether or not she wanted to cross the platonic line. She liked everything about Aidan, but the fact remained she *loved* everything about Nicholas. He was the one who really held her heart, filled her thoughts and her dreams. She missed him—missed his touch, his smile, his lips. Callie hoped that by the end of the summer, Nicholas would make Sycamore his home again. However, it would be the long, lonely gaps in between their times together that would make nights such as tonight with Aidan very dangerous and very tempting.

Observing a car parked in her driveway put an end to Callie's musings over Aidan. The hair on her neck stood on end, and her skin prickled up her arm and down her spine. Suddenly, the unlit country seemed more menacing at midnight than the big city and its open threat of crime. She re-locked her car doors, flashed her brights at the back of the sedan, then honked the horn to alert the driver of her presence. The door of the sedan opened, and the driver stepped out of the car. To Callie's utter surprise, Nicholas emerged.

"Nicholas! What are you doing here?" she asked, scurrying from the car into his arms. "What a wonderful surprise!" She nestled into his embrace and breathed in the spicy scent of his cologne. "You should've called."

"Then it wouldn't have been a surprise now, would it?"

"No, but I wouldn't have stayed out so late."

"Actually, I did try to call you, but I couldn't get any service on my cell phone."

"Yeah, there's a dead zone here at the house."

"So, happy Valentine's Day," he said, tipping up her chin for a soft kiss. "Though, I do believe it's not the 14th anymore."

"I'm sorry." Callie waited for Nicholas to retrieve his bag from the car, then they walked to the front door. She pointed to the planter box next to the door. "I keep a spare key in there. Use it if I'm ever not here."

Once inside, Callie poured some wine as Nicholas started a fire. They worked in sync, tossing pillows on the floor, glancing at one another, smiling, hurrying, as if they had done it a hundred times as their nightly ritual. Finally, they settled down in front of the fire. Nicholas tipped his glass in a toast.

"Here's to a beautiful night in front of a beautiful fire with the most beautiful woman."

"Thank you for making the trip."

"Sweetheart, there's no distance I wouldn't travel to be with you. If you sat on the top of Mt. Rushmore, I'd climb it."

Callie smiled and clinked her glass to his.

"How long do we have? When's your flight home?"

"Tomorrow afternoon."

Callie felt the pout form on her face.

"I miss you already."

"No sad faces." He kissed her again. "One day—"

"I know. Maybe by the end of the summer—"

"I count the days till I can fall asleep with you in my arms and wake up with you in my bed."

He spoke no more for his lips said everything she wanted to hear. The way he kissed her with such desire sparked shards of color to appear before her closed eyes. The most vivid of hues pulsated from her heart and danced in sexy waves, dipping and twirling in an erotic tango. Her body hugged him in methodical motion as his mouth moved to her ear lobe and down to her neck. Then suddenly the music stopped; he stopped.

"Where were you tonight?" Nicholas shot the question with an irritable bow.

"Why?"

"I smell smoke in your hair."

Callie felt the sting of the arrow as she sniffed at her hair. It wasn't just smoke he smelled. There were traces of Aidan's cologne, too.

"At Nick's restaurant," she replied with a half-truth, hearing the guilt in her voice.

"Alone or with *News, Sports, Work, and Weather*?"

"He has a name, you know."

"I don't want to know it. I don't want to know anything about him."

Nicholas's tone forced her upright and away from him, stunned by his jealousy.

"Then why did you ask about—"

"He was there, wasn't he?"

Callie looked away towards the flames.

"Yes, he was there. We're friends. We spend time together."

"On Valentine's Day?"

"We kept each other company. I couldn't be with you." She heaved a long, sad sigh. "Nicholas, do we have to talk about this?"

"I'm sorry, Callie, but I love you. I hate that someone else is the recipient of your smiles, your laugh, your touch."

She gazed into his honest brown eyes, and said, "We don't touch."

"Have you kissed him?"

Callie looked down into her wine glass, the deep burgundy becoming a black abyss of sad frustration.

"It'd be so easy, Nicholas, if you were here, if you lived here. It'd be a no-brainer. There'd only be you."

"So, it's my fault?"

"No, I understand that you're in the middle of a school year, and you can't move yet, but it's just—"

"Wait a second, Callie. I never said I was moving. I can't move, not now. I'm locked to South Carolina till Adam graduates high school."

She sat for a moment and just stared off into the fireplace. It crackled and snapped then jarred her from silent contemplation.

"Then what're we doing? This is pointless, Nicholas. We can't have a long-distance relationship."

"I thought *you* were gonna move."

"Me? I can't move. My whole life is here—my family, friends, the gallery."

"I'm not saying do it tomorrow. I know these things take time." He touched her shoulder and ran his fingers down her arm. "Let's just get on the same page, Callie, agree to be together, and then worry about the details later."

"Those details are major worries, Nicholas. You're asking me to give up my life."

Fear penetrated her eyes, and she edged away from him as she reached to put her glass on the end table.

"No, Callie, I'm asking you to consider a life with me. God, we're so good together. Everything is so right with us. We can't let the geography get in the way. We have to somehow work through this and be together."

She stared again into the fire. Her quiet scared him that she was thinking about *News, Sports, Work, and Weather.* Reaching for Callie's hand, Nicholas folded his fingers through hers, and she moved again into his arms.

"I'm sorry, Callie. I didn't mean to pressure you. Just think about it, okay? Think about us and what a great life we could have together."

"I don't have to think about that. I already know how wonderful it would be. I've imagined it since that day in the coffee shop."

She looked happy and sad at the same time. Nicholas kissed her hand as she stood up.

"Where are you going?"

"I'm going to go take a shower and wash the smoke out of my hair."

But Nicholas knew she wanted to wash off the scent of *News, Sports, Work, and Weather*. Taunted that Callie had the possibility of love in her own state, Nicholas didn't want to let go of her hand and risk losing the connection they had made. She gave him a half-hearted smile and pulled away.

"You'll be back?"

"Nowhere to go. It's my house."

He couldn't hide the surprise of hearing her statement, a little cold and detached.

"Hey, I love you," he reminded her.

"I'll be back in a few minutes." A sweeter tone, perhaps, yet Callie was far too eager to remove herself from the living room as she darted up the stair.

Hearing the water running through the pipes, Nicholas put out the fire and went upstairs. He wanted to sleep in bed with her, hold her, spoon her, hear her every breath, feel every subtle movement. The floorboards creaked in the hallway as he followed the sound of water to Callie's bedroom, which he found very tidy except for her red dress heaped on the floor.

It was a white room with white walls and white lace curtains—simple and art-free except for the angel sculptures that adorned her night table and dresser. Color spilled forth in an heirloom patchwork quilt covering her four-post bed and in the chair cushions on the rocker and on the windowseat.

Nicholas sat on the bed and listened to her sweet voice humming, resonating from inside the bathroom. With the door ajar, temptation drew him inside the steamy blue-and-white room bearing a pedestal sink and old-fashioned porcelain tub. He could see her nude body, well-rounded and provocative, silhouetted against the white shower curtain. Beads of sweat beginning to form on his brow, Nicholas pulled a blue towel from the metal rings, which caused the circular hook to clank against the wall. Callie moved the curtain slightly aside and poked her head around it.

"Nicholas," she said with pleasant surprise, her pouty, voluptuous mouth broadening with a smile. "Coming to join me?"

"N-n-no. I just—"

She reached out with one hand, her body still hidden behind the curtain. It was an invitation he found himself hard pressed to resist.

"Please."

Her fingers caught his arm, and she tugged him gently towards the shower. Fully clothed in shirt, pants, and socks, Nicholas stepped inside the tub as Callie rotated to face him. Water streamed down her slender frame as she pressed close to kiss him, teasing and tempting, pulling off his sweater and unbuckling his pants. Passion erupted in her provocative kissing and licking, working her way up his torso until she met his lips in burning desire. The water's vapor encircled them in an erotic, humid mist that began to overpower Nicholas's conscience.

"I shouldn't—we shouldn't," he thought aloud, opening his eyes as his subconscious screamed *I should! We should! Stop thinking man and just go with your heart!*

"I want you to." Callie smiled shyly at him, her long black eyelashes clumped together in wet triangles. Her auburn hair, weighted by the wetness, hung straight to the middle of her back. She reached for the soap and began lathering his chest with erotic circles. Her fingers swept slowly across his shoulders and down his arms. Stroking and massaging, she foamed his upper body then worked lower and lower until his desire filled her hands.

"Make love to me, Nicholas," she whispered in a sexy, sultry voice.

Nicholas's eyes followed the trickle of water streaming over Callie from her cheekbones to her full bosom, down her pure, snowy flesh until it bounced off her thighs. He could resist her no more. Nicholas kissed her again, then moved to her neck and suckled on the tender muscle. Her moans of pleasure provoked him to caress her breasts, toying with the hardened pink crests until Callie's body ached so that she squirmed to be free of the stimulation. He continued with one hand and moved the other hand down her stomach to where she throbbed for his touch. She gasped and clung to Nicholas's shoulders as his fingers relentlessly pleasured her.

"Oh, God, Nicholas," she purred, as his mouth left her neck and nibbled down to her breasts. He kissed and licked those glorious tips, then bestowed a line of kisses down her stomach, and he heard Callie breathlessly panting his name. "Nicholas, oh Nicholas."

Burning, yearning, gasping, grasping, Callie moaned as Nicholas suckled and tasted the essence of her being until she slipped over the edge of desire. Callie pulled at his very short hair, coaxing him up to meet her quivering lips with yet another ravenous kiss. They stepped more fully under the hot water and let it rush over them like a tropical waterfall cooling their heated bodies.

Nicholas reached around Callie and turned off the water. He carried her from the tub, leaving behind his soaked clothes, and she grabbed for the towel on their way into the bedroom. When set on her feet, Callie pulled down the covers and watched Nicholas dry off his water-drenched body before climbing onto the bed. He kissed her again, and felt her warm fingers gliding over his throbbing mass of tissue and muscle.

"You're so unreal, so beautiful," he whispered between kisses as his lips again traveled to her ear and neck where he playfully gnawed on her sweet flesh.

Nicholas breathed deeply, smelling the scented soap and shampoo, and felt her body pulsate with exciting force. Exhilarated by their heightening passion, he rolled on top of Callie. She looked up at him with soulful eyes. He had to say the words that filled his heart; maybe she would say them, too.

"I love you, Callie."

She smiled, but spoke no words, just closed her eyes and opened herself up to him as their lovemaking soared to a higher plateau, before reaching that comfort zone of satisfaction. And although Nicholas desperately wanted to remain awake, listen for her proclamation of love, and cherish every moment of this night, Callie's sweet purrs and rhythmic breathing served as a lullaby, and he drifted into sleep.

Callie woke up in Nicholas's arms and realized how perfect her life was when they were together. She felt whole. Everything had meaning. Sunlight crept into the room from behind the shades and danced in bright prisms on the bare walls.

"Good morning, beautiful," he said, nuzzling his lips through her hair to her cheek. "How did you sleep?"

"I can't remember a better night's sleep."

"Me, too." Nicholas pulled her into his arms. "You see what I mean when I say how right it is for us to be together? Every day should be like this."

"Mmmm," Callie purred, absolutely comfortable lying there in bed with him, not needing or wanting any words at this particular moment.

"How come there's no art in this room? Why no paintings?"

She let out a sleepy sigh.

"My bedroom's my retreat, my blank canvas. I think in here and don't want any distractions."

"Oh." He kissed her hand again. "What're you thinking now?"

"That last night was wonderful."

"God, Callie, you're so incredibly sexy. How I'm going to miss you."

"Oh, I'm sure there's a few southern belles who'll keep you occupied till the next time we're together," she teased.

"No, there's no one—no one like you." He rolled her on top of him and peered into her naked eyes. "I don't want to see anybody else. I want us to be exclusive, Callie."

"I know I told you I would seriously consider moving—" she began as the impossibility of the situation presented itself again "—but the bright-morning reality is that that's going to take some time."

"I know."

Callie rolled off him and sat up on the edge of the bed with the quilt covering her legs. The tiny patchwork squares caught her attention with their intricate stitching interlocking them all together. She wished her life could be so easily sewn together.

"We live in separate states, Nicholas, a thousand miles apart. It wouldn't be fair or right to ask you not to date other women during that time."

"I don't want to be with anyone else." Sitting up behind Callie, Nicholas wrapped his arms around her and pulled her to his chest. "I want to pursue this relationship with you, only you." He kissed her hair, and Callie let his love envelope her as she thought about their situation.

A relationship with Nicholas was what she really wanted, but the thought of moving displeased her. Callie liked her life, and it all revolved around Sycamore—family, friends, Appassionata. She had everything she wanted except love, and that was something she desperately desired … someone to share it all with. Callie wanted love; there was no denying that. But she wanted it in Massachusetts.

"A long-distance relationship. Is that really going to make us happy? We're never going to see each other. I'll be honest with you, Nicholas. I love your words—they're very sexy and romantic—but they run a close second to holding hands, kissing, actually being with someone."

"So, what're you saying? Do you want to date other men? Do you want to be with *News, Sports, Work, and Weather*?"

"No—yes—maybe." Callie squirmed free of his arms, got out of the bed, and put on her robe—her frumpy red robe.

"Well, which one is it?" he asked nicely, a poor attempt to mask his annoyance.

"I just need to see if love is an option for me here in Massachusetts. Before I upset the apple cart and turn my life upside down—"

"You talk like moving in with me is some great catastrophe."

"I didn't mean it that way at all. What I'm trying to say is that I need to explore what love holds for me here. My life is here. Maybe love is here, too."

"Yes, it's right in front of you. It's me, Callie. *I* love you. Can't you see that? No one is going to love you like me. Look, Callie, I know exactly how I feel and how being with you makes me feel. I'm not going to hide that or lie about it. I'm not a kid; I'm not in high school; I just don't play those kinds of games. I never did. I love you, Callie, plain and simple. That may scare you. Actually, it scares me a bit, but it excites me more. I want us to be together. I'm not saying let's get married tomorrow, but let's not waste tomorrow either. You're right about the long-distance relationship. It's going to be hard on us for a while, and it's certainly not going to predict our future. We need to be together in the same state to see if what we have can be sustained through everyday life. What we have now is somewhat surreal—the longing, the desire, the precious hours together focused completely on each other. That's not real life. We need to date like an ordinary couple and let the world in on us.

"Your moving in with me, Callie, would do exactly that. You could see me as I really am—a teacher, a coach, a friend, a dad to Adam. You'll get to spend time with my son and see how you two get along, which I'm sure will be wonderfully. I know my son, and he's gonna love you as much as I do."

Callie smiled, still not knowing what to say.

"Most importantly, Callie, you'll have a chance to scope out the area for art, see the museums, visit the university gallery. You'll get a true feel for how you'll fit in and where you could open your own gallery. You can't do that from here."

"But here, I have all that. I'm settled. This is my home."

"Home is where your heart is, and I know your heart is with me. You can fight it, deny it, but one day you're gonna realize it. I just hope when you do, it's not too late."

Callie wished she had worn her mittens for the short walk from her house to Appassionata. The cold stung her knuckles, and she shoved her hands deep into her pockets for a little warmth. Feeling and hearing the crinkle of paper, Callie pulled what she thought was a misplaced receipt from her pocket. It was a love note from Nicholas:

*Indescript moments, like ambers in a fire that no one notices till there's a moundful of ash, are what I carry in my heart when apart from you. Till the next time we touch, I'll be missing you so much ... xoxo Nicholas*

Warmed by his note, Callie pushed open the gallery's front door and found Deardra on a ladder dusting the frames of the higher-hanging pictures. Tiny particles, almost iridescent, floated like cherubs in an aimless rise and plummet to the floor.

"Deardra, tell me again that anything is possible."

"How about I jump from the ladder, and you catch me?"

"I can't do that."

"Some things *are* impossible." Deardra smiled down from her high perch, pleased at having made such a clever point. "Why do you ask? What's happened? I saw an unfamiliar car parked in your driveway this morning when I opened the gallery. I assumed it was Aidan. And let me say how pleased I am that you two finally hooked up."

"Sorry to disappoint you, but it was Nicholas. He flew up to surprise me for Valentine's Day."

"How sweet," Deardra replied, more effort put in swiping the pictures for dust than sounding happy for Callie. "Any details you care to share?"

"He wants me to move to South Carolina."

"Oh." Deardra climbed down the ladder. "What'd you say?"

"I told him I'd think about it."

As her foot hit the floor, Deardra looked Callie directly in the eye. "And?"

"And I'm thinking about it. God, that's all I've been doing since he left. Thinking." Callie sat down on the bottom step of the staircase and buried her face in her hands. "I don't know what to do."

"So don't do anything. Just let it be for a while. You can't let yourself be pressured."

Callie looked up and confided, "The thing is, Deardra, I really believe he's the one for me. I have this amazing connection with him that I've had with nobody else. That's not something I want to walk away from."

"Callie, I'm not telling you what to do. By no means, I'm no expert on love and relationships, but you've got to keep a practical perspective. You worked very hard to achieve what you've achieved." Deardra gestured grandly towards the ceiling, her stick of feathers releasing a gazillion fragments that rained down on Callie like diamond dust. "This gallery didn't happen overnight. It came to be because of years of sacrifices, *your* sacrifices, *your* talent, and *your* determination to make a dream come true. How many years did you sideline your painting to work two jobs to save up enough money to buy this place and renovate it?" She paused to do the mental math. "I count five. That's a tremendous sacrifice. I couldn't have done it. I couldn't have stopped being a photographer the way you stopped being an artist to teach."

"I did what I had to do."

"Exactly. And you're still doing it." Deardra knighted Callie with a tap on the shoulder with the feather duster. "Apassionata was built with your sweat, and you didn't do it just for yourself. It's not Callie's Gallery. It's Appassionata where every local artisan can display and sell their work. You've brought art to Sycamore and enriched every life that has entered through these doors. And now you want to walk away from that?" Deardra sat down on the step next to Callie in a show of sisterly support. "It behooves me—"

"Behooves?"

Callie sneezed and swatted at the invisible dust for some clean air.

"It boggles my brain why a smart, beautiful, successful and financially independent woman would consider leaving behind this wonderful life she's created for herself in order to pursue a relationship with a man you've been dating for only six weeks."

"Seven."

"Whatever. You've known Aidan longer than that and he's not asking you to make life-altering changes."

"No, but it's different with Nicholas," Callie explained. "We have history; we grew up together. We skipped the getting-to-know-you phase and jumped right into a relationship."

"So, you've been in relationships before. They never progressed this way this fast."

"No, but it's different with him. I trust him so I don't have up any of my usual boundaries. I don't think when I'm with him; I just feel."

"You said it; I didn't it."

"No, no, not that way. I haven't lost my mind or common sense. It's just that I go with the flow of feelings when I'm with him, and that feels amazing. I'm not afraid of getting hurt, but I am afraid of hurting him."

"I don't know what to say, Callie. I haven't seen you two together, but I have seen you and Aidan together. He likes you. Why aren't you giving him a chance? God knows he lives in the state."

"There's nothing wrong with Aidan; he's nice. But when you compare the two, he's simply a smear—smudged pigment on a canvas. Nicholas, on the other hand, is crisp, intense—a clear portrait of defining strokes of color and personality. He's alive and vibrant, and makes me feel alive and vibrant. He's sexy and passionate. He's everything I want in a man, a lover, a husband."

"Well, I think Aidan has all those qualities, too, but you can't see them because your eyes are closed to him." Deardra stood up and wiped her hands on the back of her pants. "Nobody can tell you what to do. You're a smart girl, Callie. Your future is your choice, but those choices need to be made with as much your head as your heart."

"I know."

"And what about me and the rest of your fiends? Gonna ditch us for a guy?"

"Not for a guy … for love."

At her parents' house, Callie followed her mother into the kitchen and sat on the stool bordering the counter between the kitchen and family room. The shutters were closed halfway, and Callie spied her dad asleep in his chair in the other room.

"Mom, remember Nicholas Ashton, the fellow I went sledding with a few weeks ago?"

"Yes, dear." Her mother busied herself with taking an apple pie from the refrigerator and then searching through the utensil drawer for a sharp knife.

"Well, we've stayed in touch since then, you know, over the phone, via e-mail. He's even been up to visit."

"That's nice, dear. Do you want a piece of pie?" she asked already in the process of serving Callie a slice on a paper plate.

"No, Mom."

"Take a few bites; it's delicious. I used a different kind of apple than the recipe called for." She put down the knife, opened up a tin box, and rummaged through several dozen index cards. "Where is that recipe? I know I put it back in here."

Callie hated her mother's unintentional distractions, especially when Callie was trying to discuss something important.

"Are you listening to me? Mom, will you stop for a second and just listen to me?"

"Yes, dear." She closed the tin box and handed Callie a fork. "Do you want me to zap it a minute in the microwave to warm it?"

"No, Mom, it's fine." Callie took a conciliatory bite of the pie. "I—"

"How is it?"

"Delicious." Callie forced a smile. "Mom, sit down, I want to talk to you about Nicholas."

"Yes, dear." She poured herself a cup of coffee then retreated to the stool next to Callie. "Go ahead, dear. What did you want to talk about?"

"Nicholas. I really like him, Mom. We have such a wonderful time when we're together." Callie hesitated. This was not an easy subject discussing with her mother. "It's getting rather serious between Nicholas and me."

"What do you mean?"

Her mother pulled a paper napkin from the holder and began folding it into subsequently smaller squares. Callie smiled.

"I think I'm falling in love with him."

"You think?" she asked with deliberate shock.

"I know. I am. I have."

"Really?" Her mother avoided eye contact as she diligently unfolded the paper squares then refolded the napkin into triangles. "Have you told him this?"

"I think he knows."

"Think?" Another tone of mixed surprise and agitation.

"He knows. Gosh, Mom, why do you have to make this so hard?" Callie groaned. "We've fallen in love with each other."

"He lives down south, you told me. I remember you saying that. I can't see how it can possibly work unless he moves. Is he willing to move?"

"He has a son, Mom, a five year old. He can't move. The little boy's mother lives near them, and Nicholas can't take him away from his mother."

Unfolding the triangles, Callie's mom smoothed the napkin across her lap then smiled as a calm curtained her face, like a thick muslin cloth thwarting ultraviolet rays.

"I'm sorry for you, dear. Some things are just not meant to be."

Callie took a deep breath of courage.

"He's asked me to move, Mom. Not permanent yet, just on a trial basis to see how we mesh as a family."

"And you told him no."

"Actually, I told him I'd think about it."

Callie saw the tiny stress lines form around her mother's mouth as she gritted her teeth.

"You can't be serious, Callie. You want to raise another woman's child?"

"Mom, that's besides the point. I love Nicholas, and his son is an extension of that love. He's a great little boy."

"But what about your life here? Who's going to help with the house if you're not here?" She pointed toward the family room where Callie's father sat in his recliner chair asleep. "Your father's knee keeps giving out on him and—" She lowered her voice to a bare whisper. "I think he's getting Alzheimer's."

"What?"

"He keeps forgetting things."

"Mom, Dad is as sharp as the knife on the table."

"You're not here all the time, Callie." She leaned closer to her daughter. "Every Saturday he forgets our bridge game with Rhonda and Harold Williams and then he can't find his shoes and forgets where he put the deck of cards."

"Mom," Callie chuckled with relief, putting a comforting arm around her mom's shoulder. "Dad hates playing bridge. Haven't you figured that out by now? Those lapses in memory are done on purpose. I don't know about his knee, though. Has he seen a doctor?"

"Not yet. He's afraid of nothing except hospitals since that bout with pneumonia. Thinks once he goes in, he'll not be coming out again."

"That's silly. I'll try to get him to see a doctor but, Mom, all these things can be taken care of from South Carolina. I don't need to be here. The Farleys' boy who plows our driveways is more than capable of helping out with the spring yard cleanup and the leaves in the fall. Any other house problems, you'll have to call the plumber or electrician or mason, just like you do now."

"What about your sister?"

"What about her?"

"Who's going to look after her?"

Callie inwardly cringed. She didn't have an answer to that one.

"And what about Appassionata?" her mother continued. "Have you thought about that?"

"I don't know about that yet."

"Well, missy, you better think long and hard about it. You put too much time and money into that building to just walk away from it. Your father has always said you were short on good sense, and closing the gallery for a man would prove him right. Get a hold of yourself, Callie. You're smarter than that."

♥        ♥        ♥

Sunday morning breakfast with Nick at Callie's house seemed to be the perfect time to talk to him about Nicholas and her thought of moving. Despite her non-stop consideration of the pros and cons of leaving Sycamore, Callie still found herself at a crossroads and needed some real guidance from a more objective person.

"Good morning, Callie," Nick said as he hooked his coat and scarf on the rack. Impeccably dressed, he wore a white fisherman's knit turtleneck sweater and black pants with a crisp crease. "I smell something cooking. Do I dare assume that *you* cooked breakfast for *me* today?"

"Yes, I did. I was feeling a bit domestic, plus I wanted to try out that Belgian waffle maker you gave me for Christmas."

"It's fool-proof." Nick followed Callie into the kitchen. "Just pour the batter and flip a switch."

"I know, but I'm sure you make a better batter than me."

Callie pulled two plates from the cabinet and set the table while Nick poured himself a cup of coffee.

"I don't know about that. There's something special in this kitchen 'cause when I make batter here, it always tastes better."

"What's special is the milk. It's farm fresh from next door. You can't get that in Boston, but I can get you a few bottles to take back with you."

"It's really the milk?" he asked, skeptical.

Callie retrieved a glass bottle from the refrigerator and poured Nick a small glassful.

"Here. Drink up."

He downed the entire glass.

"That is creamy."

"And that's two percent, not even whole milk." Callie busied herself at the counter with arranging the waffles on a serving dish. "Nothing like country living."

"The city has its plusses." Nick forked one of the waffles and moved it to his plate. "So, what's new in the life and times of Callie Emerson? How was your dinner with Aidan the other night?"

"Fine." She sat down at the table. "Nicholas surprised me with a visit. He was here on my doorstep when I got home that night."

"Was Aidan with you?" he inquired with a raised eyebrow, expecting a juicy, soap-opera scene.

"No, just me."

"Oh." His face dropped. "When did Nicholas leave?"

"The next morning. Just a quick Valentine's visit."

"How romantic," Nick said with understated displeasure. "Nice of him to give you five minutes time."

"It's not his fault. It's just the circumstances."

"The circumstances are deplorable—you here; him there." He sliced a small tab of butter and spread it over the waffle, the butter melting into the square crevices. "Why waste your time?"

"I could change the circumstances. I could move."

Nick reached for his coffee cup.

"Don't be foolish, Callie. You don't leave a great life to start another one—not for a man."

"I think I love him."

"Of course, you love him. That's why you're not thinking clearly."

Callie opened her mouth to defend herself but Nick waved her to silence.

"Let me tell you about love, Callie. Love is a matter of choice. You choose who you fall in love with and—"

She didn't know if that statement was true.

"Nick, I don't think—"

"Hush, girl, let me finish." He made a zipper gesture to quiet her. "Love is a choice, and it's gonna be your choice to willfully walk away from an extraordinary life you've created for yourself, say goodbye to your family, turn your back on your friends, all for sweaty palms and a pounding heart."

"God, Nick, you make it sound so cheesy, childish."

"Sorry, but I'm just more practical-minded about these things."

He took a bite of the waffle, and Callie seized the opportunity to speak.

"Then practically-speaking, isn't love—true love rare, against the odds? The bars, the personals in the newspaper, the matchmaking web-sites are all full of people still searching for it, and it's found me. Shouldn't I be hanging onto that brass ring with both hands? And he's an amazing man, good to the core, who completely loves me for me. I can't say I've ever had that before. And you want me to walk away from that?"

"Maybe you should deplete your options here before leaving the state." Nick tipped his fork at her like a teacher with a pointing stick at the chalkboard. "What about Aidan? That guy's a catch, if I do say so myself, and top it off with him already having eyes for you."

"He's a friend, just a friend."

Callie didn't want to divulge the kiss at the parking garage, though for a second, remembering that shared intimacy made her smile. Nick shook his head, put down the fork, and waved an objecting hand in apparent expertise on this subject.

"Wrong, my dear, very wrong. He doesn't look at you like a friend. He wants more."

"No," she protested.

"Yes. He's told me."

"Really?" Callie's skin goosebumped at hearing that Aidan had confided in Nick about his desire for her. "When?"

"That night in the bar when you were on your cell talking to Maisy."

*So the kiss had been premeditated.*

Callie had blamed it on wine and Valentine's Day, but Nick's slip of the tongue confirmed that it was pure seduction on Aidan's part, and she didn't quite know how to react to that. Callie leaned closer for more information.

"What did he say?" Callie asked.

"It doesn't matter. Have you really given him a chance?"

"Nick, tell me. What did he say?"

Nick responded with his own question.

"Why aren't you exploring a relationship with him? Aidan's a nice guy."

"Aidan and I are friends. Besides, even if we did start a romance, it would take months to develop into the close relationship that Nicholas and I have right now." Callie picked up her fork and stabbed the tines into the syrup-covered waffle on her plate and used the utensil to make her point. "We're at a fork in the road, Nicholas and me. Our relationship can't progress unless I move."

"And he won't move because of his son, I presume."

"Exactly. It's all on me. I have to make a decision."

Nick tilted his head in that profound professor way.

"We're talking about the rest of your life, Callie, and decisions like that can't be made in a hurry. If Nicholas really loves you, he'll give you enough time to sort through your options and make that decision."

"You mean enough time for my friends and family to convince me to stay in Massachusetts."

The corners of Nick's mouth turned up into a mischievous grin. "Exactly."

*Dear Nicholas … As always, it was good to see you and spend time with you. I began missing you the moment you drove away. It seems that is much our story … the long, lonely gaps in between our reunions.*

*I've thought a lot about our last conversation and your invitation to move in with you. Believe me, you do make many valid points, and I will continue to consider making that move. However, I can't give you an answer now. I need time. A decision like this cannot be made overnight. While I'm contemplating my future, I'm hoping you'll let us take one giant step backwards to the point where we can continue to develop our friendship without the romantic complications … Artfully yours, Callie*

Callie waited four days for a reply. She knew it would be hard for Nicholas to understand what she was going through, the indecision, the torn feelings of desire and complacency. When his e-mail arrived, Callie read it with trepidation.

*Sweetheart,*

*I never thought of love as a complication, and were it defined that way, I would still welcome it with open arms. But that is the difference between you and me. I know what I want and how special our relationship is and how very blessed we are to have found each other. One giant step backwards? How do you go back in time with a full memory and pretend things didn't happen and deny feelings that have drenched my heart in love? I don't know how, but for you—I'll try.*

Love, Nicholas

# CHAPTER 12

Nearly six weeks had passed since Nicholas's Valentine's visit. The spring thaw had begun—the warmer temperatures, the melting of the snow, and the buds of trees and flowers coming back to life. Callie's thaw too had occurred. Thoroughly missing Nicholas, she found herself in desperate need for passion, and Aidan's innocent kisses just didn't satisfy her. Their courtship was moving at a snail's pace, partly due to their busy work schedules as well as Aidan's guarded heart which didn't allow for Callie to delve into more intimate conversation that inevitably would heat up their relationship to something more than French-kissing friends.

Now, with spring in the air, Callie wanted some passion in her life. She knew she could even be persuaded to resume her affair with Nicholas and have a long-distance relationship that would involve an occasional romantic weekend. However, Nicholas didn't seem to have the same desire. His e-mails had progressed from erotic love letters to cordial exchanges. Callie accepted the blame for his change of heart, aware that her steadfast plea for a chance to pursue her in-state love options had pushed him away. But with Nicholas on her mind and ever in her heart, she found it hard to be with anyone else, even Aidan.

On this particular Sunday afternoon, Callie turned on her computer and saw an e-mail from Nicholas. Hopeful that he, too, was missing her, Callie eagerly opened his e-mail only to find a three-line text inquiring about her work and the weather. Sadly, she wrote a similar non-romantic reply then headed out the door to her parents' house for Sunday dinner.

April traditionally brought cloudy skies, and today the sky hung with thick charcoal clouds, heavy with rain. Callie immediately regretted not bringing an umbrella for the walk to her parents' house. A few yards up the street, it began to drizzle and she quickened her pace before the entire sky emptied itself on her. A sports car sped past Callie and splashed up a dirty puddle of melted snow that nearly soaked her pale pink, mid-thigh sweater dress. She looked back over her shoulder and saw the car pull into her driveway. Callie watched and waited for the driver to step out. It was Aidan.

"Aidan!" she shouted, waving him toward her. They met at the edge of her driveway by the rock wall. "What a nice surprise."

He wore a blue and green striped shirt unbuttoned at the neck and tucked into his jeans. Casually handsome with that Cheshire grin like a child on Christmas morning, Aidan palmed Callie's waist and pulled her to him for a kiss on the cheek.

"I wanted to take you for a spin in my new car."

Callie looked past him at the black car.

"It's pretty."

"It's a *Maserati*."

"Oh, Maseratis can't be pretty?" she teased.

"Sleek, powerful—"

"*Expensive*."

"Come on, Brown Eyes. Let's go for a ride. We'll stop somewhere and have dinner."

"Actually, I'm on my way to my parents' house for dinner. Why don't you come along? You haven't met them yet."

"No, thank you." Aidan's decline held such resistance as if she had offered him a ticket to a cult brainwashing.

Irritated at his not wanting to take this step and really become a part of her life, Callie bit her tongue and stood there, silent, just staring at him, hurt and confused. Suddenly, the drizzle turned to hard rain, which sent her running for Aidan's car.

"What're you doing?" he asked following behind.

"Getting out of the rain." She tugged on the door handle but it was locked. "Can you drive me to my parents' house?"

He looked down at her mud-covered shoes and visibly cringed.

"But you're all muddy."

Maybe it was Aidan's dinner rejection or Callie's gritty Sicilian roots pushing through. Whatever it was, it launched her boldness.

"Is that all you see?" She stepped closer to him and touched his clean-shaven cheek. "Is that all I am to you? A muddy mess? Someone to hang out with? A casual distraction?"

The rain continued to fall, pounding them with a steady force. Her hair soaked and dripping at her shoulders, Callie stood gazing up at Aidan and blinking away the water raining into her eyes. He leaned down and kissed her, soft and gentle, the way he always did. However, being pummeled with water caused Callie to be transported back to the shower with Nicholas, and she lost herself to the wetness of the moment. Suddenly, the sheeting rain pouring over them, binding them, intensified her desire, and their kiss grew deeper and hungrier.

Wet and wonderful, Callie opened her heart and let herself be drenched in champagne kisses as he moved his mouth from her lips across her cheek to her ear. His hands worked their way down her back to her ass where he gripped her tightly and moaned his pleasure. His unexpected sexual aggressiveness sparked her willful submission as their rising passion forced her back against the Maserati. The metal, cold like the shower tiles, felt exquisite against her hot skin. The sky's chilly wet drops kissed her face as he licked at her neck, following the trickle of water down to her breasts.

"God, that feels so good," Callie whispered and ran her fingers through his wet hair as the downpour drowned out her subconscious.

His hands explored her thighs, rising higher under her dress with each provocative purr of longing she emitted. His fingers were strong, squeezing and caressing, gently pushing her upper legs apart as he pressed himself against her. Bound in clothes, he continued to kiss her while every throbbing muscle of his beckoned to be freed. Callie moaned.

In an instant, as quickly as it came, the rain stopped … and so did Callie's response when she opened her eyes and saw Aidan.

*Oh, my God. What am I doing?*

Her heart felt Nicholas, loved Nicholas, and the guilt overwhelmed her for wanting another man to satisfy those desires. They stood there, dripping in desire, just looking at each other. Aidan's eyes bore similar regret as he looked up at the gallery, yet he was too kind to reject her.

"Shall we go inside," he began with a wry smile, "and get you out of those wet clothes?"

The invitation Callie had been waiting to hear for the past few weeks, and now—now she knew she couldn't take him up on his romantic offer, not with Nicholas at the forefront of her thoughts and Grace obviously on his mind.

"I've got to get to my parents' house for dinner," Callie mumbled as she pulled her hair into a ponytail and wrung out the water, purposeful not to meet his stare.

Aidan didn't press the issue nor rethink her dinner invitation. He simply walked to the driver's side of the car and stepped inside. Callie trudged along the stone path back to the road, oblivious to her soaked attire, deaf to the Maserati's motor as it drove away past her, and numb to her lonely core.

*What's wrong with me? Why can't I just stop thinking and be in the moment?*

Over Drew and Annie's house for Easter dinner, Nicholas watched Adam play with the boys on the jungle gym in the backyard while Annie cleared the dining room table inside.

"So what's going on with you and Callie?" Drew asked as he fetched a football from the plastic bin of balls. He lobbed it to Nicholas who caught it and returned the toss.

"Nothing. She writes occasionally to say hi, and I respond politely, holding back everything I want to say in order to honor her request. We've been reduced to *News, Sports, Work, and Weather.* I feel like I lost my best friend."

"You've given up?"

It was more a statement than a question.

"No, I have hope. I'm just giving her the space she needs."

"It's really none of my business," Drew said, rocketing the football to Nicholas, "but keep in mind that the longer this goes on this way and the more comfortable she becomes with you and her not being a couple, the less likely you're ever gonna be anything more than friends."

"I know, but I can't make her be with me. All I can do is love her and wait and hope that this is all gonna end happily. And God knows I want the happy ending. Damn it, I deserve it; *she* deserves it."

"Yeah, you both deserve to be happy."

"I only want the best for her, ya know, Drew. I love her that much."

"What're you saying?"

"Maybe I'm not the guy for her."

The words choked him as the ball left his hands.

"We both know that's not true. And if she can't recognize that you're one terrific guy, then maybe *she's* not the girl for you."

"No, she's the girl for me. I know that, but I also know she's scared."

"Scared? From what you told me, she's the ballsy-est woman I know. She put her entire life savings into that gallery." Drew flipped the football to Nicholas. "That's a helluva risk."

"That's her business life. On the personal side, it's a whole other story. She's scared to take a chance on love outside of her backyard, scared to get hurt, scared to love and be loved." He sighed. "It's so weird, Drew. The best part of loving Callie was just loving her, no filters, no holding back. It was natural, easy, just us being open, completely ourselves, simply enjoying every moment together." He shrugged, beside himself with frustration. "Now, every word I write to her in those stupid e-mails is strained. I give so much consideration to every f-ing sentence, afraid that if I let any feelings through it will push her away. It's a freakin' mind game, and I hate it. Why can't it be easy? Why can't it just be *I love you; you love me; let's be together and be happy?*"

"Welcome to the real world, my friend. It's not easy, but some people are worth the effort. You gotta go see her again, man, lay it all out on the table." Drew walked over to Nicholas's side and patted him on the shoulder. "You can't live in limbo like this."

"I know. The semester ends next month, and I'm gonna take Adam with me and spend a week or two on the Cape with my folks. That's when I'll go see Callie and let her meet Adam. I'm sure everything will fall into place then." Nicholas tried to keep a positive attitude. "Look at this face," Nicholas said as Adam ran over and tugged the football out of his hand. "What's not to love?"

But Nicholas wasn't worried about Callie loving his son. He feared she had fallen out of love with him.

"Watch me throw it, Daddy!" Adam heaved the ball, and it dive-bombed about ten feet in front of him. Crinkling his nose into a silly expression, the toddler laughed and charged to Nicholas's side. "I'm thirsty, Daddy. Can you get me a drink?"

"Sure." Nicholas lobbed the ball to Drew. "Be right back." In the kitchen, Nicholas found Annie crying over the sink as she washed a pot. "What's the matter, Annie? What's wrong?"

"Nothing, Nick." She sniffled and used her wrist to wipe her eyes. "What can I get you?"

Hesitating a moment, wondering if this might just be a hormonal time of the month, Nicholas assumed something worse and pressed Annie a bit further.

"Something's wrong, Annie. Tell me. Is Drew's cancer back?"

Annie dropped the sponge and looked up at Nicholas. Her big blue eyes held the burden of the world.

"It's not Drew. It's my mother."

Wiping her hands on a towel, Annie dabbed the cloth at her eyes. Furtively, she glanced out the window at Drew, then began explaining in a very quiet voice.

"Back in the beginning, Nick, when Drew was first diagnosed, my mom noticed a lump under her arm. She ignored it; it got bigger."

"Why didn't she tell someone or see a doctor?"

"I don't know. She says mostly because of everything going on with Drew at that time. She didn't want to add to my problems' cause I had my hands full taking care of him and the boys and everything. But this lump got bigger, and my mother told me last week, and I made her go to the doctor, and—and—" Her voice cracked and the tears started to flow again. "It's gotten into her lymph nodes, and it's spreading, rampant."

"No, Annie, not cancer."

"She's gonna die. Nick, she's 55 and she's gonna die."

"There's gotta be something they can do, some treatment. Look at Drew. He's beaten it."

"It's different with my mom. She waited too long."

"There's chemo and—"

Annie shook her head and used the dishtowel again to dry her eyes.

"She knows her options; she saw what Drew went through and knows those prescribed poisons are only going to make her sicker and weak. You saw what they did to Drew."

"Yeah, but he got better."

"For her, it'll only prolong the inevitable. It's too far advanced."

"So you're giving up? You're gonna let her accept defeat? That's not the Annie I know."

"She doesn't want to spend however much longer she has waging war against something she can't beat. I've got to respect that, Nick." She glanced out the window. "Ssh. Drew's coming."

"He doesn't know? You have to tell him, Annie. You can't go through this alone."

"I know; I'll tell him. Just not today. He's been through so much, and I just hate that that word *cancer* is gonna be part of our lives again."

"God, he loves you, and you'll get through this together."

"I know."

It was times like these that Nicholas was struck with the enormity of how precious love and life truly are. A thousand miles was just too damn far.

♥                    ♥                    ♥

Callie transported the finished painting from the conservatory to the gallery. Oversized, she struggled with the weight of the canvas as she clumsily maneuvered through the main doors and into the backroom where she busied herself the remainder of the morning with framing the picture When Callie was finished, she rested the painting against the wall, near the front doors in the lobby, to admire it for a short while before her customer came to pick it up.

Deardra emerged from the side room carrying a rolled-up tapestry as the prospective purchasers lagged behind her in casual observance of art displays. Before Deardra could reach the front desk, she saw the painting and broadened her smile.

"Callie, it's beautiful! What a fantastic rendering. Do you still have the photo?" she asked, referring to the snapshot the customer had given Callie of his grandparents' property in Spain.

Callie took the photo from the envelope on the desk and held it beside the painting.

"My God, Callie, it's nearly a perfect duplicate."

"I know. I love it."

Even Callie, ever the perfectionist, couldn't find fault with the painting from its proportions to its colors—colors that made it a perfect fit for the walls of her own house. She couldn't deny that she wanted it for herself.

"It's going to be hard, Deardra, to let this one go."

As the customers prepared to pay for their tapestry, a little boy pushed his way through the big oak doors. He grunted in his struggle but emerged with a bright smile. Wearing gray shorts and a red t-shirt, he approached the front desk but saw that he would have to wait, so he walked over to Callie and handed her a quarter.

"I'd like to buy somethin' for my mommy."

"Well," Callie pointed to the coin in her hand, "that's a lot of money, and it can buy almost anything in the gallery. Is your mommy here with you, waiting outside?"

"No, my daddy's outside." He shook his brown head of hair. "We walked up the street to see the cows and sheep, and he stepped in somethin' that didn't smell so good, so he's trying to clean his shoes. Daddy said I could come in and pick somethin' out for Mommy."

"Okay then." Callie giggled at his absolute honesty. "Would you like me to show you around?"

The little fellow craned his head up and down, darted to the doorway of one room then ran across the lobby to peek into the other room. Deardra's customers glanced over their shoulders at the sound of the scurrying feet.

"Wow, you got a lot of stuff in here, Lady. What's upstairs?"

"More pictures and paintings and angels."

"Angels?" His brown eyes widened in boyish curiosity. "Wow! You got everything here—cows and sheep *and* angels!"

Before Callie could explain about the angels, the front door opened with a sharp creek and jingle of the bell. The fresh smell of spring blew through the entry.

"Daddy! This place is so cooool. They got angels upstairs. Can we go meet them?"

Blushing in her embarrassment for having confused the little boy, Callie turned to his father to rectify the miscommunication.

"Nicholas! Oh my God! What a wonderful surprise!" Callie fell into his arms in a long embrace. She breathed deeply, her soul infused with his sexy scent. "It's so good to see you."

He pulled out of the hug and looked deep into her eyes in a silent exchange of longing. His strong hands framed her face as his thumbs caressed the sides of her cheeks. Callie melted in the moment, happy to be in his eyes once more.

"I hope you don't mind us just popping in on you," he said with a haphazard glance over his shoulder at the customers lingering at the front desk.

"No, not at all," she murmured, her subconscious fighting to be heard.

*Kiss me, just kiss me! Kiss me here, in front of everybody. I don't care. I want to feel your lips.*

"We thought—"

"Dad, come on! The angels are waiting." Adam waved his hand as he began to climb the stairs.

"Come here, Adam." Nicholas released Callie and motioned to his son. "Come meet, Callie."

Adam reluctantly obeyed his father, and trudged over to his side.

"Hi, Callie."

"Nice to meet you, Adam."

Callie offered her hand, and surprisingly the tot shook it in the most gentlemanly way. Nicholas smiled.

"We came up to spend some time with my parents on the Cape."

"Can I see the angels now, Daddy?"

"They're not real angels, Adam," his father explained. "They're ones Callie made."

"Oh." He folded his lips into a half-pout. "Can I see them anyway?

"Of course, you can," Callie answered. "They're upstairs in the back of the loft."

As Adam hurried for the stairs, Nicholas called after him, "Don't touch any of them. They can break."

"Oh, don't worry about that, Nicholas. I can always make more."

"I better follow just in case," he replied. "Do you have any plans for lunch?"

"No, but I can't go far. I have a client coming to pick up a painting at two. After that, I'm all yours."

Nicholas liked the sound of that.

Within three hours—three movements of the hour hand—Callie had resumed her love affair with Nicholas as if they had never been apart. The conversation and intimacy flowed as natural as ever. Adam took instantly to Callie, as comfortable with her as he was with her property, which he explored all the corners and crevices of, especially the creek where he traipsed right into the water, shoes and all. Adam reminded Callie so much of Nicholas when they were growing up. Exuberance finally turned to exhaustion as Adam fell asleep in the hammock stretched between two giant oak trees, leaving Callie to enjoy Nicholas without any distractions.

"You can spend the night and head out to the Cape tomorrow morning," Callie offered in a soft voice not to disturb Adam. "You know I love your company."

"And I love *you*."

Nicholas tugged Callie into his arms and kissed her. It was the first time all day that they had some privacy from Adam's cheerful presence. Questions and answers and more questions kept him rooted at their sides, but now with Adam conked out in the hammock, Callie could do what she wanted to do all day—kiss Nicholas.

His lips, spongy and inviting, beckoned him with one soul-drenching kiss after another. Deep, ardent kisses, and sweet, soft kisses kept her tangled in his arms, feeling his body so perfectly fit against hers. Callie playfully found her way under his shirt and massaged his chest with rhythmic strokes that produced groans of pleasure.

"I want to be with you," she whispered and folded her fingers through his.

"I've waited so long to hear that. I knew you'd change your mind."

"Change my mind? What'd you mean?"

"About us being together. About you moving."

Nicholas kissed her hand.

"I was talking about tonight." Callie attempted to redirect the conversation with pure seduction as she laid a path of kisses down his neck to his chest. "I want you to make love to me. I still think about that night in the shower. If you stay the night, we—"

"I don't want you for a nighttime, Callie. I want you for a lifetime. I've been waiting for you forever. Please make a decision. We've played this game long enough. Tell me what's in your heart."

"Why does everything have to be decided today? Why can't we just let life happen and be together? Stay tonight and make love to me, Nicholas."

"Tell me you love me, Callie. I don't want your body without your heart."

Callie loved him; that was a given. However, actually voicing the words would launch their relationship in a direction that Callie feared could not have a happy ending. It would require a thousand mile move … and that just seemed impossible at this point in her life. Nonetheless, she didn't want this to end; she didn't want to say goodbye to this wonderful man.

Callie heard the trill of a bell.

"I think that's my phone," she said as she dashed inside only to discover it wasn't her phone after all.

She stood by the stairs and looked at the picture on the wall over the loveseat in the living room. Framed in oak, it captured an amazing sunset on a hill in Tuscany. To the untrained eye, the painting was perfect with brilliant hues of a cascading sun and green valley. However, to Callie, it was flawed with too much yellow and a landscape slightly out of proportion with the horizon. She was aware of her own imperfections, as well, with too much restraint and introspection that overshadowed her crux of spontaneity. Yet Nicholas prized her and their relationship—a seemingly perfect picture—but Callie knew better. She saw the black smudges of her family, friends, and work that dared to ruin their masterpiece. She wanted to fix it, make it beautiful again; she just didn't know how.

Callie returned to Nicholas and the oak tree, sat down and rubbed at her forehead as if that would somehow coax her brain to make the right decision.

"What's the matter, Sweetheart? Do you have a headache?"

"Just a touch," she exaggerated.

"Here, let me rub it."

Nicholas pulled his sweatshirt onto his lap, and Callie rested her head on it. With long, relaxing strokes, he gently pulled his fingers through her hair and massaged her neck and forehead. He felt awful for having been the source of her tension for having pressed the conversation. Callie loved him; Nicholas felt it in his heart. And at that very moment, he knew she wanted no other man but him, and every ounce of his being wanted to make passionate love to her. Yet he needed a commitment, a verbal promise of love. He didn't want a repeat scenario as he had with Pru. However, he realized that pressing too hard might just push Callie away, and he just didn't want to say goodbye to this wonderful woman. Inasmuch, Nicholas promised himself not to bring the topic up again ... at least not for a few more days.

"Come out to the Cape this weekend," Nicholas suggested still rubbing her head.

"To your parents' house? I don't know. I wouldn't want to intrude."

"We're thinking about a future together. I want them to get to know you."

"Ummm," Callie hedged; Nicholas persisted.

"It'll be fun, Callie. We'll go out on the boat, you, me, and Adam. Then I'll pick up some lobsters and crabs. My mother has a way with them."

"Of course, she does. Look how you turned out," Callie joked.

"Very funny." He poked at her ribs. "My mother's really good at cracking hard shells. She may even crack yours." Nicholas turned serious. "Please say you'll come. I really want you there."

"I won't be a bother?"

"Bring a bottle of wine and some pastries from Puccini's, and you'll be most welcome."

# CHAPTER 13

"Nicholas, if you look out that window one more time—"

From her seat at the kitchen table, his mother stopped reading the newspaper to scold him.

"I know, but she's late."

He looked up and down the street for Callie's car before turning his attention to his mother. She wore a blue silk scarf around her neck that camouflaged any signs of aging. She looked good for a woman approaching sixty; however, she seemed fragile in her older years, not the wrestle-me-to-the-ground mom he adored growing up.

"Want something to eat?"

"No, Mom, I'm fine. We'll have lunch when Callie gets here."

She focused again on the day's news and mumbled, "Probably traffic on the bridge. Why don't you go out back and see what your father and Adam are up to."

Nicholas gave another quick look up the street then took his mother's advice and headed outside, down to the dock where his son and father sat with their fishing poles dipped in the water.

"Catch anything?" Nicholas called out to them.

"Sshh, Daddy. You'll scare the fish," Adam said in a voice loud enough to frighten a pair of ducks feeding near the shore.

The little boy didn't seem to notice, though. He kept his focus on the end of his pole as Nicholas realized his son was growing up and taking on interests outside of his own. Nicholas never liked fishing, never liked sitting for hours and waiting and waiting. Never found pleasure in wondering about the day's outcome. Nicholas wasn't one to wait and certainly didn't like not knowing his fate. More like his mother, Nicholas preferred to grab life by the hand and run with it. He reasoned that that was probably why he struggled everyday with Callie's indecision over their future. He knew what he wanted … how could she not know?

"Hello!"

Nicholas turned around to see his gorgeous, indecisive girlfriend walking down towards the dock. Wearing a bright yellow shirt, white shorts, and sandals, Callie waved at them as she scanned the neighboring yards and coastal views in her trek to the pier.

"Hi, Beautiful," Nicholas said giving her a hug and kiss.

"Sorry I'm late but I hit some traffic. Your mom said I'd find you all down here."

"Sshh!" Adam hissed.

"Oh, sorry," Callie said, kneeling down beside Adam. "Catch anything yet?"

He shook his little head.

"Nope."

"Let me see your hook."

As Adam reeled in his line, Callie introduced herself to Nicholas's father.

"I'm Callie."

"Yes, you are. We've heard quite a lot about you," the elder Ashton commented, smiling up at her from under his Red Sox cap.

"All good I hope."

"All good. How's things in Sycamore these days?"

"Much the same except for the town shops. They spruced up Main Street and added a video store and florist, and further out near the highway, they built a supermarket and department store."

"Here, Callie," Adam interrupted.

Inspecting his hook and seeing no bait, Callie reached into the bucket of worms and baited his hook.

"There. You can't catch fish if they've got nothing to eat."

"Thanks, Callie!" Adam cast his line and dunked his pole back into the water. He looked up at Nicholas. "She touched worms, Daddy, and she didn't puke or scream or anything."

Everyone laughed.

"I used to fish with my dad when I was a little girl."

"Well, men," Nicholas addressed his father and son, "we're going to leave you two to your fishing, and I'm gonna show Callie around."

He took Callie's hand and led her away from the dock. They walked along the shore past some simple summerhouses like his parents' home where fat cats laid on cement patios trimmed with potted plants. Canvas awnings offered back-yard shade in addition to the scattered trees adorned with rustic and copper birdfeeders hanging from low branches. As they continued along the shore, they came upon the upscale homes—expensive retreats with impeccable lawns bordered by rock walls and artistically designed flower gardens of roses, impatiens, daffodils, and daisies. Towering decks and walls of windows provided unobstructed two-mile views. Callie wished she had her sketchbook because the scenery was picture perfect, so alive yet peaceful. She wanted to capture it for eternity.

Pointing out the summer retreat of a celebrity or two, Nicholas played tour guide and shared a few stories from his childhood summers spent on the Cape. The sun beat down with its high noon rays but the breeze from the water balanced out the climate into a perfect June day.

"I'm so glad you came," Nicholas said and pulled Callie into his arms.

She smiled and kissed him, deeply, passionately, as if she had missed him though it had only been four days since his visit to Sycamore.

"What I wouldn't do for you," she replied as they resumed their stroll.

"Move," he whispered and hoped the waves would wash his persistence out to sea for he had promised himself not to pressure her.

Preoccupied with the scenery, Callie seemed not to have heard his plea. Squinting through the brightness, she shielded her eyes with her hand and gazed out toward the horizon.

"Here, beautiful, want my sunglasses?"

"No, I rarely wear sunglasses. When I do, everything looks one color, so for me as an artist, that's the worst possible thing. I like to see the water and the sky in their various shades of blue and aquamarine, and the grass in cascading emerald with burnt umber patches and the flowers with pinkish purple petals and flaming red roses."

"Are you always an artist? Don't you take any time off?"

"It's like writing, I suppose. It's in my soul. I can't escape that."

Nicholas understood what she meant. Callie was in his soul, and from that he wanted no escape either.

The day seemed to move at rocket speed when all Nicholas wanted was to stretch it out into forever. Before he knew it, Nicholas had put an exhausted Adam to bed, and he and Callie had teamed up to beat his parents at Scrabble. Unfortunately, Nicholas's mother and father had a few perfectly placed double and triple word scores that out-totaled his and Callie's.

After the game, his parents settled in front of the television while Nicholas invited Callie for a moonlight stroll. They left the house and the laugh tracks of some television sitcom and walked down the street in the summer night's silence. The rippling waves could be heard with gradual clarity as they headed toward the beach. Their conversation drifted in and out, like the tide, discussing the day's events, Adam's silliness on the boat, and their planned strategy for the next rematch of Scrabble.

"I love you," Nicholas said. "I think it's time I thank you properly for spending the weekend with me and my family."

"What did you have in mind?" she flirted, then lost her footing and fell down in the sand as Nicholas pulled her into his arms.

"Blanket you with kisses."

"That sounds very poetic, Mr. English Professor."

"Oh, no poetry, just passion."

He kissed her softly at first and tasted the sweet cherries of her lipstick. He loved the fruity way she lingered on his mouth and felt Callie inching under him for a more soulful kiss.

Callie had told him she'd never made love in the outdoors before, and he wanted to be her first. At 34, there weren't many opportunities to be a lover's first.

"Never outdoors?"

"Does an enclosed porch with all the windows open count?"

"No." He shook his head.

"I'm all about privacy, ya know."

"We have privacy," Nicholas assured her by pointing out that the nearest neighbors were in their 70's, nearsighted, and bedded down by 9:00 p.m.

Callie found the atmosphere purely provocative. With the Van Gogh sky as her ceiling, the sand her bed, and the warm ocean breeze her blanket, she lost herself in the romance of the moment. Water lapping against the shore lulled her into a peaceful afterthought as Nicholas mused aloud living oceanside the rest of his life in order to experience more nights like these.

"With me?" she teased.

"Of course, you. There's nobody but you." He paused. "Can we talk about this now?"

"Not tonight. It's late and we should be getting back."

"When then?"

Callie smiled and pulled on her shirt. She kissed him again, a reassuring touch of the lips that everything was perfect at this very moment.

"Before you leave," she whispered.

"I'm going to hold you to that."

Callie knew he would.

The next day, while Nicholas dressed Adam, Callie took her morning coffee and walked down to the dock for a few peaceful minutes before the long drive back to Sycamore. She hadn't sat but a minute when Nicholas's mother joined her. With denim shorts, a white t-shirt, and her blonde hair tied back in a long ponytail, she appeared much younger than the 59 years Nicholas confided as her age.

"Beautiful morning," the woman commented as she lowered herself onto the pier.

"Beautiful year," Callie said. "I just love New England."

Nicholas's mother was quiet for a moment, staring out at the water, calm like a sheet of glass except for an occasional ripple from a darting fish.

"You know, Callie, some people can't ever leave their roots. They're dug too deep to ever be cut, and no matter how much another tries to tug and pull and prod, it probably won't happen. Everyone has his own reasons, and no one should judge what's right or wrong."

Callie knew what she was alluding to in her vague terms. Nicholas obviously discussed Callie's indecision.

"I love Nicholas," Callie confided as an orange butterfly settled on the pier post.

"And he loves you and so does Adam. And I love you, Callie. I couldn't have asked for a better woman for my son."

"He's a fine man."

"And I have you to thank for some of that. I don't think my teenage, sleepy-head son would've gotten out of bed on Sunday mornings and gone to church if it wasn't to see you sitting in the pew in front of us. He may not have heard every word of every sermon, but at least he heard something because he was in the building." She sighed. "I know your life has a lot of dynamics, Callie, and—woman to woman—I can see all the directions you're pulled. No one is going to judge you, but you have to remember that life is short, and if you can't leave—well, love him enough to set him free."

♥            ♥            ♥

"Appassionata Art Gallery, good afternoon," Callie said, cradling the phone as she worked to frame a painting while the picture shifted this way and that, fighting against being put under glass.

"Hi, Sweetheart."

"Hi, Nicholas."

"I'm running a little late. I'll be there in an hour."

"No problem. Take your time."

"My parents are babysitting Adam, so we'll have the whole night together before I leave tomorrow. I thought we'd go for a walk and talk." His voice held hope.

"Sure. See you when you get here."

Callie hung up the phone and closed her eyes, genie-like, hoping to wish away the day. Though usually happy in the moment, she now wanted to go back in time or fast-forward to the future. Any day would be better than today because today required a decision. Nicholas wanted an answer, and she had stalled him as long as possible. He deserved to know her decision. The problem was Callie still didn't know. She had an hour to decide her future. The most important 60 minutes of her life.

Callie looked at her watch: 58 minutes left. Leaving the frame behind, she took a sketchpad upstairs to the loft, wanting to sit by the angels for heavenly guidance. Drawing a line down the center of the paper and labeling one side PROS and the other side CONS, Callie began with the benefits of moving to South Carolina.

Nicholas. The ultimate man. Kind and gentle, smart and funny, thoughtful and romantic, sexy and passionate. He was everything she wanted in a man, boyfriend, husband. He offered her unconditional love—on the condition she reside in South Carolina, but Callie knew that if he were able, Nicholas would move in a heartbeat. There wasn't anything he wouldn't do for her, and that set him apart from all other men. His kind of love made him extraordinary, and that made her feel very blessed to have him in her life.

Adam. Nicholas's son. The sweetest little boy. Adorable, innocent, playful, curious—all the traits of a toddler that made him fun to be around and impossible not to love. He had squirmed onto her lap and into her heart with his pudgy cheeks and dimpled smile. She would be proud to have him in her life.

Nicholas's family. A very warm and loving family. They welcomed Callie into their lives with only Nicholas's word of how wonderful she was. They accepted her at face value and extended their friendship with food, wine, and conversation. A different sort of family than her own, but one that she would love to call her own.

Nicholas's friends. Without a doubt, without ever meeting them, Callie was sure that the people he chose as his friends would certainly be extensions of Nicholas's exuberant personality and would welcome her into their special circle of love.

Art. Her passion. The center of her life. Finding a niche in a new community presented an exciting challenge where Callie could once again create a dream gallery. Without the pressures of living expenses, she could reside with Nicholas and take her time exploring the area and finding the perfect place to situate her gallery. And while pursuing that dream, she'd have the leisure to concentrate on her own art, her own paintings, her own sculptures and not be worried about financial constraints. It would be the ultimate experience for an artist.

Callie glanced at her watch: 42 minutes left. She started doodling on the other side of the paper as she considered the drawbacks of moving to South Carolina. There was no down side to moving. It was a beautiful state, and she knew she could continue her art and be happy there. However, several obstacles, including leaving behind the things she loved in Massachusetts, in Sycamore, seemed too high to hurdle. Responsibilities to her family and the consignment artists topped her obligations. She began writing them down one after another. They began with Appassionata and ended with Aidan.

Callie hadn't even thought about Aidan, but then again she rarely did when Nicholas was around, except to remind her that there was a man interested in being a boyfriend to her right there in her home state. Aidan, so different than Nicholas, yet wonderful in his own way. Nice to be with, do things with, talk with … an all-around nice guy. But not the love of her life.

Callie sighed and glanced again at the time: 28 minutes to decide. She re-read her list of obstacles. Her family and friends seemed scalable. They would be all right without her, and she would miss them terribly but knew the power of communication. They would not lose touch. Appassionata. It all came down to Appassionata. It was not just a gallery. It was not just an assemblage of artistic works. Appassionata was her child. It was her creation, birthed with sweat and focused energy, and raised with love. It became a molding, developing, shaping of many styles of art into a magnificent exhibit that benefited all who entered, both sellers and buyers. But the artisans benefited the most. They depended upon the sales to continue creating, buying supplies, feeding their families. How could she abandon all who drew life from Appassionata?

20 minutes.

*Why is time rushing me? Why can't it slow down and let me think? Time. Just a little more time to figure it all out. What am I going to tell Nicholas? Do we have a future? I want a future with him. But my past and present is here, like a Sycamore tree.*

Callie looked at the angels, their splendid colors refracting tiny arcs of hope on the walls. Apassionata. Callie circled the word.

*I can't close it. I won't close it. There. One decision made. But does that mean I can't move? I love Nicholas, and I want to be with him, so who can care for Appassionata? Who can I trust to manage my business?*

The phone rang, and Callie called to Deardra to answer it.

*Deardra. She's the only one capable of caring for Appassionata. She loves the gallery as much as I do, and she knows all about its finances and the artists. Deardra could manage the gallery successfully. With knowledge of the art world and a business sense, she's a perfect replacement for me. It's an awfully big undertaking, but Deardra could do it. Liam would be starting school in September, and she would have the extra time to devote to work. Would she?*

Callie summoned her nerve and hurried downstairs to talk to Deardra. She saw Deardra on the phone, and she waited a patient minute for her to finish her conversation.

"Okay, honey. I'm so excited! We'll talk about it some more when I get home. Love ya!" Deardra put the phone down. "Callie, can I have some time off?"

"Sure. Nicholas is on his way over, but I'll just close up early."

"No, not today. Keith just called, and his company is sending him to London next month to oversee the opening of their new office. Can you believe it? London in the summer! And me and Liam can go with him, virtually all expenses paid."

Callie stood there dumbfounded.

"A free trip to England, Callie!" Deardra hugged her with excitement. "This is so thrilling!"

Callie put aside her own disappointment and congratulated her friend.

"Gosh, what a great surprise and opportunity. I'm so happy for you. You took some great pictures the last time you were there."

"I know. And now I can experience it with my husband and son. Well, Keith will be working most of the day, but me and Liam can walk and explore." She was quiet for a moment, a bit introspective. "God, I have a great idea for a magazine piece: 24 Hours of London. I'll take different pictures at every hour of the day. Can you see it? Big Ben at midnight, Winchester Cathedral at 3:00 pm."

"Yes, that'd be great. Very unique."

Callie tore the sheet of notes off the pad and into tiny pieces, ripping and ripping till she had a handful of white confetti.

"Oh, I'm so excited. Can you manage without me for a few months?"

"Absolutely. I'll manage just fine. Quint already agreed to intern this summer, and I bet he could use some paid hours. Appassionata will be fine." The next words were much harder to say. "Besides, I'm not going anywhere."

Nicholas walked in the door.

"I'm early."

Callie didn't bother to look at her watch. She was literally out of time because she was out of answers. There was nothing left but consequences.

"Hey, sweetheart," Nicholas planted a kiss on her cheek. "Wanna go change?" He looked her up and down, not appreciating her black pencil skirt, white satin blouse, and very high heels.

"Do I need to change?"

"Well, I thought we could go for a walk."

Callie stepped out of her heels and smiled at him.

"Problem solved."

They walked across her property, through the woods, along the path to the waterfall. An uneasy feeling snaked through her as she remembered their last conversation at the stream 15 years earlier. Nicholas had wanted a commitment then, and she knew he wanted one now.

"You know" he began as he sidestepped a rock, never letting go of her hand. "I'm going home tomorrow."

"I know."

Callie didn't need to be reminded. It screamed inside her head with every thought. She tried thinking about something else—the crackle of twigs beneath his feet, the warmth of his hand, the fresh air deep in her lungs. They moved silently along the stream.

"So, have you made a decision?"

"About what?"

They came upon the waterfall, trance-like in its rushing over the rocks, a peaceful acceptance washing over her.

"About moving to South Carolina."

"I thought we already discussed that."

She let go of his hand and walked towards the creek, carefully stepping in her bare feet. White balls of foam battled their way through a maze of boulders before disappearing under the muddy water, blacker in this area, the sun obscured by a mesh of trees.

"I know what I said the other night, Callie, but I can't live in limbo. I want to get on with our lives. I want you to come home with Adam and me. He was the last piece in our puzzle, and he absolutely adores you, and I know you adore him, too. I've seen you with him this week."

"He's a sweet little boy. You've raised him well." She picked up a rock and sent it flying into the creek with a splash. Nicholas came up behind her and touched her hair. Callie continued with her sidetracking. "Adam told me all about his new bike that he got for his birthday. He didn't mention training wheels. Does it have training wheels or is he already riding on two wheels?"

He kissed the curve of her neck as she peered out to the falls.

"Are you changing the subject, Sweetheart?"

"No, we're talking about Adam. You didn't tell me about your visit to the aquarium yesterday. Did he like all the fish? What did he say about the penguins with the spiky hair and the giant eel in the center tank?"

He kissed her again and whispered in her ear, "I want you to come home with us, Callie. You don't have to make it a permanent move right now. Just come and spend a month. See the area and how your art will fit in there. I know you'll—"

"I can't." She stepped away.

"Why not?" His voice held frustration, a teacher tone as if he had heard too many times her excuses for not doing her homework.

"Please don't do this, Nicholas. Don't spoil our last night together."

"That's just it. I don't want it to be our last night together. And I know you feel the same way."

"It doesn't matter how I feel."

"What do you mean?" He stepped in front of her and forced her to look into his eyes. Callie ducked around him and continued to meander along the creek. "Don't walk away, Callie. Talk to me."

"What's there to say, Nicholas? You've heard it all before."

"I don't understand what's going through your head. I wish—" He held the *sh* like a brow-beating librarian. "There's someone else, isn't there? That guy, huh? What's his name? I want to know his name. I want to know everything about him."

"No, Nicholas." Callie shook her head. "This has nothing to do with him."

"Then what is it?" He stepped again in front of her, those brown eyes of his commanding honesty. "Do you love me?"

"Of course."

"It'd be nice if you actually said it."

Nicholas moved closer to kiss her, but Callie turned her head and offered only her cheek.

"What is it, Callie? In the beginning, your heart was open, and we communicated and bonded on every level—emotionally, mentally, spiritually, physically. Even this weekend at the Cape was great." He smiled. "Since December life has made sense, and you were the one giving it meaning. But today—I just don't get how you can push me away. Don't you know how special our relationship is?" He didn't allow her to answer, steaming straight ahead with his vessel of reasoning.

"Don't you know, Callie, that most people never have a relationship like ours, and if they do, they have to work very hard over many years to get to this place? Yet for us, it's just so easy, and it was like this from the very beginning. In high school we were too young to appreciate it, to fight for it. Now I know its value, but you all of a sudden have all these doubts, have all these protective barriers up. You're pushing me away. You won't let me in." Narrowing his focus directly to her eyes, he deepened his voice with purposeful emphasis. "But the fact is, Callie, I'm already in—inside your heart, dancing in the warmth of your soul."

She stepped out of his stare, out of the corral of his arms.

"Nicholas, this is all very easy for you, very romantic, but for me, this relationship is very complicated. Moving is monumental. I have a business; people depend upon me."

"It's as easy as you want it to be or as complicated as you want it to be. Love is your choice, your willful decision. Our future's in your hands, Callie; it always has been. You're the one who chose not to see me when you came back that summer."

"That's not fair. I was young. I explained that to you."

"I understand now that there were more important things in your life. Relationships, love—they just weren't a priority at 18. But here we are 15 years later, all grown up, still single, unbelievably brought together again with the same passion that existed all those years ago. I can't ignore fate, Callie. One second earlier, one second later, we wouldn't have met again. I gotta believe God had a hand in that."

She turned her head to look at the water.

"I wish I knew."

Nicholas tipped her chin with his finger, refocusing her attention upon him.

"If you think the Almighty is gonna reach down and touch you on the shoulder, it doesn't work like that. I believe He brings people together, and then it's our willful decisions where to go from there. Love is a choice, and in this case, it's your choice. I'm bound to South Carolina for 12 years till Adam graduates high school. I won't take him away from his mother, and I can't abandon him, leave him behind."

"I know. I'm not asking you to."

"I would understand if you had a similar situation here, but you don't. There's nothing tying you to Sycamore."

Dumbfounded, she rolled her eyes. Had he not been listening to anything she said?

"Appassionata, my parents, my sister, my friends—those are ties."

"You're an artist. You can work anywhere in the world. Don't close the gallery; open another in South Carolina. And as for your family and friends, they're an e-mail, phone call or a plane flight away. If they truly cared about you, they'd be encouraging you to let this happen."

"It's just not that easy, Nicholas. You say 'Don't close the gallery,' yet who's gonna take care of it if I'm not here?"

"What about Deardra?"

"She's going to London for the summer." Callie bowed her head, weighted by the pressure. "It's very complicated, Nicholas. Don't you see?"

"All I see is that you've caged yourself in Sycamore, Callie. Taken the key and tossed it somewhere, and you won't even try looking for it. It's so sad. You have a life that should be lived, and to put it bluntly, without me, without us being together, it's no life at all. You're just fooling yourself if you think any other way."

"It's easy for you to say. You're not the one who has to uproot his entire life."

"If it weren't for Adam, I'd do it in a second. You mean that much to me."

"This is one of those life-altering decisions, and you expect me to make it just like that." She snapped her fingers.

"You've had months to think about. How much more time do you need?"

"I don't know."

He laughed, almost mockingly, as if knowing that nothing, no words, no amount of time could change her mind.

"The great thing about us, Callie, was that we saw into each other's hearts and knew how special those moments together were. Having to convince you now that being with me is the best thing totally destroys the magic. Maybe—" Nicholas began to walk from her, slowly stepping backward but his eyes still holding her. "Maybe I was wrong about everything. Maybe—" He now turned his back to her. "Maybe I was wrong about you."

"Can't we just *be*?"

"Be? Be what?"

"Be in each other's eyes, be in each other's arms, be in each other's conversation."

"Those three things require us *being* in the same room, Callie. Now what?

"I don't know." She pushed a stone with her toe and feigned attention to the ground before looking up at him again. "I'm tired and I don't want to argue with you."

"I'm tired, too. Tired of this situation, your indecision."

"Let's just slow it down for a while, talk about it again in the fall."

"Are you serious? Slow it down? We're already at a crawl. Now you want a standstill. No, I can't do that." He walked away from her. "Nicholas, don't go like this. It's our last night together."

He turned again towards her.

"No, Callie, this is our last moment together. This is goodbye."

"No, you can't mean that." She maintained her calm despite his upset. "We're friends. We'll always be friends."

"Friends?" He shook off her foolish statement with a shake of his head. "I don't think I know you anymore. You have walled up your heart so much that you can't even feel how much this hurts. You can't even cry a single tear."

"Please tell me we'll stay friends." Within arm's distance, she reached out and grasped his wrist, a bit panicked that he was serious. "Please, Nicholas."

"I can't be your friend, Callie. I'm sorry I can't be that guy. I don't want you calling me or e-mailing me. I don't wanna hear about the new love of your life, what man you're settling for or, worse yet, who's breaking your heart. I just can't do that. It's all or nothing. Goodbye, Callie."

"Please, Nicholas." Pulling at his arm, she begged for their friendship. "Please don't do this."

"*You* did this."

Nicholas shrugged out of her clasp, turned and walked away, trudging up the dense hill, out of the murkiness of the woods and into the light, never bothering to look back, never seeing the tears running down Callie's cheeks, never hearing her say *I love you.*

# CHAPTER 14

"I know what you need," Nick said as Callie and Deardra sat at his bar waiting for Brianna and Jill to arrive for their annual girls' weekend.

"My head examined? Or better yet, Nicholas *in* Massachusetts?" Callie said.

"Get over that one, Callie." Nick untied the white apron, tossed it on the counter, and slipped on his sport jacket. "It's three weeks now. Not a single word from him. It's over; accept it. He's moved on; now it's time for you to move on."

"Exactly," Deardra agreed. "He ended it. You gotta quit sulking and come to terms with that. And that's what this weekend is all about—a little drinking, a little eating, a little shopping, a lot of girl talk from your best friends reminding you there are other fish in the sea."

"Aidan, for one," Nick added.

"He's right, Callie. Are you still going to that wedding with him in New Hampshire next weekend?"

"I was hoping you'd talk me out of it. We're supposed to stay overnight at a bed and breakfast."

"Perfect!" Deardra exclaimed. "Time to get on with your life, Callie, and some hot sex in a B&B is perfect."

"I don't think Aidan and I are at that point yet."

"If he's planning an overnight weekend, you're at that point," Nick assured her. "Go buy a thong, a pack of condoms, and toss your tissues away. No more crying for you. Move on."

Callie looked at Deardra for her practical-minded opinion.

"I'm with Nick on this one. Aidan's a nice guy, and this is the perfect time to take it to the next level."

"I don't think I'm ready."

Nick patted her hand and dished some advice.

"Buy some sexy underwear—bra, thong, satin and lace. The skimpier, the sexier. Believe me, you'll feel spectacular, and it'll surely put you in the mood for some nocturnal delight."

"Speaking from experience?" Deardra laughed.

"Four sisters," Nick replied.

"Callie! Deardra!" Brianna exclaimed with Jill at her side. "Start the party! The New Yorkers are in the house!"

Brianna's smile extended the length of her beautiful face. She loved these weekends. Married with two children, Brianna enjoyed the three-day escape from pre-school videos and jungle gyms at the park. She still dyed her hair blonde, but now it was shorter, *more mommy length*, she had said last year.

Jill, on the other hand, had black hair that hung to her butt. A mother, too, with a one-year old that happily came after she retired from dancing and started teaching. Jill, though, had to be pried away from her husband and son, preferring the domestic, married life to the carefree, single life that they pretended one weekend once a year.

Callie didn't need to pretend.

"So, what's the plan," Brianna asked, hopping on the stool next to Callie.

"Well, as I understand it," Nick said, "a little drinking, a little eating, a little shopping, and a lot of girl talk."

"Sounds good to me. Let's start with the drinking. I'll have a Cosmopolitan," Brianna said happily. "One for Jill, too."

"How are the kids?" Callie asked.

"Let's get through this quick." Brianna pulled some pictures from her purse. "Get yours out, too, Jill and Deardra. Five minutes for kid chit-chat, then we're single for the rest of the weekend."

As Callie looked at the pictures of their adorable toddlers and husbands, she wondered if they truly appreciated the married life.

"You're so lucky," Callie commented, handing Brianna back her photos.

"Oh, that sounds way too sad. You're not still moping over Nicholas, are you?"

Callie saw Deardra nod.

"Well," Nick said, setting the cocktails in front of the women. "Callie's spending next weekend with Aidan, and I suggested she stop in the lingerie store and pick up—"

"A thong." Callie finished his sentence and punctuated it with a smirk.

"Among other things," Nick said.

Callie knew what she really needed to buy—a one-way ticket to South Carolina. But since that part of her life was definitely in the past, a romantic weekend with Aidan became increasingly more appealing. She was starved for love, and maybe Aidan could give it to her.

♥              ♥              ♥

Aidan stared down at the gold-embossed invitation to Tony and Eve's wedding as he buttoned up the shirt of his tuxedo. Dread poured through him, and he tried to dilute it with some positive thinking, but nothing seemed to take off the edge and settle his angst at having to see Grace again, forced to share company as mutual guests of the bride and groom.

His only hope lay in a long, scenic drive to New Hampshire. Maybe by the time he arrived at the church, he could resolve his anxiety and have a pleasant time.

"Where's your date?" Tony asked, leaning into Aidan's parked car in the church lot. "I want to meet your Brown Eyes."

"Oh, my God! I forgot to pick her up."

"You drove two hours, and it didn't occur to you at any time that you were alone?"

Aidan shook his head as his friend doubled over in laughter.

"Nothing against your wedding, Tony, but I've dreaded this day."

"Seeing Grace again really that bad?"

"Really." Aidan used his cell phone to call Callie. "Hey, Brown Eyes."

"Where are you?" she asked with hesitation and concern. "I've been worried. We're gonna be late."

"I—um—I'm here."

"Where?"

"At the church."

"The church? In New Hampshire?" Each question took Callie's voice to a higher octave as she grasped for the reality of the situation while Aidan dodged the truth. "Aidan, I thought we were going together."

"I know. I forgot. Look, I'm sending my car service to pick you up."

"No, don't. I don't need to go. These are your friends."

"I want you here." He tried to convince himself of that. "I'm sending the car. It's two o'clock now, so we'll meet up at the reception. You'll be here in plenty of time."

"I can drive myself."

"No. We planned on a relaxing drive home tomorrow. I'd rather not be in separate cars."

There was a long silence as Callie considered her options and Aidan prayed for an end to this day.

"Okay," she said. "I'll see you later."

"Bye."

Aidan snapped his phone closed and forced a smile.

"Good work on the damage control," Tony remarked, sarcastic, with a demeaning, what-are-you-doing look of disappointment.

"She'll be here in a couple of hours."

"Not if you don't call your car service."

"Oh, my God. What's wrong with me today?"

Aidan needed no answer to that question, and Tony, being the good friend that he was, let it go. That was the kind of friend Tony was, the one who picked the phone up at three o'clock in the morning that first week after the breakup to talk Aidan down off the figurative ledge, to tell him it would be okay. Here it was six months later, hoping for closure with Grace amidst a beginning with Callie, and Aidan just didn't know if he could get a handle on okay.

Inside the church, the pews full with guests, Aidan tried not to look for Grace but there she sat in the sixth bench with several other people. Looking like one of the angels in the stained glass windows with her blonde, curly hair falling over her shoulders like a reverent shawl, she sat still, focused on the altar. She wore a thin-strapped, pale yellow dress or gown—Aidan couldn't see the length from where he was standing—but he could see the pearl necklace that he had given her on their first Christmas together.

Grace sat so calmly, staring at what appeared to be the flowers surrounding the altar. Occasionally, she'd blink—a long, lazy flutter of the eyelashes that momentarily obscured her blue eyes. So beautiful, as he remembered. He wanted to talk to her, tell her so many things, and began rehearsing what he would say when they met up face-to-face later. *I'm sorry. I miss you.* The same heartfelt sentences that he thought every single day since their breakup. *I'm sorry. I miss you.*

Aidan's peripheral vision caught the man sitting next to Grace leaning over and whispering something to her, something that produced one of her most endearing smiles.

*Are they together?*

The man had a dusting of blond hair in a military-type haircut, and a square face but kind eyes, especially when they looked at Grace. And now Aidan was painfully aware of how often this man looked at Grace.

*Don't look. She's mine.*

But she wasn't, and Aidan's heart felt the hurt of knowing she was seeing someone else. He stood quietly for what seemed like a thousand agonizing hours, then suddenly his self-pity gave way to self-hate. He was a hypocrite—the worse kind of double standard. The fact was he was seeing someone else, too.

*Maybe this guy doesn't mean anything to Grace. Maybe he's her crutch, her safety net. Even I have one of those. Callie doesn't really mean anything to me.*

As soon as Aidan thought it, he regretted it. Was that all Callie was to him? A crutch? Had he really used her? He hated himself for thinking that, and cursed himself, damned himself for knowing it was true. He began seeping into an irreverent vat of perverse justification, trying to reason his relationship with Callie against his love for Grace. Aidan knew it was going to be one long, horrible day.

Callie's thong and its uncomfortable presence reinforced the purpose of her weekend with Aidan—forget about Nicholas by having a wonderful time at Aidan's friends' wedding and then completely put Nicholas in the past by having a passionate night with Aidan at the bed and breakfast. That was the plan, simple enough. Unfortunately, Callie thought the plan required too much work. She didn't know why relationships demanded so much effort to work. Everything with Nicholas had been easy—except the decision not to move.

The chauffer drove up to a quaint inn owned by Eve's family. Situated on a few lush acres of former farmland, the inn no longer housed traveling tourists. Its function served now as a retreat for Eve's family and as a banquet hall for their annual family reunions, holiday gatherings, and special occasions such as weddings.

The first thing Callie's artist eyes noticed was the atypical color of the house—a gray blue—framed by brick red shutters and trim. It was a vision of Americana complete with flagpole, porch swing, and a dozen kids playing football on the front lawn. Callie took a mental snapshot of the house and yard for a post-wedding painting for the bride and groom.

Leaving her overnight bag on the porch, Callie looked in through the front doors and saw a rather barren foyer, hinting that the party was somewhere in the back of the house. Music from the band led Callie along a stepping-stone path to the back of the house where a parquet floor had been laid over the grass to provide for a dance floor as well as a clean, flat surface for the outdoor tables that bordered the area.

People danced in tight embraces while others looked on as they ate off white china plates or sipped champagne from crystal goblets. An artful palette of color, the female guests' dresses ranged from the shimmering designer dresses to the even more chic satin gowns. By far, the most stunning woman—besides the bride—was a curly haired blonde in a yellow calf-length dress with clear, Cinderella-like sandals. She stood near the band on the opposite side of the dance floor chatting with a tall, good-looking man.

Feeling like the ugly stepsister in a rather plain, pale blue, off-the-shoulder sundress, Callie stepped towards the house to find Aidan who was sure to make her feel beautiful with one of his *You're stunning!* compliments. An eruption of laughter from the blonde woman prompted Callie to look yet again at her, this time realizing who she was: Grace Sullivan.

*Aidan's Grace!*

Immediately, Callie scanned the guests to find Aidan.

*Where is he? Does he know Grace is here? My God, this is awful!*

And then Callie's angst turned to herself.

*What am I doing here? I can't be in the same room with Aidan's ex!*

Callie stopped mid-stride and began to retreat along the same path around the dance floor. Maybe, just maybe she could escape this party, sight unseen, and ask Nick to come pick her up.

Just as Callie reached the end of the parquet floor, someone yelled, "Conga!" and another faceless person pulled Callie onto the dance floor. The next thing she knew, Callie was in the middle of a conga line circling the dance floor as she desperately tried to flee the wild procession.

"I don't conga," she said trying to squirm from the fellow holding onto her waist.

"Everyone congas!"

Callie finally broke free but, as she stepped back, her heel slipped off the floor and sunk into the soft grass. Completely off balance, with no one to catch her, she fell onto her butt as the conga line continued in full force. She lay there for a moment stunned as the front of the line danced her way. The leader was Aidan, and he laughed and kicked his legs to the side, so absorbed in his alcohol-induced good time that he didn't notice Callie on the ground nor the tears in her eyes.

An older, silver-haired gentleman in a gray suit helped Callie to her feet.

"Thanks," she said, her head bowed in embarrassment as she brushed the grass from her backside and felt the raw sting of her thong wedged in a most uncomfortable place.

With blurred vision, she hurried around the house, hopping from one concrete paver to the next till she arrived at the front porch where the playful shouts of the children drowned out the band. Callie saw black slacks and men's shoes in her direct path. She closed her eyes real hard then looked up with a clearer focus.

"Callie?"

Callie didn't recognize the face of the tall man in the black tuxedo with a white rose boutonnière pinned to his lapel. He wore a smile befitting a groom.

"Callie? From the gallery." His definitive tone warranted honesty.

"Yes, I'm Callie."

"What're you doing here?"

"I—" She hesitated to find a reply from her racing mind. "I—I'm here for a wedding."

"Yes, mine." He smiled. "I'm Tony Fiore, the happy groom. So, you're a guest? I don't remember your name on the invitation list."

"Actually, I'm a guest of a guest."

"Who?"

Tony deserved an answer, but Callie wished him away. She wanted to be alone—far away and alone.

"Who?" she repeated the question. She had to think hard again for his name. "Aidan. Aidan McGregor."

"Brown Eyes," Tony said softly as his eyebrows lifted in shock. "Sorry for the surprise. I knew Aidan was seeing someone but he never said—well, he was rather vague."

Just what Callie needed to hear to make her feel even more awful. Nothing like the word *vague* to make one feel totally insignificant.

"Where's Aidan?" Tony asked. "Does he know you're here?"

"No." She forced a smile. "He's around back. I just got here."

"Well, you're heading in the wrong direction."

"No, I—I need some air."

Tony laughed at her, totally mistaking her seriousness for joking.

"You're outside. Just breathe."

A tear trickled down her cheek. She couldn't breathe. It seemed like all the air, all her thoughts, her entire heart ceased to be.

"What's wrong?" Tony asked, now concerned as he looked into her wet eyes.

"Grace is here, and Aidan's making a spectacle of himself on the dance floor, and all I want to do is get the hell out of here."

"He's been drinking."

Callie rolled her eyes in disgust. Did he really believe that justified Aidan's behavior?

"Come on, Callie, let's get you something to eat."

Tony took her hand and eased her in the direction of the back yard.

"No, I'd rather not see him right now. I'm just gonna sit on the porch for awhile." She felt another tear slip down her cheek.

"Callie, don't take it personally. Aidan and Grace—"

"Are supposed to be broken up. He's supposed to be over her, not pining for her. I don't understand it."

Tony's pained expression mirrored her own upset and confusion.

"I'll bring you a plate of food, Callie," he said and walked away.

Callie remained on the front porch for a long while, long after she finished picking at a heaping portion of pasta and roast beef, long after the kids returned to the back yard, long after the sun set. She sat in a cushioned swing thinking and watching the sky turn black and the moon rise high.

Aidan kept his distance, never even acknowledging her presence with a hello, or maybe it was just that he was too inebriated to even care where she was. Callie tried calling Nick, but her cell phone registered "no service" and she didn't want to step a foot inside the house and risk running into Aidan. Consequently, Callie decided to suck it up and somehow get through the night—a very long night that came to an end about eleven with the announcement of "It's time to cut the cake!"

Callie sent up a heavenly thank you too soon because an old woman came out on the porch and snagged Callie by the arm.

"Come on, dear. Eve's going to toss the bouquet."

Callie's heart sank deeper to the pit of her stomach as the woman prodded her into the house despite Callie's polite protests.

"Don't be rude, dear," the woman scolded. "It's tradition."

Callie's dragging of the feet saved her from the bride's bouquet toss but not from what she next saw. As Grace stood holding the rose bouquet, about 15 eager men poised themselves to catch the garter that Tony prepared to toss. Callie knew that tradition held that whoever caught the garter would slide it up the leg of the woman who caught the bouquet—Grace. Reluctantly but discreetly, Callie glanced around the room and saw Aidan on the sidelines, and she breathed a sigh of relief.

*Maybe he's come to his senses and realizes Grace is his past and I'm his future.*

Tony positioned himself in the center of the room, and pulled back on the garter, shooting it over his shoulder like a lacey elastic band. As the men reached up to catch it, Aidan darted across the floor, pouncing like a hungry lion and tackling a young man in his way as he snatched the white and blue garter. Callie cringed, as did the other guests, at the collision.

Retreating out of the house, back to the porch, Callie sat on the steps, gazing up at a hundred stars whirling in lazy circles. She couldn't help thinking about Nicholas and their night on the beach under a similar sky. God, she missed him, and hated herself for ever letting him out of her life. The next thing Callie knew, a wad of keys landed in her lap.

"You're my designated driver," Aidan said in deliberate slowness to mask his drunkenness.

Callie wanted to slap him, yell at him, curse him, tell him that she had given up a great guy for him, but she held her tongue. Shouting and blaming would only worsen a bad situation.

"Aidan, we have to talk."

"Can we do it tomorrow? 'Cause I have a feeling that it's gonna make a lot of sense, and right now I don't give a damn about anything."

# CHAPTER 15

Callie couldn't sleep. With no shades on the windows at the Rosetta Bed & Breakfast, the bright moonlight filtered in through the lace curtains, and Callie found herself counting the roses in the room. Over 300 hidden in the wallpaper, the bedding, the artwork, and even a dozen real ones on the night stand. The house dated back to the early 1800's as far as she could tell from the pamphlet they received at check-in.

Callie tried to relax and close her eyes, but her upset over Aidan and the reception kept her awake most of the night. Sharing a strange, unfamiliar bed with a strange, unfamiliar boyfriend pushed her to the couch under the window. Even worse, Aidan's deep breaths of sound sleep from the bed added to her aggravation.

*How dare he sleep!*

At the first rays of dawn, Callie grabbed her overnight bag, slipped out of the room, and crept down the hallway past all the closed doors. The floor creaked with her every step no matter how light-footed Callie tried to be. The stairs proved to be even squeaker as the 200-year-old house showed its age with stiff joints and joists.

"Who's there?" Molly Brennan asked in an early morning whisper, shuffling in her slippers through the dining room.

Wearing a green floral housedress and a yellow kerchief covering her plastic curlers, the inn's proprietor appeared old enough to be Callie's mother. Her eyes—a silver blue—squinted to focus in the dimness of the morning shadows. She greeted Callie in the living room.

"It's Callie, Mrs. Brennan, from the Rose Room," she answered in her most quiet voice. "I was heading out for a morning walk."

"Would you like some coffee or juice first?"

"Oh, no, thank you. I'm not going far. I'll be back before breakfast." Callie looked around the room. "Is there some place I can change down here? I didn't want to make any noise upstairs and wake the other guests."

"Sure, dear, the bathroom is this way through the kitchen."

Mrs. Brennan shuffled off in her yellow terry cloth slippers, mopping the dust from the wood floor as she maneuvered through the dining room around the china cabinet, buffet, and large table cut by the morning sun. Callie followed behind the rather small and lean woman into the kitchen where it sparkled under the glow of a pierced tin chandelier. Oranges sat in a wicker basket next to a juicer while the coffeemaker perked with a delicious aroma of hazelnut.

"The bathroom's in there."

Mrs. Brennan pointed to an oak door bearing a dried flower wreath of daisies and babies breath with a blue plaid bow. Potpourri sweetened the air in the tiny bathroom nautically decorated with different size plaques of painted boats and lighthouses.

Quickly changing into white Capri pants and a red and white pin-striped shirt, Callie brushed her hair and teeth before reluctantly looking in the mirror. Her reflection begged for makeup to hide the dark rings under her eyes from a sleepless night. Callie looked away, not wanting to see her pained face and the person she had become—the imperfect, irritable girl alone in the imperfect, coupled world. God, she missed Nicholas and the happiness he brought to her life. The room began to close in on her, and Callie hurried out the door.

"I'll be back before breakfast," Callie mumbled, fleeing to the outside as Mrs. Brennan looked up distractedly from a mixing bowl.

Callie charged down the lawn and broke into a full sprint past a small pond and eventually past other houses on similarly large pieces of property with rainbows of color in various types of flowers. The town was quiet except for a stray dog that sought out Callie's affection and trailed behind her as she ran in spurts trying to escape her thoughts and mistakes; however, she soon realized she couldn't outrun herself. Two miles out, Callie turned back on the road, using the return walk to think about Aidan, which only led to thoughts of Nicholas. For the first time in Callie's life she had regret, and it was going to be an awful thing to live with.

When Callie arrived back at Rosetta, she entered through the kitchen door. Mrs. Brennan, now dressed in a green dress with her hair combed and styled and hooked back on one side with a pearlized clip, sat at the table reading the newspaper. She appeared much younger, her face dusted with makeup and her slippers replaced with beaded sandals. The woman looked up and smiled.

"How was your walk, dear?"

"Fine. It's so beautiful around here with everything in bloom and the country breeze. It reminds me of home."

"And where is that?"

"Sycamore, Massachusetts. I've lived there my whole life, though I traveled a bit in my twenties. I'm an artist. I have a gallery there."

"How interesting. You paint?"

"Yes, and sculpt."

"The next time you're in the living room, dear, take a look at the rendering of Rosetta. Someone painted it for me a long time ago."

"Rosetta. Is the house named for all the roses? I counted at least ten different kinds around the house."

"Yes, when we bought the property and decided to make it a bed and breakfast, it seemed the perfect name considering all the rose bushes. Since then, I've planted more, different hybrids with different colors. I like to putter."

"Me, too. Something therapeutic about gardening."

"Yes, yes. When my husband—"

"Died."

"Oh, no, he's very much alive. He's just fishing this weekend. I couldn't manage this place without his help. In fact, I don't think I could manage a lot of things without his love and support."

*Another happy couple.*

"Mind if I have that coffee now?"

Callie moved towards the counter where a wooden peg rack held four ceramic mugs.

"Sit down, dear. I'll get it for you."

"That's okay. I can get it." Callie filled her cup, added milk and sugar, then joined Mrs. Brennan at the table. "Can I help you with breakfast?"

"What's wrong, dear?"

"Nothing," Callie replied in her most cheerful voice.

"You can tell me. I know upset when I see it. I'm married 38 years, and if you rise at the crack of dawn, walk miles, then prefer the kitchen to the bedroom, that's someone who's clearly avoiding her significant other upstairs."

*Am I really that easy to read?*

Callie chuckled with shame.

"Oh, it's a long, sordid story. I'd rather make scones."

"Scones!" Molly folded up the newspaper. "You have a good recipe for scones?"

"The best. My friend's a chef."

"The one upstairs?"

"No, not him."

"Well, let's get baking then."

Within an hour, sufficient rustling in the dining room signaled all Rosetta guests showered, dressed, and hungry for breakfast. Callie didn't want to go in there and sit with Aidan. Worse yet, she didn't want to drive the long way home with him. She called Nick to come and get her.

When Callie pushed through the doors into the dining room, Aidan immediately smiled at her. She forced a smile and sat down next to him, trying not to notice his clean-shaven face and brute musky scent.

"Hi, I'm Monica and this is my husband Keith," a young blonde woman said to no one in particular.

She had a round, tanned face with thin, arched eyebrows, painting her with a surprised expression, and long blonde hair pulled into a high ponytail that bounced with every subtle head movement. She wore a skimpy white tank top that allowed everyone a good view of her ample breasts, and all the men at the table seemed to take a long look, except Aidan. He kept his eyes on Callie.

"I'm Pete and this is my wife Donna."

A rather staunch-looking gentleman set his glasses on the table and pinching the corners of his eyes above his nose. Tiny wrinkles gave way to a serious scowl as something pained him. Gray ran through his hair, streaks of color that meshed with his silver short-sleeve shirt showing arms dotted with age spots. His wife, of a similar age, patted his shoulder then poured orange juice into his glass.

The two couples simultaneously glanced in Callie and Aidan's direction, but Callie didn't care to make any introductions.

"I'm Aidan. This is Callie." His voice was edgy, and it served to silence the room till Molly Brennan entered with a plate of pancakes and a platter of scones.

"This all looks and smells so delicious," Monica chirped, filling the uncomfortable silence. "Molly, you've outdone yourself from the last time we were here."

"Oh, scones!" Donna exclaimed and reached for two. "I absolutely love scones. You don't get breakfast like this at a hotel."

"We have Callie to thank for the scones. She was an early riser this morning," Mrs. Brennan said with a wink.

"Callie, do you cook?" Pete asked between sips of coffee.

"Yes, among other things."

"More coffee anyone?" Mrs. Brennan inquired as she took the carafe from the buffet table.

While the innkeeper set about re-filling cups, Aidan leaned over to Callie.

"Sorry about yesterday."

*What?*

Callie couldn't believe her ears. His simple *sorry* peeled away her layer of early morning peacefulness derived from her walk.

*Does he really think that's going to make me feel better?*

Outraged, she tried to contain her anger and focused on the quilt hanging on the wall over the buffet table. Bold-colored calico hearts intertwined with rings signified love and marriage—something she realized her life might never have.

"Sorry about what?" Callie said in quiet disgust, turning to look at his sad face. "Sorry for forgetting to pick me up? Sorry I missed the church ceremony? Sorry for tackling those guys for the garter? Sorry for drinking too much? Sorry for embarrassing yourself? Or sorry for still being in love with Grace?"

"Sorry for—"

"Ssh!" she hushed him. "I don't want to hear it. I just want to go home."

"As soon as we've eaten breakfast, we can—"

"I called Nick. He's coming to get me."

"Why did you do that?" he whispered. "I thought we could—"

Callie kept interrupting him. She didn't want to hear his excuses or an apology or anything remotely hinting at a future relationship. He loved Grace. Six months since their breakup, and he still loved Grace. Why couldn't he love her—Callie? Nicholas loved her. Why couldn't Aidan love her?

"I thought we could do a lot of things, Aidan, but—"

"Why are you so angry?" He reached to touch her hand, but Callie moved it abruptly to take a scone from the platter. "I've never seen you like this before."

"Probably because you never hurt me like this before."

"I didn't mean—"

"Callie, Molly tells us you're an artist," Monica piped in over their hushed arguing.

"Yes," Callie feigned happiness and broke the scone in half. "I have a gallery in Sycamore, Massachusetts, called Appassionata."

"Aidan, what do you do?" Pete asked.

Callie answered. "He's a lawyer."

Aidan spent the remainder of breakfast listening to legal jokes and fielding questions about his legal practice. Callie didn't say another word to him, not even goodbye, as he left the inn carrying his duffle bag swung over his shoulder. Hunched under the load, Aidan lost his noble stride, and left Rosetta under much more weight than that of his suitcase.

Callie sat on the porch rocker and waited for Nick to arrive. She dosed in and out of sleep as the late-morning breeze caught the windchimes and lulled her into white dreams—a colorless abyss of serenity. A horn sounded. It was early afternoon before Nick pulled up to Rosetta in his black car with the sporty hubcaps that seemed to turn counterclockwise when the car drove forward. He parked and met Callie on the porch.

"I guess the thong stayed packed in your suitcase," he said smartly, giving her a strong hug.

"Thanks for coming."

"No problem. Some time apart will do him good."

"It's over. He's in love with his old girlfriend."

"And you're in love with your old boyfriend, but life goes on, and—you'll see—you'll get past this, both of you."

"I can't believe I gave up Nicholas for him."

"Well, if Aidan's out of the picture, go be with Nicholas."

His statement seemed more like a dare. Callie stared at Nick.

"There were other reasons."

"Exactly. Don't blame Aidan for your breakup with Nicholas."

She took her scolding and stood quiet on the porch for a long while thinking, listening to the chimes and the flag whipping in the breeze. The roses smelled glorious, lofting their scent in a calming perfumery.

"Why can't I make a relationship work, Nick? I'm so good at so many things," she sighed and resumed her seat in the rocker. "Why is this so hard for me? What am I doing wrong?"

"It's not you, and it's not him. It's just that love is complicated."

"It shouldn't be. I'm not asking for much, just someone to love me for me, all of me and understand my responsibilities."

"Then you can't have a double standard. Grace is part of Aidan's life; she's his baggage."

"Ugh!" she groaned. "I don't know why I even bother. Why is this so important to me? I'm a completely independent, successful woman yet I feel like I've accomplished nothing unless I succeed at a relationship. It's completely absurd!"

"It's just that you're missing the last piece of your puzzle, and won't feel happy till—"

"The thing is I am happy, very happy till I start dating and some guy makes me sad."

"That's transference." Nick halted her rocking with his foot. "Don't blame someone else for your feelings. More importantly, don't scrap the whole puzzle for one piece. You gotta just have faith that it will all work out in the end."

"Suddenly, Mr. Practical-Minded, believes in *happily ever after?*"

"I *believe* and *wish* that for you."

♥            ♥            ♥

Still upset over the way they parted and missing Aidan's companionship, Callie sought him out. She felt she had been wrong to not let him apologize, and now two weeks later she realized he couldn't be blamed for loving someone else. She, of all people, knew that some loves never leave your heart. Callie hoped Aidan would be pleased to see her and that they could resume their friendship … or more. She missed the time they spent together, and hoped he missed her, too.

Stopping at Aidan's office unannounced, Callie found him hunched over a box, packing stacks of green and burgundy leather books. Other boxes labeled with client names and case numbers had been stacked near the door. In jeans and an untucked blue-striped shirt, Aidan worked feverishly piling book after book into the box and then securing it shut with a long piece of the tape.

"Hey, handsome."

Aidan looked up and smiled.

"Brown Eyes, my God it's good to see you!"

He stopped his packing to get up and hug her. It was a long, heartfelt embrace where no words were needed to apologize for what had happened to split them up. Lingering in his arms for a second, enjoying the male-to-female touch, Callie kissed his cheek then pulled out of his arms.

"It looks like I caught you at a bad time." She glanced around his office at all the taped up boxes. "Moving in or moving out?"

"Moving away," Aidan replied, his voice flat, matter-of-fact.

"Away? Where to?"

"California, near my sister."

Sadness lodged in her throat and she couldn't speak for the longest while

"Why?"

Aidan redirected his attention to clearing off the shelves. He reached for a gold scale, blew some dust off it, and set it upon his desk.

"I'm simplifying my life—selling the house, downsizing expenses. Maybe I'll teach a law class or two at UCLA. I'm making a few changes for the better."

"You're serious," Callie said, her knees feeling weak as if they would cave beneath her. The lone chair in the room was buried beneath a stack of files, so she sat down on the floor to absorb the news. "Why?"

"There's a lot of ghosts here."

Callie looked at her hands. They seemed very pale.

"Am I one of them?"

Aidan shook his head, then came and knelt at her side.

"You're an angel, Brown Eyes. You were the best thing that ever happened to me, and I blew it—completely blew it because I couldn't get over Grace. I wanted to fall in love you; God knows I was attracted to you from the first day we met, but I never stopped thinking long enough about Grace to really appreciate you." He patted her hand. "I hate myself for that. I hate the way I acted at the wedding. I hate the way I hurt you. I'm so sorry, Callie. I never meant to hurt you."

Hearing Aidan use her real name made her tear up.

"It's okay," she managed to say. She touched his hair, then his cheek. "I'm glad we met."

"God, you're amazing. Why couldn't I—"

"You love Grace. I suppose true love never ends."

"Maybe, but I've got to put her behind me, and I just can't do that here with daily reminders of her. Maybe in six months with new surroundings and a new job, I'll get a second chance at meeting someone as wonderful as you. And this time, hopefully, I won't screw it up."

Callie tried to smile, but it felt like a personal rejection. It felt like Nicholas all over again. She bowed her head to hide her upset.

"I wish I could be happy for you," she mumbled.

"And you're not?"

"If you leave, that really means we're over."

Aidan tipped up her chin, and she felt a tear slide down her cheek.

"We never really began, Brown Eyes. We never really began."

# CHAPTER 16

The hardest part about losing Aidan was losing a friend who had successfully occupied Callie's time and thoughts. Now, her unforgiving subconscious tortured her with regret over Nicholas and made her question every decision she'd ever made in her life. Callie agonized over her choices, realizing the worst one would be one she'd have to live with the rest of her life. She had turned her back on love. In quiet moments, Nicholas's voice echoed through her head, playing through her mind over and over again.

*All I see is that you've caged yourself in Sycamore, Callie. Taken the key and tossed it somewhere. It's so sad. You have a life that should be lived, and to put it bluntly, without me, without us being together, it's no life at all.*

Those were the most difficult times, and since Deardra had left for London and the summer brought an end to the elementary school field trips, Callie had so many more of those awful, introspective interludes. Consequently, she immersed herself deeper into work … and turned the radio up just a little louder.

"Callie, do you mind if I leave early today?" Quint, the college intern, asked.

He had eagerly taken on Deardra's hours and had even offered to help with the bookkeeping. He was an artsy sort with a short shaggy haircut and a clean-shaven face except for a dot of hair under his bottom lip. It looked more like a piercing than a dyslexic goatee. An artfully designed

Celtic cross inked his upper right arm marking him with a spirituality one might dismiss if it were a cross hanging from a chain around his neck. Young and vibrant with a *nothing is impossible* attitude made him good company in the gallery. Always willing and able, Quint had been a God-sent assistant, and Callie couldn't deny him his request even if it would leave her alone for the rest of the day.

"Sure, Quint. Where you off to?"

"My grandmother moved into a retirement home last month. She wanted me to stop by for a visit. It's bingo night."

"Sounds like fun. Go on. Have a good time."

Heading for the front door, he stopped in the lobby and asked, "Want to come along?"

"No, it's your grandma."

"It's bingo night, Callie. I'm gonna be stuck in a room with a hundred senior citizens. Someone else under 30 would be good company."

"I'm over 30."

"Really? Well, you know what I mean. Come on. My grandmother will love ya."

"How far away is this place?"

"Forty minutes to Waynesport. Come on. What do you say?"

"All right," Callie conceded without much prodding. She reached for her car keys. "But only if I drive."

"What? You don't like my Datsun?"

"Is that what that is? I didn't think they made those anymore."

"I wouldn't know. I bought it used. It gets me from point A to point B."

"I suppose you enjoy being the paradigm of starving artist, but let's talk about a raise on the way over to Grandma's." Callie smiled.

The retirement home was a luxurious adult living community comprised of condominiums, a convenience store, dry cleaner, coffee shop, and mini theater. Multi-colored gardens of sweet-smelling flowers adorned the front of the building in a park-like setting with benches and old-fashioned lampposts.

Quint's grandmother, Nina, welcomed their arrival and gave them a grand tour of the facility, pointing out each charming detail from reupholstered sofas and decorative rocks lining the outdoor pathway to the fresh-cut flowers in the vases on the dinner tables.

"So you like it here, Grandma?"

"Yes, darling, I love it. The best part is no yard to maintain."

"Any drawbacks?" he asked.

"Well, a few of the ladies are a bit snobbish, but what can you do about that? We're all at the same point in our lives, living in the same place, so I don't see why anyone thinks they're better than the other. They use their kids and grandkids to brag about their successes. Today, I'll be one of the Joneses and show off my talented grandson and his artist boss. Can't wait to introduce you, Callie, to Adelaide. She's always going on and on about an artist friend of hers from way back when named Matty. Matty this and Matty that. Personally, I doubt he even existed, but today, she can meet my real artist friend. Anyway, if nothing else, it'll be good for her to get out of her room. Adelaide's 90, and her only relative, her son, died last month, and she's been mopey ever since."

Callie nodded politely, understanding all too well about heartbreak. She happily continued to listen to Nina's idle chitchat about the other residents before heading off to dinner and bingo. Driving home that night, Callie couldn't help wondering if a community like that would be something her parents might like. No house to maintain, no property to upkeep, and plenty of activities to entertain them.

Two weeks later, Callie returned to the retirement village and lugged a large painting into the lobby. Immediately, an elderly group surrounded her.

"I'm here to see Nina in apartment 120. I'm a friend of her grandson's."

"Emil, go call her on the reception phone," one of the ladies instructed as the suited gentleman left the group to make the call. "You were here a few weeks ago to play bingo, weren't you?"

"Yes, I was. I brought a gift for Nina to thank her for her hospitality."

"How nice of you," a gnarled voice emerged from somewhere behind Callie.

"What a beautiful painting. It's the front of our center," another woman commented.

"Yes, I painted your village. I thought it was so picturesque."

Callie set the picture on the arms of a chair as they crowded around her to inspect the framed work.

"You paint? You're an artist?"

"Yes, yes, I am."

"Hey, Adelaide, did you hear that? A real artist. Tell her about Matty."

"Oh, Matty, he was a nice old man in my day when gentlemen were gallant." Her teeth slipped and she paused to use her tongue to resituate her bridgework. "He had cancer and didn't get around much in his wheelchair, but he sure painted pretty pictures. He gave me one."

"I'd love to see it," Callie admitted.

"It used to hang in my son's home, but he's gone now. All his things are in storage. Maybe you could drive me there some time, and I could show you."

Before Callie could answer, Nina called out to Callie, "Callie, dear, what a nice surprise!"

"Hi, Nina, good to see you." The group barely parted to let Callie pass to Nina's side for a hug. "Sorry for not calling ahead."

"No, Dear, this is wonderful."

"She brought you a present," a white-haired woman announced. "A very nice painting."

"Let me see." Nina gently pushed through the gathering to view the picture. "It's the front of our center. Callie, it's so perfect; it could be a snapshot."

"Thank you. I'm glad you like it. I wanted to thank you for including me in your dinner with Quint." Callie remembered how Nina had talked of the other residents and their occasional boasting. "Nina's grandson is one of the most talented young artists I have ever met. He's been interning at my gallery in Sycamore while he prepares to graduate from the Art Institute of Boston. He has an exceptional eye for color and detail. I predict he'll be one of the up and coming artists of the new millennium."

Callie smiled at Nina whose eyes watered with gratitude.

"What's going on here?" a younger sounding voice pierced the group.

A middle-aged woman with her black hair balled in a bun stepped through the people and emerged at the chair. She wore navy slacks and a lighter blue button-down shirt with the sleeves cuffed up. Running her hand over the frame, the lady perused the painting.

"This is really beautiful," the woman commented. "Where did it come from?"

"Callie gave it to me. She painted it," Nina said proudly pointing to Callie.

"Oh my," the woman said and extended her hand to Callie. "How do you do?"

"Nice to meet you. I'm Callie Emerson, a friend of Nina and her grandson."

"Pleased to meet you. I'm Valerie White, the activities director." She turned again to the painting. "You really did a splendid job, Callie. Do you paint for a living?"

"Yes, I own a gallery in Sycamore."

"I've heard of the town but I didn't know there was an art gallery there." She turned back to Callie. "How long have you been painting?"

"Seriously since college. I have a BFA and a Masters in Visual Arts Education."

"You teach?"

"I used to teach in a school. Now I host elementary classes at the gallery during the school year once a week."

Valerie's eyes brightened.

"I'm just thinking out loud here, but how would you feel about teaching an art class here for the residents?"

"Oh, what a great idea, Valerie!" Nina and Adelaide exclaimed at the same time.

The group's creative juices began to flow with discussion of location and supplies needed. Before she knew it, Callie had agreed to teach a

weekly art class in the center's solarium. It took two weeks of preparations to ready herself for this new group of students, but Callie was more
than up for the challenge.

Twenty women and seven men registered for Callie's art class at the
retirement center. The sunroom proved to be perfectly situated as the
late morning light cast a slight shadow across the front of the room.
Though Callie began her classes by explaining color, lines and shadows,
depth and perception, by the third week the residents didn't care much
for instruction on technique. Behind their easels, they just wanted to
create with their pencils or paintbrushes. Callie didn't mind; she had the
same resistance from her elementary students who were eager to pro-
duce a masterpiece. Consequently, she indulged her adult students'
childlike behavior and let them draw or color or sketch or paint on their
large white pads. She had brought some inanimate objects to begin with
but Mr. Johnson wanted a real model.

"I want something with a face," he complained.

"Draw Mrs. Johnson," Callie suggested.

"Someone with a *pretty* face," he replied as his wife smacked him on
the arm, which prompted him to immediately correct himself. "Young
face. I meant young face. Like you, Callie."

Callie did not want to be painted. A vein of insecurity kept her from
being the subject of anyone's art.

"Can I draw you?" Mr. Johnson pleasantly persisted.

"Very well," she relented. "Draw me."

"Can you take your clothes off?" he asked in a mischievous tone,
flashing a pirate smile that evoked a howl of laughter from his male
classmates and another smack from his wife.

"I thought you wanted to draw a face," Callie said.

"Well, what's a face without the body?" he teased and grinned.
"Could you take your clothes off?"

"No, Mr. Johnson, I won't take my clothes off. It'll take a lot more
than that smile to charm me out of my pants. Draw me as I am."

"But I want to do a nude," he challenged.

"Well, the day will come when your talent has progressed to that point, and we can hire a model, but for today I'm all there is, and you'll just have to draw me as I am with my clothes on."

"Can I draw you, too?" Adelaide asked.

"Yes, Adelaide. You all can draw me, if you want, just as you see me. Try your best. Raise your hand if you need any help or have any questions."

"Do you have a beau?" one woman asked, seated at a table with a spectrum of colored pencils laid out before her. The bleached-blonde lady with perfect hair, smoothed and upturned, pinned with a diamond clip, smiled at Callie over the top of her bifocals. Her nametag, stuck to the front of a white silk blouse too fine to paint in, read Penny.

"A ribbon, Penny?"

"No, a beau, a suitor." Penny smiled again and picked up a red pencil and began to draw, presumably Callie's scarlet shirt, which now matched the blossoming color to her cheeks.

"No, I don't have a boyfriend."

Before thoughts of Nicholas completely flooded Callie's mind, Mr. Johnson asked, "Why is that? No boyfriend? A pretty girl like you."

"Just not the right time, I suppose."

"Well, if I were 20 years younger—" Mr. Johnson began.

His wife interrupted. "Forty years younger, you mean."

"Well, if I were 20 years younger, I'd be chasing her around that table. If I were 40 years younger, I'd might actually catch her." He laughed a hearty, contagious laugh that infected the entire room.

Amidst the impish giggles from the females, Callie tried to keep everyone focused on their work. However, Mr. Johnson began a discourse describing his life that spanned over seventy years as he told the story of his marriage, beginning with how he met his wife in high school. Callie listened and watched as his wife's eyes gleamed with love while he talked about their courtship and 50-year marriage, their five children and eleven grandchildren. Callie realized that, despite his teasing and deliberate flirting, he loved his wife very much.

When the hour came to an end, Callie walked around the room to see the residents' drawings and paintings of herself. Each had a distinct style. Some were variations of stick figures or simplistic caricatures of just her face. Others were more mature in their efforts like Mrs. Johnson who obviously displayed a natural talent or former lessons in art. The last picture Callie looked at was Adelaide's.

While the other residents were busy gathering their supplies into a portable plastic container, Adelaide continued to use her colored pencils, feverishly finishing her picture with a shaky hand. When Callie peered over the woman's shoulder, she saw a drawing of herself—quite a remarkable resemblance of Callie standing in the front of the room, except for one thing: Adelaide had drawn Callie with wings ... angel's wings.

♥          ♥          ♥

When Callie entered Nick's restaurant, the ceiling fixtures and bar bottles rattled from the boom of Nick's yelling from inside the kitchen. It being late afternoon, the restaurant was empty, awaiting patrons for the dinner hour but, nevertheless, the bartender and maitre de both seemed embarrassed that Callie had heard Nick's outburst. She had expected as much that this was not going to be a good day for Nick. When he emerged from the kitchen, he was in the process of rolling down the sleeves of his blue shirt and fastening the white cuffs. His eyes softened at they settled upon Callie. Nick followed her outside.

"I'm so angry." With a clenched jaw, he pursed his lips to cap an eruption of profanity. "Another recipe has gotten out. Biscottis, three blocks over, is serving my chocolate blini and my prosciutto-wrapped salmon crepes."

"Are you sure? How did you find out?"

Nick's eyes deepened two shades of green.

"*I'm sure*, and it doesn't matter how I found out. What matters is that I've lost two more recipes. This is killing me!" His augmenting tone sent pedestrians jaywalking to the opposite side of the street. "These are signature recipes. I just want to know who's doing this to me."

"And why."

"I know why. For money, of course. Five star recipes such as these bring fat cash payoffs."

Desperate to comfort Nick in some way, Callie hugged him—a long consoling embrace that seemed to calm his temper.

"I'm so sorry, Nick, that this is happening. I wish I could do something to help."

"Thanks."

"Do you have any idea, any clues?"

He pulled out of her embrace and shook his head. His eyes, sad, expressed utter helplessness and frustration.

"That's what so damn irritating. My kitchen staff seems completely loyal. No one's quit or been fired."

"What about the wait staff? They're all rather young, maybe tempted to do something for a little extra cash."

"They don't have access to the recipes in the kitchen. It has to be one of the assistant cooks."

"Or chefs," Callie interjected, suspicious that it was Michael, but she couldn't voice her theory to Nick, not with him so happy about that relationship. But the fact remained that the surfacing of Nick's recipes happened right around the time Nick and Michael began dating.

"No, I refuse to believe that it's one of my chefs. I've known them for years; they're all my good friends and have worked with me to create some of these recipes. I know they're as upset about this stealing as I am."

"So, who do you suspect?"

"Everyone—no one. I just can't believe one of my employees would do this to me. We're like a family, you know."

"Even families have their weak links."

"I think we just segued to a new topic," Nick laughed as he picked up on Callie's hint of frustration. "Family troubles? Or should I narrow it down to Maisy troubles?"

"Oh, I don't want to talk about that. I came here for another reason. It's a year today," she said, softening her bluntness with a pat on the shoulder as they walked a bit farther from the restaurant.

"You're the only one that remembered. I went to the cemetery this morning."

"That couldn't have been easy, Nick. He was your brother. I know how much you still miss him."

"It's time to say goodbye, time to let go. He's not coming back, and I can't keep holding on, blaming myself."

"It wasn't your fault. You can't ever think that."

"I know, but I was his brother, his best friend, and he didn't come to me for help. I could've helped him, you know, loaned him money, listened to whatever problem that he felt killing himself was the only solution to."

They continued down the street, pausing at the crosswalk for the light to change.

Callie laid her head briefly on Nick's shoulder and whispered, "You're still angry and hurt."

"I know. Michael keeps telling me that, so today I went to the cemetery." He exhaled an excruciating sigh that seemed to dim the noonday sun. "There was a lot left unsaid. That's not easy to live with, Callie."

"I know."

She tried to focus on Nick but she kept thinking about Nicholas. There was still so much to be said.

*If only it ended another way, maybe I'd be able to deal with the loss and get over him.*

"Though he got the last word when he took those pills that night. He said he didn't give a damn about himself, me, or anything else in his life."

Callie strained her mind for something intelligent to say, something that would ease Nick's pain, something that would make it all better, but there wasn't anything she could say, just as there was nothing anyone could say to her. Her eyes glazed over and she fought back the tears.

"Oh, don't cry, Callie. I didn't mean to upset you."

"No, it's not you." She cleared her throat and blinked furiously to dry her wet eyes, trying to force a smile that just would not come to her lips. "I'm just so weepy lately."

"Well, if I were wearing that outfit," he flicked her skirt, "I'd cry, too."

"That's not funny. What's wrong with my outfit?"

She glanced haphazardly at her reflection in a storefront window and saw nothing wrong with her red and yellow shirt and black print skirt. But standing next to Nick, Mr. Madison Avenue, wearing an Italian black suit, starched blue shirt with white collar, and crisp purple tie, Callie looked flea market drab.

"Did you get shampoo in your eyes this morning and dress blindly. Really, Callie, all those colors may work well on your canvass, but in one outfit, it's far from stylish."

"I wasn't going for stylish. I was trying for neat."

"Well, you're neatly mismatched." He moved his gaze to her feet and let out a gasp.

"What's wrong with my sandals?" Callie looked down at her feet and her black sandals.

"I guess we can take the girl out of the country but we can't take the country out of the girl. Those clunky hooves have got to go. Come on."

"Where are we going?"

"Up the street to the shoe salon." Nick gave her a persuasive tug, and they walked one block to their destination.

"Some shoe store," Callie commented as they entered through French doors paneled in lace.

"Not store. *Salon.* They cater to the feet."

"Whatever." Callie tagged behind him as he began his search for the perfect sandal. He made his way around the shop, stopping to finger a particularly fashionable silver sandal with a four-inch stilletto heal bedazzled by rhinestones sewn into the leather strap. "Please not that one."

"Well, it's certainly not for day-wear, girlfriend, but you'd look stunning in it in the evening for an upscale event, perhaps."

"Oh, yes," Callie mocked playfully, "perhaps the Ball, and the Prince and I can dance all night, but wait—I don't need to buy those. My fairy godmother could zap me up a pair."

She laughed; Nick rolled his eyes and set the sandal back in its display. A young, long-lashed saleswoman, wearing a chic pair of pink sandals and matching sundress, approached them.

"Can I help you with something?"

"Yes," Nick answered as he picked up another sandal with a lower heel in Callie's favorite color, red. "She'll try these on in a size—"

"Eight," Callie said, sitting in the nearest chair.

Nick sat down next to her and watched her remove her own sandals then wiggle her toes.

"You have pretty feet," he complimented.

"Thank you. You're such a woman connoisseur. It's surprising you're—" Callie lowered her voice, "—gay."

"I am what I am, and what I am is a man of good taste."

He smiled when the sales clerk returned with the red sandals. The young girl sat down on a black plush stool across from Callie and proceeded to massage her feet, one foot at a time. When she finished, the girl helped Callie slip on the sandals. Her feet felt and looked fabulous.

"They're gorgeous," Nick said.

"I know. I love them."

Callie took a few steps and admired them in the full-length mirror. She absolutely loved the sandals, but didn't like the three-digit price tag.

"So, you'll take these?" the clerk asked.

"I don't know," Callie hedged and resumed her seat. "My own sandals are perfectly good."

"These?" Nick reached down and picked up her thick-heeled black sandal and snapped off the heel. "Ooops."

"Nick!"

"Sorry, Callie, but just think if you had been wearing them when the heel fell off, you could've broken your ankle, and then you'd be knee-deep in a plaster cast. Just awful!"

"I can't believe you did that. Remind me never to go shopping with you again." Callie looked at the saleswoman. "I guess you can wrap them up."

Nick handed the girl his credit card.

"It's my treat."

"No, Nick."

"I insist." As the girl walked off to the cash register to ring up the sale, Nick tossed Callie's old sandals in the shoebox. "You should put a little more effort into your appearance. You're so beautiful."

Callie shrugged and thought of Nicholas and Aidan, both gone from her life.

"Who do I have to look good for?"

"Yourself. Where's your self-esteem?" He tried to sound sympathetic but his eyes betrayed his false empathy. "Still pining away for Nicholas?

"This isn't about Nicholas, but it goes without saying that I've tried to put him in the past, tucked him into that box of special memories, but I keeping thinking, hoping, that he'll resurface, you know, send me an e-mail, call me, walk through my door." Her sigh stretched a thousand miles. "I just wish we could've stayed friends."

Callie lost her train of thought as snapshot remembrances clicked through her mind.

"A lot left unsaid."

His sigh mimicked his own painful situation.

"Exactly, plus that whole notion of absence, the emptiness. One of my friends moved away a few days ago, and I didn't realize how much I was going to miss him until he said goodbye." She didn't want to confess it was Aidan. Somehow, by explaining it to practical-minded Nick, it would all seem so foolish crying tears over a man once again. "I need a change of scenery, Nick," Callie moaned, closing the book on her love life. "An escape."

"Come on Callie. Let's go back to my restaurant and have something to eat. I have just the thing to cheer you up."

"I was thinking of someplace outside of Boston, maybe a beach, me in a bikini under a tiki umbrella," she joked as they strolled back to his restaurant where Nick escorted her to a side table and motioned to the bartender.

"Chris, bring out a serving of that molten chocolate cake with the pomegranate sauce," he instructed before sitting down across from her.

"Pomegranate and chocolate? Not so sure about that combination."

"It's erotic, sensual, stimulating—just what you need to get your blood flowing to all the right places." Nick smoothed his hand across the tablecloth, deliberate long strokes as he eyed Callie with sympathetic eyes. "You know, food is like people. You've gotta push past your comfort zone and try new things."

"I can't move on till I let go, and it's so hard to let go." Callie tried to hide the sadness from her voice.

Nick patted her hand, his touch saying more than any words. His apparent empathy, despite his own misery, was noble and gallant. Always her church, her waterfall, her respite … just being in his company eased her angst.

"Life is so unfair," she mumbled.

"No, no." Nick shook his finger at her. "You can't be blaming *life* as if some unknown force swooped in and caused your relationship with Nicholas to end. *You* did it. You chose to end it."

"No, I chose not to move."

"And that theoretically ended it."

The waiter brought out a plate of sliced chocolate cake dripping with the red sauce and set it on the table. Three layers high, topped with a dollop of whipped cream and a coating of grated chocolate, the slice defined itself as an artful delicacy, worthy of exhibition in Callie's gallery. Nick handed her a fork.

"Enough talking. Eat up. Welcome to the tropics."

Callie tasted the cake and was pleasantly surprised by the tanginess laced with certain sweetness.

"It's delicious."

"Exotic, huh?"

"Chocolate and pomegranate, who would've thunk it?" She pointed the fork at him. "You, of course."

He dipped his pinky in the sauce and tasted it.

"Think of yourself as chocolate, Callie. You're classic, delightful, completely lovely. But you keep thinking that you're only good with strawberries, so you've limited yourself."

"I know you're making some wise point here, but if I had to spend the rest of my life with strawberries or pomegranates, I'd choose strawberries."

Nick shook his head and changed the subject.

"How's Maisy? I haven't heard you complain about her in a while."

Despite biting her tongue to take a holier road, Callie blurted out, "I hate my sister."

"I see nothing's new there," he laughed.

"No, I don't hate my sister." Callie continued to take small bites of the cake. "I just hate the things she does."

"And what did she do this time?"

"Well, I was beginning to think that she had pulled her life together. Not a single crisis in a few weeks; she got a promotion at that sports agency she's been working at; she stopped smoking, cleaned up her apartment, but in the process it looks like she moved her new boyfriend in." Callie grimaced. "My mother called me this morning hysterical because she dropped by Maisy's place unannounced, and she nearly had a heart attack when some strange guy opened the door and said Maisy wasn't home. My mother's mad at me for not *watching* her, and my father's having a conniption that she's living with someone who they never even met. Maisy mentioned that she was seeing someone, but I don't think she's known him very long."

"Not to side with her or anything, but Nicholas asked you to move in with him not long after you started seeing each other."

"Oh, Nick, don't go there." She waved the fork at him. "You can't compare me and Nicholas to Maisy and her boyfriend. I grew up with Nicholas, plus you all met him. And at least I had the good sense to think about moving, talk to my friends and family about it. I didn't make any rash decisions."

"Point taken. But your sister is a grown woman. Nothing you can do about it. Stay out of it."

"I can't. My parents have put me in the middle of it." The bartender set two steaming cups of cappuccino between them on the table. "Maisy's not answering their questions, so they want me do a background check on this guy. Supposedly, he doesn't have a job, and my father wants to be sure he doesn't have a criminal record like Maisy's ex-husband. That divorce was hell on the entire family, and my father is determined to spare us any more suffering by knowing upfront what this guy's all about."

Nick rested his head against the back of the leather booth, gazing upward, pretending to inspect the ceiling. After a long minute, he clasped his hands on the table and looked at Callie, staring through her in a long span of quiet.

"What's his name, this guy your sister's seeing?"

"Damian Esposito."

Nick's eyes came into focus.

"Are you sure?"

"Yeah, I'm sure. Know any private investigators?"

"You don't need a PI. Go buy a newspaper and read the sports page. He's the new long snapper for New England."

Callie raised her eyebrows in wide-eyed surprise.

"And when did you start reading the sports section? Have you given up your Audrey Hepburn movies, too?"

"No, no, no, it's not like that. Charlie was having a conversation with a customer the other day, and I overheard them talking about snapper, so I naturally joined the conversation because I thought they were talking about fish. Much to my chagrin, they were talking about football and—"

Callie laughed.

"Football."

"Glad you think this is so funny, but you weren't the one who had to listen to the wily predictions of the Patriots season."

Callie tried to control her laughter, but Nick's face showed all the pain of having to endure a conversation of sports.

"It's just so funny. It reminds me of the time that guy asked you to the park, and he took you to Fenway for a baseball game."

Nick could no longer suppress a smile.

"Well, I'm happy to be your entertainment today. It's not that I don't like sports; it's just that—"

"You're gay."

"No, that's not it. There's plenty of gay men who enjoy sports. I'm just not one of them."

They commiserated for a minute, then Callie got back to her trouble with Maisy.

"So what did they say about this Damian?"

"Nothing bad, so I'd say your sister's in good hands."

"That's a relief."

"Can I say something else?" He didn't wait for her permission. "You've got to take control of *your* life, Callie. No one can take advantage of you without you allowing it. It's noble of you to look out for your sister, but the fact is you're not your sister's keeper, and you're not your parents' obedient servant. You have a mouth, a brain, and the conviction to live your own life."

Callie nodded her agreement but couldn't admit out loud that she was none too interested in living something so empty.

"How's the gallery these days?" Nick asked.

"Real good, busy. I just sold 30 of my angels to be used as centerpieces at a wedding reception next month, so I guess I got to get started on sculpting replacements."

"That'll keep you up to your elbows in clay for a while."

"Yes, but that's a good busy. I love doing that work. Did I tell you I may get Quint full time in September?"

She deposited the last forkful of cake into her mouth, scraping the fork against the plate to scoop up the remaining drops of the pomegranate sauce.

"Quint's worked out well for you, huh?"

"Good for me, but he's struggling with the tuition money for college. He's afraid that when he graduates he won't be able to be an artist and make enough money to pay down his school loans."

"Well, that's a sad fact of an artist's life."

"We're not all *starving* artists," she retorted trying not to feel insulted. "Quint would rather take a semester off to work and save up the year's tuition. I convinced him to at least register for two classes this semester."

"Resourceful kid."

"Yeah, Quint's a good guy." Callie sipped her coffee. "That reminds me. Remember the old woman in the retirement center who drew me with angel's wings?"

"Yes, I do believe that shook you up a bit. Did you ever ask her why she did that?"

"No, and now it's too late. She died yesterday; God rest her soul. They're having a memorial service for her tomorrow. She didn't have any relatives, and the director of the retirement village asked me to participate in her eulogy." Callie heard the dread in her voice. "The thing is I barely knew her except for the art class. I don't know what I'm going to say about her." Stretching her arms over her head, she groaned. "I feel the weight of the world right now."

Nick tilted his head and winked.

"Maybe that isn't a cross you're bearing after all, Callie. Maybe it's just the weight of your angel wings."

# CHAPTER 17

Callie listened from the back row as Valerie, the retirement center director, dressed in a black pants suit, eulogized Adelaide by reading random entries from the woman's journals which she had written in faithfully since her teenage years. Adelaide had traveled extensively, lived in France for a good deal of her young life, and had returned to the United States when a love affair with a Frenchman ended. This glimpse into Adelaide's life through her diary memoir touched Callie, and she wished she had taken more time to get to know the woman and not just the artist.

When Valerie finished her reading, she motioned to Callie who approached the podium and looked out over all the sad faces.

"Hello, everyone," she said in somber greeting. "I was asked to say a few words about Adelaide. She was one of my students here at the center, and she would devoutly show up to my class every Tuesday morning. Sadly, I didn't know Adelaide outside of her art, and I just learned through her journal entries what a fascinating woman she was. She and I shared no long talks over tea or strolls through the flower garden. Adelaide and I found our camaraderie through her paintings, and her paintings spoke volumes about who she was...."

Afterwards, Valerie pulled Callie aside from the refreshment table.

"Callie, I'd like you to meet David Strysko. He's the attorney for the center."

"Nice to meet you," Callie said and shook his hand.

"Do you have a minute, Miss Emerson? I'd like to talk to you about Adelaide's Last Will and Testament."

"Sure."

Valerie led them into a small conference room and closed the door.

"As you know, Adelaide only had one son, and he predeceased her several months ago," the attorney began.

"Yes."

"And she didn't have any other surviving relatives, so she met with me recently to revise the provisions of her Will and make certain bequests. One of them was you. She left you several paintings that she acquired over the years which she kept in storage with some of her other possessions that couldn't fit in her residence here at the center."

"Oh, I'm surprised she included me."

"She told me, Miss Emerson, that you were her art teacher and that you would find the value in these paintings."

"That was very kind of her."

"Once things are settled, I'll have the paintings delivered to your gallery."

Two weeks later, eight paintings—each individually wrapped in brown paper—arrived at Appassionata. One by one, Callie and Quint tore away the wrapping to reveal an eclectic collection of artwork painted and signed by obscure foreign artists ripe with talent. However, when they uncloaked the last painting, she and Quint gasped.

"It looks like a Picasso," Quint whispered.

"No," Callie's voice trailed off as she examined the oil painting of a red-hatted young woman sitting in a chair with a piano in the background. "Look at the colors, the aquamarines and the vermilions. And the woman in the chair, look at her face and body, and the chair with bold red and tan stripes." It reminded her of a masterpiece she had seen before when she was in France. "This is definitely not a Picasso. This looks like a Matisse."

"Henri Matisse?" Quint recoiled his hands, afraid to even touch the frame. "Do you really think this is an original?"

"I don't know." Callie inspected the painting again, holding it up closer to her eyes. "It just could be. The strokes, the colors, the body image of the woman and the chair—it's all so Matisse."

Quint stepped farther back from the desk and the painting.

"Is it signed?" he asked.

"There's a smudge of some sort in the corner but nothing definitive."

"How would Adelaide get her hands on an original Matisse? You think it's a reproduction?"

"Well, it appears genuine, and the frame shows age. You know, Adelaide lived in France when she was younger. At the eulogy, remember the journal entry—" Callie stifled another gasp. "Her diaries, Quint. We could use her diaries and have a museum authenticate the painting. I'll contact the Matisse Museum in France. Hopefully, they'll send a representative here."

"Hey, little sister," Maisy said to Callie's surprise, not having heard anyone enter the gallery. "What's going on?"

Before Callie could give a fake answer, Quint's excitement spilled forth.

"We may be looking at an actual Matisse painting. Callie could be rich!" he exclaimed.

Maisy pulled her hands from her jeans pockets and clapped them together.

"That's so exciting." She threw her purse on the front desk and pushed her sunglasses on top of her head. "Is this the painting?"

"Yes," Callie hedged in tone and movement, carrying the artwork to the back office for safekeeping. When she returned to the front desk, Callie interrupted Maisy and Quint's conversation about the painting.

"Listen, you two, you can't say anything about that painting. First of all, we don't even know if it's an original, and second of all—"

"If it is, you've got to sell it," Maisy instructed, fidgeting with her gold cross necklace. "Damian has some friends that are art collectors. We've been to their house, and it's filled with all kinds of paintings like these. I could help you find a buyer."

Callie didn't want to brush aside Maisy's uncharacteristic kindness but she didn't want the news of the painting going any further than the three of them, at least for now.

"Thanks, Maisy, but for now, I've got to see if the museum can authenticate the painting. After that, we'll talk about selling it."

♥               ♥               ♥

Adelaide's diaries proved to be vital in authenticating the painting as an original of Henri Matisse. Her journal entries put her in Nice, France, and she even referred to him by name; although, as she aged in years, she recalled him as *Matty,* a talented artist she had befriended after his confinement to a wheelchair. The museum appraised the painting at $50,000.

Maisy and Damian convinced Callie to sell the painting to his wealthy friends, Hayden and Lana Dimitri, who maintained a private collection of art. They were willing to pay $50,000 for the painting, and Callie had Maisy arrange for a meeting in person. Callie wanted to make sure this precious painting was going to a good home.

The restaurant Maisy selected to meet at was considered one of Boston's trendiest, catering to the chic and fabulous—a clientele of walking fashion statements demanding no less style from the establishments they dined at. The Rave offered these culinary socialites a hip, art deco atmosphere and an assortment of artfully-created dishes with whimsy and color and served with a heaping of charm.

A block-long line of patrons waiting entrance to the restaurant hugged the storefronts in an effort to keep dry from a summer rainstorm. Callie hurried past them, her hair dripping and tangled in wet strands. The maitre'd led her to Maisy's table where Callie brushed a kiss to her sister's cheek, slipped off her coat, and sat down across from her. Beautifully dressed in a black designer cocktail dress, Maisy wore her red hair pinned up with strategic curls draping her face.

"Are the Dimitris here yet?"

"No, they're running late. What happened to you?" Maisy asked, unable to mask her appall and embarrassment. She tossed Callie a cloth napkin. "You look like hell."

"I had a flat tire. I tried calling you on your cell." Using the napkin, Callie damped her hair. "I tried changing it myself, but the nuts, bolts—whatever they're called—were on too tight, so I had to call a service station." A chill ran through her, and she reached for Maisy's wine. Maisy picked up the glass and took a drink herself.

"Callie, why don't you go home? I'll make an excuse. These people are very important friends of Damian's, and I'd rather not make an introduction with you in such a state."

"Oh, no, I'll just go to the ladies' room and pull myself together. I really want to sell the painting as soon as possible. I'm afraid of word getting out and it being stolen."

"We'll do this another time. Really, Callie, go home. You look awful."

Callie's mouth dropped open.

"Is that all you can say after all I've done for you? I've had a day from hell, Maisy. I could really use some cheering up."

"If you want the fuzzy hair and red nose, go to the circus or," Maisy chuckled, "look in the mirror. I'll call you tomorrow. I want to talk to you about Mom and Dad's anniversary."

Defiant and hurt, Callie stood up.

"No, Maisy, don't call me. You're a big girl. You obviously can take care of yourself and make your own decisions. If you want to give Mom and Dad a trip for their anniversary, then just do it. I'm throwing them a party. I'll send you an invitation." She rebuttoned her coat. "And as for Mr. and Mrs. Dimitri, tell them the painting is no longer being offered for private sale. It's going to be auctioned off at Appassionata."

"What?"

"You heard me. I'm gonna auction if off myself."

"You can't do that."

"Of course, I can."

"When?"

Callie noticed the attention she was drawing from the other patrons and lowered her voice as she pulled on her coat again.

"As soon as I can pull it together."

"You're being stupid, Callie, to turn down a guaranteed $50,000 for who knows what you'll get at auction."

"It's not about the money, Maisy. Don't you know that about me?"

Despite a hot bath and glass of wine and the relaxing, rhythmic pelting of the rain on the roof, Callie found it hard to fall asleep that night with her mind racing with doom-and-gloom thoughts over how to manage a successful auction. An endless list of details formed as her brain ticked off things to do. At number 39, Callie closed her eyes and turned her thoughts to Nicholas who always seemed to soothe her regardless of the fact that he no longer was part of her life. He was part of her heart, though, and that in itself produced a smile and an instant calming effect. Soon she fell asleep, leaving behind the worry of the auction and the upset she felt for having argued with her sister.

Somewhere in the midst of a wonderful dream of being on a beach with Nicholas and basking in the hot sun, the sound of drums penetrated the peacefulness. The pounding became progressively louder until Callie realized that someone was knocking on her front door. She glanced at the clock: 3:30 a.m.

*Who could that possibly be?*

The thumping continued with a persistent force as Callie tripped out of bed, grabbed her robe, and dashed down the stairs. She thought it might be her father with an emergency; her mother didn't have the physical strength to knock that loud. As Callie hit the last step, she saw the back of a man's head from the side window. He had a familiar haircut—very short, military style. Callie's heart came alive.

*Nicholas!*

# CHAPTER 18

She opened the door to the stark expression of a young-faced policeman. Immediately, panic infused her body, and she began to shake as every conceivable tragedy came to mind.

"Miss Emerson?" he asked in authoritarian tones justifying her angst that something awful had happened.

"Yes. Are my parents all right?"

He must have noticed her trembling and used a more calming voice.

"This isn't about your parents. My partner and I were on patrol, and we noticed the front window to your gallery is broken."

Relieved, Callie glanced over towards the two-story gallery and saw the whipping beam of the other policeman's flashlight as he walked the grounds surrounding the building.

"Oh, I don't know how that could've happened."

"When was the last time you were in the building?" the cop inquired, taking a pen from his shirt pocket to scribble notes on a pad.

"About 5:30 is when I closed up, but I came home around eight, and I didn't notice the window broken then."

Giving no mind to the soggy, rain-saturated ground, Callie grabbed her keys, closed the door behind her, and trudged off barefoot with the policeman to inspect the damage. The downpour of earlier had diminished to a light drizzle, so fine a mist that it could be felt but not seen.

"Maybe you should get an umbrella—and some shoes. There's a lot of glass."

"I'll be okay."

"You don't have an alarm for the gallery?"

"No, it's such a quiet town, and the gallery only houses local artists. There's nothing in there that can't be replaced."

"Nothing of significant value?" he asked.

"No."

"No Picassos?" he said playfully.

"Oh my God!" Callie screamed and sprinted the last hundred feet to the gallery.

"Hey, Lady! Wait up!" the cop yelled, running behind her.

Callie slipped the key into the lock, but before she could enter, the cop caught up to her and grabbed her around the waist.

"Hold on a minute," he shouted, lifting her off the ground to prevent her entrance. "You can't go in there like gangbusters. Someone could still be inside, and you'll cut your feet on the glass."

"I just gotta check on something," Callie cried as he set her back on her feet. "I *do* have an expensive painting; it's an inheritance I just received a few days ago."

"All right, but you have to wait here first. Let me look around the premises." He called out to his partner who had scurried to the front of the gallery when he heard his partner's shouts. "Hey, Sam, we've got access now."

Callie waited as patiently as she could while the two cops scoured the darkened building, illuminating different rooms as they found the light switches. She hoped that the Matisse was still there.

*Please, please let it still be there.*

She needed to get to the back office where she kept it, but glass from the large arched window had scattered everywhere across the main foyer. She couldn't cross the floor without seriously cutting her feet.

"Hello?" she called out in an effort to speed their search along. "Are you done? Can I come in now?"

The officer known as Sam appeared in the foyer.

"We just want to check upstairs."

"Can't the loft wait? I really need to get to the back office over there."

"Do you have money there?"

"Yes, in a locked box, but that's not what I'm concerned about. There's a very expensive painting I got as a gift a few days ago, and I have to see if it's still there."

"Okay, let me sweep some of this glass aside. Do you have a broom?"

"Sir, I really don't want to wait anymore. That painting's worth about $50,000, and I'm going to have a heart attack if I don't check to see if it's still there."

The original police officer entered the foyer to hear Callie's agitation.

"A rare painting," he reiterated. "I'll check on it."

"Excuse me, Sir, but there's a dozen paintings in that room." Callie grew more exasperated at each passing minute. "Would you recognize a Matisse from any other painting?"

"No, but you could describe it to me."

She shook her head and huffed, "We're wasting time. Just carry me across the floor."

He looked at her as if she had asked him to part the Red Sea.

"I-I—" he mumbled.

"Please, just carry me. I promise not to tell anyone you did a gallant thing."

Callie took one tiptoe inside the foyer. Her boldness prompted the cop to hurry to her side and lift her up. The glass crackled under his feet as he carried her to the back office. As Callie flipped on the light and he set her down, she immediately saw the painting missing.

"Oh, no! It's gone!"

"Are you sure? Take a minute to look around."

Callie had set the painting against the wall by her desk so she could look at it while she performed her office tasks, finding a peacefulness in the simple picture of the young woman wearing the red hat.

"Ma'am?"

Callie's chest tightened as breathing became difficult and she shifted into a panic attack. Sweat beads formed on her face, and her hands and legs shook.

*This can't be happening!*

The most precious painting ever in her possession, and it was gone.

"I think I'm gonna cry." She leaned against the wall and tried to breathe.

"Is it insured?"

"Do you think I'd be this distraught if it was insured?"

"Before you go to pieces, let me ask you a few questions." He sat down at her desk and began jotting notes onto his pad. "It doesn't seem that anything else was touched in the gallery, so whoever stole the painting came only for that. Who knew about the painting?"

"Umm, me and Quint—he's my assistant here at the gallery, and—"

"Quint what? What's his last name?"

"Quint Sheehan."

"And what's his address?"

"He lives in Wheaton. His address is on the rolodex there, next to the phone."

As the officer turned the wheel to retrieve the address, Callie clutched the wall. Feeling faint, she fought the lightheadedness and tried to think of who could have done this horrible thing to her.

"I don't think Quint would've stolen the painting," she mumbled, moving from the wall to the nearest chair.

"I'm not saying he did. What I'm trying to do is pinpoint who knew the painting was here. He may have told someone. Who else knew?"

"Well, the people at the museum who identified the painting as an original."

"Do you have their names?"

"Not all of them. My liaison is Alex Winston."

"Okay." He scribbled the name on his pad. "Who else?"

"I think that's everyone. Oh, wait. My sister Maisy knows. She was helping me find a buyer."

"So she could have told other people."

"Maybe, but I was very clear with her to be very vague about who owned the painting, to say that a friend of hers was looking to sell an original Matisse."

"Is your sister involved in the art world?"

"No, but her boyfriend plays on the Patriots, and he knows a lot of influential people who could afford to buy a painting like this."

"What's her boyfriend's name?"

"Damian—"

"Esposito, the long snapper," he said matter-of-factly. "So he knows, too."

"I suppose so."

"Do you have a picture of it?"

"The painting? Yes, I do. I have a Polaroid in my purse back at the house."

"Well, we're going to need it. And I suggest we go speak to your sister and her boyfriend, then we'll go interview this Quint fellow. Hopefully by then, we'll know more, then we can talk to your museum contacts."

"You want to go talk to my sister now?" Callie glanced at the clock on the wall. "It's nearly four in the morning."

"The sooner the better. If you want to get the painting back, we've got to act fast."

"Why don't we just issue a press release and e-mail every museum in the world advising them that this painting has been stolen?"

"We can do that, too."

He flipped his pad shut, and Callie followed him to the door. Pausing for the cop to carry her back to the front door, she realized that the glass had been swept to the side.

"What did you do?" Ed asked his partner Sam.

"I cleaned a pathway," he answered.

Callie observed the cleared floor and the remnants of smudged footprints.

"Footprints!" she exclaimed.

"*Smudged* footprints," Ed said, none too pleased. "I don't know if these will do us any good, but there may be some clear ones outside. Radio the sergeant and apprise him of the situation. He'll send someone out to cast some molds."

Back at the house, Callie changed into shorts and a shirt while the officer waited downstairs talking on the phone with his police supervisors.

*I just can't believe this is happening, how something so wonderful has turned into something so awful.*

She glanced in the mirror to comb her hair and realized at once that she was over-reacting, that things could be worse, and this wasn't such a tragedy afterall.

*My parents are healthy, I wasn't hurt. It's only a painting.*

Callie had to say that last part at least ten more times.

*It's only a painting.*

As soon as she stopped thinking about the money and put it in proper perspective, she calmed down. After dressing, she found the officer in the living room and suggested to him that they split up.

"How about I go to my sister's place, and you go to Quint's? That way we'll save time and energy."

He agreed without argument, probably tired and not wanting to push his midnight shift into overtime, maybe wanting to get home to that special someone who made nights like this tolerable. Callie wished she had someone like that in her life, but considering her dating luck, she figured she had a better chance finding the Matisse painting than finding love.

When Callie arrived at Maisy's condominium, she found the entire building cloaked in the early morning darkness and stillness apropos to 4:25 a.m. Reverent of the sleepers, Callie lightened her step and knocked softly on Maisy's door. No answer and no murmur of rumblings inside prompted her to ring the bell. That, too, brought no response.

Callie reached inside her purse but realized she had left behind her cell phone in a rush to leave the house. Opting to use her spare key to get inside Maisy's condo to access the phone, Callie opened the door and was immediately greeted by the cat.

"Hello, kitty." Callie stooped down to pet the cat. "Where's your mommy?"

She looked about the apartment, and there were half-packed boxes everywhere. Callie assumed that Maisy and Damian had spent the night at their new house, not wanting to sleep amidst the clutter accumulated during the moving process. But Callie didn't want to drive almost an hour to their new home. All the questions she needed to ask could be relayed over the phone … if she could find the phone! Callie finally found it by the computer but couldn't remember Maisy's cell phone number from memory.

*That serves me right for relying on speed dial.*

She rummaged through the papers and envelopes on the desk looking for a cell phone bill, then turned her attention to the drawers where more stacks of papers filled the space. When she opened the bottom drawer, Callie nearly screamed with shock.

"No!"

The cat charged from her side in fright as she pulled the entire drawer from the desk and took it to the couch to search through. Under her sister's flute, Callie found a neat pile of papers bound by an elastic band and labeled *Nick of Time.* Page by page, Callie read through Nick's recipes, his prized recipes, *his stolen recipes!* She couldn't believe they were here in her sister's drawer and that Maisy had been the one who had stolen them and sold them to his competitors. Every single emotion that Callie could possibly feel from anger to disappointment to shame flowed through her.

*How could Maisy have done this?*

Callie waited until 6 a.m. to call her parents for Maisy's phone number. She explained to her father that the window of the gallery had been broken and that Maisy would help her find the best deal on a replacement window. Callie purposely left out the detail about the Matisse being stolen.

"Maisy, it's Callie."

"Callie, it's six in the morning."

Maisy yawned and moaned, clearly annoyed at having been woken from her sleep.

"I know. It's important. I need you to meet me at your apartment."

"I'm at the house."

Her tone, unwavering, held that she didn't care to leave her bed.

"I know, Maisy, but I'm not driving there. You need to meet me at the apartment."

"Why? What's wrong? If it's about our fight last night, just forget it."

"It's not that." Callie stared down at the recipes in her lap. "I'll tell you when you get here."

Before Maisy arrived, Callie returned the drawer to the desk and put the recipes in her purse. Her sister barged through the door visibly upset but her appearance—from styled hair to makeup to French-manicured fingers—was impeccable. Wearing a white linen jacket over tight-fitting blue jeans and wedge sandals, Maisy bore the look of a well-rested businesswoman.

"Tell me what's going on, Callie. Is it Mom or Dad?"

"How could you do it?"

"Do what?"

Hurt, shame, disgust—all spewed forth in one word: "Steal."

Callie watched as Maisy closed the door behind her, trying to appear nonchalant about the accusation as she busied herself with opening the curtains.

"Maisy, I want an answer. How could you steal?"

"You have no proof."

"I have lots of proof," Callie said reaching for her pocketbook. "It's the most shameful thing you've ever done in your life."

"I just had to take the painting, Callie. When you said you were going to auction it off, I knew you were serious, and I had already promised it to the Dimitris."

Stunned at the confession, Callie stared blankly at her sister.

"You stole the Matisse?"

"You already knew that."

"No," Callie mumbled, completely dumbfounded. "I was talking about Nick's recipes."

"Oh, me and my big mouth." Maisy turned and looked out the window. "It's no big deal."

"It's a great big deal!" Callie jumped up but kept her distance, angry enough to slap her sister. "Maisy, I can't believe what I'm hearing. You stole my painting? You broke my window? What's wrong with you? How could you do such a thing?"

"I'm sorry. I promised the Dimitris the painting. I couldn't tell them you'd changed your mind."

"Why not? It's *my* painting. I can do whatever I want with it." Callie tried to control her temper by inhaling deeply. "Where is it? I want it back right now."

"It's not here."

"Well, go get it."

"It's at the house. I can't get it now. Damian's in the car. We have to meet the movers at his apartment."

"Does Damian know about this?"

"No, of course not," she said as her voice took a pleading tone, "and please don't tell him."

"Then why in the world would you risk doing something that could destroy your relationship with him? God, Maisy, you actually have a chance for a happy life. He's a great guy who actually loves you."

"You say that like it's frickin' unbelievable."

"What's *frickin'* unbelievable is that you stole from me and Nick. How in the world did you get your hands on his recipes?"

"I found your key to the restaurant and the code to the alarm."

"I kept that in a drawer in my bedroom!"

"I'm sorry. You weren't home one day, and I used the spare key in the planter to let myself in."

"And you rummaged through my drawers?" Callie couldn't believe what she was hearing. "I don't even know you!"

"I'm sorry, Callie. I was short on cash, and—"

"You were going to steal it from me, but then you found the envelope with Nick's key, and you got the crazy idea to steal from him!"

"I'm sorry. Really, I'm sorry. It all just happened. I never meant to do it."

"You do what you do, Maisy. Be accountable for once in your life!" Callie took a second to calm down. "I thought you were pulling your life together. You finally meet a great guy like Damian, and, well, it's like you keep sabotaging your relationships."

"Maybe he deserves better, not someone who was raped when she was 17."

"I can't believe you're still dragging that around with you. Let it go, Maisy. Damian deserves someone who loves him *today, tomorrow,* every day going forward. Your past is your past. You can't change it, so quit dwelling on it. Lots of bad things happen to good people."

"I'm not so good." Her eyes welled up with tears.

"You'll never appreciate the good in life unless you've been dragged through the mud."

"Always the philosopher," Maisy remarked in a tone unappreciative of her little sister's wisdom. She wiped the tears and re-composed herself. "I've had enough mud."

"So do something that makes you happy. I found your flute today stuffed in the drawer. You used to play it when we were little and that always made you happy." Callie remembered how she had asked her parents for flute lessons, but they thought she was too young. Instead, they had sent Maisy for lessons, wanting to try them out on her first. After the rape, Maisy never played again and the subject of Callie playing never resurfaced.

"I'll play it again someday when I'm happy."

"What have you not to be happy about?" The last thing Callie wanted to do was give her sister a pep talk, and Damian's entrance through the door and into the apartment saved her from doing just that.

"Maisy, we've got to get over to my apartment before the movers arrive." He saw Callie on the sofa. "Callie, you don't look so good. What's going on?"

"The Matisse painting was stolen last night from my gallery."

"Oh, man, that's awful. Did you call the police?"

"Yes, they're already involved. I wanted to tell Maisy in person and let you both know that if I do get the painting back, I won't be selling it privately anymore. I'm gonna hold a public auction."

"Do you really think you're going to get it back?" he asked.

"Well, unless the thief stole it for his private collection, he won't be able to sell it legitimately. All the museums across the world have been notified. I'm just hoping that whoever took it will come down with a conscience and do the right thing: return it to me."

"Well, if you do get it back," Damian moved to Maisy's side and put his arm around her shoulder, "we'll help out in any way with the auction. You can count on us."

"Thanks." Callie stood up. "Well, I'll let you guys be on your way. I know you have a busy day ahead of you with all the moving." She took a few steps to the door and made a dramatic gesture with her hand, pointing to the boxes but looking directly in Maisy's eyes. "Say goodbye to your past, Maisy."

♥          ♥          ♥

Nicholas arrived at Drew's house exactly at 7:30 a.m. On time and very much looking forward to a day of golf, he hurried Adam to the front door.

"Let's go, sleepy-head; ring the bell. Jason and Ryan are waiting to play with you."

Adam pressed the doorbell, then yawned.

"When will you be back, Daddy?"

"Later this afternoon. I think Annie is going to take you boys to the pool to go swimming. That'll be fun, won't it?"

"Yeah."

As Drew opened the door, Adam scrambled past him to find his playmates.

"They're in the family room watching TV," Drew called after him as Adam disappeared from sight. Still unshaven and wearing a t-shirt instead of the usual golf polo shirt, Drew motioned Nicholas inside. "Come on in. I need a favor."

"Need some time to get changed?"

"Annie's mother took a turn for the worst last night. She's at the hospital with her now, and I was hoping you could watch the boys."

"Sure, no problem," Nicholas answered. "How bad is it?"

"Pretty bad. They don't think she's gonna make it through today."

"Well, get going. I'm fine with the boys. Don't worry about a thing."

Drew closed the door and headed toward the kitchen.

"I need a cup of coffee first. Want some?"

"Sure." Nicholas followed behind and took a seat at the counter. "How's Annie holding up?"

"She's a saint, Nick. After all she's been through with me, she's going through it again with her mother, and I just haven't been there for her. I know that's shitty of me, but even now, I'm dreading going to that hospital. I walk in there, and I smell death."

Drew pulled two cups from the cabinet and filled them with the hot brew. He pushed one over to Nicholas, then turned on the television to the morning news. They were quiet for a long while, Nicholas wanting to console his friend but knew that no words could do that.

"It's gonna be okay. You'll get through this, you and Annie."

"I just wanna forget about the cancer, but it's in my face every day with what her mother's going through. And worse yet, she's not gonna make it like me."

"You're blessed, Drew. You beat it."

"Yeah, I know. I just wish I could forget about it." He shook his head as if trying to rid himself of the memories. "It was a living hell, ya know, all those months. I don't know how I got through it. Well, it had everything to do with Annie, and now I feel like a louse for not being more supportive."

"I'm sure she understands."

"Yeah, it's the unspoken understanding. She doesn't even ask me to go to the hospital, but I gotta go today." He sighed. "Death is horrible. That's the way I want to go," Drew said, pointing to the television that showed an accident scene of mangled wreckage. They fell silent a moment to listen to the breaking news.

"We're live in Coolidge, Massachusetts, where a drunk driver has claimed the life of New England Patriots player, 32-year-old Damian Esposito, and his female companion. Her name has not been released yet pending notification of the family...."

"That's exactly the way I want to die, quick and painless. Make a wrong turn when I'm 80 years old, and wham, lights out," Drew said.

"Yeah, but this guy was 32. Just makes you realize the value of life, to not waste a day."

# CHAPTER 19

It looked more like a socialite wedding than an art auction on a cool September afternoon. Callie's property had been transformed with a huge white tent and 500 chairs to accommodate the bidders gathered and media camped out for the auction of Matisse's painting. Using the press valiantly to attract publicity, Callie had been surprised by the overwhelming response and attention given to the auction. She even had to hire security guards to protect the painting.

Despite her parents urging that this auction not take place out of reverence to Maisy's death six weeks earlier, Callie prodded the process along through hours of preparation. Deep in her heart, she knew that her sister would've wanted and supported Callie's success and sale of the painting. Yet, further down in her heart, Callie struggled with the guilt of their last conversation at Maisy's apartment. Though Maisy had returned the painting, Callie hadn't had another opportunity to sit down with her sister and talk. That unsaid gnawed at her stomach.

Callie looked around at the crowd of people; her parents were noticeably absent. At four o'clock promptly, Callie stepped to the podium and tapped the microphone to silence the crowd. TV crews turned on their video equipment.

"I welcome all of you here to Appassionata where we have been blessed with a gift of enormous value that drills to the core of art and history and passion. Behind me sits a newly discovered work of Henri Matisse. Art aficionados know his paintings are poetry, lines of symbolism drawn to evoke the purest of emotions. His paintings are novels—great colorful stories of truth and love and passion, and this long undiscovered work is no exception. Henri Matisse was one of the most prolific artists of all time. He lived from 1869 to 1954, and during most of that time, created images rooted in tradition yet transcending all time.

"I could go on and on about the man and artist called Matisse, but I know how anxious all of you are to begin this auction. That being said, we'll start the bidding at $50,000." Callie nudged Quint, who proudly stood next to her in a blue shirt with a Picasso-inspired tie, and whispered to him. "Your college tuition is no longer a concern.…"

In the heart of South Carolina, Nicholas tucked Adam into bed and returned downstairs to watch TV and grade some papers. When the phone rang, his heart jumped in anticipation of hearing Callie's voice but, like every other phone call since June, it was not her voice on the line.

"Hey, Nick, it's Drew. Turn on the news. Your Callie just put Sycamore on the map. Call me back later."

Nicholas changed the channels until he saw Callie's face on the TV. The camera zoomed out as Nicholas watched Callie hug some guy in a blue shirt, then the camera panned the throng of people in her yard before settling its focus on the reporter.

"That was Callista Emerson, the owner of *Appassionata*, where tonight another page of art history has been turned. She unearthed a treasure and has auctioned off the original painting by Henri Matisse for $228,000. The new owner, Brad Ford, an avid collector, says he'll add this piece to his private collection."

Nicholas used the remote to turn off the television. It was nice to see Callie's face for a moment, happy, smiling in that carefree sort of way that labeled her life perfect just the way it was. However, seeing someone else receive her attention and her hug—no matter how innocent—though, it didn't look that innocent—hurt.

*Another page in art history*, Nicholas thought, *and another page in Callie's life written in a book that I can no longer read.*

The two-second glimpse of her on TV confirmed she had survived the breakup and gotten on with her life.

*Maybe it's time I do the same.*

A week later, Nicholas had taken the picture of Callie that he kept by his bed and put it in the drawer. He was moving on, and tonight marked a monumental moment: a first date with a woman name Zendra Potter. Annie had played matchmaker, and convinced Nicholas that Zendra would make him forget about Callie.

Glancing at his watch—7:45 pm—waiting for his blind date, who was now 15 minutes late, Nicholas doubted this was the way to forget about Callie. Ready to flee the restaurant with an onslaught of good judgment, prepared to justify his escape by blaming Zendra's lateness, he downed his drink before catching sight of the young woman entering the restaurant. Rather pretty with long black hair, Zendra wore white pants and a long pink wispy-tailed shirt that caught the breeze as she hurried to the table. Nicholas was glad he hadn't left.

"Hi, you must be Nick. You're just as Annie described."

She plopped her purse and keys on the table and nearly knocked over her water glass. Nicholas reached out to steady it.

"Hi."

"Sorry I'm late, but I was out of perfume. I just feel naked without my perfume, so I made a pitstop at the mall. It was so crowded, and I couldn't find a parking spot, so I just said 'F' it, and parked in the handicap zone." She barely took a breath and sat down. "The store I usually buy my perfume in, The Scent Factory, was out of stock, so I had to go to The Nose Knows. Have you heard of it?"

"No," he answered, struck dumb by her babbling.

"Well, good thing. Let me tell you that it's this overpriced store for sure, and I wound up paying $20 more than usual, but at least I don't feel naked. Wouldn't want to be naked on a first date—well, at least not at the beginning."

Zendra laughed—a sultry, manly type laugh, atypical of her girly-girl attire and personality.

Nicholas forced a smile, wishing he could ask for the check and be on his way.

She continued with her story and after what seemed like an hour later, began another long yarn about Annie and her matchmaking. He glanced at his watch again—8:00 pm! Nicholas motioned for the waiter. He needed another drink.

Three unfortunate blind dates later, Nicholas sat at the Thanksgiving table at Annie and Drew's house searching his mind for something to be thankful for besides his son … and his family … and his friends … and his job … and his home …

*Okay, I have a lot to be thankful for, then why do I feel so sad?*

He knew the answer to that, and it had everything to do with love, and he just didn't want to think about it anymore. There was a void that no one seemed to fill.

"Earth to Nick. Did you hear what I said?" Annie asked as she passed him a basket of bread. "You're a million miles away."

"No, Aunt Annie," Adam piped in. "Dad's a thousand miles away. He says that all the time."

Annie smiled and rolled her eyes, mumbling under her breath, "Get over her already."

Drew carried in the turkey and began carving it. The skin crackled as he separated the legs, and juices poured from the breast with every slice of the knife. Drew's sons, oblivious to the artful carving of the turkey, pretended to be samurais and fenced playfully with their forks until their mother walked into the dining room with the last serving bowl and set it on the table.

"Boys, behave yourselves," Annie scolded as she sat down next to Nicholas and waited for Drew to finish carving the turkey.

"You baked a beautiful bird, Annie," Nicholas complimented as he refilled his glass with wine. "Thanks again for inviting me and Adam."

"We're happy to have you here with us."

"It's getting to be a regular occurrence. It seems I spend all the major holidays with you. I'm going to have to think of some way to repay you or at least start chipping in for your food bill."

"Don't be silly," Annie chirped as she began to prepare her sons' plates, dishing out mashed potatoes, stuffing, corn, and biscuits. "Well, ya know," she said confidentially in a hushed voice to Nicholas, "you could do me one favor."

"Anything."

"Take out my friend Shannon."

"Not another blind date," he whined softly.

"It's not a blind date," Annie whispered. "You already met her. She was the pretty brunette at Drew's birthday party last month."

"Oh her." Nicholas remembered her as being slim and attractive and having a rather sexy, pouty mouth. "I'll think about it."

"Please think about it. She's pretty and nice, and the holidays are approaching and you don't want to be alone. How about we double date on Saturday?"

"No, I can't," Nicholas said, relieved to have an honest excuse. "Adam and I are going to New York City. One of my former students published a book, and he's having a booksigning at the Barnes and Noble there."

"What kind of book?" she asked.

"A non-fiction, *Cooking for Kings*, which relates the history of France through the chefs of the palace kitchens. I'll bring you back a signed copy."

"What about your writing?" Drew inquired. "Finished with that manuscript yet?"

"I'm working on it. Considering I have no social life, I hope to be done by Christmas."

Annie leaned over Nicholas's shoulder and whispered, "I have a remedy for that social life problem. Her name is Shannon."

♥          ♥          ♥

New York City stood cold among the blistering winds that ran down the avenues with fury, chasing typical tourists indoors for escape from the cold. Two days earlier the wind would have wrecked havoc on the giant balloons that graced Fifth Avenue during the Macy's parade. The temperature had dropped from an unseasonably 50 degrees on Thanksgiving to 21 degrees with a wind chill factor that dipped into the teens. Trying to keep Adam sufficiently warm, Nicholas battled the crowds inside the stores before facing the winter weather as they made their way down the city streets.

"It's cold, Daddy," Adam said with his face buried behind his scarf.

"This is nothing compared to the cold weather where I grew up," he replied, realizing that his son had already grown accustomed to the more mild climate of South Carolina.

"Can we see the Christmas tree now?"

"After the bookstore, we'll head over to Rockefeller Center. But the tree's not lit up yet. They light it up next week."

"But we'll be home by then," he whined at they stood at the corner waiting to cross the street, his eyes two snow globes wide with curiosity at hearing music being piped to the streets from some nameless store.

"We can watch it on TV, and you can tell all your friends at school that you saw the tree in person."

"When are we gonna put our tree up, Daddy?"

"Soon, Adam."

The fact remained that Nicholas was not in the Christmas mood and had hoped this trip to New York would put him in the holiday spirit. The light changed to green, and Nicholas scooped up Adam to save him from stepping in a puddle. They kept pace with the horde of people moving along the sidewalk. The cold bit at Nicholas's face, and he welcomed the sight of the bookstore, festively decorated with huge wreaths, pine swags, and elaborate gold and red bows.

Inside, glimpsing his former student sitting at a table with a stack of books on either side of him, Nicholas weaved through the customers and the velvet ropes and took his place at the end of the line. Adam pulled off his hat and gloves and unzipped his blue jacket.

"Daddy, where's the kids' section?"

"After we talk to my friend, we'll find the children's section and pick out a few books for you." Nicholas patted Adam's head and smoothed the staticy strands of hair standing on end.

Bookstores provided an instant warmth, a comfort of home that Nicholas loved. The writer in him came alive as he looked about the building and all the books that lined the shelves and tables. Appreciative of all those who opened their souls to publish their works, Nicholas glanced around at these written legacies which stood at varying heights, saluting, commanding respect and piquing interest with their attractive covers and intriguing titles. He smiled knowing that his own contribution to the literary world sat among these others, and he reaffirmed to finish his next manuscript before the end of the year.

"Daddy, it's our turn." Tugging at his father's hand, Adam pulled him to the author's table.

"Professor Ashton! What a nice surprise!" the young man exclaimed and stood up to shake Nicholas's hand. The college student had aged into a man with a mustache, serious eyes, and hearty handshake.

"Stephen, congratulations on your book. I'm so proud of you."

"Thank you. That means a lot to me." He sat back down. "Are you still teaching at the university or are you living in these parts now?"

"Still teaching. My son and I planned this trip around your booksigning. I just had to say in person how happy I am to see you live out your dream. How's the marketing going?"

"The plan is eight cities in two months. Lots of booksignings and a few radio and TV interviews. I hope I can keep up with the schedule. It doesn't leave me much time for writing."

"What's your next project?"

"I'm working on a US version: *Cooking for Presidents*."

"Sounds like another bestseller." Nicholas smiled. "Do you have any plans tonight? Would you like to have dinner with me and my son?"

"I'd love to, Professor, but my wife is in town, and we have tickets to a show." He opened up the book and turned to the title page, busying himself with an inscription. After a minute he looked up and handed the book to Nicholas. "It's really great to see you again."

"You, too. Good luck with the book and call me when you're in my neck of the woods. We'll have you as a guest speaker in my English classes."

Stephen laughed, sounding much like the student Nicholas remembered, jovial and witty.

"Everything I learned, I learned from you, Professor. You're the expert, not me."

Nicholas walked with Adam towards the children's section of the store and thought about what his former student had just said. *An expert?* On English perhaps, but an ignorant on relationships.

*He's married; I'm not. What am I doing wrong?*

As Nicholas passed the art section, he glanced down the row of books. At the end of the aisle, he saw the back of a brunette and instantly thought of Callie, feeling her presence as if she were blowing kisses on the back of his neck.

*Maybe that's what I'm doing wrong.*

"Come on, Daddy. I see the kids' section!"

Nicholas flipped open his cell phone and called Annie. No one answered but he left a message.

"Hi, it's me. New York is great—cold, but great. I've been thinking about—well, lots of things. Go ahead with that double date with Shannon. Any day this week is good for me. We'll be home tomorrow, so call me then. Bye."

It was time to make changes, and today seemed like a good day to start.

♥         ♥         ♥

"Merry Christmas," Callie said as she took a seat at Nick's bar and pushed a red wrapped present in his direction.

With a furrowed brow, Nick eyed her suspiciously.

"You're about a month early for that. We're still eating turkey leftovers at my house."

Callie pointed to the Christmas tree in the corner of the restaurant.

"The tree's up, so it's official. The holiday season is here."

"It's a Douglas Fir. It smells great, doesn't it?"

She stared a moment at the tree and commented, "I think it's a bit skewed; it's leaning slightly to the left."

"Obviously, it's a male tree. Why don't you go brush up against it, Callie? I'm sure it'll stand erect," he joked.

"I'm way out of practice," she laughed, wishing it weren't so funny. "You have a better way with men than I do. How's Michael? How was your Thanksgiving?"

"He's great." Nick poured her a cup of coffee. "We drove down to Connecticut to my mother's house, and my sisters showed up with their families, and it was really nice to all be together."

"They like Michael?"

"Everyone loves Michael, including me. I'm real happy."

"I'm glad you're happy. You deserve it."

Callie tore open two packets of sugar and emptied the contents into her cup.

"And how was your Thanksgiving?"

"It was wonderful not having to spend it with my parents. They're still so doom and gloom about Maisy's death, so it was great being in New York with Brianna and her family. She and I traveled into New York City yesterday, did some shopping and saw a show. Which brings me to this." Callie tapped Nick's gift. "Open it."

"It's not Christmas."

"It's *early* Christmas. I'm doing all I can to get myself in the mood. I have *three* trees to put up—mine, my parents, and the gallery, and I just dread having to untangle all those lights."

"Just do what I do every year. At the end of the season, I simply toss all the lights in the garbage. It's cheaper and less stressful to buy them new each year."

Callie laughed.

"I do believe the Christmas tree lights may be the only thing that keeps me out of heaven."

"There's probably a Christmas tree hell where there's thousands of trees waiting to be decorated, and then afterwards the devil walks by and zaps a bulb, and the whole strand of lights go out," he joked as he ripped open the present. "Hey, a cookbook, *Cooking for Kings*."

"Signed by the author. It's the history of France through the recipes of palace chefs."

"You didn't see a book titled, *Nick's Recipes*, did you? I still think someone's out there publishing my recipes."

"You haven't heard of anymore restaurants copying your dishes, have you?"

"No, it's been quiet since the summer. I hope whoever stole them got hit by a bus."

"Nick, that's an awful thing to say," Callie said as Maisy's tragic death crossed her mind. "Let's just hope that whoever did it had a moment with the Lord and shredded the recipes."

"I can only hope." He flipped through the pages. "This is really nice, Callie. Thanks."

"I had to stand in a long line to have that signed, but for you," she breathed a dramatic sigh, "anything."

Nick leaned in toward Callie and whispered, "Don't look now, but a rather good looking man just walked in, and I do believe you've caught his attention."

Callie looked over her shoulder at the young man in a green plaid sweater and black pants. He had black hair, kind eyes, and charming smile.

"He's not my type," she replied softly to Nick.

"Nonsense. You haven't dated since—" he swallowed the words, and Callie appreciated his avoidance of speaking the name. "It's time you got back on that horse, my dear, and started riding again. And let's select a different breed; your usual *types* don't seem to be working. It's time for a change, Callie, and today seems like a good day to start."

# CHAPTER 20

The package had sat on her desk all afternoon, teasing her with its shiny green and red paper. *Open me! Open me!* It kept calling to her, beckoning her to view its contents, but Callie wanted to wait till she was in the privacy of her home.

"You haven't opened it yet?" Deardra asked impatiently. "I would have tore into it by now. Aren't you the least bit curious what your old boyfriend sent you for Christmas?"

"I still can't believe you opened the UPS box it came in."

"I'm sorry, but I told you I needed the box for one of your angels I was shipping out. It was the perfect size."

"Are you sure there wasn't anything else in the box? A card or something?"

"No, Callie, just the book."

"And how do you know it's a book?"

"It feels like a book. It's shaped that way, and there's no jingle or rattle."

"You shook it?" Callie asked with surprise.

"I was curious. Besides, me and my son do it all the time. We're getting pretty good at figuring out what's inside the boxes under our Christmas tree."

"That's horrible," Callie said with mock disapproval as Deardra bowed her head in similar remorse. Callie pulled out a present from under her desk and handed it to Deardra. "Here, shake this. What did I get you?"

Deardra gave the box a gentle shake, then looked up and whispered. "A digital camera."

"Oh my God! You knew that by shaking?"

She shrugged; a rosy facial tone revealed her embarrassment.

"Not really. I peeked a few days ago."

"You didn't!"

"I did. I'm sorry, Callie, but I'm so excited about it. I really wanted a new one. Thank you."

"You're welcome."

"I feel so foolish, you know, at 34 still getting excited over a camera."

"It's your passion, Deardra. It'll excite you your whole life. Now go home and have a Merry Christmas and start taking pictures with that camera."

"Thank you again." She pulled on her coat and hugged Callie. "Merry Christmas and go open your book."

Deardra left and Callie locked up the gallery. Walking through the shoveled path to her house, Callie smiled at the thought of Nicholas sending her his book or manuscript. He had reached out to her, and that meant everything to her. It warmed her to the core of her lonely heart. He was ready to be friends again.

Curled up in front of the fireplace, Callie peeled away the red foil paper; Deardra had been right in her deduction. It was a book—an unpublished manuscript entitled "Borrowed Time." Callie turned the title page and read the inscription.

✑

*Dear Brown Eyes,*

*When I returned to California, I resumed my writing—something I had shelved in my pursuit of law and the niceties it afforded me. I suppose I learned from you that the most important things in life are not for sale.*

*Anyway, here's my attempt at fiction. Hope you enjoy the story. I have a meeting with a literary agent after the New Year. Call me with your thoughts as I value your opinion. (831-555-1143)*

*Missing New England and your brown eyes, Aidan*

*Aidan.*

Not Nicholas. Callie was immediately sad and happy at the same time. When Deardra had said *old boyfriend,* Nicholas came to mind, not Aidan. To hear from him after all this time, to know that he had gotten his life together, to remember their time together, all brought a smile to her face. She didn't waste a minute, and began reading his story. It was the next day, Christmas Eve, at 9:00 p.m. that Callie slammed the book shut and reached for the phone.

Aidan had just arrived home after a five-mile jog and was headed for the shower when he heard the phone ringing. He thought about letting the answering machine take a message—it being Christmas Eve and he was already late to his sister's house for dinner—but he opted to answer it.

"Hello?"

"You killed your heroine? Aidan, you can't kill your heroine!"

He recognized the voice at once, though he was more accustomed to a less agitated tone.

"Brown Eyes, I'm fine. Thanks for asking."

She chuckled at his pointed sarcasm, and when Aidan closed his eyes, he could almost see her smile. He missed that smile and those brown eyes.

"Oh, sorry, Aidan," she apologized. "How are you?"

"I'm great. How's everything in Massachusetts?"

Continuing up the stairs, taking them two at a time, he maneuvered through the hallway blindly as he pulled his t-shirt over his head. Aidan sat down on the bed and unlaced his sneakers. Sweat dripped from his forehead onto the floor, and he used the t-shirt to wipe his face.

"Everything's fine. Cold. It's snowing as we speak."

"I'm jealous. It's warm and sunny in California. In fact, I just got in from a jog."

"Oh, is this a bad time? You can call me back."

"No, it's a fine time. Actually, it's long overdue. I should've kept in touch." Now it was he who was apologizing. "I got out here and immersed myself in anything and everything to keep from thinking about what I left behind. But I learned you can't run from ghosts; they tend to follow behind. I was pretty miserable the first three months out here, then I started writing, and it turned out to be very therapeutic, a catharses of sorts."

"No more ghosts?"

Aidan laughed.

"Writing tends to chase them away. And how about you? How's the art business?"

"Business is good—great, actually. Ever since September with all the publicity over the Matisse auction, the gallery's been so busy. In fact, we created a website with an online catalog to serve the out-of-state customers."

"Matisse auction?" he asked, pulling off his socks, one by one, and tossing them into the heap of dirty clothes sitting in the laundry basket near the entrance to the bathroom.

"I can't believe you didn't read about it or see it on TV. I think every major television station and newspaper had reporters camping out in my yard that weekend."

"Really?"

"It was crazy. Looking back, I still can't believe that I pulled it off, but I did. It was a lot of work, but it was a great success."

"So what was the final bid?"

"$228,000."

"Amazing! Someone paid that much for a painting?"

"Not just a painting. A Matisse."

"Well, good for you." Aidan congratulated her. "I guess that diamond ring I gave you last Christmas had some mythological power after all. How did you get your hands on a Matisse?"

"Gosh, that's a long story, but suffice it to say that it was a kind gift that turned out to be a magnificent discovery." Her apparent excitement turned to sarcasm. "So, Aidan, you don't watch TV out there in the land of TV? I suppose the next time we're out together and someone asks what you do for a living, I can tell people that you're a monk."

"Always a jokester," he chuckled. "I'm still practicing law, but I spend a lot of time writing."

She took a deep breath as if summoning courage.

"I got your manuscript."

"Yes, I see that. And you don't like the ending?"

"I *hate* the ending. You can't kill her off, Aidan. Why in the world would you kill her? I just don't understand it. She finally comes to terms with her life, and you go and end it, take it all away from her. Why? Why did you do that?"

"I was making a point," he replied.

"A point? What point?" Her distress returned. "That you don't like happy endings?"

"That sometimes life passes you by." He knew that was the story of his life, and putting it in print helped him remember not to make the same mistake twice, if he was so lucky as to actually get a second chance. "It underscores the title of the book, *Borrowed Time*. We're all living that way, just some make better use of their time than others."

"Oh, Aidan."

Her voice faded off and then he heard sniffling.

"Are you okay? Are you crying?"

"I think life's passed me by."

"How so? You have a wonderful life."

"Oh, you know," Callie said quietly as the words caught in her throat. "I'm sitting home alone on Christmas Eve reading your manuscript. That's not quite the life I planned for myself at 34. This used to be my favorite holiday; now I just want it to be over. I feel like life's passed me by, that I let it pass me, and it took with it my chance for love."

"You're being melodramatic. I'm sure if you look out your window, there's a line formed all the way to your gallery with men wanting to date you."

She let out a little laugh, almost dutiful to acknowledge his wry sense of humor.

"Do you believe in soulmates, Aidan?"

"I can't."

"Huh?"

"I can't," he repeated. "I can't believe that there's just one perfect person for me out there, because I know who she is and where she is, and she's no longer in love with me."

"Grace?"

Aidan thought he was over her, at least over the pain, but the simple mention of her name stabbed at his heart.

"It's never too late till you're dead." It was an odd, morbid statement masked in romance. "Isn't that the point of your book? A year gone by, a thousand—three thousand miles doesn't keep someone from loving, not when it's true love."

She paused for his answer, but her soul-evoking questions sucked the speech from him.

"She loves you, Aidan; she'll always love you. Believe me, a day hasn't gone by that she didn't think about you, what she gave up, what she's missing."

"So much time has passed."

"Don't look at that as a bad thing. Sometimes people need time and distance to realize what's truly important, what they can live with, what they can't live without. Call her."

"Maybe."

Aidan didn't have the heart to tell Callie that he had called Grace a month ago when he finished writing the book. It had a different ending then. Needless to say, 330 pages suffused him with sufficient courage to make the call. He began with *I miss you*, and Grace ended it—ended all hope of them ever being together—with *I'm in love with someone else.*

It was at that point that Aidan realized that the *something* missing in their relationship had been Grace's love for him. It hadn't been enough for her to re-prioritize her life and marry him. She may have been his soulmate, but he wasn't hers. No wishing, no wanting, no pleas for compromise could change the reality—she didn't love him enough to share her life with him, and until he could trust another woman enough to hurt him like that again, he had no possibility for a happy ending.

"I'll say a prayer for you."

Aidan scoffed at the irony.

"God doesn't waste His time on a guy like me."

"A guy like you? They don't get much better than guys like you, Aidan. You're a good soul under all that handsome marble."

He laughed again before turning serious.

"Good guys don't hurt sweet girls like you. I'm sorry about that."

"It certainly wasn't your intention; I know that. Besides, you're not the first good guy to make me cry."

Aidan thought it kind of Callie to let him off the proverbial hook, but he didn't like that he had made her cry or that anyone else had either.

"So, who's this other good guy that broke your heart?"

"It's me that broke *his* heart, and in that process I broke my heart. It's another long story—a long, *sad* story—with one of your tragic endings."

"He's dead?"

"No, but I feel like I am."

"I don't know what to tell you, Brown Eyes. I'm sure as hell no one to be giving advice about resurrecting relationships. Maybe you should be saying one of those prayers for yourself."

"Oh, I couldn't do that. It'd be like saying *God, you brought this great guy into my life, and I was too stupid, too headstrong, too preoccupied to make it work.*"

"So what? Everybody deserves a second chance."

"Yeah, I already had my second chance, and I blew it. Twice in my life; twice out. It's over now, and not a day goes by that I don't regret it."

Aidan heard her sniffle again.

"Brown Eyes, all I can say is keep trying till there's absolutely no hope. Until he tells you that he's in love with someone else, it's not over. And girls like you and Grace are hard to fall out of love with."

"Thanks."

"I don't want to cut you short, but I better be going now. I'm late to my sister's house."

"Sorry to have kept you and cried on your shoulder."

"We monks are here to serve," he teased. "It's my fault anyway. I think my manuscript precipitated all this talk about lost loves."

"What about the ending?" she asked, a hint of plea in her voice. "I want a happy ending."

He tried to catch the words, but they hit the air wrapped in a thick coat of cynicism.

"Don't we all. Bye, Brown Eyes."

Aidan knew he needed to shower and get dressed, but he sat on his bed and continued to think about Callie and what she had said. If anyone deserved a happy ending, she did.

> So, God, it's time You and I had a little talk. I know You've been watching me, and I've probably disappointed You with some of the choices in my life, and maybe that's why I'm where I am—single in California instead of married in Massachusetts. I don't want to believe that You punish people for their mistakes, and God knows—and You know that I've made my share. But my life is different now, on the right track so to speak, and it has everything to do with a girl named Callie.
>
> Now, God, I'll be the first one to admit that there's a lot of things I don't understand—may never understand, and I don't want to be pointing fingers or playing the prosecutor, but this world You made has a lot of flaws in it. So, I'd contend that You've made Your share of mistakes, too, so that's why I feel I can ask for a favor. And it's not for me; it's for Callie.
>
> If You don't know her, You should. She's part of that army of angels You sent down here to make this world a better place, and she has. I don't think I'd even be having this conversation with You if it wasn't for her, so that in itself says an awful lot about her. Anyway, if You're looking down at her now with Your almighty eyes, You'll see she's sad, and

*she shouldn't be sad, and those brown eyes of hers are too beautiful to ever cry tears. So that's where You come in....*

# CHAPTER 21

Callie set aside Aidan's book and reached for the art book that she had bought on her visit to New York. Flipping through the pages of master paintings always eased her sadness, and this particular night, alone on Christmas Eve, Callie found herself in need of some cheering up. She thumbed through Monet, Van Gogh, and Picasso, but slowed her skimming when she came upon the Matisse section. He now had a special place in her heart.

The more Callie read about Matisse, the more she learned how much he had relied on instinct. Looking through the pages of some of his best-known works, Callie lingered on her favorite, "The Red Madras Head-dress" which Matisse had painted in 1907 and showed a woman sitting in quiet reflection. Then she turned the page and came upon "The Conversation" and it seemed to speak to her. As Callie studied the picture like never before, she saw herself in the wife's chair, imprisoned in the context of the painting and not being able to live as the subtle French word on the rail's scroll "*non*" seemed to dance mockingly around her. *No, no, no, no!* Callie's life seemed to be a continual denial of emotions.

She sat on the floor and cried, not liking the path she had paved for herself. She had cemented herself into a corner—a cold, lonely corner. Callie loved Nicholas. She was tired of denying that. She had chosen everything but love, thought of everyone but herself, had denied her own emotional needs. Simply, she had lied to herself for too long. Yet, facing the facts didn't make it better.

Night closed in on Callie, and the fire died out along with her desire to stay awake. She needed to quiet her thoughts, and sleep seemed the sensible solution—if only her subconscious would refrain from torturing her with dreams of a life never to be.

From the bedroom window on Christmas morning, wearing a winter white ski sweater and jeans, cuddled up on the padded seat, Callie looked out upon the landscape blistered by the prior day's blizzard. The woods loomed with sadness. The pine trees crouched as their white branches hung low, heavy from their icy needles. Even her favorite towering oak with the tire swing, which always heralded the sky, struggled to keep its frozen limbs outstretched.

Callie's breath had steamed the window, and she wiped the glass clean to watch the new falling snow. Its pristineness blanketed the ground as far as she could see. A perfect picture of pure white. The top of the rock barrier, fencing the back of her property, had been tipped by four-foot drifts that had scaled it. The stone path from the house to the gallery was no longer visible. Even the road lay hidden beneath the snow's coating. No fences, no paths, no roads—no markings hinting at boundaries. Her world seemed to stretch far beyond the white lawn laid outside. It was a blank canvas waiting to be painted.

Callie's excuses, her reasons for staying in Sycamore no longer existed just as her footprints of yesterday had vanished. There were no trails to follow or preset holes to step in; all paths needed to be forged again. Every snowflake suddenly presented an exciting opportunity to shape her life into what she wanted and needed it to be. Ifs and buts evaporated into the wind as it swirled and danced her cares far out of sight.

Callie left the window to find a suitcase to pack her things. She pulled open her drawers and transferred the contents to the large black nylon bag on her bed. Sweater upon sweater, jeans and dresses, boots and shoes—it was more than she needed but Callie didn't want to leave anything behind although she knew that she'd have to return to square the management of Appassionata.

Callie thought about heading straight for Logan Airport without saying goodbye to her parents. Having to rationalize her decision and justify her feelings was not going to be easy.

*How am I going to explain love to practical people who don't believe in romance and passion?*

As Callie sat in her cold car and waited for the engine to heat up, she blew warm air on her mittens and once again debated heading directly for the airport. She wanted to surprise Nicholas, hug him, tell him how much she missed him and loved him. And because of the snow, she knew there would be major flight delays that might have to route her through New York or Atlanta if she wanted to get to Nicholas by the end of the day. Callie turned on the radio and listened for the weather report that indicated the snow would taper off by late morning.

Callie pulled out of her driveway, which had been plowed at daybreak by the boys down the street. A few inches had accumulated since then but Callie didn't seem to have any trouble making treads to her parents' house. Smoke plumed in curlicues from the chimney as Callie knocked on the front door, hoping against hope that Christmas had somehow put her parents in the mindset to understand her need to be with Nicholas.

Her mother's face lit up when she opened the door and saw Callie standing there.

"We didn't expect to see you so early, Callie. How nice. We can all be snowbound together on Christmas," her mom said, bolting the drafty door closed.

"Actually," Callie hesitated, mentally choosing the right words, "I'm just staying for a little bit. I'm on my way to the airport."

"Airport? What in heavens for? It's snowing out there." She put on her glasses that hung from a chain around her neck and peered out the window. "You better call the airport, dear. All incoming flights have to be delayed."

Callie pulled off her scarf, coat, and boots. She followed her mom through the kitchen to the family room where her father sat in his recliner in front of the burning fireplace watching television. He wore an unbuttoned, plaid flannel shirt with a white tee shirt underneath it. A few remnants of a cornbread muffin lay on an empty plate on his lap.

"Hey, Callie." He nodded to her. "Take this dish for me."

"Hi, Dad."

Callie brushed a kiss to his cheek, then took the plate and returned to the kitchen for a cup of coffee.

"Jake, tell your daughter that there's no sense going to the airport in this weather. No flights are going to be coming in on time."

"Oh, that goes without saying. Better just settle yourself in for a while," he said. "When your friend's flight arrives, I'm sure she can take a taxi out here."

Callie took a cup from the cabinet and poured herself some coffee, trying not to be irritated by their remarks. However, she hated when her parents started jumping on that trampoline of conclusions.

"Who said anything about me picking anybody up?"

They looked at her sideways, perplexed.

"Well, *you* just said you were going to the airport."

"Yes, but not to pick anyone up. I'm flying out."

"On Christmas? Where to? What for?" her mom asked.

"What the hell's going on, Callie?" her father demanded, almost getting up from his chair.

"You never mentioned any trip before," her mother added.

"I know. It just came up. I'm flying down to South Carolina to be with Nicholas."

"Nicholas?" Her mother wrinkled her brow. "I thought you and him weren't seeing each other anymore."

"We weren't, but that was because of me, and—well—I want to see him again."

"You're acting ridiculous, Callie." Her father scowled at her. "Just get that dumb notion out of your head. You ain't going nowhere on Christmas, let alone in a snowstorm."

"Dad, it's not a snowstorm. It's just a little snow, and it's supposed to stop by noon."

"Why the sudden urgency, Callie? Surely, this trip can wait till after Christmas."

"I love him, Mom. I don't want to wait anymore. I want to be with him."

"I want to be with him," her father mocked her in a falsetto voice.

"The roads are awful, very slippery," her mother warned.

Callie's parents continued to talk over one another, each the definitive expert on what was right. It got to the point where they began a morbid bickering of imagined catastrophes.

"In this weather, your car will spin out and you'll crash head on with a truck."

Callie's mother used her hands in a theatrical gesture to mimic the crash and make her point.

"More likely she'll slide off the road and crash into a tree," her father said flatly. "Do we need to lose another daughter to a tragic accident?"

"And instead of celebrating Christmas, we'll be planning your funeral."

Her mother's eyes welled with tears.

"Stop! Please stop it, both of you! You're driving me crazy!"

"Don't use that tone in this house!" her father yelled.

"Why not? You use it all the time. It seems you don't hear me unless I shout." Callie lowered her voice. "I didn't come here for your permission. I'm going to South Carolina whether you like it or not, but I much prefer if you like it and support me."

"When will you be back?" her mother asked quietly.

"Mom, this isn't a vacation. I'm moving."

"Moving?" her father growled.

"Yes, *moving to* South Carolina."

"What in heavens for?" Her mother reacted with tears. "You can't leave us. Your whole life is here."

"No, Mom, *your* whole life is here. My life is wherever I want it to be, and I want it to be with Nicholas."

"He has a son."

"Yes, Adam. He's a wonderful little boy."

"You're going to raise another woman's child?"

Her father's stare burned through her.

"Yes, Dad. I love them both."

"So you don't love us anymore then," her mother whined like a child.

"No, that's not true. I love you and Dad very much."

"But you're choosing—"

Callie interrupted her mother.

"I'm choosing love, Mom. I'm choosing marriage and family. I'm choosing life. I don't have a real life here."

"You're being selfish."

"Maybe I am. Maybe for once I'm thinking about my needs. All I have is my art, and that's not enough anymore to make me happy. I love Nicholas, and he loves me." Callie hoped the latter was still true. "I'm not going to spend another minute pretending I don't have those feelings. They're wonderful. He's wonderful. I'm alive when I'm with him." She looked from one parent to the other, both now silent, both expressionless.

"I'm not going away forever," Callie explained. "I'm keeping the house and Appassionata. Between Quint and Deardra, the gallery will be just fine. I'll probably fly up once a month to check on things. And then in the summers when Nicholas and Adam have no school, we'll come up for long visits and stay at the farmhouse."

"You're making a mistake," her father snarled, still walking that line of pretension.

"No, I'm making a life for myself, making the best decision for me. Can't you understand that? Callie looked from her father's angry face to her mother's pout. "Be happy for me. For once in your lives, let me live *my* life."

♥         ♥         ♥

"Goodnight, Adam." Nicholas pulled the blue quilt snuggly around his five-year-old's body as his son squirmed to find a comfortable spot on the pillow.

"Goodnight, Daddy."

"Did you have a great Christmas?"

"Yeah, it was a lot of fun, and Santa brought me a lot of cool toys. I really love the football and baseball mitt." He raised his head off the pillow. "How does Santa know that these are my favorite sports and not basketball?"

"I suppose that while he's watching to make sure you've been a good boy all year, he notices the things you like to do."

"I like to watch Nascar, too, but he didn't get me anything with my favorite driver."

"Let's not be complaining about what you didn't get," Nicholas said in a parental voice sure to hush any whining. "I really like these pajamas Grandma and Grandpa sent you."

"Yeah, they're cool, Daddy. When're we gonna visit them again?"

"In a few months when the weather gets warmer. They have a lot of snow right now."

"But I love the snow!" With enough energy to start the day all over again, Adam sat up and pushed off the quilt and blanket and knelt on the bed in a pleading gesture. "Please, Daddy, pleeease, take me to Grandma and Grandpa's house. I love making snowmen and sledding."

Nicholas lay his son back down on the bed and re-tucked him in.

"I know you do, but—"

"And I miss Grandma and her cookies and fishing with Grandpa."

"I know, Adam, but it's too cold to fish now. We'll go when it's warmer."

"Can we visit Callie, too? I miss her."

Taken by surprise, Nicholas felt as though Adam pounded him with a dozen snowballs. He sat there on the bed for a moment not knowing how to respond to his son. Though Callie was never far from his thoughts no matter how much he denied his feelings, Nicholas had wrongly assumed that Adam had forgotten about her. His innocent question showed the impact Callie had made on both their lives.

"I miss her, too," Nicholas finally said and kissed Adam on the forehead. He pulled the quilt up and under his arms, then turned off the light. "I love you, little guy. Now get some sleep."

When Nicholas reached the bottom of the stairs, the phone rang.
"Hello?"

"Merry Christmas, honey. It's Shannon. I wanted to stop by."

"No, not tonight," he replied. Ten minutes ago, Nicholas probably would have enjoyed the company, but now he had Callie on his mind, and all he wanted to do was lay in front of the tree and fireplace and have her memory blanket him from the cold night.

"It's Christmas, Nick. I really want to see you."

"Tomorrow, Shannon. I'm tired," he said flatly.

"It won't be Christmas tomorrow."

Nicholas looked over at the wrapped present he had bought for Shannon. It had taken him an hour to decide upon a necklace, and then he spent the next week wanting to return it. He didn't know why. He just didn't want to give it to her.

"It doesn't matter." Nicholas used the poker to turn the logs on the fire. A blaze of orange flame crackled.

"I have a present for Adam, too," Shannon continued. "I got him a basketball."

"He's already asleep. Look, Shannon, I'll talk to you tomorrow."

"What's wrong with you, Nick? You're treating me like I'm nobody. I'm your girlfriend."

Her pushiness annoyed him.

"We've only been dating a few weeks."

"I thought I meant something to you." She sounded more angry than hurt.

"You do," Nicholas responded, not really sure that she actually did, at least not at this minute with Callie filling his thoughts.

"Good, then I'm coming over."

"No, Shannon, I don't want any company."

"It's Christmas."

"I don't care."

"Fine. Be that way!"

Shannon hung up the phone with a slam that echoed through Nicholas's head. He considered calling her back to apologize, but he didn't. He just wanted to be alone.

Replacing the metal poker into the stand, Nicholas took Callie's angel from the mantel and sat on the floor holding it. As he rested his head against the couch, he stared at the ceramic face, which greatly resembled Callie's pretty face except that the angel's eyes were blue. He remembered Callie's eyes, those brown sexy eyes that crinkled at the corners when she smiled at him. It was as if she could see into his heart, feel what he was feeling, and have it reflect back to him in her eyes.

Their connection, their bond, their love had been so powerful. Even now after all these months dating different women, his heart still responded to her memory. Nicholas began to wonder again, as he had so many times before, how Callie could have walked away from their relationship and resumed her life without ever looking back, without the compulsion to fight to be together, without a single phone call or e-mail or plea for another chance.

Shaking off those upsetting thoughts, he refocused on happier remembrances. He smiled when he thought of Callie's lips, their pink upturned softness, and the way it made him feel when she kissed him. He loved the feel of her hair and the way she purred when he stroked her head or massaged her neck. He missed the touch of her hands and how wonderful her fingers felt folded through his as they sat talking. He wished he could hold Callie now, snuggle next to her, nibble on her ear, kiss from her lips to her breasts then continue all the way down to her—

The phone rang and barged in on his arousing fantasy. Hopeful of a miracle, he answered the call in a welcoming voice.

"Hello and Merry Christmas," he said.

"It's me again. Are you still mad?"

"Shannon, I'm not mad. I just want to be alone."

"But I don't want to be alone. I want to be with you. Can I come over?"

Her persistence turned to pleading which only irritated Nicholas more.

"No, you can't come over. You've got to hear what I'm saying and respect that."

"I *hear* what you're saying, and I don't like it, not one bit. You're acting like an ass, on Christmas no less. Do you *hear* what I'm saying?"

"Shannon, I'm tired and I don't want to argue. Goodnight."

Returning to his seat on the floor, Nicholas found he was far too aggravated with Shannon to relax and think about Callie.

*Why can't she respect my wishes and leave me alone? Callie had done exactly that.*

Nicholas swallowed hard and stared into the fire, six months of wondering finally making sense. He picked up the phone and called Callie. It rang four times then he heard her voice.

"Merry Christmas! It's Callie. I'm out and about being Santa's elf, delivering a few presents, so leave me a message and I'll call you when I get home."

He thought quickly for a message.

"Hi, Callie. It's Nicholas." He paused, filled with disappointment at her not being home, sad that she was spending her time with someone else, and a bit annoyed that her message sounded happy while he was so sad. "I wanted to wish you a Merry Christmas."

Callie stood on Nicholas's front porch, wanting to knock on the door, wanting more than anything to go inside and just be with him. His Victorian-style house oozed warmth and coziness with a wide wrap-around porch and rocking chairs. Through the curtain of the front window, she glimpsed Nicholas, as handsome as ever, kneeling beside the Christmas tree and talking on the phone. His hair was two inches longer since she had seen him last summer, and Callie smiled at that, remembering how Nicholas said he'd let it grow in when his friend had beat the cancer.

The flames of the fireplace and dim lights of the tree cast a soft glow upon Nicholas's face. Callie sat down on the porch step and looked up at the sultry smile of a crescent-shaped moon. A light rain added to the chill in the air, but she wasn't cold, not with the fire in her heart that sizzled with every glimmer of her new life with Nicholas. Callie couldn't wait to be in his arms again, tasting his lips, feeling his body, enjoying his conversation, being bound by a love so passionate that it actually freed her.

As happy as she was, Callie felt sad over how much time she had wasted, precious hours and days, gone forever, never to recapture. She looked up at the sky as storm clouds obliterated the moon, and pondered those missed moments, life-altering moments that would have had her inside the house right now instead of sitting on the porch....

When Nicholas hung up the phone, the doorbell rang. He knew it was Shannon determined to push herself on him. Seeing the back of her brown hair as he opened the door,

Nicholas barked, "I don't want to see you. Go home!"

Callie heard the slam of the door and felt the cold breeze cut through her. It was the worst possible scenario, something she hadn't even considered in all her imagination that Nicholas would turn her away. She thought, hoped—yes, expected—he would welcome her. Frozen in place, two Christmas presents in her hand, Callie didn't know what to do. She could leave and let this be their final scene, a horrible ending that would haunt her for many nights, or she could turn around, knock again and hope to somehow salvage a friendship from all his anger.

Callie knocked ... and waited ... then knocked again....

Nicholas tried to ignore the rapping at his door. He didn't want to argue on Christmas. The third time she knocked, he forced himself to answer the door; however, his irritation spiked.

"What? What do you want?" Nicholas huffed as he looked up from her black boots to her blue jeans to the red and white wrapped presents with green foil bows.

Her hands shook slightly, and he couldn't tell if it was from nervousness or the chilly December night. He didn't want to look at her face for Shannon had those pouty, risqué lips that would get her through airport security despite her radioactivity. Probably why he had continued to date her these past few weeks when he knew she wasn't the woman for him.

"Merry Christmas, Nicholas."

He immediately recognized the Massachusetts accent and looked up into Callie's brown eyes. Surprise paralyzed him. He couldn't even smile as a thousand thoughts ran through his head. He noticed immediately that Callie had no luggage, and his heart dropped. Nothing had changed. She was just a lonesome soul on Christmas seeking a night of love. And as much as he wanted to give that to her, to be intimate with her, to kiss and hold her, Nicholas couldn't let himself love her and then hear her goodbye as she walked out of his life again tomorrow.

"Hi," she began softly. "I know you're mad at me and want nothing to do with me." Callie paused for composure, trying not to cry. "But I—I hoped that we—" She glanced down for a moment then gazed up again at Nicholas's face. "I miss you. I miss having you in my life, and—and if nothing more, I want us to be friends." She inhaled deeply, siphoning courage from the air. "But I want more." She smiled but his face held a blank expression of indifference.

"I'm seeing someone."

"Oh."

The pain in her heart manifested in misty eyes.

*It's really over. I'm too late.*

Avoiding Nicholas's stare, Callie glanced haphazardly at the floor of the porch then up to the ceiling then at the black iron lantern over the doorbell. The porch light momentarily blinded her sad, wet eyes. With her hands occupied with the gifts, she blinked furiously to stop the tears. One by one, they fell. Callie bent down and placed the presents by the door and wiped her tears before rising again to her feet.

"They're for Adam," she said meekly. "Just some Nascar stuff."

Callie turned around to go. She hoped Nicholas would stop her, run to her in a dramatic, romantic gesture and sweep her off her feet, tell her he still loved her and couldn't live without her, but each remorseful step took her further from him.

Callie remembered what Aidan had said about it not being over till he's in love with someone else. She hesitated mid-stride, pride pushing her towards the steps and the car, but she turned about-face and returned to Nicholas at the door, stepping up on the jam to meet him face to face.

"Do you love her?" she asked, her breath taking form against the cold night as she wiped her tears once more.

"She didn't break my heart twice."

"I'm sorry." She looked down then up again, vulnerable, cold, afraid. "Do her brown eyes make you smile?"

"Her eyes are blue, and your brown eyes made me cry in June."

Callie stood quiet for a moment; another tear drifted down her cheek.

"I'm sorry, Nicholas," she whispered then placed her trembling hand up against his. "Does her hand fit perfectly in yours?"

"At least I have her hand to hold."

Callie wanted to move her hand away, to run from him before she imploded, to keep that tiny spec of pride that would get her back to Massachusetts in one foolish piece, but the flow of her love kept her fingertips touching his.

"I want you to hold my hand."

"You had a lot of reasons in June why we couldn't be together, Callie. What's changed?"

"Everything and nothing."

Callie struggled to find the words to plead her case and champion her love for him. As she searched his face for some encouragement, some hint of love—that love that had spanned years, miles, even heartbreak—albeit her heartbreak—she couldn't believe it was over, yet his stoic eyes said it all.

"So nothing's changed."

Nicholas's tone bit into the wintry air. Callie didn't think she could be any colder. She shuddered.

"What hasn't changed is my love for you. I never expected when you left last June that I wouldn't be able to get over you. I thought that with enough work to fill my days and time to forget our nights, I would be able to meet someone else. But I don't want anyone else. Every day that goes by just makes me love you more, want you more, and hate myself for ever letting you out of my life. I chose wrong last June. I chose every-thing but love, and now I realize that everything is nothing without love."

"Why are you here?" he persisted with another tortuous question.

"Because I love you, Nicholas, because no one compares to you, because I want no one but you."

Callie stepped in through the open door and slightly pressed herself against him so that her mouth was mere inches from his. Nicholas stood completely still as she reached around his shoulders and fingered the hair behind his neck. Even closer now, she gazed deeply into his eyes and spoke in a whisper to hide her quivering voice.

"Because I'm longing for a passionate kiss—the kind that ignites my heart and burns to my soul, a deep and tender kiss where your lips linger on mine in a crescendo of desire, and I know no man could kiss me like that but you."

Nicholas still didn't move, but Callie could feel his heart beating, a rather vigorous pace paralleling her own. He blinked once yet said noth-ing. The silence was deafening.

"Say something," she pleaded, blinking back the tears. "Just not good-bye."

He closed his eyes for an eternal minute.

*He can't even look at me.*

Callie's sadness erupted again, the wet drops spilling down her face, taking with them all hope for her happy reunion. She continued to hold onto Nicholas, not for the intimate closeness she desired but for sheer preservation, knowing her legs were too weak to keep her standing.

Nicholas finally opened his eyes. He smiled.

"Marry me."

# CHAPTER 22

The Massachusetts sun smiled on Callie and Nicholas's June 24th wedding. They decided to marry in Sycamore in the church they attended as children. Most of their relatives still lived in the northeast, so it was much easier to have the wedding in Massachusetts rather than in South Carolina. Besides, neither one of them could think of a better place to have the reception than at *Appassionata* … except maybe at Callie's new gallery in South Carolina. Callie would have loved for everyone to see the newly christened *Artfully Yours.*

With a certain southern flavor, *Artfully Yours* captured the essence of the local community with artisans displaying their works in a grand but rustic environment similar to *Appassionata.* The money raised from the Matisse auction helped turn Callie's dreams into a reality with a gallery housing an eclectic array of art on a piece of property with an old house that they restored to its plantation charm before moving in as a family. Callie achieved all the comforts of Sycamore but with the added pleasure of Nicholas and Adam.

"I now pronounce you husband and wife."

Outside the church as the bells clamored in celebration, Callie stood with Nicholas at her side. Wearing an off-the-shoulder ivory gown with a beaded corset bodice and cathedral train that dripped over the stairs, she hugged her mother and father.

"I can't wait to make you grandparents."

Her mother smiled, her eyes wet with stymied tears.

"Did you hear that, Jake. She wants to make us grandparents."

"As if we'll ever see the kid with her living down south," he mumbled as they walked away to stand next to Nicholas's parents.

"What did your dad say," Nicholas asked.

"Nothing worth repeating. Just Dad being Dad." Callie preferred to think of her father at the moment before he had walked her down the aisle, when he told her he was proud she was his daughter.

As they prepared to greet the exiting guests in the reception line, Callie and Nicholas waited for Drew, the Best Man, to park his boys with Annie who watched over them and Adam, all their hands bulging with rice.

Callie whispered to Nicholas tiny details of approaching relatives.

"This is my Aunt Sharon from upstate New York. Next to ours, she has the best porch—two white rockers and great view of the lake," Callie said softly. "She's such a sweetheart with a quirky sense of humor. I just love her; you will, too."

"Callie, darling, congratulations!" The long-haired woman hugged her niece. "I'm so happy for you. It was such a touching ceremony, and the music and that flutist—ah, Pachelbel always brings a tear to my eye. It was really beautiful."

"Thank you, Aunt Sharon."

"Nicholas, welcome to the family."

He extended his hand, but the genial woman opted for a hug.

"Callie tells me you're a writer," she said, pulling from the embrace to look at him directly.

"Yes, I dabble in prose," Nicholas replied.

"Any Vikings?" she asked, catching Nicholas with a confused look upon his face. "I just *love* a good Viking with a jewel-encrusted sword."

Callie interjected, "Aunt Sharon loves historical sagas."

"Oh, I see." Nicholas smiled.

"Yes," the woman added, pulling a paperback from her purse. "I should've been born in another era, twined around the leg of some handsome Viking."

"You're my Viking," Callie murmured to her husband as the line of greeting continued. "Nick!"

"Callie, gorgeous, I'm so happy for you!" He hugged her. "What a perfect ceremony." Nick paused to shake Nicholas's hand. "Nice touch with the flute. I hope my catering the reception completes the day."

"Nick, at this moment, I'm so happy that I could eat hot dogs and never stop smiling."

"Hot dogs." He shook his head at her silly statement, then glanced down at her feet. "You may be a country girl at heart, content with chili dogs and steak fries and cut-off shorts and flip-flops, but today, Bella, you're wearing the gown *and* the glass slippers, and you couldn't look more beautiful."

Nick kissed her again and then joined Michael and the other imminent rice-throwers.

The reception line finally came to an end as the last two guests approached. Callie smiled.

"This is my friend Aidan and his girlfriend, Arielle," she quietly confided to Nicholas. "He took time off from work to fly out here from California for our wedding."

"Brown Eyes! Congratulations!" Aidan's hug lifted Callie a foot off the ground. He whispered in her ear, "You got your happy ending."

Callie kissed his cheek.

"And it looks like you're working on yours. She's very pretty."

Aidan set Callie back on her feet and shook Nicholas's hand.

"Congratulations! I'm happy for the both of you." Aidan put his arm around his girlfriend's shoulder. "This is Arielle Mateese. Not related to *your* Matisse, Callie, but every bit as precious."

"Hi, nice to meet you. Thank you for including us in your special day." Arielle bubbled forth with enthusiasm. "It was such a beautiful wedding ceremony, and I have to say the flutist was amazing."

"Yes," Aidan agreed.

"And your dress is so pretty."

"Oh, thank you," Callie replied. "I can't wait to sit down with the two of you and chat later at the reception. You remember Nick, don't you, and how to get to his restaurant?"

"Of course, Brown Eyes. See you later, and save me a dance." Aidan took Arielle's hand and led her towards the group on the grass.

"He's nice," Nicholas said, referring to Aidan.

"Yeah, quite nice."

"Is he an artist like you?"

Callie smiled, remembering all the fake careers she had given Aidan. She could've told Nicholas the truth that Aidan was *News, Sports, Work, and Weather*, that he was a lawyer and a writer, but she preferred to tell him what she truly believed Aidan was because if it weren't for his guiding influence that Christmas Eve, Callie wouldn't be married to Nicholas now.

"He's an angel."

The reverend emerged from the church and approached the happy couple at they prepared to meet fistfuls of rice.

"Thank you, Reverend, for everything today," Callie said.

"My pleasure. May God bless you with love, happiness, health, and prosperity all the days of your marriage."

"Thank you."

Nicholas reached into the inside pocket of his jacket and handed the priest two envelopes.

"One's for you and one's for the organist. I didn't realize we were going to have a flutist, too, so I don't have an envelope for her."

"Yes," Callie added. "She was exceptionally talented, and we've gotten so many compliments about the music. We would've liked to have met her and thanked her personally, but please pass on to her our thanks, and we'll drop off an envelope for her tomorrow."

"I didn't arrange for the flutist," the reverend replied and furrowed his brow at the confusion. "I thought she was someone you two had hired."

"No, we didn't," Callie shared. "Do you know who she is?"

"I didn't see her. She must've been up in the choir loft."

"Well, she was amazing. I haven't heard flute music since I was little and my sis—"

Callie stopped mid-sentence and realized that God had truly blessed her this day. She cast a smile upwards and plotted her next angel sculpture. This one would hold a flute, have blazing red hair, and her sister's brown eyes.

## THE END.

# ABOUT THE AUTHOR

Mary-Jo Holmes is the award-winning author of *Gianna ... a love story.* She is a Regional Representative for the National Association of Women Writers, publisher/editor of a newsletter *Musings,* and host of a writers group. Although her writing has spanned many genres, her passion remains focused in the romance genre. As a freelance writer, Mary-Jo penned dozens of fiction and non-fiction articles for local publication, interviewed the New York Yankees, as well as critiqued and judged manuscripts for the Romance Writers of America's local and national fiction contest.

Other credits include scriptwriting where she collaborated on a police drama series pitched to cable television as well as written scripts for episodic television and The Romance Channel. More recently as an educational consultant with a background in English, Mary-Jo lectured and tutored prospective college students on the components of outstanding admissions essays. She's a member of Romance Writers of America, and a volunteer for the National Center for Family Literacy.

Outside of writing, Mary-Jo maintains a balanced life with her family and friends, managing time to travel and participate in various community service organizations such as the American Cancer Society and St. Jude's Children's Research Hospital.

www.Mary-Jo-Holmes.com

978-0-595-47700-5
0-595-47700-3